MAXWELL'S GRAVE

School can be murder...

When Peter 'Mad Max' Maxwell took the kids from Leighford High on an archaeological dig, all should have been about learning and fun. The professionals were very excited – was the grave they had found that of Alfred the Great? No, because the corpse was not Saxon, but an altogether more recent murder. No sooner has the first body been unearthed than another is discovered: a policeman on the case is found dead at the wheel of his car. What knowledge did he possess that led to his death? And does his colleague, Maxwell's partner Jacquie Carpenter, unwittingly have the same information?

MAXWELL'S GRAVE

Maxwell's Grave

by

M. J. Trow

Magna Large Print Books
Long Preston, North Yorkshire,
BD23 4ND, England.

British Library Cataloguing in Publication Data.

Trow, M. J.
    Maxwell's grave.

    A catalogue record of this book is
    available from the British Library

    ISBN   978-0-7505-2715-6

First published in Great Britain in 2005 by Allison & Busby Ltd.

Published in Large Print 2007 by arrangement with
Allison & Busby Limited

Magna Large Print is an imprint of Library Magna Books Ltd.

Printed and bound in Great Britain by
T.J. (International) Ltd., Cornwall, PL28 8RW

To my favourite archaeologist –
you know who you are!

Chapter One

Five days before All Saints' Day, in the Year of our Lord 899

Eadric Clayhand stalked the ridge against the darkening sky, a silhouette in the coming night, black on purple. The rough basket had long worn the left thigh of his leggings so that the wicker chafed his skin. At least the load was lighter now as he scattered the grain by the handful, the strap cutting less deeply into his shoulder.

The rain had stopped driving from the south west, but his hair still clung to his forehead, matted and cold under the leather cap. His feet still squelched in the Wessex mud, lifting the sucking clay with each stumbling step he took. One by one they had left him, calling their farewells and wending their way homeward as dusk fell and the last rays of light had died away to the west. As he trudged his furrow, he had watched them, the men who were boys when he was a boy, their hoods pale against the darkness of the Downs, disappearing over Staple Hill.

Then he stood alone, silent before the stars came out, feeling the wind in his face. The strip fields fell away from him to the sea, a slab of cold silver waiting for the moon. He heard the last gulls call as they wheeled over the shingle headland. They would not be back before dawn and by then, perhaps, the wind would have blown soil over his precious seeds and God would be in His Heaven and his family would eat for another season. His shoulders ached, his back felt like a ridge of iron. Time to go home; to make his way down Staple Hill to the little hut smoking in the darkness – to his dogs, to his children, to his wife.

Then, suddenly, Eadric was on one knee in the cold clay, his eyes trying to focus in the darkness of the valley below him. He counted five, six helmets in the lower field, moving steadily down the winding road that led to the ford of the Leigh. Men on horses. He could hear the jingle of their bits now, the wet thuds as their hoofs chewed up the ground. He could see their spear points – two, was it? Three? He checked the dagger in his belt – four inches of iron against six mailed men. He didn't like those odds. Iron men on horses were always trouble. His father had spoken of them, and his grandfather. Men with hoarse voices and foreign tongues who came to raid and burn, loot and pillage. They spread-eagled women on the hayricks and split men's skulls in their laughter. No priest, no king was safe from them. No babe in the cradle. He could hear their muffled voices, not what they said, but how they sounded – secret, furtive, guilty. They spoke Eadric's language, but it was not a dialect he knew. Mercian? He'd heard it once. It was not the tongue of Wessex and he was wary of it. He watched the horses splash across the silver, twisting ribbon of the river before it turned one last time to rush headlong for the sea. The dark riders reached the stand of ash trees that flanked the west bank and they dismounted. Those trees were sacred to Eadric's grandfather. The mad old man had worshipped wood and stone before the Lord came to him, in a vision one night. There were spirits there, men whispered, elfin circles in the coarse grass. Eyes looked out from knot-holes and ghosts huddled together in the branches, their dead breath stirring the leaves. Eadric didn't like the ash grove. He had forbidden his boys to play there and no one tilled the strips that ran the woodland's edge.

Horses snorted in the blackness. He could see their nostrils flaring wide, their breath curling away as the evening dews developed and the cold of night took hold. Eadric was lying on his front, giving no tell-tale outline on the headland of Staple Hill. His basket lay forgotten, the seeds that were all that separated his family from starvation fending for themselves under the stars. His knife was in his hand, blade-naked, ready. The horsemen were all on foot now, one holding the animals' reins, patting flanks, soothing necks. The others, he could just make out in the cluster of trees, were carrying something – a bundle, wrapped dark and heavy. They laid it on the ground, beyond the tangle of the tree roots and they began to dig. Two of them worked, grunting with the exertion, spades biting into the unforgiving clay. He knew what that felt like. This was his land, this stretch of upland called the Downs, this little corner of Wessex above the drift of the Leigh. He saw them take off their helmets and unsling their cloaks and swords, swearing and cursing. They wouldn't feel the night cold with the job they had. They were burying a man, not as men should, by the light of day, with a mass-priest intoning the service for the dead and the bells tolling. They were burying him in the darkness, out of the sight of God, a grave deep enough to hold a man's soul, deep enough to outwit the scavenging wolf. Deep enough to find a way to Hell.

And Eadric did not hear the footfalls padding behind him and above. He did not see the tall horseman wander away from the rest and creep up the hillside to his left. He did not see him swing his axe to the sky with both hands. And he was still watching the gravediggers at work when the great iron blade sliced through his hood and parted his hair and split his skull and hacked through his brain. The dull-bladed knife flew from his grasp as the blood spurted and gushed into the clay.

The seeds blew away on the wind. Ashes to ashes; dust to dust.

March 16 2004

Arthur Wimble stalked the ridge against the darkening sky, a silhouette in the coming night, black on purple. All evening, he'd been scanning the field on Staple Hill, listening for the longed-for, tell-tale click of his metal detector, fiddling with the dials, fine-tuning his way to the fortune he'd always hoped would be his one day.

Arthur Wimble was an anorak. He was an anorak before they'd invented anoraks and he'd spent a fortune over the years investing in more elaborate and high-powered detectors. He'd faced the lot – furious farmers, angry archaeologists, copulating couples – in his quest for the Great Find. Let them scoff; let them chuckle over their pints when he walked into the pub; let the women snigger in the supermarket queues. *One day* he'd make it. Make it big. There were hoards out there, he knew. He'd read all about them. Celtic torques at Snettisham, silver coins in Jorvik – more than enough for a man to retire on. What would they say then, in the council offices where he checked their cars in and out? Where would those chuckles go when he bought a round for everybody in The White Ferret? No, when he bought The White Ferret? And those women in the supermarket, what would they be whispering then?

'There's that Arthur Wimble. He's a millionaire, you know. Found some buried treasure with his metal detector.'

'Never!'

'Straight up.'

'What a brilliant bloke.'

'Yeah, he's been made Honorary Professor of Archaeology at Wessex University, you know.'

'Well, fuck me!'

And he was still smiling at the thought, was Arthur Wimble, when his foot landed awkwardly on a flint outcrop and he stumbled forward, detector clanking to the ground, anorak flying over his head.

'Shit!' He'd twisted his ankle and both hands were slimy with the wet clay he'd gouged into. But there was something else – a sharp edge

13

under his left wrist. He sat upright against the scudding clouds over the headland, looking left, looking right. Below him the lights of Leighford twinkled into life at the end of a spring day, the cars heading homeward along the flyover; a sleepy seaside town shaking off the cobwebs of winter and hanging out its shingle for the season to come. He fumbled in his pocket, risking a torch on the blackness of the Downs.

Its beam flashed on the ground. It was a knife blade outlined there, old, iron, badly corroded. It was a knife; not a dagger, exactly, nothing as exotic as that. But a knife, nevertheless, and old. Encouraged, he crawled further, edging his way down in the gathering darkness to the stand of ash trees on the uneven mound. Here was the centre of the dig that was about to be – a give-away exploration trench.

Arthur Wimble had been hanging around archaeologists for years. He knew how their minds worked. Box systems, grid systems, horizontal approach, open area, narrow trench, vertical approach, frozen sites – these were just jargon to outsiders, but Arthur Wimble understood every word of it. He had a book on the subject.

He never knew, when they asked him in the days and weeks ahead, what made him cross the first trench and climb the ancient embankment below the trees. The ash trunks rose before him like silent sentinels, watching the intruder in their midst. Perhaps he felt drawn to them in an odd, inexplicable way he couldn't put into words. And it was here that he found it. Virgin, untouched. Before the archaeologists got to it. Something that had lain undisturbed for centuries. He scraped away the wet soil with his free hand, peering over the rims of his glasses at what he'd found. It was stone – or was it marble? It was smooth certainly and rectangular, most of it under the tangle of roots he was sitting on. And there was writing on it. He teased the ochre clay out of the carving with the old knife blade, still clutched in his left hand. It was words all right, but it was gibberish. He spelt out the letters aloud, one by one –'H-i-c j-a-c-e-t A-l-f-r-e-d-u-s-...'

'Oi!'

He hadn't heard the footfalls padding behind him and above. He had not seen the tall black figure loping over the ridge of Staple Hill and swing his shotgun to the level with both hands. He was still trying to make sense of the carving when he felt the kiss of both barrels against his neck and a voice hissed in his ear.

'What the fuck d'you think you're doing?'

'So,' the teacher had his back to the class, his gaze on the sunlit sea and the silken sails and the happy hunting ground of early retirement. One day, he'd be there himself; in the Never-never land of lump sums and enhancements. 'Picture the scene.' He swivelled back to the class, the bright eyes of Year Nine focused on him, the guru, the *éminence grise*, the *fons et origo* of all their historical wisdom (except that Year Nine didn't understand any of those words).

'October, 1940. The Battle of Britain is over. If you'd been here then, you'd have seen it all – lazy vapour trails in the cloudless blue that marked

15

the lines of battle. A thousand dog fights, Spitfire against Dornier; Heinkel against Hurricane. The Few against the Many. The bottom line, my children, is that our young men shot down more of their young men than vice versa. England one, Germany nil – where've you heard it before?'

The bell shattered the moment. The damn bell *sans merci*. No one moved. He folded his arms, leaned forward and said softly, 'So Winston rang Adolf and said "Does this mean you're not coming over?"'

He was Peter 'Mad Max' Maxwell, a legend in his own lunchtime. And he was wasted here. Four hundred years of his life he'd given to Leighford High School and here he was, in another late spring that was turning to early summer, throwing pearls before swine. He smiled and nodded. They closed their books, chattered among themselves, made their plans, passed the minutes of their lives.

Charlie put on his hood, the badge of the oddball, the misfit, the weirdo. He'd pick up his skateboard from the Front Office on his way out and terrorize little old ladies on his way home, rumbling along the tarmac like the tanks that Mad Max had talked about. See, Charlie *had* been listening all along. Jade was away fast. She had to feed her siblings, catch *Home and Away*, get tarted up and down the Front by seven. Maybe she'd meet Lars again, just like she had last night. It never occurred to her that Lars was 27, with a wife and kids; he was nice to her – that was enough. Bought her saveloy and chips and a vodka and Coke. And if he got his hand down her front a few times, well – it was a small price to pay.

Sarah smiled as she waddled past her favourite History teacher – she was all dimples and smiles– 'Bye, sir.' But she was always careful not to do PE, so that she wouldn't have to show the purple weals her stepdad gave her when he came home drunk. And that was most nights now that he'd lost his job and nobody talked to him any more.

'Mad Max' Maxwell watched them go – the rag, tag and bobtail that was Nine Ex Four. Their massed IQ wouldn't reach room temperature, but he loved them, in his old-fashioned, never-admit-it kind of way. And he'd teach them some History if it killed them all. He wandered to the window of Aitch Four, the room with a view he called his own. It was his Tardis, his padded cell, his kingdom. In the car park below, Newly Qualified Teacher Edwin Lapidge was having no luck at all stemming the tide of herberts streaming out of the wrong gates. Perhaps he was talking Swahili to them; perhaps they were deaf. Someone – Karl Marx wasn't it? – had once told the masses they had rights. And, sillies that they were, the masses believed him. So it was their *right* to go out of the wrong gate. Nine Ex Four had Advanced Vocational Certificates in Rights. But don't ask them to die on some long-forgotten Marxist barricade – that smacked of a Responsibility. And Nine Ex Four didn't *do* Responsibility. Come to think of it, neither did most of the world. Wasn't that why Mr Blair, that great Headmaster at Number Ten, was introducing citizenship?

Maxwell could hear his phone ringing in his office and trotted along the corridor, past the fluttering notices of the History Department.

Cambridge was offering essay prizes again. And a new course was burgeoning at Thicko University – Double Honours History with skateboarding. The queue must be round the block. Maxwell caught sight of the cleaner out of the corner of his eye.

'These bleedin' kids get worse, Mr Maxwell,' he heard her grunt between inhalations, No-Smoking school though this was. 'I could fill a slot machine with the bloody chewing-gum they leave behind – and the toilets! Well, you don't wanna go there, honest you don't.'

'They do indeed, Mrs B.,' Maxwell waved at her without turning round. 'Yes, I'm sure you could. No, I'm all right at the moment, thanks – bladder like a battleship, you know the type.' Mrs B. doubled up as Maxwell's cleaner on the Mezzanine floor at Leighford and his private apartments at home; what that woman didn't know about Peter Maxwell could be written on the back of a UCAS form. 'Hello?'

He tried to do that thing all women and most men can do, cradle the receiver between his shoulder and his ear. It fell out, but he caught it with a dexterity surprising in a man who would never see fifty-five again, a dexterity born of the Slips and Silly Mid On. Long years ago Peter Maxwell had indeed been a flannelled fool at the wicket. Now, he was just a fuddled oaf in a hole.

'Mr Maxwell?' a male voice said.

'Indeed.'

'Mr Peter Maxwell, Head of Years Twelve and Thirteen at Leighford High?'

'The same.'

'Peter Maxwell who is in the History Department?'

'Yes.' Maxwell's tether-end was never terribly far away. 'Look, who...?'

'I'm so sorry. This is Dr David Radley,' said the disembodied voice. 'Wessex University. Would you be interested in a corpse at all?'

Chapter Two

'Well, I have to admit,' Dr David Radley was saying, 'there is an ulterior motive.'

'Which is?' Peter Maxwell passed him a coffee mug.

'Recruitment. Retention. Resources. The new Three R's of the twenty-first century.'

'Say on.' Maxwell lolled on the nasty L-shaped piece of county-bought office furniture they'd let him have back in the heady days of 1975. Radley had rung the Great Man only yesterday and here he was, bearded, fresh-faced, the epitome of everything everyone expected from an archaeologist of international repute, except he wore shoes rather than sandals and seemed to be able to afford a tie. 'I assume,' Maxwell went on, 'we're talking bums on seats?'

'That's about the size of it. The more budding archaeologists we can have, the more of the research grant cake we get. Cynical, but the way of the world. You must have the same problem.'

'Ah, well,' Peter Maxwell was the Head of Sixth

19

Form at Leighford High School. He'd seen it all, done it all for all those years that he'd clung to the chalkface. He'd begun as an oik in a grammar school History Department, making the tea, doing the marking. Taking the classes nobody else wanted – the Remove and Lower Classical Six Ex. Then, Wham! The Maoist revolution, a little red book and the great leveller called comprehensivization. It had come later to Maxwell's school than many, but it had come nevertheless. The more stoic of Maxwell's superiors had stuck it out for a while, but they had been no match for the egalitarian explosion of flower power and free love and people bonking in Hyde Park. They'd quietly done the decent thing and shot themselves and Peter Maxwell found himself as a Head of History in a bog standard comp (as people who didn't teach in them called such schools). His drift into the Sovereignty of the Sixth Form was another story, but it gave him the nicest job and the nicest office in the school. 'Today,' he said, 'we have this little scam called EMA – an old-fashioned bribe to keep the hopeless off the streets and out of the dole queues for that teensy bit longer.'

'You sound disenchanted, Mr Maxwell,' Radley said, gazing at the film posters that filled the man's office walls. Was that Clark Gable holding up a snow-swept Loretta Young in *The Call of the Wild?* And surely Vivien Leigh and Robert Taylor weren't canoodling on *Waterloo Bridge?* In a similar vein, Gene Tierney and Don Ameche had clearly decided that *Heaven Can Wait.* 'Do I detect a man who has rather missed his way?'

Maxwell looked at the archaeologist, with his

Gucci loafers, his corduroy trousers, his engaging smile. When professors were younger than you, it was time to hang up your trowel. Then the Great Man laughed. 'How very perspicacious of you,' he chuckled. 'And it's not often I get to say *that* these days. Yes,' Gloria Swanson leered down at him from *Sunset Boulevard* and an unrecognisable Katherine Hepburn peered over the leaves that choked the passage of *The African Queen*. 'Yes, I wanted to be Steven Spielberg before they invented Steven Spielberg. Instead of which ... well, it's a long story.'

The door swung open and a good-looking woman stood there, silver flashing at her waist. It was difficult to say how old she was and she wanted it to stay that way. Under the starch of her frontage beat a heart of gold and a bosom, as the old pop song had it, like a pillow.

'Sylv.' Both men got to their feet. 'Dr David Radley, this is Sylvia Matthews, our school nurse. Dr Radley is Professor of Archaeology at Wessex.'

'Professor?' Sylvia Matthew's face said it all. However old she was, she was within syringe distance of Peter Maxwell's vintage and David Radley had to be all of eleven.

Radley smiled. 'That's David, please,' he said, shaking her hand.

'Problems, Nursie?' Maxwell asked. It wasn't often that the Florence Nightingale of Leighford High wandered, lamp ablaze, into his particular ward.

'No, no, nothing vital,' she smiled.

'David's trying to get me to bring a few of the Sixth over to a dig he's working on.'

21

'Oh, how exciting,' Sylvia beamed. 'Sort of *Time Team*. I've got a real thing for Mick Aston. That cotton-wool hair!'

Radley's face said it all this time. 'In a manner of speaking,' he said. 'So. Max, isn't it? This time tomorrow, then. I think I can promise your students some excitement.' He finished his coffee and shook Maxwell's hand. 'It's okay. I'll see myself out. You guys must have a ton of stuff to sort.'

'Is it all right if I bring our Head of History, Paul Moss?' Maxwell asked. 'Archaeology isn't quite his bag, but I'd hate to leave him out of the loop.' And of course, Maxwell failed to add, Moss was quite a useful driver of the school minibus.

'Of course,' Radley said. 'The more the merrier,' and he smiled and was gone.

'I'm sorry Max,' Sylvia perched on the edge of the man's desk, sliding a wodge of essays to one side. 'I didn't mean to break up the meeting.'

'No sweat,' Maxwell was switching on the kettle again, hunting for a cleanish mug. 'Cup of the brew that cheers?'

'No, thanks,' she was rummaging in her pockets. 'Any more caffeine today and I'll be hanging from the chandeliers.' They'd been queuing up all day, the lame and the halt. She who suffered little children had seen more suffering than usual since nine that morning. Two morning-after pills; one fainting in Health and Social Care; overturned wheelchair on the Business Studies ramp circuit; and a Chemistry-test-induced general malaise (eight kids at once).

He looked at her. There had been a time, she'd told him, when Sylvia Matthews and Peter

Maxwell had been an item. He'd never actually been aware of it himself, but she had, and it hurt. That had been long, long ago, before she'd met Guy and he'd met Jacquie. Love had changed, as the poet said, to kindliness.

'What do you make of this?' She passed him a piece of folded paper from her pocket.

He looked closely, held it to the light, sniffed it. 'Consortium,' he nodded. 'Lined, narrow feint. A4 certainly...'

'Max,' she growled, her eyebrows curling to reach her hairline.

'Sorry,' he sniggered, like the overgrown school-boy he was. 'God.' He was reading its contents now.

'Exactly.' Sylvia sat on his sofa with the air of a woman who's been proved right. Not that that, in this particular instance, gave her any satisfaction.

'Where did you find this?' he asked her, cross-ing his office to close the door.

'It fell out of a folder carried by a girl in Year Eleven. She didn't know she'd dropped it.'

'Who?' Maxwell wanted names. He wanted details.

'Max, I'm not sure...'

'Sylv,' he looked into her eyes. 'If this little missive is genuine, it could mean the end of a man's career. You know that as well as I do. Isn't that why you brought it?'

'You know the handwriting?' Sylvia asked.

The Head of Sixth Form nodded. 'As do you. It's the Memo King. It's John Fry. Who's the girl?'

She sighed. Sylvia Matthews had been the

23

school nurse at Leighford High for more years than she cared to admit and she'd seen it all. Tears and tantrums and love affairs and hatreds and suicide bids and knife attacks – outside the staff room, it was even worse. Kids had told her things in the quiet confines of the Nurses' station that would turn white the hair of the most blasé confessional priest. She wiped eyes and blew noses and slipped morning-after pills when she judged that that was best. She could have made a fortune writing for any Agony column in the land. But this was different.

'What worries me is the "we all" bit,' she said. 'There's two of them.'

'I'll settle for a single name, Sylv.' Sylvia Matthews looked at Peter Maxwell. She knew that tone. She knew when the man she'd once loved was serious.

'Annette Choker,' she said, afraid suddenly that Katherine Hepburn and Gene Tierney and Don Ameche high on their respective posters might be listening.

Maxwell nodded. 'Annette Choker in Eleven See One?' It was a pointless distinction to make, really. Leighford High School didn't boast any other Annette Chokers – life would just be too confusing. He could picture her now, a cheeky little girl with large teeth and big knees who had grown up, as so many do, into a surly tart with attitude and a bum that half Year Twelve would die for.

'I'm sorry, Max,' Sylvia said. 'With all my experience, I just didn't know what to do with this one. Giving it to Annette's Year Head would be like signing John's death warrant.' Maxwell nodded in agreement. Graham Hackett was surprisingly old-school for a young man. Ex-soldier, he was also a Methodist lay-preacher and his absolutism was of the distinctly black and white variety. 'Giving it back to Annette,' Sylvia was still outlining the possibilities, 'smacked of procuring. Giving it to John ... well, I haven't got the bottle to give it to John.'

'Unlike Annette, apparently,' Maxwell mused.

'It might not mean...'

'"See you tomorrow night,"' Maxwell read aloud, '"usual place. There'll be enough room. We can all have some fun. No knickers." Yep, sounds like a whist drive to me.'

'What will you do?' She looked into his sad, dark eyes, into the face that had launched a thousand problems for the Senior Management Team.

Maxwell looked at the clock on the wall. 'I shall go home,' he said, pocketing the note and neatening the pile of reports on his desk. 'It's the end of another perfect day. Let me sleep on this, Sylv. There's some weighing up to do.'

'Eleanor Fry,' the Nurse nodded solemnly, standing up and straightening her dress.

'And a little thing called under-age sex. Annette's still fifteen, isn't she?'

'What'll he get?' Sylvia asked.

'You know as well as I do. Loss of job,' Maxwell said. 'Pension up the Swanee. His name on the Register. Time probably, during which he'll be the target for every "normal" thug on the inside. Razor to the genitals whenever he goes to the bog. Then, when he gets out, assuming he does,

25

that's when his troubles really start. The paparazzi, local and national, will have his photo, his name, his address, his inside leg measurements. He's a teacher, so he's fair game. Tagging will be the least of his worries.'

Sylvia sighed. 'I thought you'd say that,' she said.

He reached forward and patted her hand. 'You did the right thing, Nurse Matthews,' he said. 'My problem now.' He brightened, changing the subject. 'You out on the razzle tonight? You and Guy?'

'Wednesday,' she mused. 'Bathroom. Grouting.'

'Ah, you young things,' he punched her shoulder tenderly. 'Never a dull moment, eh?' He winked at her, catching the worry behind her eyes. 'I'll sort it, Sylv. Go home.'

And she did.

White Surrey lay at a rakish angle in the little niche that Mad Max had made for himself. He'd named the bike after the courser that carried the much-maligned Richard III on his helter-skelter charge against Henry Tudor at Bosworth. When he was a younger man, Peter Maxwell could get up to the original's speed on the contraption, down hill and with a tail wind. He wasn't sure it was much of a contest any more. When the cares of the day became too much and the prattle of the staff room lost its allure, knives glinting dully in the sun, the Head of Sixth Form would come here, wedge himself into the old chair he'd half-inched from the old Head's study, in the days when Heads were Heads and teachers were glad

of it, and chew wistfully on his banana sandwiches. He had a good view of smokers along the
North hedge and if he stood on one leg on
Surrey's saddle and leaned left, he could just
catch a glimpse of the sea. Faithful Surrey waited
near him, patiently waiting for the off, as now.
And if the old metal animal could have pawed
the ground in its puissance, it would have.
Maxwell's cycle clips flashed silver in the afternoon sun as he swung his good leg over the cross
bar and pedalled out of the quad (Surrey was his
quad bike in moments like these) and hurtled out
of the gates with a hearty 'Hi-ho Silver'.

'Who was that mad man?' passers by would
stop and ask each other.

'That's Mad Max,' someone in the know would
say. 'Step wide of him. For all sorts of reasons.'

Knots of children were wandering homeward
as he sped past them, snatches of their conversation coming to him on the breeze.

'He fuckin' did. I fuckin' saw him.'

Maxwell half-turned in the saddle. Janet Eking-
ton, daughter of the Unitarian Minister.

'It was Ronaldo's call. He bloody blew it.' That
was half Year Ten.

'You bastard!' Could have been anybody.

'But Utilitarianism is essentially a hedonistic
concept.' He half-turned again, but there was no
one there. Had he just made that one up, or was
old Mr Senility coming to call at last? He took
Antrim Road at a steady pace, feet like beeswings,
scarf, even in the glad, mellow days of May,
flapping like a battle flag in the wind of change.
The colours of his old College, Jesus, Cambridge,

proudly floating even this far south. It was nearly five as he reached the flyover, slow with traffic as the inaptly named rush hour crawled by like years. He sliced past them, dicing with death, waving at their merry horns and smiling at their scowls. All this and no road tax either. What a boon for cyclists like him and other lycra-minded people. Then he was breasting the hill over the Dam, that happy-hunting ground of winos, weirdoes and wildlife that every seaside town boasted. He heard the irritating toot of the Dotto Train far below him, newly unwrapped from its mothballs, and could almost smell the floss of the candy wafting up from the Front. He took in the breakers' sparkling silver to his right and the far green of the Downs to his left. He heard the gulls cry as they wheeled, like him, into the evening, gold of the dipping sun gilding their razor wings. Then he'd gone into the dip, the sea a series of dappled snatches now through the tall towers of the Barlichway Estate, the sink of iniquity out of which half his kids crawled every day. In all the south, this was a black spot, one of the poorest wards in Europe, a blot on the scutcheon of Wessex. But it was probably listed in some ludicrous EU diktat and it would never come down.

He hauled Surrey's handlebars in the tight circle that took him into Columbine and home. Number 38, he mused, had rarely looked so lovely, his front lawn sprinkled with the pink petals of the season. He heard his tyres hiss as he swung gratefully out of Surrey's saddle, landing on his good leg and sliding the sleek beast into the awning alongside his shed. He patted the saddle and jerked free the panniers that carried his marking and his empty lunch box. What it did not carry was tomorrow's lesson preparations. Peter Maxwell had not prepared a lesson in 800 years.

He watched the Great Man from the afternoon shadows, eyes narrowed to slits. He could kill him at a stroke – well, three or four. Teeth that would gouge his throat; claws that would rip his abdomen open. He settled for raising his leg in the air and licking his own bum. This time, Maxwell, you can live. *This* time. But there will come a day, and it won't be long now, when you'll turn too slow. That chain will come loose, those brakes will fail. And *I'll* be waiting. Blood on the mat.

'Afternoon, Count,' Peter Maxwell raised his shapeless tweed cap to the black and white Tom licking his arse under the acacia.

He glanced at the mail on the mat as he threw open the front door. Saga holiday offer; be bored to death in the company of really old farts – incontinence no object. Promise of another gargantuan prize draw from Tom Champagne; imagine, Peter Maxwell, a brand new Lexus GTI FX84 pulling up to the kerb outside 38 Columbine. A red reminder for the electricity bill; surely he'd paid one of those a couple of years ago? He threw his hat and scarf vaguely in the direction of the stand and took the stairs two at a time. Off with the jacket, tie and cycle clips as he skirted the lounge, a quick detour to the kitchen to pick up a clean glass and he was on, up to the next floor, beyond his bedroom to the Inner Sanctum that was his attic.

There they sat under the skylight, the 54 millimetre plastic warriors of the Light Brigade stretched out on the diorama table, with sand glued to its surface, looking for all the world like the dust of the Causeway and the Fedioukine Heights in that distant Russia of the good old days. At their head, astride the chestnut Ronald, Lord Cardigan fretted and fumed, all dash and fire, waiting for his fourth order on that fateful morning in October, so long ago and so far away. The order that was now coming to him, in the flying plastic hoofs of the troop horse of the 13th Lights, ridden by the impetuous Captain Nolan, pelisse flapping behind him, sabre bouncing on the animal's flanks. 'He was an ugly man,' someone who knew him had written, 'and he made an ugly corpse.'

Maxwell crouched to see them all at ground level. Three hundred and eighty-nine to go and he's collected the set. Would he make them all, all the riders into the jaws of death, before death took him too, or would the paltry pension that teachers got these days freeze his assets and leave him with half a brigade, the glittering squadrons under strength? He relaxed into his modelling chair, pulling down the gold-laced forage cap he'd bought in Brighton years ago and tilting it on his thatch of greying hair. He reached across and poured himself a stiff one, the amber nectar that was Southern Comfort and which lent a cosy, rosy glow to the world.

He picked up the grey plastic figure on the desk in front of him. 'Private Ryan,' he said softly. 'No one to save you, was there?' He fitted the plastic body onto the plastic head, muttering to nobody in particular. 'Enlisted, 1847. Sailed for the

30

Crimea on the troopship *Shooting Star*, April, 1854.' He placed the rider into his saddle, careful to get the balance right, buttocks to leather. 'Seriously wounded in the Charge... Died of wounds at Scutari. When can their glory fade? Shit!' Maxwell slammed the horseman down and the soldier's unglued busby rolled onto the desk. The Great Modeller was on his feet, the forage cap back on its hook, the Southern Comfort untouched in the cut glass, Private Ryan waiting impatiently on his horse without stirrups, weapons or reins. The best laid plans of mice and men. And there was a damning note burning a hole into Peter Maxwell's pocket. He had places to be.

'Eleanor, isn't it?'

'Yes.'

'Peter Maxwell, from Leighford High,' the Head of Sixth Form tipped his legendary hat. 'Is John in?'

'Um ... yes.'

Eleanor Fry was a good-looking woman, in a flowery dress that was rather eighteen months ago and smacked of the M and S Revival period. All a little too Stepford Wife for Peter Maxwell. She led him through the hall of the unadventurous semi in the leafy, shady side of Duncombe Street and into the kitchen. Beyond the sliding doors, John Fry was sitting in a steamer chair, a lager in his hand and shades hiding his eyes. He was thirty-something, like his wife, with a floppy, Hugh Grant sort of hair-do and a laid back manner synonymous with being head of Business Studies. He always wore a suit when Visitors were around or he was

31

appointing somebody new to his Empire. Like Vespasian with no class.

'Mr Maxwell, John,' Eleanor announced him as though she was the housekeeper.

'Maxwell...' Fry was on his feet. 'Good God.' This was a first. Along with half the kids at Leighford High, John Fry had always believed that Peter Maxwell lived in a cupboard somewhere on the History floor.

'We know where you live,' Maxwell winked, sensing the man's surprise.

'Clearly.' Fry wasn't smiling. 'Er ... d'you want a drink?'

'No thanks,' Maxwell told him, although the three or four fingers of Southern Comfort he'd just left behind wouldn't have come amiss about now, 'I'm cycling.'

'Are you? Oh, of course, you can't drive, can you?'

Maxwell smiled. He smiled at the memory of a pretty, dark-haired girl and her baby. Their faces smiled back at him every time he opened his wallet. Their faces said, 'We're still here, darling. Darling Daddy.' But they weren't here. Not any more. They were dead, slewed across the wet tarmac on a deadly bend, long, long ago. And ever since, Peter Maxwell had never sat behind the wheel of a car.

'No,' he said softly. 'No, I can't.'

'Well,' the Frys stood in their back garden looking at Maxwell as if he were a Jehovah's Witness. 'What do you want?'

'Er ... oh, it's boring stuff, John. Those AVCE students...'

'Who?'

'Duke of Edinburgh Award. Bronze. Just crossing t's, dotting i's you know. Bernard Ryan's been on my back.'

If John Fry had not been suspicious before, he was now. Bernard Ryan was Leighford High's Deputy Head and Fry knew that rather than being on Maxwell's back, he was usually under Maxwell's shoe. And as for the Duke of Edinburgh Award, Leighford High hadn't gone in for that since the said Duke of Edinburgh got engaged to the Princess Elizabeth.

'Get me another, then, El, would you?' Fry raised his empty can in the air and they watched his wife turn on her heel and go indoors. 'We don't do Duke of Edinburgh, Max,' Fry said. 'What's all this about?' He waved the man to another chair opposite his.

'Annette Choker.' Maxwell cut to the chase, checking that, Eleanor Fry-wise, the coast was clear.

'Who?'

'Well, I don't know why Bernard wants the report now,' he suddenly said, a little too loudly. 'Some sponsorship bid or something. It's all about kite marks these days, isn't it? In my day, a kite was something you went out with on a windy day.' Eleanor Fry had emerged silently and with alarming speed onto the patio steps and hurried past Maxwell to bring her husband his beer. Her body language said it all and a line of G.K. Chesterton crept into Maxwell's mind. 'Silence itself made softer by the sweeping of her dress.'

'Yes.' Fry's smile was frozen behind the shades.

'Yes, it is. So, what do you need?'

Eleanor had gone again, the door clicking behind her.

'The truth.' Maxwell leaned forward. There was a hedge to his front and a hedge to his back and God knew how many neighbourly eavesdroppers beyond each one; the kind and the caring who also doubled as the vigilantes of the Neighbourhood Watch.

Fry wasn't having any. He lolled back on the steamer, hissing open his can. 'You've lost me.'

Maxwell had expected this. He pulled a crumpled note from his jacket pocket and passed it to his man.

'So?' Fry shrugged. It was easy to hide behind dark glasses, even if the eyes had it.

'It's your writing, John.'

'Bollocks,' the Business Studies teacher snapped.

'I've had more memos from you than hot dinners,' Maxwell was patience itself. 'Remember last year? Taffy Iliffe gave you a special award at the Christmas dinner. You were the Memo King, weren't you? The man voted most likely to pop pointless pieces of paper into everybody's pigeonhole. I just want to know two things. Where is this confined space of yours? And who else is involved?'

Fry was sitting upright now. 'Look, Max. This ... note or whatever it is,' he handed it back, 'is nothing to do with me, and what's it got to do with Annette Choker?'

'So you do know her?'

'I know of her. She's in Year Eleven, isn't she? I

don't teach her myself.'

'John,' Maxwell began, '...look, will you take those bloody glasses off? I need to see the whites of a man's eyes.'

Fry took his time, then he whipped the shades away. 'Just what is it you're accusing me of?'

It was Maxwell's turn to sit back. 'Got any kids, John?' he asked, looking round at the neat garden, with its borders, its shrubs, its privet boundaries.

'No,' the Head of Business said.

'Maybe, if you had...'

'Unless you've got some specific allegations,' Fry was on his feet, 'I'd like you to leave.'

Maxwell glanced across to the kitchen window where Eleanor Fry was moving about, wiping this, polishing that. Displacement for the displaced. He stood up, then closed to Fry, toe to toe, head to head.

'I'd like to think you're the victim of a vicious schoolgirl scam,' he said softly. 'The sort the *Mail on Sunday* dredges up occasionally. But I've got a nasty feeling you're a pervert meeting a couple of fifteen year-olds for sordid sex sessions. Starting to sound pretty *News of the World* now, isn't it? I'll see myself out.'

He toyed with going back through the house, making his excuses, commenting on the lovely microwave, engaging in small talk, but the side gate suddenly seemed strangely appealing.

Bernard Ryan stood in the foyer of Leighford High School that morning, still, for reasons only he understood, wearing his name badge. He had been at the school as Second, then First Deputy, for too many years now and time, that Grand Illusion, had passed him by. He wasn't really old enough for redundancy, but he'd asked the Head anyway if he could go, on the grounds of his obnoxiousness and ineptitude. In a moment of unusual and dazzling quippery, the Head had told him no; he was not quite incompetent or obnoxious enough.

'Forgotten who you are, Bernard?' Maxwell tipped his hat as he swept past him.

'Morning, Mr Maxwell,' Bernard Ryan bridled; he had all the sense of humour of a walnut.

The Head of Sixth Form hopped down the main corridor, removing his cycle clips as he went, much to the delight of a gaggle of Year Seven girls on their way to registration. 'I'll have you know,' Maxwell rounded on them, 'that this dance was all the rage back in the Summer of Love. Called the Bee Hip Hop. Ask your grand-dads about it.' Just a little more confirmation, were it needed, that Peter Maxwell was mad. And he was gone into that Inner Sanctum, that haven of peace that is the staff room. Bolt-hole of sanity, oasis of calm.

'I don't give a flying fuck!' were the first words that Maxwell heard. 'You sort it out.'

A decidedly rattled John Fry crashed past him, shoulder-barging Maxwell aside as he disappeared through the doors.

Dierdre Lessing stood there, open-mouthed. She was the Senior Mistress at Leighford High, or Head Procuress as Maxwell occasionally called her when he was feeling very tried. Live cobras hissed and writhed on her head and most people avoided her deadly gaze lest they be turned to stone.

'Dierdre,' Maxwell whispered, smiling. 'Mouth. You're gaping, dear.' It was like talking to his cat.

'Did you hear what that man said?' she shrilled, hands on hips, still staring at the still-flapping door.

'I did,' Maxwell nodded, tutting. 'Most un-Businesslike. What did you say to upset him?' It was the sort of stupid question the sillier Year Heads asked the pulverized victims of bullies.

'Well, nothing.' Dierdre was mentally unravelling the conversation of the past few minutes. 'We were talking about progression; you know, Year Eleven into Year Twelve. Each Department Head is supposed to... I just asked him to be a little more proactive...'

Maxwell inhaled savagely, recoiling and clutching his throat, steadying himself against the wall. 'You ... you used the p-word?' he hissed in disbelief. 'Dierdre, how could you? I must rush and console Mr Fry. Poor dear, he's in need of counselling.'

Dierdre Lessing's face said it all. 'You're the end, Maxwell,' she growled and stormed out, to a gentle ripple of applause.

Maxwell bowed to his assorted colleagues and turned to his pigeon-hole. Ben Holton, the Head of Science, was at his elbow. 'Wanker,' he chuckled. Holton was bald as a badger, the wrong side of a messy divorce and would never see fifty again. Laughs didn't happen often in his life.

'You talking about me, Dierdre or John Fry?'

Maxwell didn't glance in the man's direction, but started to sort his mail.

'Take your pick,' Holton said.

Maxwell laughed, carrying a telephone-directory's thickness of bumf to the bin. 'Let's do Thursday.'

The slope of the headland above Leighford that was called Staple Hill was like a battlefield. Vehicles lay at rakish angles, among them Leighford High's minibus, the ghastly Nineties logo emblazoned on the side, sponsored by everything from Nike to Leerdammer. Tents littered the skyline, canvas flapping in the stiff spring breeze, straining against the guy-ropes, like those of Maxwell's beloved Light Brigade in the Crimean Autumn in olden times.

A host of sixth formers clustered inside one, around Mr Moss, their Head of History, that old bastard Mad Max and an odd-looking tall bloke with a ragged beard and sandals. They were all looking at a dead man, his bones splayed out on the table under the shade of the tent's roof. He looked like a construction kit, with his body parts exploded prior to cementing.

'If you look here,' the bearded man lifted up the grey-brown skull, 'you'll see what killed him. A single blow has shattered the cranial area. Probably an axe.'

Cecily Jenkins pulled a face. She'd never liked hittie-hittie things and often had to leave Mr Moss's or Mr Maxwell's lessons when the history got a bit rough.

'Is this a battlefield, Mr Russell?' Paul Moss

38

wanted to know. He'd only been a historian for nine years. He was still wet behind the ears.

'No evidence of that,' Douglas Russell told him. 'No, we're investigating a Saxon cemetery. But this body was found much further up the slope, outside the perimeter trench. We've no idea why it was separate. Some sort of taboo, perhaps. We know that in the ninth century...'

It all blurred into gobbledegook in the brain pan of Robbie Wesson. This was a punishment trip. Whereas the sixth form, those privileged wankers in Year Twelve and Thirteen who were allowed to wear their own clothes were here for their edification and delight, Robbie was a pressed man. Mr Moss, his History teacher, had told him that in the olden days people were sent out to crack rocks as a punishment, chained together. They were black people, Robbie knew, and sometimes they were on a ship, picking cotton or something. So it didn't come as *too* much of a surprise to Robbie that Mr Moss had turned his detention into this boring visit. He looked at the bloke with a beard. He knew words were coming out of his mouth and he understood about one in four. Okay, so there was a dead bloke. That was mildly interesting, but when he'd picked up a bone, Mr Moss had screamed at him. There were computers in the tent, but they were all showing really boring stuff and he wasn't sure he'd get away with accessing his BMX sites.

So Robbie went on a wander. He often did it, dawdling between lessons, taking twenty minutes to go to the lav, inventing urgent embassies on behalf of Miss So-and-so or Mr Whatsisface. The fact that Robbie couldn't remember half his teachers' names spoke volumes. He found himself outside the tent. Robbie could slip out of places for England. Shit! He'd left his fags in his locker, back at Leighford. What a plonker. Never mind, perhaps he could cadge one off of one of the people up to their waists in various holes on the hillside.

'What you doing?' Even in misfits like Robbie Wesson, the flame of intellectual curiosity burned bright occasionally.

'Digging.' The woman didn't look up. She was wearing gardening gloves and her bare shoulders were pink and blotchy under the afternoon sun. She had a really silly straw hat, like one Robbie's gran had. She looked like that woman with big tits on the gardening programme on the telly, that Charlie Buttock.

'What for?'

Charlie Buttock rested back on her heels, wiping the sweat from her forehead under the hat brim. 'Who are you?' she asked, instantly suspicious of anyone who didn't reach her waist.

'I'm Robbie.'

'Are you with the school party?'

Robbie hadn't been asked to a party since he was eight. The old girl was clearly as daft as a brush. And she had to be forty if she was a day.

'Shouldn't you be with the others?' Charlie Buttock felt a vague sense of unease.

'Yeah.' This was Robbie's way in. 'But Mr Moss sent me to get his ciggies.' Robbie's razor logic told him that this woman wouldn't know that Mr Moss had never knowingly had a ciggie in his life.

40

'Only, the van's locked. You haven't got one, have you?'

'I don't smoke,' Charlie Buttock told him. 'Now, please go away. I'm busy.' And she got on with her trowelling again, hoping the ground would swallow the child up like the mountain behind the Pied Piper.

Robbie wandered away, muttering. He turned again, briefly, to stare with disbelief at the size of the woman's arse in her tight jeans. Not even Marcia Wapham had an arse that size and all Year Eight agreed that Marcia Wapham was *huge*. What was it that lured little Robbie towards the copse? The cool of the trees, perhaps, in the unseasonable heat of the May day sun. It would be minutes before they noticed he'd gone. And anyway, he was busting for a pee. He ducked past the dumper truck and balanced dangerously on the planking that led to the myriad spoil heaps, scattering a couple of mud-caked buckets in his wake. For a recidivist offender, Robbie was bloody loud. Then, he was in the shadows of the trees. This would do. He wasn't normally so coy. Usually he'd point percy at any old porcelain, from church walls to Old Peoples' Homes but he didn't want the old cow digging to see him in case she thought he was flashing her. And *that* would be just too gross to contemplate.

He was just in mid-rip, watering the ash tree roots, when he saw it. It looked like a bundle of rags at first, dark against the tangle of vegetation, except ... except there was a hand sticking out of it, the fingers curled towards him, beckoning. He clenched his muscles, stopping with difficulty in mid-pee. He whipped up his flies and peered closer, his heart thumping, his mouth dry. He'd never seen a dead body before, not one that still had flesh on it. And the skeleton in the tent didn't look real anyway. He kicked the bundle with his trainer. Nothing. Maybe it was a wino, like that old bloke who lived on and off the Barlichway, near Robbie's home, the one they threw lighted matches at to make him jump. A flap of blanket flopped aside and a face stared up at him, dark eyes sunken in the head, mouth half open as though in mid-sentence. The neck was at a weird angle, the head to one side, like some-body'd stuck it on funny. And there was dark brown stuff all around the collar.

'Fuckin' 'ell,' Robbie hissed and crashed back through the undergrowth. 'Mr Moss, Mr Moss! There's a dead bloke!'

Chapter Three

'What's that stupid boy shouting about?' Charlie Buttock wanted to know. She was kneeling up in her trench, glowing a little, as Maxwell would have put it, with the exertions of the day.

Paul Moss was probably still the right side of thirty-five. He was out of the main tent like a bat out of hell and haring across the site, mixing metaphors as he went, leaping trenches and kicking trowels like a man born to it. 'Robbie!' he screamed. 'Have you touched anything?'

Robbie was stumbling back out of the clutch of trees, his trainer-laces flapping, his hands flapping, the baseball cap that was the mark of the stupid person from George W. down, lying discarded in the dust. Moss put his career on the line by grabbing the boy's elbow and steadying him.

'Robbie,' he shook him. 'What is it? What's the matter?'

'It's a body,' Robbie was shouting, pointing to the trees. 'Over there.'

'We haven't excavated over there yet,' Charlie Buttock was explaining. 'There can't possibly...'

But Peter Maxwell was creeping over the ash tree roots, feeling his way in semi-darkness, trying to force his eyes to focus after the sharp light of the sun. He couldn't make out anything at first, then his foot hit something, soft but solid.

'Jesus!'

'What is it, Mr Maxwell?' Douglas Russell, their archaeologist guide, was standing with the Leighford sixth formers at his elbow.

'Nothing,' Maxwell turned to face them. 'Paul, get the kids in the minibus, will you?' In such moments, even Peter Maxwell was apt to denigrate his own sixth form, but in the face of death, the sophisticates of Year Twelve were children indeed.

'What?' Moss frowned, but he'd worked man and boy with Peter Maxwell for years now, almost all his working life. Mad the man may have been, but he was only mad nor' by nor'west. And when Mad Max told you to do something, he had his reasons. And you did it. 'Oh, right. Come on, people. Home-time.'

'But sir...' Robbie couldn't believe what was happening.

'Yes, Robbie. Tell me all about it later.'

The Year Twelve students, in jeans and t-shirts, had been grateful enough to take a break from the rigours of their AS revision slog to look at a few artefacts, but this was different, frightening, urgent. Had Robbie Wesson been literally burning, not one of them would have pissed on him to put him out, but there was something wrong. They all sensed it. Mad Max's face was odd, serious and suddenly grey. His voice was hard, his words deliberate, and in such moments, you didn't cross him. You just kept your head down and you moved. A couple of girls put their arms around Robbie's skinny little shoulders and instantly turned into their mothers, leading the bewildered boy back to the minibus.

Douglas Russell was in the undergrowth now, squatting with those muscles that archaeologists the world over develop in their years at the soil-face. 'My God,' he hissed, staring at what Peter Maxwell was staring at.

'That is ... *was* ... David Radley?' Maxwell needed confirmation. He'd only met the man once and the light was poor in the ash-tree thicket.

Russell was nodding. 'God in Heaven...' and his hand instinctively went forward.

'No!' Maxwell was faster, snatching the man's wrist and holding it firm. 'Evidence,' he said more softly. 'You, of all people...'

'Yes,' Russell visibly pulled himself together, 'Yes, of course. I'm sorry. An eleven-hundred-

44

year-old body I can cope with. But this...' He realized he was shaking. He was going to throw up.

'Do you have a mobile phone?' Maxwell asked, as much to give the man something to do as anything else.

'Er ... yes ... I ... I don't know...' He slapped his pockets uselessly. It would be in his jacket, in the tent, in the four-by-four, at the hotel. At that precise moment, he didn't really know.

The Head of Sixth Form stood up, lifting the shaken archaeologist with him. He led the man into the sunlight. Charlie Buttock stood there, one or two other diggers alongside her, watching the scene unfold as if in a film. Somebody else's screenplay, somebody else's set.

'Paul,' Maxwell called to his oppo, standing by the bus. All the kids were inside, peering intently out of the window. All except the two girls playing mummies to Robbie Wesson. And Robbie Wesson, owner of more syndromes than China, was trying very hard not to cry.

The Head of Sixth Form waited until the Head of History was alongside him. 'Call the police,' he said softly. 'It's a murder.'

And he bent down and picked up the fallen headgear of Robbie Wesson, as though it was Richard III's crown in the bush at Bosworth.

If he'd been asked, Peter Maxwell couldn't have told you when the blue and white police tape stretched around a murder scene had been replaced by American Yellow. Any more than he could have told you when British policemen took

45

to wearing body armour or carrying night-sticks. Something to do with global terrorism, was it? Nine eleven? Al Qaeda? Nor could he say when policemen began to look younger than he did. No, that wasn't true. *That* he did remember. He'd been 31 when a spotty kid had come to tell him, with a faltering voice and unsteady gaze, that his wife and child were dead.

'DS Toogood,' another spotty kid stood in front of him now, ears damp, tail bushy. 'You are...?'

Gagging for something alcoholic, Maxwell wanted to say, but this was hardly the time to be flippant. 'Peter Maxwell.'

To be fair to Martin Toogood, he wasn't spotty at all. He was dark and good-looking in a Massimo Serrato kind of way.

'You found the body, I understand?'

'Not exactly.'

Maxwell had stayed on the edge of the trees since Paul Moss had made his phone call. He knew the need to keep out of crime scenes and he knew that he and Russell and little Robbie Wesson at least had been crashing about all over the place. He kept the natural nosiness of the other diggers at bay, with gently raised hands and soothing words.

They'd all known Radley – his friends and colleagues. He'd insisted that the Leighford kids go home and had got them all away before the law arrived. That had taken eighteen minutes; not bad perhaps in these days of hi-tech gadgetry. Even so, Maxwell wondered whether or not in his day, an old copper on his bike couldn't have done it in ten.

'I've got a dead man here, Mr Maxwell,' Too-good snapped shut his warrant card holder. 'I don't have time for cryptic clues.'

'Indeed not, no.' The last thing Peter Maxwell wanted to do was to hinder the police in their enquiries. 'The body was found by a student from Leighford High School – Robert Wesson. Special Needs kid in Year Eight.'

'Where is he?' Toogood was scanning the site, oddly golden now in the early evening sun.

'At home,' Maxwell said. 'I sent the Leighford party away.'

'*You* did?'

'Murder sites aren't the place for children, Sergeant. Wouldn't you agree?'

'If I had the leisure for it, sir,' Toogood told him. 'What were you all doing here?'

Maxwell wandered with him down the slope of Staple Hill, past strange men in white coats and hoods, who had arrived in myriad police vehicles, sirens blaring, lights flashing, trampling without respect over the archaeological site, interested only in gathering evidence of an altogether more recent tragedy.

'Dr Radley invited us,' Maxwell told him. 'He was keen to attract students to his department.'

'The dead man?' Toogood stopped and turned. Maxwell nodded.

'When did you see him last? Alive, I mean.'

'Er...' Maxwell sighed. 'Let's see. Today's Thursday. Yesterday. Yesterday afternoon. At Leighford High. We set up this visit then.'

'What time was this?' Toogood was jotting it all down, in true text book fashion in his notepad.

'Quarter past, half past four? After my teaching day, certainly.'

'And what is it you teach, Mr Maxwell?'

'History,' the Great Man said. 'I'm Head of Sixth Form.'

'English was always my thing,' Toogood said, his face suddenly softer. 'History came a pretty close second.'

'I find it often does,' Maxwell smiled.

'Martin,' a female voice made them both turn and an auburn-haired woman stood there, picking her way over the rubble of ages in incongruous office shoes. 'SOCO want a word. In the main tent.'

Toogood nodded, slipping the book away. 'Any sign of the governor yet?'

The woman shook her head.

'We'll talk again, Mr Maxwell,' the sergeant said and was gone, up the hill and into the tent with its white-coated men.

She flashed her warrant-card at him. 'DS Carpenter,' she said.

'We can't go on meeting like this,' he muttered, wanting to catch her hand, to kiss her. 'Your place or mine? Oh, and can I put my hand down your blouse, please?'

The briefest of smiles flew across her face and her grey eyes flashed in the gold of the sun's rays. 'You,' she closed to him, 'are just a dirty old man.'

'Tsk, tsk,' he shook his head. 'And I thought you bought all that guff about how much I loved you.'

'I bet you say that to all the police officers who come to investigate a murder. Henry's going to be furious – that you're here, I mean – you know that, don't you?'

'Henry? How is the old sleuth?'

'Same old, same old,' she shrugged. 'Infuriating.' They were talking about DS Carpenter's boss, DCI Henry Hall, who had locked horns with Peter Maxwell on more than one occasion. Maxwell could picture him now, in his battleship grey suit, with his solid jaw and his impenetrable eyes, vacant behind dead lenses. Where *did* he buy those glasses? Mr Inscrutable.

'What's this all about, Max?' Jacquie Carpenter may have been Maxwell's lover, but now, today, on this hillside, she was a copper first.

'The dead man, as you know, is David Radley. He's professor of archaeology at Wessex. Paul Moss and I bought a few kids over, at his request, to see the dig. All part of Radley's personal recruitment drive.'

'Kids?' She couldn't see any.

'I sent them home. Who's this Toogood?'

DS Carpenter smiled, glancing back to the main tent where her colleagues were congregating. 'He's quite cute, isn't he? New kid on the block. From the West Country somewhere.'

'Ah, Tottingleigh,' Maxwell nodded, thinking no further than the next village along. 'Says he's an English specialist.'

'Got a degree in it,' the policewoman said. 'Don't ask me what a Medieval literature buff is doing in a blue suit. Takes all sorts, I suppose. What do you know about Radley?'

'What do you know about how he died?' he countered.

49

'Uh-huh.' It had started already, as she knew it would. She looked out from the headland to the sea beyond, gilded now in the dying sun. Vast purple bars of cloud were sliding into place along the horizon, closing down the day, bringing in the night. 'You know the rules. I cannot divulge...'

'Bollocks, heart of my heart.' It was his turn to smile. 'We go too far back, Woman Policeman Carpenter. Now, talk, kid.' It was, as always, the best Bogart she'd ever heard. She looked at the man she loved under his pointless tweed hat, his curls iron grey under its rim. She wanted, as always, to reach out and smooth that cheek with its furrows, those lips with that smile. She wanted, as always, to feel his arms around her and to bury her face into the soft hair of his chest.

'You'd better get out of here before Henry arrives,' she said. 'We'll talk later. It'll have to be official, of course – at the station, I mean.'

'And unofficially?' He fluttered his eyelashes at her, Svengali to her Trilby.

She wrinkled her face. 'Same old, same old,' she muttered. 'Your place. Tonight. But it'll be late. You don't want to know the paperwork this little lot'll generate.'

'I'll be up,' he winked at her. 'And don't talk to me about paperwork, Woman Policeman. I am a teacher.'

'How'll you get home?' she asked, glancing round. 'I don't see Surrey.'

'I came in the minibus, remember? No, the walk will do me good. Abyssinia, Woman Policeman.' And he ducked under the tape and was gone.

'Ah, Henry, nice of you to call.' Dr Jim Astley was putting away his bag of tricks. In the confines of the main tent, he looked a strange, ancient, jaundiced creature, worn out by years of forensic medicine, golf and an alcoholic wife. Almost alone among the scattering of aliens in white coats, he was in civvies.

'I thought I saw...' DCI Henry Hall's wife didn't drink and he didn't play golf. Even so, the eerie light in the tent and a lifetime sorting through the wreckage of other people's lives, lent his skin the same parchment colour.

'...Peter Maxwell.' Astley finished the sentence for him. 'Yes you did. Uncanny, isn't it, how that man can smell trouble?'

It was. Henry Hall and Peter Maxwell were like two buttocks of the same bum, drawn like iron filings to the magnet that was murder. Hall because he had no choice – it went with the territory, Maxwell because ... well, just because, that's all.

'What have we got?' Hall was scanning the table behind his man, the light of the white cloth reflecting back in his lenses. A pile of old bones wasn't very helpful.

'No, that's not ours,' Astley chuckled. He, who had been around death so long, could afford a wry smile now and again. In fact, it was vital. 'Oh, it's a murder all right, but I suspect a certain statute of limitations will have kicked in by now. Saxon, apparently. That's some time ago, now, isn't it?' Jim Astley had given up History after O levels.

Hall believed it was. And he believed there was

one man who'd know exactly, with that carbon-14 mind of his, the bastard he'd just seen sauntering away down Staple Hill in the direction of Leighford – the bastard the kids called Mad Max. 'Over here.'

Astley let his glasses dangle from the chain round his neck and trudged across the trenches to the little ash grove. SOCO men still crouched here, photographing, measuring, plotting exactly all the calibrations of murder.

'Evening, guv,' Martin Toogood stood up beside the body in question. 'Dr David Radley. He was an archaeologist. In charge of this dig.'

'Next of kin been informed?' Hall asked, looking at the corpse at his feet.

'Not yet, sir. There's a wife in Brighton.'

'Who've we got on that?'

'DS Carpenter,' Toogood told him.

'No. No, I need Jacquie on something else.' He glanced across to where his other DS was talking to a rangy, shocked looking man in sandals and a beard. 'Get the Brighton boys on it.' He checked his watch. 'The wife'll be worried by now.'

'Sir,' and Toogood was striding back to the four-by-fours and the patrol cars, phone in hand.

'Yes, Jim?' Hall wanted answers of the pathological kind.

'Neck's broken,' Astley wasn't going to kneel down again, not with his sciatica. 'So's his left ankle. I'd say he's been dropped.'

'Dropped?' Hall frowned.

Astley shrugged. Well, a fall, anyway. And not here. If you look up...'

Hall did, to the tangle of ash limbs breaking the

52

sky overhead.

'...Not enough weight in those branches to carry his body. Anyway, how would anybody get him up there? No, he was brought here. Carefully laid down where you see him now. The question is, why?'

Hall nodded. That was always the question. But there were so many questions in a murder enquiry, so many pieces of a puzzle to fit together. And somebody had taken away the box with the picture on it.

The lights of Columbine had long gone out by the time Jacquie Carpenter's Ka purred to the kerb outside number 38. There had been a time when she'd parked discreetly around the corner in the early days when she and Peter Maxwell had first been an item. And when she had a career and he had issues. Now, she still had a career and he still had issues, but somehow, there was light at the end of the tunnel of their lives together. Nobody was moving in with anybody. But they were there, at the end of the phone, at the end of the street, a bike ride away at most. They were comfortable with that.

'Evening, Count.' She waved her car keys at the black and white brute stretched like one of Landseer's lions on Maxwell's front lawn, his white bits bright under the crisp half moon. He wagged his tail, just the once, and continued to crunch his way through the ex-rodent he'd spent the last hour torturing to death. Bloody soft, these coppers; they let you get away with murder.

She rang the doorbell even though she had a

key somewhere and an apparition appeared in the frosty glass of the front door.

'Yes?' she said to him, their favourite old joke from Messrs Kenny Everett and Billy Connolly.

'Two pints please, milkman.' He kissed her on the nose. 'God, my mouth feels like a badger's arse.'

'Scrummy.' She swept past him and dragged herself up the stairs, to his lounge. 'I wouldn't know. And stop looking at my bum.'

'My dear,' he informed her. 'It's half-past five in the morning. I can't focus on anything as small as a bum until at least quarter to nine. And then,' he gloated, rubbing his hands together, 'I have a huge selection to choose from.'

'You say the sweetest things,' she laughed and hurled her handbag at the settee in the living room. Maxwell hadn't opened the curtains yet and the place had that weird light that lamp-lit early morning brings. 'Coffee in the usual place?' she asked.

'Yes,' he told her. 'Where you left it yesterday.'

She walked through to the kitchen and busied herself with the kettle.

'Fancy a full English?' he asked, vaguely trying to tie up the cords of his dressing gown, and wondering what the hell he had in the fridge.

'No thanks, Max,' she said. 'It's been a long day.'

'Thanks for coming,' he said, rummaging in the cupboard for cups.

'Well, this is sort of official,' she turned to him.

'Ah,' he slid his arms round her waist. The girl was just young enough to be his daughter. What *was* she doing in the wee small hours wasting time with this mad old bastard? 'That has all the hallmarks of dear Henry, if you'll excuse the rather weak pun.'

She wrinkled her nose. 'You might have known,' she said. 'He saw you light-footing it off the dig site.'

'I know he did. I even waved to him.'

'Nothing like being subtle.' She rubbed her nose against his.

'It was only a matter of time,' he said and his sentence died away as she kissed him.

'Oh, no you don't,' he laughed, hauling her off. 'You can't talk with your mouth full and you've got a lot of talking to do. If I've got the summons, as I assume I have, I need to be briefed.'

'Max,' she shouted. 'You do this every time. You know I can't...'

'...divulge,' he smiled. 'Yes, I know. Now, let me pour you a coffee and drive these lighted matches under your fingernails.'

Henry Hall would have liked to have set up his Incident Room on the slope of the Downs, on Staple Hill near to Dr Radley's dig, but that would have involved Portakabins and major upheavals and permissions that would take weeks to get. The Chief Constable, no less, said no. So, that Friday morning saw Hall and his team back at Leighford nick, but with the new found purpose and urgency that always came with a murder enquiry. His team sat in front of him, ready and waiting.

'Victim,' Hall was standing in front of a screen with a blown-up image of the dead man. Radley's

55

eyes were half open, his neck purple with a wound. His lips were parted too, as though in mid-sentence. Nobody commented, but one or two of the younger coppers felt unnerved by it. It was Hall's way of keeping them focused. 'What do we know?'

'I've got that, guv.' Martin Toogood waved a notepad in the air as the coffee mugs clicked and the smoke wreathed the stacks of paper in the paperless office and the VDUs flickered with a life of their own. 'David Radley was thirty-two. Married to ... Susan.'

'Has she been contacted?' Hall asked.

'Brighton CID,' Toogood confirmed. 'She's taken it badly, apparently.'

No surprises there. This was a room of hard-bitten police people. There was not one who had not seen it all before – the tears, the hysterics, the stunned silence. And each time they'd been there, talking to distraught parents, comforting forlorn spouses, holding the hands of uncomprehending children; each time, they thought to themselves, 'What if it was me?' And nothing was more calculated to keep cynicism at bay.

'Radley was an Oxford graduate. Pretty high-powered, apparently.'

'Enemies?' Hall asked.

'Sir?' Toogood was a little wrong-footed.

'Man was thirty-two,' Hall reasoned, as much to himself as to his team. 'He was a go-getter. What if somebody resented that? Where did he lecture? Wessex?'

'Yes, guv.'

'Right, Martin. Get on it. Get over to the campus at Petworth. Talk to Radley's people. I want chapter and verse. Anything from the scene, Dave?'

DC Dave Garstang was a walking shit-house of a man, but he'd made a pretty smooth transition from crowd control at football matches to SOCO liaison and most people admired him for it.

'Body was found by a kid ... er ... Robert Wesson, in Year Eight at Leighford High.'

'Anybody on that?' Hall checked.

'Jacquie Carpenter, guv,' Toogood told him.

Hall gave the man an old-fashioned look. Jacquie Carpenter and Leighford High. That meant Jacquie Carpenter and Peter Maxwell – a marriage made in hell if ever there was one in public relations terms. Henry Hall found himself, for that split second, grudgingly admitting that when it came to catching killers, it might *just* be a marriage made in Heaven.

'What else, Dave?' he asked.

'We've got more tyre marks than the parson preached about, guv,' Garstang said, sifting through his papers. 'Archaeologists, farmers, metal detectors, nosey-parkers, site security people. Plus one school minibus.'

'And footprints to match, I suppose?'

'You got it,' Garstang nodded. 'I did find out one thing, though.'

'Oh?'

'Archaeologists are addicted to chewing gum. SOCO found 68 wrappers around the site.' A ripple of laughter ran round the room. Good. You really needed that at moments like these.

'Well,' Hall said softly, 'I don't suppose they get

57

out much. Who's got the site personnel list?'

Silence.

'Somebody?'

Martin Toogood cleared his throat, wishing he'd already nipped out on his way to Petworth.

Hall's face said it all. 'Alison.'

'Sir?' a fresh-faced DC with freckles and no neck looked at him like a rabbit in the headlights.

'That's one for you, I think.'

'Well, I don't know where to start, really.' Sally Greenhow was passing an insipid cup of coffee to Jacquie Carpenter. 'I don't think it's cause for alarm.'

'Thanks,' Jacquie sat in the Special Needs office at Leighford High. It had posters of David Beckham on the wall and assorted truculent-looking bands that Jacquie had never heard of. There were trailing spider plants to reinforce the fact that this was the Jungle Room. And there was patience and endless tolerance. And love, of a sort. 'I know,' Jacquie said. 'It's difficult to tell how people are going to react, isn't it?'

'To what?' Sally asked.

Jacquie looked at the woman, with her pencil figure and her frizzy, flaxen hair. In Peter Maxwell's reckoning, this was one of the good guys, a beacon in a naughty world. But he'd never said she was *bright*. You don't get to be SENCO by being bright.

'To finding a body,' the detective said, sensing wires crossing in all directions.

'A body?' Sally frowned, putting her mug down on the table between them. 'I'm sorry, can we rewind on this conversation? I thought you were here about Annette Choker?'

'Who?'

'Oh, God. No, look,' Sally Greenhow wasn't usually fazed by anything, but today was not going well. 'Why are you here?'

Jacquie put her mug down on the table, along with her cards. Was nobody talking her language any more? 'Robert Wesson found a body yesterday afternoon, at the archaeological dig above Leighford. I need to speak to him.'

'Oh, Jesus,' Sally rummaged in the rug-bag hanging on the arm of her chair. 'Do you?' she was pulling a cigarette out of a packet.

Jacquie shook her head. 'I used to,' she smiled. 'Thought better of it.'

'Quite right,' Sally said, lips clamped round the noxious weed. 'But there are times...' and she inhaled gratefully, consigning the match to a litter-bin with an expertise born of years in Special Needs. 'No, we're at the most appalling cross-purposes here. We're hideously short-staffed at the moment. Pregnancies. Nervous breakdowns. You name it; we've got the lot. You're a friend of Max's – you know the score.'

'Some,' Jacquie confessed.

Sally knew that Peter Maxwell got himself into scrapes. She knew he had a penchant for murder. And she knew he loved Jacquie Carpenter.

'So,' Sally went on, squinting as the smoke drifted up past her eyes, 'I'm doubling up as Deputy Year Head for Year Eleven at the moment. And one of my little darlings, Annette Choker, has done a runner.'

'You've reported it?'

'Of course, that's why I assumed you were here.'

'Sorry.' Jacquie shrugged. 'One thing at a time, I'm afraid. I'm sure somebody will be in touch about this girl. How long has she been gone?'

'Where are we today? Friday. Wednesday – Wednesday afternoon. We let a full day go by, then our Student Services people ring home. Mrs Choker thought Annette was at school. She checked all the usual offices – her friends, a sister in Halifax. Nothing.'

'Year Eleven,' Jacquie checked. 'So she's ... what...?'

'Fifteen.'

'Street-wise?'

Sally rolled her eyes skywards. 'You could say that. Lives on the Barlichway Estate. D'you know it?'

'You could say that,' Jacquie smiled.

'But, Robbie...' Sally changed tack. 'He found a *body?*'

'That's right.'

What was he doing at the dig?'

'Part of a school trip, evidently.'

Sally snorted. 'A school trip? Not Robbie. He only comes to school at all for the free breakfast and lunch. He tends to last an average of eight minutes in lessons.'

'Well, that's as may be,' Jacquie said. 'But he found a body, nonetheless. I need to talk to him. And to see the others on this list.' She handed the woman a piece of paper.

'Er ... no, these are Year Twelve. All of them.

60

That'll be Max's domain. You'll have to see him about them.'

'I will.' Jacquie finished her coffee. 'But first things first. Where can I find Robbie Wesson?' And would her visit coincide with his eight minutes in the building?

Eleanor Fry slipped off her negligee and looked at her body in the half light of her bedroom. Her breasts were still firm, her thighs still curved in all the right places. Tears rolled silver down her cheeks as she turned to round the corner into the bathroom. She took John's razor blades from the cabinet in the corner and the bottle of pills from the drawer below it. She wasn't thinking rationally any more. In fact, she was barely thinking at all.

Slowly, she sank into the hot water, the bubbles covering her body as she stretched out. How pointless, she thought, as she unscrewed the bottle and tipped the white capsules into her hand; why had she bothered to scent the water? Tonight of all nights. She glanced at the label. 'Sweet Dreams' it was called. But she was too tired to smile at the irony. She swallowed one, two, three, four, then lay back so that her head rested on the bath's rim. She felt the wall behind her and the suds surge around her shoulders and she half closed her eyes against the glare of the sun through the frosted pebbles of the window.

Then, as if in a dream of her own making, she took the blade and lowered it to her left wrist under the water. She wasn't groggy yet. She was rational, fully awake, her mind's balance totally undisturbed. And she felt every nerve scream as the blade sliced through her vein and the froth turned crimson.

Chapter Four

'Morning. I wasn't sure I'd find anyone here.'

'I'm just passing through, laddie.' The muffled voice came from the other side of a cabinet of skulls. 'Who are you after?'

'I'm DS Toogood,' the detective flashed his warrant card. 'Leighford CID.'

'Leighford? You're a long way from home. Tam Fraser.' A large man with a mane of silver hair emerged from a stash of boxes in the corner of the room and shook Toogood's hand, taking in the photo on the card at the same time. 'No, I'm just doing a bit of housekeeping.'

The accent was Lowland Scots, refined, intelligent. If Peter Maxwell had met the man he'd have been instantly reminded of the actor Finlay Currie. But Martin Toogood was far too young for that.

'Who were you hoping to find of a Saturday?' Fraser asked him. 'This is a university, man. We have the longest holidays in the world. After policemen, of course.'

Toogood ignored the jibe. 'Anybody,' he said. 'I'm making enquiries in connection with the death of Dr Radley.'

The man's bonhomie vanished. 'Aye. David.'

He shook his head. 'Appalling. Just appalling.'

'You knew him well, of course.'

'*Knew* him? Man, I made him what he is... Oh, God, isn't it funny how the most humdrum cliché sounds like a sick joke at times like these. I made him what he was yesterday. I'm Emeritus Professor of Archaeology. David was one of my protégés. Brilliant mind. Simply brilliant. Would you care for a cup of coffee?'

Toogood would. He sat on a chair Fraser swept clear of a pile of folders in the bowels of the Petworth Department of Archaeology. 'Masters dissertations,' the Scotsman said, unceremoniously dumping them on the ground. 'Plagiaristic twaddle you might just as well wipe your arse with. You a university man, Sergeant?'

'Yes,' Toogood chuckled. 'Merton, Oxford.' He hoped that no one had ever done that to *his* dissertation.

'Really?' Fraser paused in mid-kettle. 'That must be rather unusual, in your line of work, I mean. I don't mean to be offensive, but, well, Mr Plod and so on?'

'Fast-track is the way forward these days,' the sergeant said, perching on the empty chair, 'though I must admit there are those in the police who disapprove. Always been a certain fear of an officer class, an elitism. Fraser. Fraser,' Toogood clicked his fingers. 'Of course. *Saxon Identities*. You wrote it.'

Fraser chuckled. 'Don't tell me you're an archaeologist!'

'No,' Toogood laughed. 'I studied Old and Medieval English with just a threat of Norse.

Even so, *Saxon Identities* was *de rigueur.*'

'As well it might be,' the Professor smiled, modesty never his strong suit. He was boiling a kettle like an ancient wizard over a cauldron. 'Sugar?'

'No thanks. When did you see Dr Radley last?'

'David? Ooh, let's see.' The kettle shrilled to boiling point. 'Quaint, isn't it, how they've brought these whistling kettles back? If we wait long enough, everything comes round again. Now, you take dowsing...'

'Er ... David Radley?' Toogood was in a hurry. Archaeological tactics would have to wait.

'Oh, sorry.' He passed the policeman his coffee. 'Where are we today? Saturday. Monday, was it? Tuesday? No, Monday. We both had lectures here at the university. The semester ended yesterday and we were to have had our valedictory bash on the Wednesday night.'

'Valedictory?' Toogood knew what the word meant, but not the scale of it.

'Oh, just an end of term thing. Few nibbles, a wee dram. Lots of public back-slapping and even more private backstabbing. Personally, I wouldn't miss it for the world. We all try to make it if we're not in the field. David wasn't there.'

'That was unusual?'

'No, not really. He was preoccupied, I suppose, with the dig at Leighford. It happens.'

'And on Monday, when you saw him last, how did he seem?'

Fraser found a chair from somewhere too and sipped his coffee. 'Fine. I mean, same as always. With David, what you saw was what you got. He was an honest, straightforward sort of guy.' A darkness came over the professor's face. 'We're going to miss him.'

'Tell me about the project at Leighford.'

'Well, that's quite fascinating. It's a Saxon cemetery essentially, eighth-ninth centuries. David was very excited about it. Inhumations of that calibre don't come along every day. But there was ... something else about this one.'

'Something else?'

Fraser looked at his man. What was he? Twenty-six? Twenty-seven? A young man in a hurry, certainly. But the Emeritus Professor had long ago passed the point where policemen looked younger than he did. 'All right,' he said, putting his mug down with some decisiveness. 'I told you a minute ago that David was straightforward. And that Monday was the same as always. Well, neither of those statements are quite true. I've known him since he was an undergraduate, first at Cambridge, then taking his Masters right here at Wessex. He was good. Very good. Even from the first semester, I knew he had quality, the kind of intellectual rigour you come across once in a lifetime. Oh, he had newer ideas than mine, of course, but that's the way of it. It wouldn't do for us to stand still. When he got a lectureship, I was delighted – and yes, before you ask, I did put in a word with the Vice-chancellor. It's the way things work in academe – but I guess you know that.'

Toogood nodded. It was the way it worked in the police too.

'Even when he got the Chair here on my retirement, he was still the same old David. Oh, a little more circumspect, I suppose, a tad more political. That, too, comes with the territory. But recently ... well, he'd changed.'

'In what way?'

Fraser shrugged. 'I sensed he was leaving us out of the loop.'

'Us?'

'The department. His colleagues.'

'Were these ... what? Professional differences?'

Fraser chuckled. 'Laddie. You get those every day. Geophysics is about as useful as a balloon with a hole in it, but we have to live with these things. No, David seemed...'

'Yes?'

The Scotsman sighed, trying to put it into words. 'It was as if he had a secret.'

'A secret?' Toogood frowned. 'What was it?' Time perhaps to reach for the notepad.

Fraser gave him an old-fashioned look. 'I don't know, laddie,' he growled. 'Hence the word secret.' He briefly wondered how fast-track the lad actually was. And just how useful *was* Old Norse at Oxford?

'Your best guess, then?' Toogood knew better than Fraser that secrets sometimes lead to murder.

'Let me ask you something first,' Fraser said. 'How did David die?'

It was a fair enough question, one that hovered like an annoying fly in Toogood's brain. The paparazzi had asked every copper going in and out of Leighford nick the same question for the last day and a half. It was how to answer it that posed the problem.

'His neck was broken.' Toogood had cut to the chase.

'God.' Fraser put down his coffee mug quickly, for fear he might drop it.

'So was his ankle, by the way,' Toogood clarified. 'Does any of that have a bearing ... on the secrecy, I mean?'

'No, no,' Fraser sighed. 'Just a certain ghoulishness on my part, I suppose.' Yes, that was probably right. It's the first question anybody asks when faced with sudden death. How? The why of it all comes later.

'No doubt it'll be all over the papers by tomorrow,' Toogood said. Henry Hall's press people, he knew, were lining up a conference as soon as they could.

'No doubt,' Fraser nodded, as aware as Toogood of the fondness of flies for shit.

'And the secret?' Toogood was like a terrier with a rat.

Fraser suddenly stood up. 'You'll have to talk to Samantha Welland.' He finished his mug and lobbed it gingerly into the little sink to his left. 'If anybody knew David better than I, it was Samantha.'

'Where would I find her?' Toogood stood up too.

'Saturday,' Fraser said, looking at his watch. 'Karate class.'

The rain was easing off as White Surrey wheezed up the long hill that ran north-west out of Leighford. But the white metal beast with gears with minds of their own wasn't wheezing half so much as the man in the saddle. Peter Maxwell braced himself against the wind that cut cross-wise over the road as the old viaduct came into view. He toyed for a moment with cutting across country through the lower fields and Berryfold Copse, but it had been raining most of the night and he knew the mud in those dips too well. He stuck to the road, straining his back and driving his legs down to the tarmac.

Shit. He stopped on the ridge. Above him, in the grey distance, the line of ash trees along Staple Hill formed a wintry screen against the horizon and the grassland below it was a patchwork of holes and ditches, bright red and white markers littering the ground beyond the fluttering police tape in even brighter yellow. There was a police car there, white, gleaming with gadgetry, the logo of the West Wessex Constabulary crisp on its sides. But it wasn't the presence of the car that bothered him as such; it was the grey-suited man leaning against it, talking over the radio.

But Peter Maxwell wasn't the type to slink away. He who had faced the Cambridge History Tripos, sudden death at close hand, Eleven Zed Eight last thing on a Friday afternoon. He'd come this far, hoping to revisit the scene of the crime, and he wasn't going to turn Surrey round and pedal homeward just yet. A man's got his pride. Besides, he needed to talk to the man in the grey suit. Birds and stones. He slid out of the saddle at the makeshift gate and was hailed by a constable, cold and wet, who had been there, hopping from foot to foot, since the dawn. His thermos flask was empty and his relief was late.

The gatling might as well have been jammed and the colonel dead and the regiment blinded with blood and smoke. Maxwell couldn't really have consoled him, even had he been bothered, by telling him that Mafeking wasn't like this, in the good old days.

'Chief Inspector.'

Henry Hall hadn't heard the purr of his bike wheels on the heathland, hadn't caught the conversation at the gate. He'd been touching base with Martin Toogood on his two way radio as he drove into Brighton, and engrossed as he was, the bad penny had caught him unawares.

'Mr Maxwell.' Henry Hall slipped the receiver back into the car, knowing the voice all too well. 'This is a pleasant surprise.'

'Mountains and Mohammed,' Maxwell smiled, leaning Surrey against Hall's paintwork. 'I thought I'd save you the cliché of "What are you doing here?" That's usually the last thing a victim says, isn't it, before they get theirs in *Morse*, or *Dalziel and Pascoe* or *Midsomer Murders?*'

'Thank you for that.' Hall had only smiled five times in eighteen years. He wasn't about to add to the record. 'I was going to send someone to see you on Monday.'

'*Someone*, Chief Inspector?' Maxwell raised an eyebrow. '*Monday?* Tut, tut. I thought at very least I'd merit a DI. And isn't four days after a murder a *little* on the leisurely side, bearing in mind result quotients and so on.'

Hall looked at the man in front of him. Come wind, come wrack, Peter Maxwell always wore the same battered tweed hat. Only on the warmest summer days would he shed his (Jesus, Cambridge) scarf and his bow tie. Only when he was not on the road would the famous cycle clips ping off into a pocket and his turn-ups flap to their furthest extent, eternally collecting fluff, bits of gravel and hayseeds. He'd known the man for years, ever since they'd found the body of one of Maxwell's own sixth form in the Red House. Funny. Henry Hall couldn't quite remember where the Red House was now after all this time. He only knew they'd demolished it. Like Ian Huntley's house at Soham, like Fred and Rosie's place at Cromwell Street, Gloucester, it had gone under the bulldozers. Lest, in the ever-more-sickening world of the twenty-first century, some lunatic made shrines of them.

'So you've come to snoop?'

Maxwell looked at the man in front of him. Henry Hall was a master of blandness. Whatever emotions he possessed were locked behind that firm jaw, that grey suit, those blank glasses. If Hall's wife and three sons were to be machine-gunned in front of him, Maxwell swore the man would just adjust his tie and get on with solving the crime. But he *would* solve it. And that, in the maelstrom of murder, was common ground for them both.

'Saxon cemetery,' said Maxwell, jerking a thumb at the spoil heaps and trenches behind him. 'Can you imagine how exciting that is for us old-stuff buffs? You know what Domesday says about Leighford? Of course you do. Like me, you know it by heart – "Hugh holds Ley Ford of William of Warenne. In the time of King Edward,

70

there was land for twenty ploughs, in demesne...'"

'Get to the point.' Ancient history had never been Henry Hall's suit and he *did* have a murderer to catch.

'The point is that Leighford before 1066 is a closed book. So, Saxon bodies here present a wonderful opportunity to...'

'Ah,' Hall cut in, wagging an upright finger at the man. 'But it's not *Saxon* bodies that you're interested in, is it, Mr Maxwell? You want to know all about Dr David Radley.'

'As do you,' Maxwell nodded.

'It's my job.' Hall stood his ground.

Maxwell could have fenced with this man all day; the cut and thrust of involvement in murder was bread-and-butter to him. But time, even if Henry Hall didn't seem to think so, was pressing. 'I spoke to this man on Wednesday, in my own office at Leighford High,' he said. 'A little over 24 hours later, he was dead, and his body lying yards from where I was standing. That makes it sort of personal.'

'That makes it a job for the police.' It was not the first time that Hall and Maxwell had had this conversation. Would it, one day, Hall wondered, be the last? 'What were you hoping to find?'

You not here, Maxwell thought to himself, but he was too much of a gentleman to say so. 'Vibes,' he said.

'Vibes?' Hall repeated, disbelievingly.

'Yes, I hate the phrase too. "A sense of the past", if you will,' Maxwell explained. 'Real or imaginary. Ancient or modern.'

'So little things like forensics are a no-go area to

you, then?'

'Oh, I don't know,' Maxwell smiled. 'I like to think I have an open mind. And of course, any titbits that your SOCO people and Dr Astley want to pass my way...'

Hall clicked open the car door. 'I should hold onto your bike, Mr Maxwell,' he said, 'in case it falls over as I drive away.'

'So what are *you* doing here, Mr Hall?' Maxwell asked him, resorting, after all, to the cliché of the television crime dramas, 'if you don't believe in vibes, if you don't find answers blowing in the wind, what price this visit?'

'Checking on the lad on the gate,' Hall said, nodding in his direction. 'Keeping away nosy parkers like you. By the way, you *do* have lights on that thing?' He pointed to Surrey.

'Oh, yes,' Maxwell said. 'For when I sneak back here after dark, you mean? Don't worry about me, Chief Inspector. I'll be fine.'

Hall lowered his glasses slightly, letting Maxwell see the grey of his eyes. 'All right,' he sighed, postponing his leaving, bowing to the inevitable. Perhaps, if he just gave Maxwell a *tiny* window on the case, he'd feel sufficiently self-important and go away. Henry Hall was not an historian; otherwise he would have known the futility of Neville Chamberlain's appeasement and the pointlessness of the Danegeld of Aethelred Unraed, the badly advised. 'My understanding is that Dr Radley approached you to bring a group out to the dig.'

'That's right.'

'And you arrived at what time?'

72

'Four-thirty, five, something like that. You'd have to ask my boss, Paul Moss.' That Maxwell had a boss at all came as something of a surprise to Henry Hall.

'Did you expect to meet Radley?' he asked.

'Yes, I did,' Maxwell told him. 'His Number Two, Douglas Russell, said he hadn't seen him all day.'

'Did you believe him?'

'Why, Chief Inspector,' Maxwell was as wide-eyed as he was bushy-tailed. 'Don't tell me Mr Russell is a suspect.'

Hall opened the door wide. 'Everybody's a suspect, Mr Maxwell,' he said softly, trying not to sound *too* much like Peter Sellers as Inspector Clouseau. 'Even you. Shall I give you a lift or tell that constable to arrest you for deliberate contamination of a scene of crime? You see, that "Do Not Cross" tape is not just a serving suggestion.'

Maxwell raised his hat and hauled Surrey's handlebars upright. 'Point taken, Chief Inspector,' he said. 'A vertical movement of the head is as good as a rapid closure of an eyelid to an equine quadruped that is visually impaired,' and he pedalled away across Radley's planking, gravel and mud flying in his wake.

She advanced on him, hands in the air, circling slowly. A powerful, peroxide blonde, nudging thirty-five. He grabbed one wrist, but she was faster, spinning him sideways with his arm locked straight. There was a hiss of breath from the little audience, white robed, green belted, against the mirrored wall. Then she brought her leg forward

73

and yanked him backwards to thud painfully on the mat. To a ripple of applause, he staggered to his feet, and the pair bowed to each other. Slowly, her mask of sheer power melted into something softer.

'Next time,' he muttered as his head came up.

'Next time I'll break your arm,' she smiled sweetly.

'Miss Welland?'

She turned at the sound of her name. A good-looking dark-haired man was standing in the doorway of the gym, with what looked like a warrant card in his hand.

'DS Toogood, Leighford CID.'

'Yes,' she reached for a towel from the wall bars, and hung it round her neck. 'What can I do for you?'

'Professor Fraser said I might find you here.'

'Tam? How is the old bastard? I'm flattered he knows what I do on my days off.'

'He's concerned,' Toogood said.

'About what?' She ran the towel over her hair and straightened her top, cleavage threatening in the bright neon strip lights of the gym.

'Is there somewhere we can talk?' Toogood asked. People shrieking 'banzai' and flinging each other all over the floor wasn't exactly conducive to a quiet chat.

'I need a shower,' she told him. 'But I don't suppose you want to join me in there?'

'Perhaps some other time,' Toogood said. University lecturers hadn't looked like her in his day. There had been nothing alluring about Sir Anthony Fischer at all, but then he was 72 with a glass eye.

'All right,' she smiled, sensing his discomfort as she jutted her breasts at him. 'Buy me a mineral water. Last one in the refectory's a wuss.'

The café at The Camdens Fitness and Leisure Centre was hardly state of the art. Hard aluminium chairs littered the room with equally hard aluminium tables, topped in garish blue and orange tiles. Decidedly unathletic people served an astonishingly limited range of goodies behind the counter and the whole place, from its breeze-block walls to its metal stairs had the odour of the jock-strap and the dodgy trainer. Famous athletes grinned down from photos on the walls, biceps bulging, quadriceps quivering.

'Look, it's just awful about David,' Sam Welland was saying, 'but life has to go on. How's Susan taking it?'

'Susan?'

'His wife.' The karate star took a hefty swig from her water bottle.

'I don't know,' Toogood told her, trying valiantly to open his sugar sachet. 'That's my next port of call.'

'Well, it's a silly question, really. She must be devastated. You know that stuff will kill you, don't you?'

Toogood grinned sheepishly.

'Oh, let me do that. For goodness sake. Men!' and she ripped open his sachet before hurling its contents into his coffee.

'Professor Fraser,' he said, just about able to stir it for himself, 'was concerned that Dr Radley had secrets.'

'Secrets?' she frowned in the middle of another swig. 'What does that mean?'

'I hoped you might know. How well did you know Radley?'

'We were colleagues,' she said. 'Well, technically, he was my boss, but that wasn't his style.'

'You worked together?'

'Only in the sense that we were in the same department. Tam actually appointed me.'

'He seems to have appointed a lot of people.'

'That's what being an *éminence grise* is all about,' she laughed, mopping her cleavage with the towel. 'Tam knows everybody and everything. Oh, he's a little out of touch now, I suppose. It'll happen to us all.'

'Was Radley secretive?'

'Not that I know of,' she shrugged. 'Always struck me as being very pleasant. Up front, in fact.'

'So, you didn't know him all that well?'

'Recently? No.'

Toogood paused slightly in mid-stir. His years in the business had taught him to catch the odd nuances, the eyelash flutter, the change of tone. 'Recently?' He took her up on it. 'You mean, there was a time when you knew each other better?'

She put her bottle down. 'What are you implying, Sergeant?' she asked, an edge in her voice he hadn't heard before.

'Oh, nothing,' Toogood hedged. 'I just wondered how close you two were.'

'I told you.' She stood up, hanging the towel around her neck again. 'We were colleagues.

Nothing more.'

Toogood scraped back his chair. 'When did you see him last?'

'Monday,' she said quickly. 'He had a lecture in the morning. I had some reports to write in the department. We had coffee.'

'Did you go to the Valedictory bash?'

She looked at him in an old-fashioned way. 'That endless round of bitchiness? I did not.'

'And on the Monday, he didn't seem in any way ... odd? Different?'

'No,' she shrugged. 'Should he?'

'I don't know,' he confessed. 'I'm just trying to put together a picture of the man's last days. It's not easy.'

She turned to go. Then she turned back. 'Do you work out?' she asked him.

'Er, no, not really. Oh, a few minutes in the gym, when I can find the time. Why?'

'Oh, no reason,' she smiled, flicking him with the end of her towel. 'Only I wouldn't mind getting you on the mat sometime.'

Now *there* was an offer Martin Toogood may have to refuse.

Everybody knew the Quinton. Not because everybody had stayed there, but because it was typical of a certain brand of hotel you'd find anywhere in the country. The building was Victorian because Leighford was essentially a Victorian seaside town. The prints on the walls were sub-Constable, when they were not early Jorrocks, as though the sight of the English aristocracy thundering in pursuit of the uneatable was what

77

every holiday-maker aspired to during their annual fortnight by the sea.

The view wasn't brilliant either. It had been, before they built the new Leighs Shopping Centre and the high rise of New Look and Waterstones and HMV that had cut the Quinton off from the sea. But it *was* the sort of place that visiting archaeologists stayed while digging in the area and it was here that Peter Maxwell found himself, in a corner of the bar, swapping pints and sob stories with Douglas Russell.

'It's good of you to come to see me,' the archaeologist said. He sat hunched on the monks' bench, looking far shorter than his six feet three.

'I have to confess,' said Maxwell, wiping froth from his upper lip, 'to a certain ulterior motive.'

'Oh?'

'Had you worked with Dr Radley long?'

'Never met him before last month. No, that's not quite true. Our paths had crossed on a weekend conference in Cambridge – that would have been ... ooh ... eighteen months ago.'

'So, you're not in his department at Wessex?'

'Lord, no. I'm a geophysicist from Birmingham. We go all over the place. Have resistive equipment, will travel. I was on the Volga last year, looking for Viking settlement evidence.'

'Any luck?'

'Some. But this one is really exciting.'

'Leighford? Why?' To Peter Maxwell, the most exciting thing about Leighford was the road that led out of it.

'Well, to begin with, no one had a clue about

the Saxon cemetery. The records are peculiarly sparse for this part of Wessex.'

Maxwell knew that.

'With Winchester being so close, it sort of steals the show. The cathedral, the castle, Nunnaminster, Old and New Minsters.'

Maxwell knew that too.

'If it weren't for the golf course...'

'Yes, indeed,' Maxwell nodded, wanting to know more about this; he had never knowingly hit a golf ball in his life. 'So this is rescue archaeology, then? Three days to solve the riddle of the universe before the bunkers and clubhouse go in. And I haven't seen hide nor hair of Tony Robinson.'

'It's never as desperate as that,' Russell told him. 'That's all made up for the telly.'

'A sort of "I'm a Botanoarchaeologist – Get Me Out Of Here"?' Maxwell smiled.

'I'm sorry, Mr Maxwell.' Russell wasn't smiling with him. 'I'm finding it a little difficult to come to terms with all this.'

'Of course,' the Head of Sixth Form nodded. 'I'm sorry. It must have been a huge shock. When did you see Dr Radley last – alive, I mean?'

'Um, the day before ... Wednesday. He had a phone call.'

'At the site?'

'Yes, on his mobile. Said he had to see someone.'

'What time was that?'

'Ooh, let me see. Mid-afternoon, I suppose. Said it wouldn't take long and he'd be back here by evening.'

'He was staying here too?'

'Yes, Room 13, macabrely enough.'

'But he didn't show?'

Russell leaned back, his pint barely touched on the table in front of him. 'No. I assumed whatever had called him away had been more complicated than he thought.'

'Did he have any enemies? Radley, I mean?'

Russell was shaking his head. 'Everybody had the highest regard for him. He'll be a serious loss to archaeology. God knows who'll get his chair at Wessex.'

'So there you are, Count.' Peter Maxwell was lolling back on the settee, the pile of exercise books lying beside him screaming in an unholy unison 'Mark us! Mark us!', but Peter Maxwell's mind was on altogether higher things. 'Is that what this is all about?'

The black and white beast was stretching on the pouffe opposite, his claws reaching out tantalizingly to threaten yet more furniture. He let his legs sag, displaying his lamentable lack of bollocks as a reminder to his Lord and Master of the appalling mutilation the man had subjected him to all those cat-years before. To let him know he wasn't just going to roll over and take it.

'Is it just professional jealousy?' the Great Castrator was burbling on in the dim light of the lounge, a glass of Southern Comfort in his fist, the lamp's rays sparkling on the crystal. 'When they announce Radley's successor to his chair at the university, will we have our man – or indeed woman? Yes, I know, Count,' he caught the nuance of the ear-twitch, 'but they *have* had the vote for rather a long time now and there *has* been a woman – allegedly – at Number Ten. It can't be *too* long before they're allowed university chairs too.' He sipped the amber nectar. 'I went to his room, you know; Radley's, I mean. Number 13 – fancy that; what are the odds, eh? When I'd left Russell at the bar I pulled the old one about being a CID officer left out in the cold again. Left hand, right hand. Nobody-tells me-anything speech – you know the one.'

Count Metternich did, but he wasn't about to let the old duffer know that. He rolled over and licked his forearm intently.

'Anyway, it worked and I got a shufti. Of course, Mr Hall's ladies and gentlemen had been all over it anyway, but it never hurts to have a second opinion. Well, it's not really impersonating a police officer. I mean, I didn't show anybody a warrant card or anything. And I'm not sure I used the d-word at all. The floozy behind the bar just *assumed* I was CID. I can't be responsible.'

Metternich was aware of that after all these years. 'But I have to concede the local boys had done a good job. Place was empty. No suitcase. No briefcase. No official secrets, no love letters, no compromising photos. All in all, it's like David Radley never existed. Right!' Maxwell sat upright and replenished his glass. 'Just for your benefit, I'll go over it again, because somewhere, I'm missing something. Now, listen carefully, because I just *might* be asking questions later. David Radley is a bright young thing, mentioned in archaeological despatches from here to Vladivostok.

Monographs and papers up to his armpits. Simon Schama calls him "Sir" – you know the sort of thing. He's a nice bloke with no known hang-ups who's keen to show the world what archaeology is all about. Hence the invitation to me and my people to the dig. He gets a phone call on Wednesday from person unknown and goes off to see him/her. He doesn't come back. So,' Maxwell was on his feet now, prowling the room in a passable pastiche of the feline draped currently on his furniture, 'between fourish, when Russell said he left the site on Wednesday and four-ish Thursday when little Robbie Wesson stumbled over him, he was done to death. Cause, I hear you ask? Broken neck. Oh, and broken ankle, but that's a minor consideration. Where? Don't know. When? Don't know that either. By whom? Ah, the 64,000 dollar question. What I need, Count, is a time of death.'

'One day,' mused Metternich. 'One day,' and he turned over again and licked his bum. It's a messy job, but somebody's got to do it.

By the end of that Saturday, Martin Toogood wasn't sure he wanted to be a copper any more. All day, he'd been driving east, talking to a dead man's colleagues. Now, as the sun flushed before setting, one ironic burst of gold after a long, grey day, he'd talked to a dead man's wife.

Susan Radley was a beautiful girl with coal black hair cut short at her cheek and shaved behind. Her eyes were dark circles of loss and bewilderment and despair. She'd sat, with her mother on one side and her father on the other, trying to make some sense of it all. She'd known

David Radley since they were kids. To her, he'd been 'Boo' after the sinister, sad and, in the end, sweet character in *To Kill A Mockingbird*. And Boo Radley had come out, with her, while they were in the sixth form. University *had* been tough, because he'd gone to Oxford and she was at Reading, but they'd kept together through hideous phone bills and frantic car dashes and keeping focused on each other. Their wedding, six years ago, was all lace and froth and flowers – Toogood had been shown the photographs. They'd planned ... oh, they had such plans. He was 32, a professor already. There were books, a television series in the offing. It was a fairytale.

Now, the fairytale was a nightmare, and a darkly handsome young policeman coming to invite her to look at her husband's corpse on a mortuary slab. Somewhere, somehow, there had to be a reason.

Martin Toogood shoved his car into reverse and his wheels spun on the gravel. Saturday night and he had a body.

Chapter Five

Monday's child wasn't fair of face or anything else as Peter Maxwell wheeled into Leighford High. A soggy Saturday had given way to a sunny Sunday and the weather men had promised faithfully, running their seaweed worry beads through their hands, and in the name of Michael Fish, that things would stay that way for at least, ooh, 24 hours. After that, what with global warming, greenhouse gases, genetically modified foods, the transit of Venus, who the hell could say?

But Leighford High wasn't worried about the weather. The Tower Block always leaked, even, mysteriously, when it wasn't raining; they'd all, over the years, got used to that. No, what exercised the minds of Senior Management that Briefing Day was the absence of Annette Choker. Nobody knew quite who'd invented Briefing. Some schools, of course, had one every day, which seemed rather over-kill. Perhaps 'over-kill' was an unfortunate phrase to use in the case of a missing schoolgirl. But at least Briefing gave the staff a chance to look *all* their colleagues in the face and wonder 'Who the hell are you?'

'Taken Study Leave early, surely?' Simon Pendlebury was the new bug in charge of the Art Department, all flowery shirts and home-made shoes.

'You're a Curriculum Manager, for Christ's sake,' Bernard Ryan, who happened to be standing close, hissed in his ear. 'Act like it.'

Peter Maxwell caught most of that and nearly had time to sit down when he realized, for the first occasion in their brief lives together, he actually agreed with something the Deputy Head had said. Ranged before him in the staff room were the motley misfits who were his colleagues – the dirty six dozen who'd somehow offended, upset the gods on high Olympus, drawn the short straw, whatever analogy appealed. And now, they were paying the price – doomed forever to face

Satan's legions across some fated classroom in the name of education, education, education.

'No, it's not that simple, Simon.' James Diamond was the Headteacher of Leighford High School. Not its Headmaster – that post had been abolished when Political Correctness was born in the days when a spade was still called a spade. He was the wrong side of forty-five now, a whizz kid promoted way above his abilities because he had no whizz at all. A good classroom practitioner, an average Head of Science, he had been elevated to management by someone whose grasp of essentials had been very basic. He'd ridden it out now for too many years to turn back. And people snapped at his heels. Young climbers like Simon Pendlebury. Old bastards like...

'With respect, Headmaster,' all eyes turned to Peter Maxwell slouching in the corner. 'Would you like to tell us all how complicated it actually is?' This was pure theatre which everyone except the Senior Management Team loved. Heather Mortimer, Head of Drama, might as well forget *The Rocky Horror Show* and just charge admission to watch Mad Max in action. She'd have cleaned up.

'I don't think this is the time or place, Max,' Diamond was feeling fairly prickly this morning. And it was *never* the time or place to tangle with Mad Max.

'Again, with respect, Headmaster – and I choose my words carefully – bollocks. Annette Choker is a student at this school. We need to be told – the truth and all of it.'

There were 'hear hears' and a muted ripple of applause around the room. Diamond knew when

85

he was outgunned as he was every time against his Head of Sixth Form. He glanced hopefully at his Deputy, Bernard Ryan, but Ryan had tangled too often with Maxwell before and he still had the scars. Dierdre Lessing was his Senior Mistress, that quaint old phrase that had survived the ravages of time. She would have loved to have chewed up Peter Maxwell and spat him out, but she didn't want an audience for that. She fought dirty and the glare of the staff room on a Monday morning was not the place to do it.

'All right,' Diamond said, alone in the solitude of command. 'Annette Choker went missing from her home on Thursday night. She'd taken clothes and a sum of money. She hasn't been heard of since.'

'Any word on the streets, Sally?' Maxwell called across to the tall, frizzy-haired girl who now wore the brief mantle of Year Head to Year Eleven. If anybody could pick up the goss, it was Sally Greenhow, one of the few good appointments Diamond had made.

'Nobody's talking,' Sally said. 'But if anybody does know anything...' She looked expectantly around the room.

'...They are to come and see me.' Dierdre Lessing was keen to stamp her authority again; it had been slipping for some minutes. 'This is now a police matter.'

'It *is* a police matter,' Diamond emphasised. 'That's what makes it all rather *sub judice*,' and he glowered at Maxwell, hoping that a sense of decorum would quieten him, and that his lofty grasp of Latin would impress everyone else. 'But, as Dierdre says, anything you may overhear in the course of the day...' That man could repeat for England. 'Any other announcements?'

Yes, thought Maxwell; to John and Eleanor Fry a bloody awful mess.

'Just little Robbie Wesson,' Sally Greenhow reminded everyone. 'He found a body last Thursday. He's a bit shaken up.'

And it was typical of Simon Pendlebury that he was the only one laughing out loud as he left the staff room.

'Max,' Diamond caught the Great Man's eye. 'Could I have a word?' He was being particularly *sotto voce*.

'Headmaster?'

'You used the word "bollocks" just then – I'd rather you didn't.'

'Headmaster,' Maxwell was the epitome of concern. 'Just because you're paranoid doesn't mean everybody isn't out to get you. You have a nice day, now, d'you hear?'

On the way along the corridor, Peter Maxwell all but collided with Sylvia Matthews. 'My place, Nursie,' he muttered out of the corner of his mouth. 'Two minutes.'

She nodded and he bounded up the stairs. 'Keep to the right, Barton, if you want to see another lunchtime.'

Barton did and he complied pronto.

Mad Max was in his Heaven again and all was right with the world.

Twelve Bee One were already waiting as he hurtled in, 'Good morning, boys and girls,' he boomed.

There was a twitter of response. 'Not hearty enough,' he shouted. 'Good morning, boys and girls.'

'Good morning, Mr Maxwell,' the unison was impressive. Not quite Greek chorus, but it would do.

'Better, better. Now, work on that. Get yourselves into groups – God, how educationally switched on is that? Why is there never an Ofsted inspector around when these flashes come to me? Ponder this one; Uncle Joe Stalin, man or myth? You've got five minutes to exercise your little grey cells,' – it was pure David Suchet – 'while I brew something hot, wet and brown next door and then I shall expect your words of wisdom – got that, Janet?'

'Yes, Mr Maxwell.'

'Good,' and he winked at her, slapping her shoulder with the utmost tenderness as he left. 'Oh, and Jeff?' He paused at the door.

The lanky lad at the back looked up. 'Sir?'

'Love you!' and he blew him a kiss.

Twelve Bee One fell about. Monday morning. Mad Max. An unbeatable combination.

The kettle was already thundering to a crescendo in the Head of Sixth's office when a panting Sylvia Matthews appeared.

'Late, Nursie,' he chided her, checking his watch. 'I'm on my fourth cup.'

'Sorry, Max.' She flopped onto his indescribably uncomfortable furniture. 'Three Morning Afters and a Possible Impetigo and it's only...' she checked her watch, '...twenty-past nine.'

He passed her the steaming mug – as predicted:

hot, wet, brown. 'I feel I've slept through an entire day,' he said. 'Annette Choker. What news?'

'The police were here on Friday.'

'The police are always here.'

'Jacquie...'

'Jacquie?'

'Haven't you seen her?'

'Since Friday, no.' He closed the door and sat opposite her, mug in hand. 'I rang her a couple of times over the weekend. No reply. It's like that when she's on a case.'

'Well, she wasn't here about Annette. She was here about Robbie and finding the body. But you know all about that, surely?'

'I do,' he told her. 'I was there too. That's common knowledge, presumably.'

'Well,' she leaned back, raising an eyebrow. 'Of the twelve or so people from Leighford High who were at that dig, only one of them has any sense of discretion – and that's you, Max. Year Twelve have got verbal diarrhoea, Paul Moss is including it in his memoirs and Robbie ... well, no, actually, Robbie's pretty quiet. But he will talk about it. He's talked to me. He's talked to Sally. He's talked to Jacquie.'

'What about Annette?'

'Friday afternoon we had another visit from a DC McCormick, pretty little kid, not long out of nappies...'

'Why didn't I know about any of this?' Maxwell wanted to know.

'Perhaps you were busy teaching, Max,' Sylvia suggested. 'I believe it's what they pay you for.'

'Oh, that.' The Head of Sixth Form took a sip

that scalded his mouth.

'She talked to Sally, as Annette's stand-in Year Head. And her Form Tutor.'

'Who's that?'

'Simon Pendlebury.'

'God help us!'

'Quite. She also talked to me.'

'Ah,' Maxwell looked at her. This was more promising. 'And what did you say?'

'Max, I didn't know what to say. And all week-end I've been agonizing about it. I picked up the phone to you more than once.'

'What did Guy say?'

'Talked me out of it.'

'Hmm.'

'What does "hmm" mean?' Sylvia screamed at him, then remembered that Maxwell had a History class next door. 'Max, we're involved in this. We ... I should have told somebody.'

'*You* did,' he said calmly. 'You told me. If anybody is carrying any cans here, it'll be me.'

'No, no,' she shook her head. 'That's not fair.'

'All's fair in love and teaching,' he reminded her. 'What *did* you say to this girl detective?'

'She was in uniform. I said ... God help me ... I said it was possible that Annette was having a fling with someone, but that it was only a rumour and I didn't know who.'

'But it's not a rumour,' he corrected her. 'And you *do* know who.'

'Max!' she screamed again. 'For fuck's sake!'

'Sorry, Sylv,' he smiled and reached out to take her hand. 'I notice our Mr Fry is absent today. As he was on Friday.'

'Of course he is. They've run off together. It's obvious.'

'It would seem to be.'

'And we're...'

'...Accessories before, during and after the fact.' He finished the sentence for her. 'I went to see him, you know.'

'Who?'

'John.'

'When?'

'Wednesday.'

'What did you say?'

'I confronted him. In a bizarre little scene like something out of Chekhov. Showed him the note.'

'Jesus!' Sylvia hissed. 'What did he say?'

'He denied it, of course.'

'Denied it?' Sylvia was beside herself. 'How could he? It's in his handwriting.'

'Exactly.'

'Then...'

'Oh, that was only Round One. Round Two I'd planned for Friday. I was going to tackle him again, away from the home environment. Away from wifey.'

'Oh, yes, Eleanor, isn't it?'

'She didn't seem a very happy lady.' Maxwell remembered her cold stare, the wandering around the kitchen, the sweep of her dress.

'Would you be,' Sylvia asked him, 'if your husband was knocking off a fifteen-year-old?'

'No, indeed,' Maxwell conceded. 'Anyway, Round Three was a bit banjaxed by events at the dig.'

'Round Three?'

'Well, it would have been difficult and I'd have probably brought you or Sally in. I was going to confront Annette.'

'Hmm.'

Maxwell smiled. 'And what does "hmm" mean?' he asked her.

She screwed up her face. 'It means you ought to know better than exposing yourself to a teenaged girl.'

'I beg your pardon?' Maxwell was good at mock outrage.

'It would amount to the same thing. You'd get about as much co-operation as if you'd dropped your trousers.'

'Always used to work behind the bike sheds in the good old days,' Maxwell said, finishing his coffee.

'Those were the Fifties,' Sylvia said.

'Fifties?' Maxwell frowned. 'I'm talking about last term. See yourself out, Sylv. I've got a classroom of young hopefuls next door in desperate need of enlightenment. And don't worry. I'll sort it out.'

'Oh, no you don't.' She stood up to face him. 'Tell me *exactly* what you intend to do.' Sylvia Matthews had been here before. She'd loved this man once. Loved him still in a different way. She'd seen him hurt too many times. She didn't want to see it again.

He held her by the shoulders and kissed her on the tip of her nose. 'I intend to make a rookie policewoman very happy and possibly earn her promotion and a few brownie points on her way crashing through the glass ceiling.'

'I hope you know what you're doing, Max.' She shook her head.

'Trust me, lady,' he said. 'I'm a Head of Sixth Form.'

'What have you got for me, Jim?' Henry Hall was up to his eyes in paperwork and it was only day five of the Radley case.

'Precious little, I'm afraid, Henry.' Jim Astley was sitting at a desk too, at the other end of a phone line, his paperwork rather less intensive, but his problems no less daunting. 'Radley's vertebrae snapped at the third, spinal cord cut cleanly. Commensurate with hanging.'

'He was hanged?'

'No, no. Figure of speech. In the glory days before '65. Judicial hanging always produced a clean break in the third vertebra – if it was done properly. Brilliant practitioners like Pierrepoint. Ah, good times.'

'Come off it, Jim,' Hall said, tilting his glasses back onto his hairline in a rare moment of relaxation. 'Before your time, surely.'

'Ah,' Astley chuckled. 'You say the nicest things, Chief Inspector. No, I was a mere shaver when that great government of ours decided to give murderers a second chance – none for their victims, you'll notice...'

'I'd love to talk ethics with you all day, Jim,' Hall told him. 'But I *do* have a body. Or rather, you do.'

'*Habeas corpus.* Yes, indeed.'

'Cause of the neck break?'

93

'Blow to the side of the neck, left. Single blow, sharply delivered.'

'Blunt object of some kind?'

'Yes, and I'm damned if I know what. Wood? Iron? There's nothing on the skin. Other than extensive bruising, I mean. Slight break and some bleeding commensurate with trauma like that.'

'Do you know when he died? Where?'

'One question at a time,' Astley said. 'Miracles take a *little* longer, you know, Henry.' Hall had heard that one before. And from this man in fact. Pretty well in every case they'd worked together. 'When?' Astley began with that. 'I would hazard a guess late on Wednesday night or early Thursday morning. I'd say he'd been dead about fifteen or sixteen hours when that deranged little child found him. Although, as you know, time of death is an infuriatingly inexact science.'

Hall knew that. 'What about place, then?' He moved Astley on.

'Your guess is as good as mine. Where did he live?'

'Near the Petworth campus, University of Wessex,' Hall said. 'Are you saying he died at home?'

'Not necessarily,' Astley told him. 'But it's possible. What was he wearing?'

'Sorry?'

'When anybody saw him last – what was he wearing; any idea?'

'Not as such, no,' Hall conceded. 'Is it important?'

'It could be. You see, his shirt buttons weren't

done up properly. Now, I don't know about you, but the last time I did that I was still in Infant School. Somebody stripped him and put on different clothes. Spooky, isn't it?'

'I'm very busy, Mr Maxwell,' Alison McCormick had just scraped into the police service on account of her height. She was more than a little sensitive about it and resented looking up at the bow-tied, weirdly capped man standing over her, peering through the Perspex. It had been a long, long day.

'I understand you're working on the Annette Choker case.'

Alison McCormick was suddenly all ears. 'That's right.'

'I have some information.'

'You are?'

'Quietly desperate for a cup of tea,' he beamed at her across the front desk at Leighford nick.

She blinked, glancing desperately at the desk man, filling in ledgers to her left.

'Sergeant Wilson,' Maxwell recognized the man above the stripes. Their meetings had not always been the marriage of true minds. 'Good to see you again. How *is* Captain Mainwaring?'

'Interview Room Two, Constable,' Wilson growled at the girl. He had no taste for Maxwell's humour and no time for Maxwell's nonsense. 'And I'm afraid we're all out of tea, Mr Maxwell. Home Office cutbacks. We've got so many civilians in the station now, there's no money for anything else.'

'Do you know,' Maxwell smiled as the door

buzzed to let him in, 'it's just the same in teaching. LSAs we call them, Learning Support Assistants – I just don't know how we managed without them all these years. Christ alone knows what they do.'

'Bloody right,' the sergeant concurred. And Maxwell followed the little policewoman, marching away down the corridor ahead of him, regulation shoes clacking on the concrete below the black-tighted legs. Interview Room Two hadn't changed since Peter Maxwell had seen it last. Windows too high to peer out of. And in case you were tempted, the glass was frosted. There was a table and four chairs – two for the Nice Policeman and Nasty Policeman, one for the Felon, one for his Brief, all of them of course, to varying degrees, members of the criminal fraternity.

'Have a seat,' she ordered curtly.

'Shouldn't I have a man policewoman with me?' he asked. 'Lest you forget yourself and leap upon me in a moment of passion?'

She looked at him for a moment, confused, lost even. 'You wish!' she sneered, in command again. A little puerile, perhaps. Not *quite* up to Maxwell's level of wit and repartee.

He sat down opposite her. 'Tape?' he nodded at the machine in the corner, fully aware of FACE and other pieces of legislation forced on the government in recent years.

'This is only a chat, isn't it?' she asked him. 'Unless you've got something to confess.' Alison McCormick wondered what kind of madman she'd got here. He was a funny age, well-spoken, with a twinkle in his eyes that spelt trouble.

Could she, she wondered, disable him with a well-timed blow to the crotch, reach the door before he did, bang the emergency button on her side of the desk. And wasn't DS Carpenter knocking off a bloke called Maxwell?

'Well,' he reached inside his jacket pocket. 'In a way.' And he passed her the note from the Memo King.

'What's this?'

'All part of the riddle that is Annette Choker,' he told her, leaning back and folding her arms.

'Do you know her?' she asked, still not looking at the note.

'Yes.' He leaned forward. 'But not, I must emphasise, in the Biblical sense. I taught her, I think, in Year Seven. Or was it Year Nine?'

'You don't know?' Alison asked.

Maxwell clasped his hands on the desk, doing an excellent stool pigeon impression from a Thirties social conscience picture. 'Don't ever tell their parents, Woman Policeman,' he said, 'but there are nearly twelve hundred kids at Leighford High and I have to admit, I don't know them all. Besides, Annette has, I believe, blossomed, since she sat in my classroom.'

The Woman Policeman saw all sorts of promotional possibilities pass before her eyes and leaned back, choosing her words. 'Like that, do you, blossoming girls?'

'Not as much as some of my colleagues,' he tapped the note.

'What is this?' she asked.

'Read it,' he suggested.

'"See you tonight. Usual place. It'll be a bit

97

cramped, but we'll all have some fun. No knickers." Who wrote this?' Perhaps it was the light, but Alison McCormick seemed to have turned pale.

'John Fry, Head of Business Studies at Leighford High.'

'It's not signed,' she noted.

'Spot on, Miss Einstein,' he said, 'but take it from me, that's Fry's writing.'

'Where did you get it?'

'It fell out of a folder I have reason to believe belongs to Annette Choker.'

Alison McCormick sat there, frowning, trying to make sense of it all. 'So you're saying...'

'I'm saying that John Fry, Head of Business Studies at Leighford High appears to be making an assignation with a girl who has now gone missing from home. It's a common enough situation, Woman Policeman – the Sundays are full of it.'

'Why wouldn't he text her?'

'Sorry?'

'This John Fry. If he was having a thing with Annette, why didn't he text her? Talk to her even?'

'Why did Leopold and Loeb decide to kill Bobby Franks? Why didn't Dr Crippen use the right kind of lime to dispose of his wife? Why isn't the moon made of green cheese? I'm giving you John Fry's head on a plate, Woman Policeman. Find him and you'll find Annette.'

'I'll think about it,' the girl was on her feet.

Maxwell sat back, looking up at the bright eyes, the clenched mouth. If ever a woman was on her dignity, this was it. 'Are you telling me you're not going to follow this up?' he asked, incredulous.

'I'm telling you I'll think about it,' she told him. He reached for the note.

'No,' she said sharply. 'No, that stays here. It might be important evidence. Good evening, Mr Maxwell. I'll show you out.'

'It's not my case, Max,' Jacquie said across the wires. She was in her kitchen, wrestling with the spring cleaning she'd been meaning to do now for weeks, her cordless tucked between her head and her shoulder, which was a woman thing. 'I'm on the Radley business.'

'Look, Jacquie, darling,' she heard him wheedle, 'is there anybody at your end who speaks English? Is it money? Can I give you a stash of my earth pounds?'

'All right,' she sighed. 'I'm sure Alison's onto it. For all your appalling, chauvinist views of womankind, she's nobody's fool. Might make a reasonable DC in twenty years or so. She'll be onto it. Trust me.'

'All right.' He held his hand in the air as a gesture of peace, lolling back in his modelling chair in his attic as he was. 'All right. Let's hope she will be. I'm washing my hands of this now.'

'Good, good. Thank you, Pontius.'

'Jacqueline,' he sat upright. 'Do I detect the bum's rush here? You sound preoccupied.'

'Max, I'm cleaning the kitchen.'

'It's half-past eleven at night.' He checked the clock to make sure.

'So I'm nocturnal.'

99

'Yeah, right. To change the subject just a threat; what news on the Radley business?'

'Now, Max...'

'Come on, Jacquie.' Maxwell checked the paintwork on the jacket of Private Ryan. Buttons needed highlights. 'I was the second person to reach him, for God's sake. After daft Robbie, and I can't see him solving anything. You know I just can't walk away.'

'Yes,' she stood up, feeling her back in half, and held the phone again. 'Yes, I know that,' she nodded, her eyes suddenly moist. That was Mad Max all right and she loved him for it. He had never walked away and never would. 'But you know my position.'

'Now, don't change the subject,' he scolded. 'Sex later. Let's get to cases first.'

'Behave!' she growled at him. 'Look, I've got a briefing at the nick tomorrow morning. I'll know more by then. Now, I really have to go, Max.'

'I bet you say that to all the men who love you and keep interfering in the cases you're working on.'

She laughed. She could picture him now, with that silly old military cap on his head, kicking the furniture between dabs with his paintbrush and doing his hurt, schoolboy routine. 'I love you, Peter Maxwell,' she whispered.

'I love you too ... er ... er ... Jacquie, is it?'

'Bastard!' and she hung up.

Martin Toogood was tired. The VDU screen was flickering in front of him, words jumping before his eyes until they weren't making sense any more. He logged off, stretched for the first time in what seemed like hours and grabbed his jacket from the chair. He checked his watch. Christ, it was nearly Tuesday morning. And he had a briefing at eight. He couldn't remember when he'd slept last and when he had, all he saw was the pale, dead face of Susan Radley, alone in the world for the first time in her life.

He grunted something at Wilson, stirring his cocoa at the front desk. He pushed the necessary buttons and made for the car park. The interior lights came on as he clicked the remote. Must clean the bloody thing, he thought as he got in, kicking aside the Ginster's wrapper and the Coke bottle. One day, one day.

He turned the wheel full lock and purred out of the gate. Traffic was slow this time of night, all the drunks extra wary as they passed Leighford nick and the slightly less legless wary of the unmarked car that came out of its car park. The lights were with him at Cross Street and again at the flyover. This was good. He'd be home by half-past twelve. Quick shower. Something slimy from the freezer – thank God for microwaves. Then bed. What an invention.

He checked his speed. There were cameras on Gravel Hill, and they had film in them. Still, he had mates in Traffic. They wouldn't be asking too many questions. He put his foot down, catching the sea like a slab of silver under the half moon. The lights were still twinkling along the sea front away to his right, tiny bulbs bouncing on the breeze. He flicked his way through the radio channels. Some bollocks about the EU; a particularly crap rap; ah, this was all right – a band his mum had told him all about; The Moody Blues.

'It's not the way that you say it when you do those things to me,' Justin Hayward was singing as he began the descent. Hayward was still looking for a miracle in his life, singing of the silence of the mountains and the crashing of the sea when Martin Toogood put his foot gently on the brake. Nothing. He pressed harder. No response.

And Justin Hayward was still singing about the dead and the sleeping when the car left the road, roaring with a scream of tyres through the hedge, to roll and bounce over and over on the ridges of the Down, circling in all the slow motion of death.

There was no eruption of flame, no spurt of fire. Just a long, dying hiss of steam and the relentless squeak of a slowly turning wheel. The rest was silence.

Chapter Six

Milk bottles growing daily in number. A parcel too long on the step. Mildred Hanson wouldn't have classed herself as a nosey neighbour, but she couldn't help noticing how oddly still the Fry house seemed as May edged towards June and the blossom passed and the sun warmed the earth. You could normally set your watch by John. His car was always growling along the gravel at eight-thirty, back around five, later sometimes.

Eleanor was different. Mildred knew that John was a teacher, but Eleanor didn't appear to work. She'd go shopping most days; Mildred had often waved to her in Asda, but her car came and went at irregular intervals. Occasionally she heard her radio in the garden. When the two of them were there, they didn't seem to talk much. But now there were no cars coming or going. No John at eight-thirty and five; no Eleanor at any time. So Mildred, the non-nosy neighbour, sent Keith round. And Keith had gone – anything for a quiet life. He had taken retirement too early – he knew that now. And, love Mildred though he undoubtedly did, she was just beginning to grate on him a little. She was just so ... daily.

Six pints stood in the plastic thingy on the front step. There was a parcel addressed to Mrs E Fry alongside. The free Leighford paper that advertised crap that nobody wanted jutted from the half-open letter box.

'Hello!' Keith called through it, risking his old trouble by bending so low. Nothing. He knocked the paper through to land with a thwack on the pile of unopened mail on the mat. He could see the hall was empty, the whole place silent except for the ancient tick of the grandfather clock one of the Frys had inherited as a wedding present. Keith had retired years ago, but he still had a powerful pair of shoulders and he tested one of them against the door. Solid.

He tried the side gate, the one that led to the garden. No obstacle here. A hose lay uncoiled across the lawn, the lawn that could do with a mow. There were daisies and butter-cups sprouting with a glory that Solomon might have envied. But then, Solomon was no gardener. He looked in through the patio doors to the kitchen. No one there. He tried the handle and the door opened. That was odd. A loaf of bread lay discarded on its board, its cut face grey with mould; a half-full (or was it half-empty) cup of cold coffee stood nearby, its surface mottled with turquoise blotches. The room seemed oddly cold on this bright Thursday morning, unlived in, abandoned, dead.

'Hello?' he called again. 'Eleanor? John?'

It wasn't half term for another week so he knew John would be at school. But why hadn't he collected the milk? The post? The letters lay in front of the door where the postman had been dutifully slotting them through for the past few days. The lounge was empty. Telly off. Papers, days old, on the coffee table.

'Hello!' the old man called again. 'I'm coming up.' And he made for the stairs. He felt more awkward now than he had on the ground floor. There was something half-sacred about other people's bedrooms. He'd only ever once been in next door's downstairs and never up here. He felt like an intruder. 'Hello?' the call was softer now, as if he was afraid of an answer. He tried the first door. Spare room. Bed made. A pair of trousers on the duvet. He tried the second. The master bedroom – a double kingsize, the covers pulled back, pillows rumpled. No sign of life. There were more doors. One, he knew, was the airing cupboard, because his and Mildred's house was a mirror image of this one. The other would be the bathroom – no point in looking in there. The third was the second spare room. This was the junk heap, what estate agents incomprehensibly called the box room. There was an old computer here, parts of an exercise bike, piles of books.

Something made Keith go back to the master bedroom and he opened the wardrobe. Her clothes were there – dresses, tops, sling-back shoes. His seemed to have gone. No shirts, no jackets, no trousers. So that was it, then; he'd left her. Done a runner. And what about Eleanor? Chased after him? Gone home to mummy? Keith was still pondering the possibilities when he pushed open the bathroom door.

For the rest of his life he wished he hadn't. Eleanor Fry lay in a bath of blood, her skin the colour of parchment, one arm resting on the edge of the porcelain, fingers slightly curled. On the floor below them, an empty bottle lay on the bath mat. Keith gripped the door to steady himself. For a fleeting, silly, shock-induced moment, he saw himself in a *Midsomer Murders* scenario. People who found bodies there always screamed and came rushing out of picturesque cottages off chocolate boxes. Real life wasn't quite like that. He couldn't make any sound at all. All he could do was stare at the dead woman's face. Her grey eyes were sunk in, dull in the half-light. Her right breast jutted from the crimson water, her shoulder raised slightly against her head, as if she'd been holding a phone there.

Keith had seen the dead before. He should have recognized the smell. As soon as he left the kitchen, he'd been aware of it, a sickly sweetness which is unplaceable at first, the unforgettable. He knew she'd been dead for days, that rigor would have come and gone, that her back and legs would be dark with lividity, that her flesh would be cold.

He turned and padded down the stairs, pausing at the phone on its cradle by the kitchen door. He didn't use it. It just didn't seem right, somehow. And he waited until he was back on his own soil before he said softly to his wife, busy at work in her flower beds, 'Mildred, you'd better call the police.'

Missing persons were always difficult. Missing girls a hundred times so. To begin with, there was that fine line between civil liberties and panic. Annette Choker would be sixteen in five weeks. And in five weeks, all the rights of adulthood would kick in. As it was, she was a minor and the law galvanized itself into action. DCI Henry Hall had his hands full with the Radley inquiry. He couldn't really spare the personnel to hunt for the girl, but he couldn't ignore her either. He didn't want to pull Martin Toogood off the murder case – the man was too useful. On the other hand, a rookie PC like Alison McCormick couldn't handle it by herself. There was always Jacquie Carpenter. But Jacquie had her uses too, on murder enquiries, especially when Peter Maxwell was involved. And Henry Hall would rather know where Peter Maxwell was at all times in these situations – and that meant using Jacquie as a sounding board.

The word of Annette Choker's disappearance

had gone out to every police authority in the country. Her description; a school photo from Year Ten when she looked more angelic than she did the day she vanished; what she was last seen wearing. It all travelled the electronic miles through cyberspace to find itself, hard copied, on police station walls, supermarket notice boards, night club billboards. Did anybody look at those, Alison McCormick wondered as she checked the wording of the description for the umpteenth time. Did anybody care? What did they see? A little girl lost, caught up in a frightening world she didn't understand? Or a tart out on the razzle, deserving everything she got? Welcome to police work.

Newspapermen had a take all their own. They snooped like the heavy, bloated flies of summer, onto cases like these. Those that weren't already bivouacked on the trench-dissected slopes of Staple Hill were clamouring for exclusives on the steps of Leighford Police Station. They circled the Barlichway Estate where the law of the jungle prevailed, wafting greenbacks under the noses of impressionable kids and mixing with the lowest of life other than each other. They hovered at the gates of Leighford High, asking all and sundry whether they knew Annette Choker or where she'd gone.

It was an ashen-faced Henry Hall who called the nick to order that Tuesday morning. The call had just come through. He waited until the fidgeting had stopped, until ciggies descended from mouths, coffees were placed on desks, faces turned away from computer screens and eyes were on him.

'I've got some bad news, people,' he said. 'Martin Toogood was found dead an hour ago. His car came off the road on Gravel Hill. If it's any consolation, he couldn't have known what hit him.'

The silence that followed was almost painful. Mouths hung open, or lips trembled. No one, for a moment, could look at anyone else.

'I'm going to sort it,' Hall said, glad to be moving, glad to be leaving the building. He heard someone crying as he swept past. It could have been anyone, but it happened to be Alison Mc-Cormick.

He'd been baulked of his prey once and he wouldn't be again. Peter Maxwell had abandoned the tell-tale Jesus scarf and the trademark tweed cap. He wore a scruffy green anorak, the one he did the garden in, and he oiled Surrey carefully, before he made for the Downs and the slope of Staple Hill.

Metternich watched him go from his lair in the privet where he was dining alfresco on rack of vole. Where was the old bastard off to, this time of night? Still, what the hey! He didn't get out enough, when all was said and done.

Maxwell crested the hill a little after midnight, the half moon still bright on the sea and the lights twinkling out on the Shingle. He noticed a gap in the gorse bushes to his left where some idiot had come off the road – and recently too; this hadn't been there yesterday. Motorists! Hate 'em or hate 'em. He dismounted at the old gate that led to the dig site. The police tape still floated there, but there was no fresh-faced copper freezing his walkie-talkie off and certainly no police car with an all-too-awkward Henry Hall in it. That was already two points up on his last visit.

The downside was that it was night and Peter Maxwell would have to resort to a torch. He wondered how conspicuous that would be, darting like a latter-day firefly against the black backdrop of Staple Hill. It was also six days after little Robbie Whatsisface had found the corpse of David Radley and the trail was getting colder. He ducked under the Do Not Cross warning and reconnoitred the site. A series of trenches to his right, leading over the brow of the hill to what had once been the river bed of the Leigh told him that this was the edge of the Saxon cemetery. They'd found nine graves so far, Douglas Russell had told Maxwell's Year Twelve, all facing east-west, all wrapped in linen shrouds. Four women, three men, two children. People who had walked the Wessex of Alfred and Edgar, who had known this land long ago, when it was dark and tangled wild forest; when it was deep and silent wild marsh. Russell was looking for a church. Experience suggested there had to be one, somewhere beyond the ash grove. But would they find it before their contract came to an end and the golf course developers moved in? Could that, Maxwell wondered, be what all this was about? Did someone kill David Radley not to allow the dig to go ahead; to halt progress and put a stop to this?

He stepped gingerly across the duckboards and the planking. He didn't want to risk his torch just yet – the moon was help enough out here. Then he was in the dark tangle of the ash copse and trying to get his bearing. He flicked on the torch beam. What was the point of this, he wondered, as he knelt painfully on the tree roots? Henry Hall's experts had been all over them with their gismos and their thingummies. What did he hope to see that they'd missed, with his feeble little torch and his historian's nose? He was still looking up at the branches above him, at the black criss-cross of the ash boughs against the pale purple of the night sky, when he felt something round and cold against his neck and heard a chilling click. Instinctively, he opened his arms wide, trying to swivel his eyes to the left.

'Would I be right in assuming that is a shotgun in my neck, or are you pleased to see me?'

'Spot on, squire,' an Essex man replied. 'Now – two questions. Who the fuck are you? And what the fuck are you doing here?'

Henry Hall took the loss of a man personally. Tom Wilson, on duty at the front desk, had seen Martin Toogood go at a little before twelve and had signed him out. There seemed nothing unusual, Wilson assured the DCI. Yes, the DS had been on duty for nearly fourteen hours, but that wasn't unusual in this business. Yes, Wilson had seen him drive out. And no, there had been nothing amiss.

Hall had stood earlier that day on the grassy ridge by the roadside on Gravel Hill, where the wind blew the stunted bushes flat as the weather roared in from the Channel. Policemen in yellow jackets had directed traffic, shooing away morbidly curious rubberneckers. A section of the road had been cordoned off where Toogood's car had smashed through the flimsy wooden rail and gone over the edge. The DCI had waited while they brought the car up by crane, a slow, agonizing job. He had listened, impassive, to the grinding of steel and the tinkling of shattered glass and the rip as the car's mangled shell tore free of the shrubbery. He had supervised the sending of bits of twisted metal to the police lab, loaded like a giant armadillo on the flat-bed, plates bent and broken. Then he had gone to the morgue.

If truth be told, Henry Hall had a thing about morgues. It wasn't a cliché, like dear old Christopher Timothy in the long-forgotten Flaxborough series on the telly. It wasn't *bodies* he objected to; it was the buildings they put them in. Cold, green, with that scrubbed and rescrubbed steel, that sense of the slaughter-house.

Martin Toogood's chest was crushed beyond hope, his ribs driven into his lungs. Both arms were broken and his pelvis smashed. Only his face remained unmarked and the boy lay on the slab as though he were asleep.

'It's a death trap, Gravel Hill,' Jim Astley was scrubbing up, ready to go to work. 'Time you people did something about it. And it's my day off.'

'Sorry, Jim,' Henry Hall was looking down at his DS, at the wreck of a life.

He felt the doctor's hand on his elbow, still wet from the ritual. He'd have to scrub again now. 'One of your own, wasn't he?' he said softly. 'It's

111

no trouble.' Jim Astley could be a bit of a bastard. In fact, he was most of the time. But just occasionally he cracked and proved he was human after all. It wrong-footed Henry Hall every time.

In the brightly lit neon corridor outside, in those areas of Leighford General where members of the public were permitted to see their loved ones for the last time, an elderly couple sat on upright NHS chairs. They'd both been crying, both trying in their own ways to come to terms with the news a uniformed copper had given them.

'Mr and Mrs Toogood?' They both stood up, she clutching her handbag, he holding tightly onto her. 'I'm DCI Henry Hall...' and it didn't happen very often, but he found himself holding a frail old lady as she sobbed into his neck.

'Mr Maxwell, is it?' The questioner was a corporate type, all suit and attitude, with what appeared to be a very expensive squirrel sitting on his head.

'It is,' the Head of Sixth Form answered, smug in the knowledge that *he* would never need the services of a rug.

'Do you mind telling me what you were doing at the dig tonight? Other than trespassing, I mean.'

'Do you mind telling me why you're asking?' Maxwell countered. All in all, it had been an unpleasant hour or two. He'd had a shotgun jabbed into his neck, then his back, and had been unceremoniously bundled into a four-by-four by two fully paid up members of Rent-a-Yob. Now he was in somebody's office, facing a large, well-

112

suited man in a huge leather chair. The place was opulent, with designer glass smouldering against a giant single-pane window and tasteful coffee tables with suede tops. The carpet alone was worth Peter Maxwell's lump sum, should he ever live to collect it.

'Because I own the land on which you were trespassing.'

'Fair enough,' Maxwell nodded, quietly impressed by anyone who handled a sentence's syntax like that. 'I'll be apologizing, then.'

'Well, that's good,' the suit said. 'Quite the in-thing, these days, isn't it, for criminals to have to apologize to their victims. All part of our blame culture society, I believe.'

'Victims?' Maxwell chuckled, looking at the heavies in the black suits, their knuckles trailing the skirting boards, still waiting in the darkened office corner. 'Is that how you see yourself? As a victim, Mr ... er..?'

'Anthony Cahill. Of Cahill and Lieberman.'

'Ah, I see. You're the golfing people.' Maxwell was *nearly* up to putting two and two together.

'No, Mr Maxwell, we're the property people,' Cahill corrected him. 'This particular site is a golfing enterprise, yes. But we could just as easily be talking condominium, retail outlets, marinas. We specialize in diversity.'

'And soundbites,' Maxwell nodded. Teaching has a jargon all its own, with its visions, its inclusion policies, its differentiated outcomes. But the world of business could leave it standing every time.

'This could be a police matter.' Cahill's smile

was wearing a little thin.

'Oh, it already is,' Maxwell told him. 'What with the body and all.'

'Yes,' Cahill's face darkened a little, as he looked at his heavies. 'That was unfortunate.'

'Then, there's the matter of the shotgun and the abduction by your two rottweilers here.'

The heavies moved forward like automata, fists flexing, lips curling – signs of aggression they'd learned long ago from the football terraces and British Party get-to-maim-you conferences.

Cahill clicked his fingers and the rottweilers stayed to heel. 'George and Julian were only carrying out my instructions, Mr Maxwell. George *does* have a permit for the Purdey and as for abduction ... well, that's putting it a little strongly, don't you think? No, I thought you might appreciate a lift back. Your bicycle *is* strapped to the roof and I know you'll take it in the right spirit when I say you are a *tad* on the elderly side for physical rigour of this type.'

'Thoughtful, I'm sure. Are you always so zealous in guarding your investments?'

'Oh, yes,' Cahill was deadly earnest. 'Make no mistake, Mr Maxwell, property is a dangerous business. No one is in it for what I believe the working class call "laffs". Now,' he leaned forward across his large, expensive desk, 'what assurances do I have that you will not again stray onto the dig?'

'None,' Maxwell said flatly. 'Mr Cahill, let me try to explain something to you. Six – nearly seven – days ago now, a boy I know found the body of a man I knew – right up there, on your

114

little patch of land.'

'And that's your business?' Cahill asked.

'My boy,' Maxwell held out his left hand. 'My man,' be held out his right. 'There's a certain ghastly symmetry to it, don't you think?'

'It's a police problem,' Cahill said.

'So I've been told,' Maxwell nodded. 'I don't know if you've been following the case on the telly, the radio, the papers? Well, I have and you know what's missing? An arrest. Or even, in fact, a suspect.'

'Ah, I see,' Cahill smiled, cradling his hands and leaning backwards. 'So you're some sort of Hercule Poirot meets Jane Marple, are you? I thought people like you only existed in fiction.'

'No, no,' Maxwell assured him. 'We're real enough. Helping police with their enquiries. You know, like Leerdammer does.'

'You mean, you work with the police?' Cahill frowned.

'In a manner of speaking.' Not a flicker betrayed the nonsense Maxwell was spouting. 'Tell me, in that context, George ... Julian – who else have you boys shooed off the site? Who else's neck have you jabbed a shotgun into? Who else's bike have you manhandled onto your roof?'

Cahill snapped his fingers again and whatever George was about to say never reached his vocal cords. Synaptic reactions like his took longer. 'My operatives and I are quite prepared to answer *police* questions,' Cahill said. 'Indeed, we have already. But until then, Mr Maxwell, let me give you a piece of advice. If you persist in straying onto any property of mine in the future,

115

then, rest assured, it won't be a cosy little chat we'll be having.'

'That sounds a *little* like a threat,' Maxwell observed, wrinkling his nose at the man.

'Got it in one,' Cahill smiled, 'as our golfing clients might say. Now you can play cops and robbers all you like, but if my lads catch you at the site again, they'll be playing castanets with your knee-caps. Julian, unship Mr Maxwell's bicycle, will you? I'm sure he can find his own way from here.'

It was early Wednesday morning by the time Peter Maxwell got home. Oddly, both his tyres had punctures and he'd had to wheel Surrey noisily from the flyover, clanking and squeaking as he went. As he reached the dark of the privet hedge outside 38 Columbine, a figure hurtled from a parked car and threw itself at Maxwell. Surrey clattered to the tarmac as Maxwell caught her in his arms and held her tight.

'Jacquie,' he tried to say through the muffle of her sleeve. He held her at arm's length. 'Jacquie, what's the matter?'

By the street light he could see the crumpled lip and runny nose and the silver-streaked cheeks.

'It's Martin,' she gulped, letting the tears fall now that she'd held in all day. 'Martin Toogood. He's dead.'

It was nearly half-past two before Jacquie Carpenter had calmed down sufficiently to talk rationally about things. She'd been talking rationally all day, to her colleagues at the nick, to nurses and doctors at the hospital, to Martin's sweet, heartbroken parents, all of them trying to understand what had happened and why.

Jacquie and Maxwell had got outside a few Southern Comforts by now and they lay snuggled on his settee in the warm lamp glow of his lounge, his arms wrapped around her as he breathed in the scent of her hair.

'Right,' he said. 'Once more from the top.'

She took a deep breath. How well he played the game, the old police ploy. Make them go over it again – and again – until the whole thing emerged. People in shock remember titbits, fragments, snatches, at random and in the wrong order. No way to solve a case; no way to get at the truth. He was her Nice Policeman and she loved him for it.

'Martin left the nick shortly before twelve. Tom Wilson signed him out at eleven fifty-six.'

'That's usual practice?' Maxwell checked.

'Technically, no. Martin should have done it himself, but we all do it. The desk man's vital in any nick in the country; knows all our comings and goings – he clocks us all in and out, man and boy.'

'Chauvinistically said,' he smiled and squeezed her.

'He drove out almost immediately.'

'Almost?' Maxwell was right – leave no stone unturned, no second unaccounted for.

'Long enough, Wilson said, for him to get into the car and get to the gate.'

'All right. What's that? Two minutes? One? Then what?'

117

'He turned right out of the station.'

'Along the High Street?'

'Yes. Nothing then until he ... until Gravel Hill.'

'What was he driving?'

'Mondeo.'

'You're the expert, Jacquie. How long would it take him to get to Gravel Hill?'

'That time of night, there'd be virtually no traffic, not once he'd left the town centre; twelve, fifteen minutes, tops.'

'So the accident happened at ... twelve fifteen?'

'Close enough. Henry said Astley's time of death was between twelve and one.'

'From what I know of Jim Astley, he seems to be pulling out all the stops on this one.' Maxwell and Astley went nearly as far back as Maxwell and Hall. They sounded like a Vaudeville act and just as jolly!

She half-turned to him. 'He was doing it for Henry, he said – a personal favour.'

Maxwell nodded. Perhaps he'd misjudged the old pathologist. 'Tell me about Toogood. Drink? Drugs?'

Jacquie was already shaking her head. 'Astley found nothing in his system at all. I worked with the man for over a year, Max. In a profession notorious for driving you to one or the other, I never saw him hit more than a Stella. And nobody does drugs in our line – we see too much of what they can do.'

'So he was sober as a judge?'

'Yes,' she nodded. 'Obviously, it was the first thing Astley looked for.'

'Road conditions?' Maxwell was covering all

the angles. 'Weather?' He knew all there was to know about people he loved dying on roads. None of it made any sense.

'The road was dry. It had been a fine day and there was no sign of any grease or obstacle at the point where the car left the road.'

'So,' Maxwell brushed Jacquie's hair back from her face and planted tender little kisses on her temple. 'Tell me about the car.'

Jacquie took a deep breath again. 'That news came through only this evening,' she said and caught the time of Maxwell's digital clock. 'Sorry, *last* evening. The police lab had been all over Martin's Mondeo. There was no doubt about it. Somebody had cut through his brake cables.'

'Are you quite sure about this, Sylvia?' James Diamond BSc, MEd was wiping his glasses already and it was only nine thirty-two.

'I still have friends at Leighford General,' the school nurse said, looking down at Diamond in his office and realizing again what a *small* man he was. 'Eleanor Fry was brought in by the police at 11.30 yesterday morning. She was pronounced dead. The post mortem has been delayed until tomorrow, but my contacts tell me we're talking about suicide.'

'Dear God,' Diamond threw his glasses onto the pile of reports on his desk. At moments like these, the target levels of Nine See Eight seemed particularly irrelevant. 'Thank you, Sylvia. I know I can rely on you to be discreet about this.'

She looked at the man with contempt. County Hall's poodle, the Secretary of State's lapdog, the whipping boy of the Chairman of Governors; why didn't he *stand up* to people?

'Yes, of course, Mr Diamond,' she said and made her exit. Diamond flicked an intercom switch. 'Bernard, get in here, will you? We've got to find John Fry before the Press get hold of things. No. No. I'm not talking about the Choker girl, dammit. I'm talking about Fry's wife. She's killed herself.'

Chapter Seven

Tam Fraser's nose was buried in a sheaf of geophys reports. Around him stood his team, Douglas Russell to the fore. He looked up in the weird, distorted sunlight of the main tent.

'People.' The man with the lion's mane of snow white hair cleared his throat and expected the world to grind to a halt. 'I'm Professor Fraser of the University of Wessex. I'd like you to have my condolences over poor David. He may have been your boss, but he was my friend. The university thought the simplest solution to this situation was for me to fill the breach, however temporarily. What's this?' He pointed to a page.

'Er ... findings of the resistivity gauge, professor,' the lanky geophysicist behind him thought it rather an odd question.

'Mr ... Russell, is it?'

The man nodded.

'You're in charge of geophys?'

'That's right,' Russell wasn't on. 'As you see, we've got clear activity down here, near the old riverbed. I was wondering whether now wouldn't be the time to start...'

'The thing about geophysics,' Fraser smiled at them all, cutting his man dead, 'is that it highlights anomalies, but doesn't actually tell you a damn thing. Have you tried bosing?'

'Bosing?' Russell didn't believe what he was hearing. Some sort of echo-sounding from the Dark Ages?

Fraser looked at him. 'The old ways are best, Mr Russell,' he said, tapping the side of his nose. 'Believe me, I know. Who are you?'

'Helen Reader.' Charlie Buttock was owning up to her real name at last.

'Are you a professional or are you just along for the ride?' Fraser could smell an amateur a mile away.

'Well I ... I worked on the Seahenge project. Last year I was at Silbury...'

'Yes,' Fraser nodded. 'Rather like the young people being at Glastonbury, isn't it? Do we have any other trained archaeologists here?'

Two hands went up.

'You are...?' the great man moved to face the first.

'Derek Latymer. Southampton. Class of '98.'

The man was young, certainly, scrawny, but with the muscle that comes from eight years at the trench-face. He hauled the broad-brimmed hat from his head.

'More importantly,' Fraser said, 'class of degree?'

121

'First.'

The professor nodded. 'Masters?'

'Ethnoarchaeology. The Pacific Rim.'

'Hmm,' Fraser commented. 'Useful here, then. You?'

'Robin Edwards,' the second hand stepped forward. The man was the heavier of the two, stolid even, with a thatch of blonde hair and a complexion made all the ruddier by his days under the sun on the slope of Staple Hill. 'University of Lancaster. I have a Two One in...'

Fraser's hand was in the air, stopping him right there. 'Right, laddie,' he winked at him, 'You make the tea, will you? Mr Russell and I have a little re-grouping to do.'

'Jesus,' whistled Helen Reader as she trooped out into the sun for another gruelling day at the clay face, clapping the wide hat over her head-scarf. A great believer in protection, was Helen Reader. 'What a bastard!'

Latymer chuckled. 'That he may be,' he said, 'but in his day, there was no one to touch him.'

'In his day?' she hauled on her gloves and collected her bucket. She pointed to the yawning graves. 'He must have known some of these people personally. And what is bosing exactly?'

'Bosing,' Latymer told her, 'is a technique Heinrich Schliemann probably used at Troy. You bash the ground with a wooden mallet or a lead-filled canister and listen for the pitch of the echo.'

The woman rocked on her heels in the little pit she'd made her own over the last fortnight. 'You'll forgive me for saying this, Derek,' she said, 'but you might as well piss into the wind.'

He leaned over her. 'Don't knock it, Helen, until you've tried it. At least he didn't ask *you* to make the tea! Now, that's progress!'

Reports came in sporadically throughout Wednesday. A man matching the description of John Fry had been seen getting on a plane at Heathrow. Almost simultaneously, he was serving himself petrol at services on the M6. An hour later, he was getting off a bus at Heanton Punchardon in Devon. There was no doubt about it, the mobile phone was a godsend to the serial nosy person and the weirdo who wanted their fifteen minutes of fame. Manning it all, with arms flailing like a demented windmill, Alison McCormick was at breaking point by lunchtime.

There is no time in a busy nick for pity, for dwelling on what might have been, for analysing the what ifs. Henry Hall's team had a murder enquiry in their laps, trying to piece together the shattered life of David Radley. They had a schoolgirl somewhere out there in a naughty world, with or without the sicko who may have abducted her. Now, in the cold, dead form of Eleanor Fry, they had a suicide too. But looming over it all, the smiling face of Martin Toogood – a colleague, a mate. That got under all their skins, the members of Hall's team, as they made endless phone calls, cross-referenced hundreds of facts, fought off the press.

At lunchtime, the DCI held his first conference with the ladies and gentlemen of the Fourth Estate. It was the usual circus. Thirty or so of the guardians of the peoples' morals, defenders of the right to know, champions of the morbidly curious, were crowded into Hall's police station, trying to read reports upside down, craning their necks to catch computer screens. All babbling together in a cacophony of noisiness. Hall was calm, unflappable, an enigma behind his blank glasses, sitting square and ready behind his blank desk. Jacquie Carpenter was the acceptable face of policing, sitting, appropriately, on the man's right hand, her lower half tucked well out of sight of the *Daily Sport* man who might be able to snap her getting out of her chair and superimpose somebody else's bum on the photo. 'Copper in naked love-romp.' Brilliant.

'Now it's one of your own, Chief Inspector,' the *Guardian* called, 'I expect everything else is on hold, is it?' The political envy of the left was apparent in every syllable.

'Not at all,' Hall told him, knowing perfectly well that every other copper in the room wanted to punch the man on the nose. 'Can I remind you, ladies and gentlemen, that this meeting has been called in connection with the death of Dr David Radley.' It wasn't a question; it was a statement.

'Are you saying there's no connection with DS Toogood?' the *Telegraph* wanted to know, believing in its heart of hearts that there was some ghastly underground conspiracy to decimate the country's police force.

'We have no reason to make such a connection at this stage,' Hall said. He'd done conferences like this without number. The ladies and gentlemen of the Press were today's sounding board, the nation's social conscience, the judge, the jury, and even, half of them wished, the executioner.

There were moans and whistles all round. 'We already know somebody tampered with your boy's brakes,' the *Leighford Advertiser* cut to the chase. This man was either a kid on the make, anxious to prove to the big boys of Fleet Street that he was a rising star, or else he was an old hack on his way down, out to prove he still had what it took to be a thoroughly obnoxious bastard. He could have been any age, really. 'Do you believe in the laws of coincidence, Chief Inspector?'

'I believe in being given time to get on with my job,' Hall silenced the hubbub with a harsher line than usual. Jacquie was impressed with that. But then Jacquie was usually impressed by Henry Hall; he knew his job. Martin Toogood had been his colleague, his mate too. 'That's all for now.'

Slowly, as the minutes of the afternoon ticked away, they pieced together the last days of the life of Detective Sergeant Martin Jonathan Toogood. Henry Hall sat slumped in his shirt-sleeves, sticky in the suddenly fierce heat of late May. Jacquie Carpenter had the floor, pointing to the whiteboard behind her, directing operations. In front of her, burly coppers sat quietly, smoke curling up from half-smoked ciggies. Unusually, in a murder enquiry, there was no photo of the deceased on the wall. Everybody knew what Martin Toogood looked like – his face was etched in all their minds. And nobody in that tense, tired room wanted to see a photo of him dead.

'According to Martin's log, he went to Petworth on Saturday morning. Talked to a Professor

Fraser at the university. That interview finished at...' she checked her notes, 'eleven forty. Then he went to Brighton, to the Camdens Leisure Centre, to talk to another of David Radley's colleagues, a Dr Samantha Welland. He grabbed lunch in the town and made some phone calls. We've traced these. One to his mum and dad – apparently he rang them every Saturday. One here to the nick. One – and this is interesting – to his garage.'

'Who's been on to them?' Hall asked.

'I have, guv.' A thick-set West Indian's hand was in the air. 'If he thought there was something wrong with the car, he didn't tell the garage.'

'Where is this, Jimmy?'

'Braddocks in Westbridge Road.'

Hall nodded. He'd used them himself. Careful people. Good track record.

'No,' Jimmy went on. 'He was just booking in an MOT for the end of the month. Routine stuff.'

'All right. Jacquie?'

'We don't know exactly where he was in the afternoon of Saturday, but he'd already arranged to meet with Radley's widow, Susan, in the evening. That interview lasted a little under an hour. He left her at ... eight twenty-three.'

'What about Sunday?' Hall moved them all on, anxious to avoid silences. Keep them busy, keep them working. Everybody would feel better for that.

'Day off,' Jacquie said. There were some people in the room who vaguely remembered those. 'As far as we know, Martin collected his papers from

126

the shop at sometime during the middle of the morning. They had weekend staff on and the kid was a bit daffy, so he wasn't quite sure. Remembered a man vaguely answering his description, but if it was Martin, he didn't pay his outstanding paper bill – that's still on their books. He had lunch at the Pilgrims, with Tony.'

Tony Campbell shifted in his seat. He was Toogood's age, but without Toogood's ambition. There was nothing remotely fast-track about Tony Campbell. He knew it and that was fine. Police forces needed Indians too. It was just an ordinary Sunday, the day before Toogood died, but one Tony Campbell would remember for the rest of his life.

'Martin rang me about ten,' he said. 'Asked if I could come out to play.'

There were a few smiles in the semi-darkness of the room. No one could quite manage a laugh.

'Anything relevant?' Hall asked. 'Over lunch, I mean?'

'You know what it's like, guv,' Campbell said. 'Trying to remember inconsequentials. Sure, we talked about the Radley case. Shop, you know.'

Everyone knew. It went with the job. They weren't supposed to do it, of course, off duty and in public like that, but what the hey...

'But we talked about other things too – you know, putting the world to rights. Martin had got this holiday planned...'

Everybody shifted uneasily. Unfinished business, plans that would never happen. A career ended. A life cut short. It was all so bloody painful; so bloody pointless.

127

'Monday,' Hall moved them on again.

'Martin came on duty at nine sharp,' Jacquie took up the narrative. 'He worked on various leads all morning here at his desk, went over to the lab early afternoon.'

'Anybody see him in the canteen?'

'Said he'd grab something on the hoof, guv.' Tony Campbell had waved to the man the last time he'd seen him, on the last day of his life.

'He was a Cornish pastie man,' somebody said.

'Ginsters. Loved them,' somebody else echoed.

'All right, people,' Hall said softly, keeping them on track, away from the memories, the folk tales. He'd be St Martin by nightfall and they all had a job to do. 'We know he left at eleven forty-eight. That's too long.' He was tapping a pencil on a notepad. 'Too long a day.'

'He was the best bloody driver I knew,' Tony Campbell said, defending his friend to the last, looking wildly around with tears in his eyes, challenging anybody to say otherwise.

'We know, Tony,' Hall looked at the man. 'We know.'

The silence they'd all been dreading fell at last. It felt like a dead weight, suffocating, choking. It made your skin crawl and your throat tighten.

'Right,' Hall broke it, bringing the *coup de grâce;* just one of the jobs you do when you're in charge and everybody's looking at you for results. Somehow, somehow, to make everything all right. 'To cases. Tony, you knew Martin better than any of us.'

'Best man at my wedding,' Campbell confirmed, clearing his throat, welling down.

'That's what his wife's always said,' somebody shouted. Great. It broke the ice and people laughed for the first time that day, Tony Campbell among them. Hall reminded himself to find the joker and give the man a medal.

'Anybody bear him a grudge?' Hall let the ripples die away before he posed the question.

'He put away his fair share of villains, guv,' Campbell said. 'But we're not aware of anybody in particular. No overt threats. Nothing out of the ordinary.'

That wasn't helpful. But it didn't surprise the DCI. In his experience, most 'honest' crooks didn't bear grudges. Everybody inside was innocent, of course, framed not so much by bent coppers, but by the bent system; the laws that were framed by the rich for the rich, the them-and-us mentality of Tony Blair's Britain. And anyway, the opprobrium of villains was usually levelled at DIs and above, the heads of investigations whose profiles were high, not the underlings who were clearly, like the Nazis of yesteryear, merely obeying orders.

'This case, then,' he said. 'Who has Martin seen, except for this Professor Fraser, Dr Welland and Radley's wife?'

'He interviewed a number of people at the site, guv,' Jacquie told him, 'when the body was found.'

'Who's got the list?'

'Guv,' Tony Campbell passed the sheet of names forward.

'Four. We'll need to see all those again. This Douglas Russell; is he running the dig now?'

'Er ... we don't know, guv,' somebody said.

'Right. Back to basics. Jacquie, you and Tony get out there later today. I want each of those four quizzed. And I mean quizzed. I want to know what they've all had for breakfast for the past week. Jimmy,' he glanced at the West Indian, 'get yourself over to the Quinton, calling at the magistrates' offices on the way. I want a warrant to search the rooms of any of these diggers staying there. Start with Russell.'

'Yes, guv.'

'Now – anything of note on Martin's computer?'

'The affairs of men,' Jacquie's voice was a little broken up on her end of the phone.

'Who's been talking?' Peter Maxwell wanted to know, perched on his office desk at Leighford High, that great centre of academe for the sons and daughters of gentlefolk. 'Dierdre Lessing and I are merely colleagues. And as for Sally Green-how, I was just whispering in her mouth,' his Harpo Marx was a *little* lost without the actions to go with it but if you were a certain age, it was un-mistakeable for all that. Had Harpo ever spoken on celluloid, he would, of course, have sounded just like the Groucho Maxwell was doing now.

'Seriously though, Max,' she said.

'Sorry, darling heart. Say on.'

'It was the last thing Martin Toogood wrote on his computer on Monday night. Mean anything to you.'

'Julius Caesar,' Maxwell said, dredging it up from the deepest fathoms of his brain, 'by a little-known playwright called William Shakespeare.'

'That would make sense,' Jacquie was scrabbling around her end in the nick for a bit of paper. 'Say on.'

'Ooh, it's been a long time since I wrestled with the Bard of Avon.' Maxwell screwed up his face in an attempt to remember. 'Um ... "The enemy increaseth every day;

We, at the height, are ready to decline.

There is a tide in the affairs of men,

Which, taken at the flood, leads on to fortune.

Omitted, all the voyage of their life

Is bound by shallows and in miseries.

On such a full sea are we now afloat,

And we must take the current when it serves,

Or lose our ventures..."

Or something like that!'

'You shit!' she smiled. 'How did I know you'd know that word for bloody word?'

'I phoned a friend,' he explained, giving her his best Chris Tarrant. He tapped on the window of his office and the snotty urchins up to no good on the ground below him vanished like ice in sunshine. 'If memory serves – and I think you know it does – it's dear old Brutus talking to Cassius. They've just killed a pretty decent bloke – Caesar – for all the wrong reasons, and they've realized their number's probably up. What's the link?'

'I wish I knew,' she sighed. 'Martin certainly lost his ventures, didn't he?'

'He did that,' Maxwell agreed, dropping back into his chair. 'You didn't tell me Martin was the poetic sort.'

'Well, he *did* read English at university.'

'Yes, I know. History would have been better, of course... Are you all right, Jacquie?' She'd gone very quiet.

'Yes,' she nuzzled her head into the phone, as well as she could in a frantic Incident Room. 'Yes, I'm fine. See you later.'

The bell was ringing at Leighford High, summoning the faithful and the not-so-faithful to Lesson Five. Perhaps in Faith Schools, they had a peal of the things chiming out Old Tom Oojah; it would certainly make the day go with a swing. Why was it, Peter Maxwell wondered, that three quarters of the way through the academic year, he still had no clear indication of who the hell he was teaching next? He checked the timetable on the wall, that great Behemoth that ruled everyone's life. God, yes, Thirteen Ay Two – the last lesson before they vanished into that glad goodnight that was Study Leave. How could he have forgotten? Maxwell's Own. Time for the pep talk, the last words of wisdom. The if-you-can-keep-your-head speech.

Mechanically, he nudged the over-zealous Year Seven kids to the correct side of the corridor and removed the white baseball cap from Jason Pillockface's head for the umpteenth time that week – 'Oh, sir!' the lad wailed as his civil liberties were taken from him. But these were the actions of a veteran of countless classroom campaigns and Maxwell wasn't even thinking about them. In his head, Jacquie's words whirled, the last sentence on Martin Toogood's computer. 'The affairs of men.' Was that it, then? Had the

132

clever, fast-track graduate cracked it? How had Maxwell put it to Jacquie? 'They've just killed a pretty decent bloke – Radley – for all the wrong reasons.' So, who stood to gain from Radley's death? It was the first question Henry Hall would have asked himself and his team, Maxwell knew that. Who would inherit the mantle? The Chair at Wessex? And a *conspiracy?* Was that what Too-good meant? The assassination of JFK – the second gunman on the grassy knoll. The murder of KFK – the gloating woman in the polka-dot dress. The moon landing, with the dear old stars and stripes flapping in a wind where there was no wind. Nobody believed that load of old tosh. Or did they, in the face of overwhelming evidence? He turned into Aitch Four as Year Thirteen settled down to be entertained for one last time. He really wanted to put the Radley case before them, get their take on it, use their fresh, young, inquisitive minds. To hit them with Toogood's enigma. As it was, he had a job to do.

'The parting of the ways, children,' he boomed as he closed the door. 'And the best bit of advice I can give you, as always, is?'

'Read the question!' they chorused.

'Damn right!' he winked.

'I want to see the man in charge. I assume it *is* a man?' the tall Scotsman stood facing Sergeant Wilson that Wednesday afternoon.

'In charge of what, specifically, sir?' Tom Wilson had been County Pedantic champion four years running back in the Nineties. You never lost it.

Tam Fraser leaned forward to look the man

closely in the face. 'I haven't time to piss about, laddie.' He said. 'You take those stripes of yours and get me somebody with pips on his shoulder – or is that analogy lost on you?'

'That'll be Detective Chief Inspector Hall,' Wilson said, unperturbed. He'd met belligerent Scotsmen before, albeit usually reeling pissed under the lion rampant shawls of the tartan army a little after the final whistle. 'Who shall I say...?'

'Tam Fraser,' the Scotsman said through Wilson's protective glass. 'Emeritus Professor of Archaeology, and you haven't the time for me to list all my publications.'

There is a God, then, thought Wilson and he'd just met him, but he couldn't say so. The desk man in any nick in the country had to be all things to all men. Lost cats, kids with their thumbs stuck up kettle spouts, Brinks Mat heists, serial murder – he'd seen the lot. A pompous old fart with a degree wasn't about to faze him.

'So what do you make of it?' Fraser asked Henry Hall when the DCI had had time to read the letter the professor had shown him. Wilson had mechanically gone through the motions of ringing through to DCI Hall who had asked him to bring Fraser through. And here they were, in Hall's office, at the end of another day, each of them trying to cope, in his own way, with murder.

'Oddballs,' Hall shrugged, passing the letter back.

'Undoubtedly,' Fraser agreed, although he'd expected a rather more penetrating analysis, 'but don't you see any implications here?'

'Implications?' It had been a long day for Henry Hall. Maybe he wasn't at his best with the amount of sleep he'd had.

'This ... organization, pressure group, call them what you will, are threatening my people at the dig.'

'Hardly threatening,' Hall reassured him.

Fraser adjusted his pince-nez to focus on the letter. "We find it reprehensible",' he read, "that you are defiling the bodies of our ancestors by disturbing their last resting places and we would like to warn you that unless you close the dig down now, we cannot answer for the consequences." Where I come from,' Fraser folded the letter again, 'that constitutes a threat.'

Hall looked at him. 'There's no address.'

'No,' Fraser agreed. 'Just as whoever killed wee David didn't leave his business card. I wouldn't have your job for all the tea in China.'

Hall held out his hand for the note to be passed back. The paper shone white in his lenses. "The Sepulchre Society of Sussex",' he read. 'All very alliterative.'

'Aye, peachy,' Fraser agreed. 'Have you heard of them?'

'I was about to ask you the same question, Professor.'

'This particular group, no.' Fraser sat back, legs crossed at the knee. 'But I'm familiar with the ethic. Aboriginals in particular get themselves in a snit about it, whiteys come along and desecrate – as they see it – the graves of their forebears. The fact that we're learning a phenomenal amount about their own ethnic past on their behalf seems

135

to have escaped them. But then, I can't say I'm surprised. Archaeology is not an option in schools, History's disappearing...'

If only, thought Henry Hall; he was thinking specifically of Peter Maxwell.

'Colleagues of mine have been roughed up in the Philippines,' Fraser went on, 'and there was a particularly nasty incident in Wyoming eight years back. You'd think the Lakota would be happy enough with Kevin Costner turning them into nice people on the big screen, wouldn't you? The bottom line, Chief Inspector, is what do you propose to do about it?'

Hall put the letter to one side. 'When did this arrive?' he asked.

'This morning.'

'At the site?'

'No, of course not, we haven't got an address there. It was sent to my colleague Douglas Russell, at his hotel.'

'The Quinton.'

'If you say so. I've only been here since this morning. I'll have to find somewhere, I suppose.'

'So you've effectively taken over from Dr Radley?'

'Taken over?' Fraser chuckled. 'Good God, no. I'm sixty-two, Inspector; my days of grubbing about in the earth are well and truly over – or so I thought. No, I'm just a caretaker until Upstairs at the university decide what to do about David's replacement. In the meantime, our window on the dig is closing rapidly. Golf course! I ask you!'

'Leave it with me,' Hall said.

Fraser leaned further back in his seat. 'I want

protection,' he said. 'For my people.'

'Protection?' Hall frowned. 'Professor Fraser, I'm conducting two murder enquiries simultaneously at the moment. That's apart from everything else going on, on a day-to-day progress at a station like this one.'

'Man, you should have been in the Gorbals in the good old days. Ach, that's another story.' He narrowed his eyes as he tried, as many had before, to get the measure of the man in front of him. 'You do know,' he said with his stately, gravel voice, pointing at the letter, 'that these people killed David Radley, don't you?'

George and Julian prowled their windy ridge again that night, their shaven heads pale under the moon.

'Fuck this for a game of soldiers,' Julian hissed, rummaging for his ciggies in the pockets of his body warmer.

'Stop whingeing,' George told him, taking a swig from his hip flask. 'Belter?'

'Nah,' Julian flexed his shoulders. 'Got to stay focused.'

'Ere, I saw that geek today.'

'Which of the many?' Julian asked, 'This is an archaeological dig. The whole fucking place is crawling with geeks.'

'That Arthur Wimble bloke. Remember I caught him helping himself to a bit of tat a few weeks back?'

'Oh, yeah. Recovered from his smacking, has he?'

'Conditional rehabilitation, Julian,' George corrected him. 'Gotta get with the jargon, y'know.'

Julian's fag glared briefly as he lit it. 'What time you got?'

'Half three,' George peered at his luminous dial. 'Hello.'

'Hmm?'

'Ten o'clock. By them spoil heaps.'

Both men crouched, making their bulk less conspicuous. George was right. A shadowy figure, dark, furtive, was flitting between the gate and the furthest of the heaps, jet against the blackness.

'Looks like fucking van Helsing,' Julian said.

'Who?'

'Van Helsing. You know, vampire hunter. Bloke in the film. What's his face? Jackman. Hugh Jackman.'

'That's all we fuckin' need. Vampires.'

'No, it's that long coat, that hat. Some bloody weirdo.'

'Metal detector?' the men's voices were at a sub-whisper. There wasn't a breath of wind below the ridge and they could hear 'van Helsing's' feet crunch on the gravel.

'Can't see one,' Julian was forcing his eyes to scan the darkness. 'Don't suppose it's a bloody ghoul, do you?'

'How d'you mean?' George asked. 'Ghoul?'

'Well, there's bodies, isn't there? I remember when I was a kid in London. There was the Vampire of Highgate. Somebody was hacking into vaults and stuff.'

'Get away.' George came from Romford. 'What for?'

Julian looked at him. 'To have sex with the corpses. It's what they get off on, these people. Necromancers, they're called. People who have affairs with dead women. Makes your hair curl, don't it? I seen this documentary on Channel Five...'

If he'd had any hair, George might have agreed with him. 'But the corpses are bloody Saxon, ain't they?' The senior security man was bringing all his powers of logic into play. 'That's like the olden times. Can't be much fun in that, surely? Where would you put your todger, for a start?'

'He's on the move.' Julian snatched at his oppo's sleeve.

The dark shadow was flitting across the site now, the long coat like a cloak flying behind him.

'Not windy, are you, Julian?' George nudged his number two.

'Me?' he said quickly. 'No fucking way. You tooled?'

He saw the barrels of George's Purdey gleam under his coat. 'I can't actually fire this thing you know,' George reminded him. 'There'd be bloody hell to pay.'

'Yeah, I know,' Julian said. 'But *he* don't. Let's do it.' And he stood up, bellowing. 'Oi. You!'

And the shadow paused for a second, looking up at the equally dark figures on the ridge.

George and Julian crawled down the ridges, stumbling over gravel heaps, sliding on shale, scattering spades and trowels. George, shotgun levelled, bounced over the guy ropes of the main tent and hurtled round the corner, only to collide with Julian, running from the other angle.

'Where'd he go?' Julian hissed, his left buttock giving him gyp where he'd wrenched it skirting the ash grove.

'I thought you had him,' George spun round, barrels at the ready.

'I thought you did.'

George straightened, smoothed down his tie and broke the gun over his arm. 'Well, that's it, then.'

'Yeah,' Julian agreed, wondering where he'd dropped his fag, then louder, 'Well, he'd better watch it, whoever he is. We'll have the dogs with us tomorrow night.'

'Bloody right,' George confirmed, suddenly as windy as his oppo. Whoever it was had vanished like a ghost. 'Got a ciggie, Julian?'

Chapter Eight

Peter Maxwell had occasionally been summoned to the Senior Management Team meetings they held every Thursday afternoon. That was when there was some post 16 initiative in the offing and they needed his unique input. They needed it again now, but it had nothing to do with post 16. The meetings were held, not in the cubbyhole belonging to Bernard Ryan, nor the bone-strewn lair of Dierdre Lessing, but in the nasty, cheap, bright office of James Diamond, BSc, Med. Some of the more acceptable examples of GCSE Art tried desperately to liven the bland wallpaper. Derry Irvine it was not.

James Diamond looked greyer than usual, of a piece with his suit. There was an untouched glass of water on the oval table in front of him.

'The crux of the matter, Max,' he was saying, 'is John Fry. We don't know what to do.'

'Supply cover, Headmaster,' Maxwell spread his arms, and got up to go. What could be simpler? If only all of life's little problems could be solved so easily. 'Will that be all?'

'Oh, for Christ's sake, Maxwell!' Bernard Ryan snapped. 'We don't need your flippancy.' The Deputy scowled at the Head of Sixth Form that he'd hated on sight.

'Exactly,' Maxwell smiled, doing up his jacket and wrinkling his nose at the Deputy Head. 'I expect, somewhere deep down, you have plenty of your own.'

'No, Max,' Diamond stopped him a look of desperation on his face. 'Please. Wait a minute. Look, you ... you've had more experience of this sort of thing than most of us. We ... we need your help, dammit.'

Maxwell looked at them, denizens of the oval office. Indeed they did. Bernard Ryan had an unerring nose for making the wrong decision and doing it without style. When Maxwell had lost it with the man last year and called him an inept Machiavellian in a governors' meeting, he'd had to go away and look up 'inept' as well as 'Machiavellian'. Every year he didn't do the timetable – the timetable did him. Dierdre Lessing coiled in her lair, slithering over the bones of dead men. Countless careers had crashed as a result of her bitching, not a few good men frozen by her basilisk stare. And then, there was James Diamond himself. Where do you start with a man like that? The truth? James Diamond couldn't handle the truth. Maxwell was nearly fifty-six; he just didn't have the time.

The Head of Sixth Form sat back down again, opening the jacket, coiling one leg over the other, like a rather macho Quentin Crisp. 'How much do you know?' he asked.

'Dierdre?' Diamond delegated.

'No one has seen John since last Wednesday,' the Gorgon said, hating herself and Diamond for having to treat Maxwell as an equal rather than the oik he so plainly was. 'He rang in to leave a message on the school answerphone. Said he wouldn't be in on Thursday. His back was playing up again. He left work for his classes.'

'And that's it?' Maxwell checked. He couldn't remember when *he'd* set work for his classes last.

'When we had no word on Monday morning of this week, Emma rang his home. There was no reply.' Emma's real name was Thingee, as Maxwell knew full well. Her oppo, Harriet, who manned the school switchboard in the afternoons, was called Thingee Two. It wasn't rocket science.

'He's got a mobile, presumably?' It was a fair assumption; everybody but Peter Maxwell did. He *had* carried one in the past, just to please Jacquie, but suddenly, one summer, he'd rebelled. He'd thrown it into the sea in a fit of Luddism. And, do you know, he didn't miss the damn thing at all.

'Emma doesn't have a list of mobile numbers –

not unless there's a trip involved and then somebody usually takes the school mobile. You know all this, Max.' Dierdre hated Peter Maxwell with a passion, hated him because she knew he knew where the bodies were buried and had a long list of her incompetences which at any moment might appear in an after-dinner speech or the front page of the *TES* or the *News of the World*. And she hated him, too, because he was always so bloody *right*.

'Yes, *I* do,' he told her. 'I just wonder how much the *Advertiser* knows as we speak.'

'Exactly,' mumbled Diamond. 'That was my next gambit. What do we tell the Press?'

'Nothing until they ask,' Maxwell said. 'Have they asked?'

'Not yet,' Ryan told him. 'But it's only a matter of time.'

'Prepare a Press statement against the day, then,' Maxwell said. 'Nothing committal. It's all in the hands of the police, blah; in whom you have the utmost confidence, etc etc and as matters are sub judice, your hands are tied.'

'Is it that simple?' Diamond asked, wondering why he hadn't thought of it.

'For the moment,' Maxwell nodded. 'One bridge at a time, Headmaster. We've got a long way to go and must be steady. Is there anything else?'

'Yes, Max,' Diamond looked nervously at his colleagues. 'Yes, there is. Look, ever since the incident, in the Red House all those years ago, you've been involved in ... shall we say, un-pleasant incidents. I ... *we* would like you to get involved in this one.'

'Involved, Headmaster?' Maxwell frowned, leaning forward and stroking his chin. 'I'm not sure I understand.'

'Yes, you do, Max,' Dierdre snapped, tired of fencing with the man. 'It must be obvious even to you that John Fry has run off with this wretched tart in Year Eleven. We're all of us anxious to keep the whole sordid business under wraps. You have a certain … rapport with lowlife like Fry. I never liked him.'

'Let me understand this, Headmaster,' Maxwell leaned further forward still in the half-circle of no-hopers. 'You want me to find John Fry?'

'Yes,' muttered Diamond. "Whatever classes you've got tomorrow, Max, we'll cover them. Tell the others you're on some conference or other. It's half-term next week...'

'So I won't need cover,' Maxwell beamed, clicking his fingers and leaning back. 'Timing's damn-near perfect, Headmaster. What with budgetary restrictions and so on. Well done!'

'Maxwell!' growled Diamond. 'Do you want me to beg?'

'Do you have so little faith in the police?' the Head of Sixth Form asked. 'They *do* have rather superior resources to mine.'

'The most vital thing,' Diamond said slowly, 'is to keep this in-house. Eleanor Fry is dead already. We don't want any more tragedies.'

Maxwell nodded, looking at each of them, making them wait.

'Well, Max?' Diamond was the first to break the silence. 'How about it?'

144

'I'll need access to Annette Choker's file.'

'Annette?' Ryan repeated.

'She'll be easier to find than John Fry,' Maxwell said.

'What if they're not together?' Diamond asked.

'Then we'll have to ask ourselves a whole new batch of questions, won't we?' Maxwell said. He saw himself out.

They built the Barlichway in the Sixties when the Four were Fab, Harold Wilson was at Number Ten and Peter Maxwell was a struggling under-graduate at Cambridge. It would be fifteen years before the social engineers who plan towns for a living realized that flat roofs, high-rise and miles of concrete created more problems than they solved. And by then, it was too late.

Peter Maxwell wheeled into Pear Court as the sun died below the Leighford gasworks. Some wag had painted letters in front of the title – Despear Court. That was rather good; Maxwell wished he'd thought of that. Come to think of it, he probably had. A knot of hooligans in baseball caps and trainers with undone laces were kicking a can around the gutter, shouting obscenities to each other. It could have been worse, Maxwell reasoned; they could have been kicking the cat.

'I hope you boys have done your homework,' he called.

For a moment, they stopped, looking at the old bugger in disbelief. It couldn't be him? Could it? Same bike. Same stupid hat. Christ, it was an'all. Then they wandered across to him. 'Mr Max-well. Gonna buy me a pint?'

'You can buy me one, Roger, in three years time when you're old enough.' Roger had been a geezer in the cradle. He was not of an age, but for all time.

'Come off it, Mr Maxwell,' another said. 'Tit's been in pubs since he was this big, ain't you, Tit?'

Roger nodded proudly. Bearing in mind where his mate had raised his hand above the ground, that would have made him an alcoholic at three. Nothing absurd about that when you're fourteen and your IQ is the same.

'Mr Maxwell ain't here for the good of his healf.' Norman was the Einstein of the Pear Court Mob.

'Sensitive of you to understand, Norman,' he said. 'I'm looking for Annette Choker.'

Roger pushed his fingers down his throat.

'That's a *little* unkind, Roger,' Maxwell frowned.

'Well, she lives up there,' Norman said, pointing to a balcony that ran, draped with washing, high above. 'With her mum.'

'That's Number 61?' Maxwell checked.

'Yeah, but she's done a runner,' Roger said. 'Gone off with that w... Mr Fry in Business.'

'You know that for a fact?' Maxwell asked him.

'Near as dammit,' Roger assured him.

'Common knowledge around Leighford High...' Norman said.

'Yeah,' somebody else chipped in. 'She was always bragging about it. How he took her out to this restaurant and that nightclub. All a load of bollocks.'

'So you didn't believe it?' Maxwell rounded on the child.

'Not that spending money stuff, no.'

'She's a lightweight, sir,' Norman assured the Head of Sixth Form. 'Wouldn't need to spend much money on her to get her to drop her knickers. You got a feel, didn't you, Tit, in Year Eight, for a jammy dodger?'

Roger nodded. 'That's on account of my sex appeal,' he said, triumphantly. The others hit him round the head.

'Any one of you guys ever see Mr Fry around here?' Maxwell asked.

'Nah,' they chorused, collectively. 'We'd have had his hub caps off if he'd showed his face round here.'

'Yeah,' Roger grunted. 'I hate Business Studies.'

'Talking of hub caps,' Maxwell chose his man with care. 'Norman, want a fiver to mind my bike?' He held up a crisp one to prove he was a man of his word.

'Yeah!' Roger lunged for it. Norman was faster. 'Not you, Tit,' and he slapped the lad's hand away. 'Just me. Mr M, your bike's safe with me. 'Ere, ain't you got no helmet?' Moron Norman may have been, but he was a safety-conscious one.

'Can't afford it, Norman,' Maxwell shrugged. 'I keep giving people fivers to mind my bike.'

Predictably, there were babies crying and dogs barking as Peter Maxwell took the concrete stairway that led to the heaven that was the first floor balcony. There were nameless stains in dark corners and nasty smells and a reminder in spray paint to Mr Blair that, despite all his hard work at Number Ten, Rod Rules. He stepped carefully over the toddler straddling a plastic trike outside

147

Number 59 and knocked gingerly on the red-painted, peeling door of 61. A dog barked inside followed by a high-pitched yell and the rattling of dead-bolts.

'Yes?' an overweight woman with her hair piled high stood there, squinting at him through the cigarette smoke that curled up past her eyes. She had another toddler in her arms. Mucus dribbled into the child's mouth and the front of her bib was like Joseph's coat of many colours.

'Mrs Choker?' Maxwell tipped his hat, a gesture the woman had probably never seen before.

'Who wants to know?' This bloke looked like a bailiff, but equally he could have been a bloody Jehovah's Witness. He had a bloody bow tie on. How up himself was that?

'I'm Peter Maxwell, from Leighford High School.'

'Oh,' the hardness vanished from the face and she grinned a gappy smile. 'You Annette's teacher?' The Mrs Chokers of this world were often over-awed by people of Maxwell's persuasion. It was all part of the race memory of when their great-grandfathers had been caned for breathing too loudly.

'Not exactly,' Maxwell said. 'But I *am* looking for her.'

'You and the whole bloody world. Look, um, Mr Maxwell, come in will you? Jenny!' she shrieked into the flat's grubby interior. 'Jenny! Get yer arse out here.'

A girl of about ten, the living spit of the missing Annette, clopped into the hall, balancing on pink fluffy mules. 'Take her, will you, love? Mr Max-

148

well and me need a moment.'

'Oh, Mum!' the girl whined.

'Just fucking do it. And shut that bloody dog up!'

She bundled the toddler into Jenny's skinny arms and pushed them both through a door. Maxwell followed her through a narrow corridor into the room at the far end.

'Won't you have a seat, Mr Maxwell?' She swept some clutter off a chair in the tiny kitchen and Maxwell sat down. Through the pointless nets on the north side of Pear Rise, he could see the Downs rise to the sky, the gorse dark patches on the paler grass of Staple Hill. To the right, he knew, just blocked by the jutting corner of the gasworks, lay the old streambed of the Leigh, and the ash grove where little Robbie Wesson had found Dr David Radley and older graves yawned, naked to the probing of twenty-first century man.

'Is there any news?' the woman asked.

Maxwell tried to gauge her age. Early thirties, probably, but it was difficult to tell. A stranger to underwear, Mrs Choker's breasts lay heavily around her waist, her nipples resting on the formica table top. She'd once been quite attractive, Maxwell realized, but the years and the kids and the Barlichway had all taken their toll.

'I'm afraid not,' he said. 'When did you see her last, Mrs Choker?'

'It's not Mrs Choker,' the woman said. 'That's just the name I gave Annette when she started school. Choker was her dad's name. I wonder where he is now?'

'Jenny's his girl, too?' Maxwell asked.

'Yeah.' The woman who was not Mrs Choker lit up a second fag, having mashed the first into an ashtray on the table in front of her. 'Do you?'

'No, thanks,' he smiled. 'So what do I call you?'

'Selina,' she said.

'Selina,' he nodded. 'When did you see Annette last?'

'Let's see.' She screwed up her eyes as the smoke filled her face. 'Week last Thursday. I told the coppers. We'd had a row.'

'Really? What about?'

'Oh, for fuck's sake! 'Scuse me, Mr Maxwell,' and Selina dashed to the door. 'Shut that fuckin' dog up, Jennifer. I've got company! Sorry about that,' and the woman resumed her position opposite the teacher from up at the school. 'She kept going out,' Selina said, rummaging in the bits and pieces of the table for a coffee mug. 'I don't mind telling you, Mr Maxwell, she was a right bloody handful. Oh, I loved her, of course I did. But talk about wilful! Still,' she snorted, 'I was just the same at her age, I suppose, looking back. Well, it's the hormones, ain't it? That and looking for a better life. Not exactly a bundle of laffs round here. D'you wanna coffee?'

'No thanks. Had she gone off before, Selina?' Maxwell asked.

'Once or twice. Oh, not for long, though.' Selina laughed. 'The first time, she was five. She'd heard about Disneyland, seen it on the telly. We'd had an up and downer – she was a little cow, even then. And she packed her bag with a towel and a toy and off she went. I caught up with her at the chip

150

shop. Mr Patel had spotted her and sent his eldest to tell me. I didn't even know she'd gone.'

'This time,' Maxwell brought her back to the here and now, 'she took a bit more than a towel and a toy?'

'Yeah,' Selina grunted, flicking ash off her cigarette. 'Half her fucking clothes and 40 quid of mine. Why do they have to grow up, eh?'

Some of them don't, Maxwell thought, but whatever else this woman was, Selina was the girl's mother. She didn't need that kind of comment; not now. 'Is there anywhere she might have gone? Her father...'

Selina shook her head. 'Annette barely knew him. He was gone by the time she started school. I can't find him and nor can the Child Support people, so I don't see how she could. Anyway, she wouldn't want to. All this bollocks about kids wanting to find their natural fathers – what's that all about? Especially when their natural fathers bugger off in the first place. You got kids, Mr Maxwell?'

Not for the first, time, Peter Maxwell saw the little face he loved, the little face he saw again sometimes in his deepest dreams, his little girl. 'No,' he shook his head. 'Or twelve hundred of them, depending on how you look at it.'

'What? Oh, yeah. Right.'

What about other relatives?' he persisted. 'Aunties? Uncles?'

'I haven't spoken to my sister since 1987. She don't even know I got Annette. My mum's dead and I never knew who my dad was – that's history repeating itself, that is. Annette's got a sister in Halifax. Well, half-sister, actually. I don't talk to her no more.'

Maxwell smiled. 'What about friends, then? Did she have a best friend?'

'Michaela,' Selina nodded. 'Michaela Reynolds. Lives out along the railway somewhere. But she ain't there. And she ain't in Halifax neither. The coppers have checked. Look, Mr Maxwell, it's nice of you to go to all this trouble, but if you ain't Annette's teacher...'

'Tell me, Selina, when you and Annette weren't off hooks, did she ever mention any of her teachers, Mr Fry?'

'Fry?' the woman frowned. 'No. I don't think so. Why?'

'Oh, nothing,' Maxwell sighed. 'Just a long shot.'

Norman had been true to his word and White Surrey still gleamed in his grubby hands as Peter Maxwell repossessed it. He checked his watch. 'Bedtime, boys,' he called and listened to their jeers die away as he purred out of Pear Court and navigated his way, via the stars, to the old railway line. 'And don't forget that homework!'

Henry Hudson, the railway king, had once walked this way, with his maps and his theodolites and minions flapping in his wake. That was in 1842 before he'd got greedy and started selling spurious lines. The Leighford-Littlehampton line was about the last honest buck Henry Hudson had ever made.

The row of Victorian cottages was still there, built above the line the navvies had laid. And for once, they hadn't just erected their shanty towns with scraps of wood and iron and dossed down with their dogs and their wives and their barrels of cider. They'd put down roots and they'd stayed. Even so, the cottages were not unlike a shanty town again. Satellite dishes protruded from every angle, half-stripped cars and bikes lay propped on bricks on what were once neat, carefully tended front gardens. The heady aroma of the Taj Mahal Balti House wafted over Hudson's old track, now a skateboard park where noisy infants defied gravity by hurtling upside down through space.

Peter Maxwell rapped on the door of the end house. More dogs. More crying children. It was nearly dark by now and the rattle and roar of the skateboards was eerier in the stark floodlights that suddenly switched on. It was a surreal scene that George Orwell might have capitalized on had he lived. *2004* he'd have called the novel. And the skateboard park of Railway Cottages would have been his Room 101.

A vest came to the door – the south coast's answer to Rab C Nesbitt. 'Yeah?'

'Mr Reynolds?'

Mr Reynolds could have been anything from twenty five to fifty. His shoulders sported black curling hair and dragon tattoos coiled menacingly over his biceps to snap and roar at his wrists.

He took in the stranger at his door. Stupid hat. Poncy bow tie. Fuck me – they weren't cycle clips, were they? Shaun Reynolds hadn't seen those since his granddad died. 'Might be. Who are you?'

'Peter Maxwell. Leighford High School.'

'Yeah?' It secretly unnerved Shaun Reynolds that them up at the school knew where he lived.

'Is Michaela home?'

'I dunno. Michaela!' The windows rattled.

A dark haired girl whom Maxwell recognized emerged from the bowels of the hall. She looked different out of what passed for her uniform at school. Her navel dripped jewellery and she wore unseasonal boots of beige suede below yards of naked thigh. 'Some bloke for you,' Reynolds said and disappeared.

'Michaela,' Maxwell smiled at her. 'I'm looking for Annette.'

'I ain't seen her.' The girl was chasing a wedge of chewing gum around her mouth and, what with negotiating the tongue-stud, this was a major feat of engineering.

'Annette's mum seems to think otherwise.' Maxwell stood his ground. He'd been arguing with Year Eleven girls for years.

'Well, she's wrong.' Michaela stepped back to close the door, but Maxwell was faster and jammed his foot in the way.

'I don't think she is, Michaela,' he said.

'Dad!' the girl screamed. Michaela knew Peter Maxwell. He used long words and talked loudly in corridors. She was afraid of him because he was so clearly Mad.

Reynolds was back, a copy of the *Daily Sport* in one hand, a can of Carlsberg in the other. 'What the fuck... Is he touching you, Micky?'

'Yeah,' the girl blurted. 'He was trying to grab

154

my breasts.'

Maxwell stepped back this time, hands in the air. What? Me?

'Is that right, mate?' Reynolds confronted him, snarling, nose to nose with his man. 'You trying to touch my girl?'

'No,' Maxwell assured him. 'All I want is some answers.'

'I know what you want, mate,' Reynolds hissed, the dark hair bristling on his shoulders. 'It's having your bollocks cut off, one by one. How do pervs like you get a job in fucking teaching in the first place?'

'Pervs like me?' Maxwell was only prepared to retreat so far. Now he stood his ground, legs locked, arms by his side. In the flight or fight split-second decision scenario, men like Mad Max always chose fight.

'Yeah. You and that Fry bloke. I read it in the local bloody paper. His wife's bloody killed herself. Preying on young girls. Now fuck off, off of my property, or I'm calling the police.'

'There's just one more thing, Mr Reynolds...'

He winced as she dabbed his nose. And she winced along with him. 'Why don't you keep your nose out of things, Max?' she asked.

'My nose,' he mumbled. 'That'll be this big, throbbing thing that's currently spreading over my face and impeding my vision, will it?'

Jacquie stood up and looked at the man she loved in her bathroom mirror. 'You're lucky he didn't break your teeth. What did he use?'

'Just his head.' Maxwell slurred, wondering

whether that particular part of Shaun Reynolds' anatomy had been made of concrete. He was also wondering what had happened to the bit that used to separate his lips from his nostrils, in that he couldn't see it anymore. 'The Railway Cuttings version of the Glasgow Kiss, I expect sociologists call it. Still, I don't suppose he'll be picking his nose with his left hand for a while.'

'Why?' She threw the bloody cotton wool in the bin.

'He got it caught in the door, I can't *think* how that happened. Those Victorian door-frames, you know. *So* dangerous.'

'Great,' she scolded. 'He'll probably do you for assault now. What were you thinking?'

'I was thinking I might find Annette Choker,' he said.

'Come into the kitchen. I'll get you some ice for that. We're onto it, Max.'

'You've found her, then?' he waddled carefully across her hall and into her kitchen, his head tilted back, plugs up his nostrils.

'Well, no, but...'

'You know where she is?'

'Well, not exactly...'

'I rest my case.'

She sat him down, lovingly, on a kitchen chair before rummaging in the contents of her freezer. 'The point I'm trying to make...'

'...Is that Annette Choker is a police matter. Yes, I know. But, you see, when I passed a vital piece of information concerning the possible involvement of my colleague John Fry in all this, the police didn't want to know.'

156

'What do you mean?' Jacquie said, a little surprised. 'Who did you talk to?' She wrapped the frozen cubes in a cloth and placed the little bundle carefully on her true love's face.

'Shit!' he hissed. 'And that's "To whom did you talk?" by the way.'

'Big baby!' She knocked his hand away.

'Woman Policeman,' he told her. 'Slip of a thing. Bit on edge, I thought. Using her dignity like a piles cushion. The sort of attitude that comes with being tiny, female and inadequate.'

'That's Alison McCormick, you uncompromising chauvinist bastard!' resisting the temptation to cuff him, lovingly of course, around the nose. 'Remind me again why I love you.'

'Ha ha,' he chuckled as best he could, 'let me count the ways. No, I'm on a quest, light of my life.'

She looked at him, dried blood all over his shirt, dark bruises spreading under his bright eyes. A quest. Yes, that would be right. Where there were windmills and dragons, there would be Peter Maxwell, mad as a snake, pen in hand, tilting from the saddle of White Surrey for all he was worth, pursuing whatever grail was shining in his vision. This one was a missing schoolgirl and a possible pervert. She shook her head, her eyes a little damp, her own vision a little misty.

'Do tell,' she said.

'Mr Diamond, no less,' he told her, feeling the blood trickle from his nose again. 'My revered Headmaster. "I don't care what it takes, Max," he said.' It was a near-perfect James Diamond, bearing in mind his obvious indisposition. '"I

157

want you to find what our woefully inadequate police force cannot. Especially that Carpenter woman. She's hopeless."'

'If you weren't an incurable cripple already,' she leaned over him, 'I'd smack you with your own handbag. You're staying here tonight.'

'Darling, I can't.'

'Yes, you can,' she insisted as only half-dressed detectives with long auburn hair can in the long watches of the night. 'You'd never make it across town with what you've got.'

'Ah, the puncture.'

'*And,*' she insisted again, 'it's the spare room for you, my lad.'

Maxwell looked even more hurt than he actually was. 'All my wounds are before, Woman Policeman. There's absolutely no reason why you couldn't take me roughly from behind.'

Morning had broken like the first morning by the time Peter Maxwell got up. The sun streamed in through Jacquie's curtains onto Jacquie's carpet and onto the note she'd left for him. She had a bitch of a day ahead of her interviewing archae-ologists with Henry Hall. There was a lasagne in the fridge, wine in the rack and probably something black, white and celluloid on the TCM channel. *On no account* was he to go home until she got back, but it could be late.

'I wouldn't dream of it, darling one,' he smiled softly and pattered downstairs to mend the puncture in Surrey's rear tyre. Norman, it seemed, hadn't been *quite* the good egg he'd promised to be last evening and Maxwell would have words with him about that. Even though it was half-term, Maxwell's memory was long. And Norman owed Maxwell a fiver.

The sun was still shining late that morning, as Dr Samantha Welland twirled at the end of the rope that stretched from her dislocated neck, up over the beam in her garage and to its anchorage on the far wall.

One of her shoes had landed on the concrete floor, kicked away from the low chair and her tongue protruded, blue and swollen, from her caked, foam-flecked lips.

'Sam Welland,' Jacquie Carpenter said, checking the list in Hall's office. 'She's the only one left to see.'

'How long has she been at the dig?' Henry Hall asked.

'A couple of days,' his DS told him. 'Came hard on the heels of Professor Fraser. She wasn't with the original team. Derek Latymer's under the impression she came uninvited. Bit of a tease, this one, according to Martin's notes.' Martin. There was that name again. He was never very far away.

'Do we have an address?' Hall asked.

Jacquie checked. 'Hove,' she told him.

Hall checked his watch. All day the two of them had been interviewing the four names on the dig list. Now, only one to go. Questions, questions. Over and over. 'Can I just go back to...?' It was endless.

'Tomorrow,' Hall said, sliding his pen into his inside pocket. 'I daresay she'll keep till then.'

Chapter Nine

'All right, Jacquie.' Henry Hall had tilted his seat back as far as the confines of her Ka would let him and he was dozing, his hands clasped across his chest. 'Let's recap. Start with that noxious bastard Tam Fraser.'

'Noxious bastard, sir?' Henry Hall wasn't normally given to expletives. 'Does that give me some clue about the way my summation ought to go?'

'Not at all.' Hall shook his head. 'I want your honest opinion.' They were driving east, the pair of them, in the warm glow of a Saturday in the dying days of May. It ought to have been idyllic, except that they were both working for the umpteenth day on the trot and the face of a dead colleague haunted them both. To cap it all, it was Whit Saturday, that magic day in the year when the number of cars on any road in the country suddenly doubles and people who haven't driven for months come out of cold storage, as though from a sleep of years, and pretend they can drive. Rip van Winkle meets Michael Schumacher.

'Wanker!' she screamed at one such, an old git who had to be a hundred, actually attempting to drive a Morris Minor.

'I'm not sure that's anything the Crown Prosecution Service can get their teeth into,' Hall had not opened his eyes. 'Give me a little precision.'

160

'Sorry, guv,' she said. 'All right. Professor Tam Fraser, semi-retired,'

'Professor Emeritus,' Hall corrected her. 'Wonder if there's such a thing as DCI Emeritus? I like the sound of that.' So did Mrs Hall. For years now she'd watched her husband get older and grumpier. He didn't sleep as well as he used to and all three boys were growing up with only the vaguest notion of who their father was.

'He's an arrogant shit, sir, if you'll pardon the expression. Trying to get a look up my skirt while being appallingly patronizing with the other eye, so to speak. I pity his female students.'

'But, that apart,' Hall posited.

'Seems to have been genuinely fond of David Radley. I think probably under that ghastly, professorial Scotsman exterior, he's actually quite cut up about the murder.' Jacquie was shaking her head at the ludicrous antics of the artic drivers, wishing just for a moment she were in a patrol car.

'Did he have anything to gain from Radley's death?' Hall was taking her through the set pieces.

'Hardly. He already outranked him. Probably ... why not indicate?' she suddenly screamed at a white van man, '...just as much of a whizz kid as Radley in his day. No, the dig's given him extra work when I don't suppose he needed it.'

'Alibi for the time of the murder?'

'That's tricky.'

'Why is it tricky?' Hall was using his DS as a sounding board, dotting i's and crossing t's, making doubly sure he hadn't missed anything himself.

161

'Jim Astley's lack of time of death.'

'Jim Astley's lack of anything,' Hall mused. 'Know what's odd about this case, Jacquie? No obvious motive, no obvious forensics. David Radley seems to be some sort of cross between Mother Teresa and Mother Teresa... Didn't appear to break wind without permission – and then in writing, in triplicate. Who would want to kill Mr Nice Guy?'

'Almost anybody,' Jacquie shrugged. 'Just to wipe the smile off his face. Oh, please!'

Hall didn't have to open his eyes. 'Agricultural vehicle,' he said.

'Combine bloody harvester!' Jacquie confirmed.

'So, when we *assume* Radley died, where was Fraser?'

'At a conference in London. Something or other organized by London University. A symposium on Saxon England.'

'Is that you yawning or is it me?' Hall asked. For the first time, he opened his eyes and glanced across at the girl gone dancing, chancing, backing and advancing along the A27. 'Oh, sorry, I forgot. Mad Max.'

She glanced back at him. 'I don't think it's his period,' she smiled, never *quite* knowing how Henry Hall felt on any given day about Peter Maxwell. She wondered how he was, with his swollen lip and squashed nose. God knew where he'd got to by the time she got home last night. His note had just said, 'Still on the trail. See you soon. Love you, Woman Policeman.' Now, she hoped, he was still curled up in his bed with that

162

revolting cat for company.

'All right,' Hall changed the subject. 'Talk me through Douglas Russell.'

'Ah, now him I liked,' Jacquie said, wincing on her boss's behalf as she crunched the gears. 'But he seemed scared.'

'I picked that up,' Hall said. 'Why?'

'Perhaps he thinks he's next. Remember the threatening letter.'

'He had *something* to gain from Radley's death.' Hall mused, playing devil's advocate and ignoring Jacquie's red herring.

'What? Not the dig – Fraser's stepped in. Not the Chair at Wessex, surely? He's a geophysicist.'

'Which means?'

'I don't think they're held in very great esteem, guv,' Jacquie said. 'Oh, great. Roadworks!' and she yanked on the brakes, waiting for the queue to disappear and the lights to turn green. 'Anyway, he doesn't strike me as the ambitious type.'

'No, indeed,' Hall agreed. 'But there's something not quite right about our Mr Russell. What car does he drive?'

'Um ... not sure. His is the Land Rover, I think. Why?'

'No reason. Alibi for Radley?'

'Hasn't got one. Or at least, he was alone in his room at the Quinton, assuming, as Astley does, that Radley died a little before midnight on the Wednesday night.'

'He didn't die at the site, we know that. And he didn't die in his room at the Quinton.'

'That's right. So why ... oh, come on, for God's sake!'

Horns were beginning to blare in the morning as the sun climbed higher and began to take its toll on tempers, already frayed by Bank Holiday lunacy.

'So why go to all the trouble to move him onto the site?'

'Symbolic,' Hall said. 'Some ... what? Ritual significance? Man's an archaeologist, so it's only fitting he's found dead, one corpse among many.'

'But Russell wouldn't have put him there, surely? Bit like shitting on your own doorstep, isn't it, guv?'

'A more distant doorstep than the Quinton,' Hall commented. 'Even if Russell didn't kill him in either of their rooms, there are other possibilities. Basement, dining room; it's got a billiard room if I remember rightly. And if you're right about the Land Rover, it's a damned handy hearse. Large, strong and its tyre tracks wouldn't be out of place at the dig site because it's there every day anyway.'

'Are you putting Russell in the frame, sir?' Jacquie asked, a little uneasily.

'No, no,' Hall fluttered his hands in the air, 'I could make a reasonable case against my granny if I felt so inclined, Jacquie, you know that. Against you. Against Peter Maxwell.'

She ignored him. 'Derek Latymer,' she said.

'Ah, now there *is* a young man in a hurry,' Hall said. 'Left at the roundabout.'

Jacquie was about to scream 'how the hell do you know' since the man's eyes were shut, but thought better of it. 'And he didn't like Fraser.'

'That makes him all right in your book?' Hall

164

asked her.

'You know what I mean, sir,' she said slowly.

'Yes, I do,' he said. 'It struck me that young Mr Latymer didn't have much time for anybody. Slagging off Fraser as something out of the Dark Ages himself. Ripping into Russell for all sorts of academic shortcomings. He seemed particularly to have it in for Samantha Welland. With colleagues like that, who needs a killer?'

It was a little before ten that the Ka crunched on the gravel of the drive of The Orchards.

'I had no idea there was so much money in archaeology,' Jacquie was staring up at the Thirties opulence of the house ahead of her, the sort of place, with its rounded corners and iron-framed windows, they used for the set of *Poirot;* she half-expected to see David Suchet waddle out of the shrubbery.

'Jesus!' Hall sat bolt upright. There was a screaming ambulance siren behind them and a white vehicle, lights blazing, roared across the gravel, sending it flying in all directions. Behind it, a squad car, lights flashing, siren blaring, took part of the gate post with it. *'That's* going to go on somebody's record,' he murmured.

Half a dozen coppers of the West Wessex Constabulary were all over the building immediately. One of them was outside Jacquie's door; another near Hall's.

'Excuse me, madam,' the lad said once she'd wound down the window. 'Would you mind telling me what you're doing here?'

She flashed her card. 'Same as you, son,' she said, though she wasn't much older than he was. 'But with a little less urgency. What's going on?'

Hall's card was all but up the nose of the constable on his side – and it had to be said, he didn't always have constables on his side. 'What's the trouble here?'

Both boys in blue were rather more upright and to attention in the unexpected presence of a DCI. We've word of a suicide, sir. In the garage.'

'Over here!' a voice called from the steps. 'This way.' A woman, smart and fortysomething with a chunky hairdo swayed on the patio above the gravel.

'Sergeant,' Hall stopped the senior man on his way across the drive. 'I'm DCI Hall, Leighford. What's going on here?'

'We got a call of a suicide, sir. But there may be complications.'

'There often are,' Hall said. 'Your patch, man. Carry on.' At least the DCI had a sense of decorum.

'Sir. Come on, you lads.'

Coppers and ambulance men went about their business, barging through the garage doors, flinging them wide. Hall could see the kicked over chair, the single shoe, the dangling feet.

'Jacquie,' he motioned his DS in the direction of the woman still standing, as though frozen, on the steps. 'Get her inside and get a statement. I need to check this one out.'

The A27 was busier by the time Hall and Jacquie were driving home. They had come to interview

166

the last of the full-time archaeologists working on the Leighford dig and they were too late. Samantha Welland was dead.

'Scenario one, then?' Hall was back in his erstwhile position, eyes closed, seat tilted, hands clasped. Jacquie didn't know how honoured she was. There weren't many men that trusting.

'Um ... scenario one,' Jacquie has been chewing it over all day; she was glad, at last, to be able to put it into words. 'Scenario one is that Samantha Welland killed David Radley and took her own life in remorse.'

'Points in favour of that,' Hall wanted to know.

'Martin Toogood interviewed her.' Jacquie was piecing it together. 'She got rattled...'

'Yes, but backtrack. Murder of Radley.'

'Broken neck,' Jacquie switched lanes to avoid the endless artics, even more of them now than on the way out. 'Caused by a karate blow delivered by Sam Welland. She was a black/brown/green – waddya want belt judo expert, had muscles on her muscles. Could have lifted him too, dumped him in the ash grove.'

'What did she drive?'

'Volvo estate. It was in the garage.'

'Room enough for a body,' Hall nodded.

'And that's why she got in on the dig,' Jacquie was in full flight now. 'Get bloody over! She had to establish her tyre tracks at the site. So she invited herself over.'

'Left it a bit late,' Halt said. 'We've got 'em all. SOCO were on the ball this time.'

'Were they, sir?' Jacquie had nearly as much experience of the Men in White as Hall had. How

167

many times, in the experience of both of them, had somebody in a lab somewhere fucked up? Guilty men had walked as a result. And in the good old days, some good men died for the same reason.

'Point taken,' he said, without moving so much as an eyebrow. 'OK, so Sam Welland hates David Radley. He's cleverer-than-thou, got more papers published than she's had hot dinners. Alternatively, he doesn't approve of his people flopping about on mats shouting *Banzai*. Or he just looked at her funny, whatever. She's got a short fuse. Loses it. They row. She kills him.'

His fingers were conducting a little mini orchestra across his chest.

Where?' she asked

'I thought you were doing the scenario?'

Jacquie smiled. She knew when a buck was being passed. 'Not Radley's room at the Quinton.'

'That still leaves his house – but his wife's statement would seem to rule that out. Radley was staying in Room 13 at the Quinton for convenience sake; although it's no drive back to Petworth. Susan hadn't seen him for days. That leaves Welland's home. It's certainly big enough to have a murder room in there somewhere.' He waved a lazy thumb back over his shoulder. 'We'll have to leave that to the Hove team.'

'They seem competent enough,' she said.

'They always do,' Hall nodded. 'Scenario one, Sergeant.'

'Wherever she does it,' Jacquie's tyres squealed as she took the roundabout too fast, 'she bundles him into the Volvo, drives to the dig, presumably

168

after dark on Wednesday night and dumps his body in the ash grove.'

'Why?'

A silence.

'Don't know.'

'You know what they say about police work, Jacquie. Ninety per cent perspiration, ten per cent speculation. Speculate.'

It was the nearest to a joke you were likely to get from Henry Hall and Jacquie settled for it. 'Symbolism,' she said. 'Aren't ash groves sacred or something?'

'Ask Maxwell,' the DCI said. 'I'd have put him in a grave.'

'Seems a *little* harsh, sir,' Jacquie smiled, her grey eyes twinkling. 'Teachers like him are hard to come by.'

Henry Hall never rose to bait of any kind. 'Now, don't mix your metaphors,' he told her in a quip worthy of the Great Man himself. 'We're talking about Radley.'

'In a grave?'

'Sure. If I remember rightly, they've found a dozen or so, haven't they? Saxon remains or whatever. What could be neater? Somebody's already done the hard work for you – the six feet under bit.'

'But he'd be found too soon,' she realized.

'Say on.' He liked the way this was going.

'That kid from Leighford High didn't find the body until late afternoon, and if he hadn't been sticking his nose in where it shouldn't have been, it would have been later still. Maybe not until the Friday or whenever the team planned to start work on the grove itself.'

'Right. But, conversely, no attempt to bury him. Radley was fully clothed, was still carrying his wallet, complete with cash and credit cards. It would have been quite easy to flick a few feet of earth over him. Chances are we wouldn't have found him yet.' There was a silence while Jacquie negotiated a few roundabouts, slower this time.

'There again,' this was the DCI's PS, 'somebody had stripped him and re-dressed him. Why?'

Silence.

'Scenario two,' Hall said.

'Er ... scenario two,' Jacquie focused, 'is that Samantha Welland took her own life while the balance of her mind was disturbed over issues we know nothing about.'

'Which brings us to Hazel Twigg.'

Jacquie snorted. 'Sorry, guv. I mean, I know it's all very tragic, but I don't know how I kept a straight face. What kind of people call their daughter Hazel if their surname is Twigg?'

'What indeed?' Henry Hall had only smiled three times in his life. He saw no need to extend that record today. 'What did you make of her?'

'Mannish lass,' Jacquie said, remembering their first sight of the woman on the steps of The Orchards. 'Clearly lesbian.'

'Live-in-lover of Sam Welland. You interviewed her first. What did she tell you?'

'My notebook's back there.'

Hall was waving a finger in the air. 'Uh-huh. Memory, detective sergeant if you please. You know how much the eminences on the Bench hate little black books.'

Jacquie flashed him a steely glance. Hall felt it, even with his eyes closed, but he wasn't giving her the satisfaction. 'Well,' Jacquie ventured, 'she was clearly distraught. I calmed her down, made her a cup of tea, the usual drill.'

The usual drill indeed, but Henry Hall knew Jacquie Carpenter. She'd have done it perfectly, as though Hazel Twigg, at that moment, was the only person in the world and that there had never been anyone so special or as wonderful as Sam Welland.

'"I loved her" she kept saying, over and over again. "I loved her". Almost as if...'

'Yes?'

'...Almost as if, somehow, her love had caused what had happened.'

'Tell me about their relationship.'

'They'd met ten years ago at the Karate Club ... um...'

'The Campdens.' As always, the DCI was a step or twelve ahead.

'The Campdens. Sam was working on a research thesis – an M.Phil. She got Hazel a job in the archaeology office at Petworth.'

'Not an archaeologist?'

'No, assistant to the Admissions Tutor; glorified typist, in fact, but she was concerned with under-graduates. She and Sam had similar interests.'

'Women.'

'I was going to say Martial Arts,' Jacquie was brave enough to correct her boss when she didn't have time to think about it. 'They dated a few times, realized they could make a go of it and

Hazel moved in.'

'To a very nice *pied-a-terre* indeed. I didn't know they paid university lecturers so well.'

'According to them, they don't,' Jacquie said. 'Oh, in your own time!' she suddenly snarled at some daffy tart in a sun hat. Here she was, up to her armpits in other people's tragedies and daffy tarts still drove badly in sun hats. It was the way of the world. She reined in her venom; she was beginning to *think* like Mad Max now. 'No, Ms Welland's family are loaded. According to Hazel, her parents are divorced and mother was killed in a plane crash – Cessna over the Downs, engine failure. Father didn't want to know so little Sam was brought up by grandparents. They in turn have shuffled off, leaving Sam with a packet, including the house in Hove.'

'Is there a will?' Hall's mind was wandering in a different direction now.

'Doubt it, guv; she was twenty seven.'

'Let that be a lesson to you,' Hall said. 'What were Ms Twigg's movements over the last twenty-four hours?'

'Well, she was at the university on Thursday until five. Came home, had supper with Sam and got an early night.' Picture of wedded bliss, really.

'They slept together?'

'Usually, yes. But not when she or Sam had early mornings. So as not to disturb each other, they each had a spare room. Sam was up early to get to the dig at Leighford.'

'This was the day before yesterday?' Hall checked.

'That's right. After that, it all gets a little hazy.

172

What did she tell you?'

The DCI had interviewed the companion after Jacquie. She'd been the Nice Policeman. He was curt, brusque even, by the book. His back was beginning to register that he was, after all, travelling in a Ka. He tried to stretch, but there was little chance of that. 'She visited friends in London later yesterday,' he took up the thread, 'Clerkenwell. Obviously, we'll need to check this out. The address is in my notebook, but of course,' he looked blankly at her, 'I've committed it to memory. She stayed over.'

'Left a message on Sam's answerphone.' Jacquie filled in from her own knowledge.

'Which is still there.'

'Yes.'

'I played it,' they both chorused.

'So she made an early start from London,' Hall went on alone. 'Got to Hove about ten, ten fifteen. And found Sam in the garage. Minutes before we arrived.'

'What did you make of the forensics, guv? By the time I got there, SOCO were finishing up.'

'From the house, you approach the garage from the utility room. A flight of steps get you down there. I counted ten. Room for three cars but only Sam's Volvo was there. Hazel Twigg's was on the drive, if you remember. Sam would have rigged up the rope from the wall to the left as you look at it, across the overhead beams and into the position we found her in. There was a chair under her body, taken from the kitchen. All very tragic.'

Another silence. None of it made much sense to Jacquie, but she was prepared to bow to her oppos' far greater experience. 'Is that it, then?' she ventured. 'Can we say Case Closed and all go home?'

For a fleeting moment, Jacquie thought she saw the hint of a smile hover around Henry Hall's lips, but on second thoughts, it was probably the afternoon sun reflected back from her bonnet as they took the long rise to the Downs above Leighford, and the run up to Staple Hill.

'Tut, tut, Detective Sergeant,' he said. 'Why kill yourself with a rope you've had to buy – Hazel Twigg said there was no rope in the house – when you've got a medicine cabinet full of tablets upstairs and a kitchen absolutely chocka with sharp knives? No, no. Young Samantha clearly had no money worries. She seemed very happy with her companion of a mile. For all we say Radley was better, she was successful in her career. No reason that I can see to kill herself. No, we are looking at scenario three.'

'We are?' Jacquie was afraid Henry Hall would say that, but at least this one he was going to expound.

'Scenario three is that Sam Welland is the third killing in a series, all part of a common plan. David Radley, neck broken, found in the ash grove at Leighford. Sam Welland, dangling from a rope in her garage – "suddenly, at home".'

'And Martin Toogood?' Jacquie said. He was never far from any of their thoughts, but neither of them had mentioned him all day.

'And Martin Toogood,' Hall nodded. 'And that's the one that breaks the mould. It doesn't fit the pattern and it's bugging me to hell.' He sat upright and what happened next was pure Peter Maxwell. 'Are we nearly there yet?' he snapped. And that was pure Bart Simpson.

Sundays in summer. Gorgeous, slim young things wandering the white beaches of Leighford, G-strings covering their modesty, barely evident breasts *just* concealed by halter-neck tops. Slabs of lard oozing onto the sand, the great beached whales of middle-aged England, listening to raucous music on their portable CD players. Hedged round by a protective barrier of groynes and wind-breaks, an ancient granddad with a straw hat and the bravery to take off his tie in the soaring temperatures. Skinny, spotty lads, mostly Leighford High's finest, kicking a football in any direction but the improvised goal.

The smells of the season wafted across the beach – instant barbecues, curling black on their foil bases, carried promise of underdone sausages and crisp burgers, tastes to harden our arteries. The slightly sickly odour of sunblock mingled with them, with just a threat of whatever problem Southern Water hadn't *quite* sorted out in Leighford's sewage disposal system.

He waited until the coast was clear, until the queue had gone from the ice cream kiosk, then he pounced.

'I'll have a 99 please, Michaela.'

She froze in mid-serve. Under a ludicrous straw hat, she barely recognized the Head of Sixth Form from up at the school. He had dark, almost purple circles under his eyes and his nose seemed to be jointed in the middle. His lips were thicker than usual and were coated, even before he'd bought his ice cream, in something white.

'Is that with a flake in it?' Michaela asked, ever the professional, regaining her composure. She didn't look much less of a tart now in the regalia of Mr Scrummy, than she had framed in the doorway of Railway Terrace the previous night.

'Yes, my dear,' Maxwell said patiently. 'That's what makes it a 99. Otherwise I'd have asked for a cone.'

'Strawberry sauce?' She was operating the EU regulated gadgetry, with an efficiency which would have astounded her Science and Design Technology teachers.

'Thank you, no,' he said. 'I'm allergic to pink.'

'You know, my dad's really pissed off with you. Hazelnuts?'

He shook his head. 'I'm not best pleased with him.'

'He says you've broken his hand.'

'I say he's broken my nose,' Maxwell countered.

'One fifty,' she passed him his 99.

'Hang on,' he rummaged in his back pocket. 'I'll have to remortgage. Why did you lie to him, Michaela?'

'What do you mean?'

'Come off it!' he handed her the coins. 'You accused me of touching you up. I don't blame your dad. In those circumstances, I'd probably have done exactly what he did.'

'You got kids, then?'

The little girl. The photograph. The memories. The pain. 'No, Michaela,' he said softly. 'You're missing the point. Look, you're Annette's best

176

friend, right?'

'Maybe,' she sniffed.

'Don't you care what's happened to her?'

'Nothing's happened to her,' she whined.

Bingo!

'So you have heard from her?'

Michaela hesitated. This was Mr Maxwell in front of her. He'd taught her back in Year Eight. Some of his lessons were actually quite interesting. And he did look a sorry state at the moment. Perhaps she had been a bit hasty the night before last. 'Yeah, yeah, I have.'

'Where is she?'

'Your 99's melting,' she commented.

He slurped his hand, gingerly. Michaela's white goo was only marginally less painful than Jacquie's ice pack. 'Don't change the subject.'

'Look, she's quite safe,' Michaela said. 'She just needs a bit of time, that's all. Her mum's gonna kill her as it is...'

'I think her mum could be the least of her troubles, Micky,' he said.

'Look ... you in the phone book? Got a mobile?'

'Yes. No, in that order. Well, I have, but I never use it.' Michaela was incredulous. How *old* must you be not to use a mobile?

'How about, if she texts me again, I tell her you want to talk to her. Yeah?'

'I'm in the book,' Maxwell said, slurping his hand again. 'Call me, Michaela. I think everybody should be more worried about Annette than they are. All right?'

'Oi, can we get some service around here?' The queue had formed again behind Peter Maxwell and the great, tolerant British public was exercising its bonhomie. All on a Summer's Day. Nonny Nonny.

Chapter Ten

'Jesus! Mr Maxwell, what happened to you?' The waiter hovered by the table, menus in hand, horror etched on his face.

'Don't ask, Hop Sing. It's a very long story,' Maxwell told him.

'You brave enough for chopsticks tonight?' The man looked as if he had enough to worry about as it was.

'Is the Pope a Buddhist?' the Great Man felt constrained to ask.

'That'll be a no, Kenny,' Jacquie Carpenter explained. Kenny had been in Britain for many years now, but no one was assimilated enough for Maxwell's repartee.

The pair sat opposite each other in the Great Wall, Jacquie stuffing prawn crackers, Maxwell trying not to cry when he nibbled his.

'Tell me again why you call him Hop Sing.' She sipped her lager. The dragon lanterns threw weirdly coloured patterns on the flock wallpaper as the breeze lifted from the sea and slipped in through the sash windows of Leighford's favourite – and only – Chinese restaurant.

'Ah, you have to be a certain vintage, darling heart,' he told her. '"We chased lady luck, till we finally struck, Bonanza." They don't write Western theme songs like that anymore. "Hoss and Joe and Adam know every rock is high." There was almost a tune to it. They were the sons of Ben Cartwright, aka the actor Lorne Greene – now there's a name to conjure with – in a cowboy series in the Fifties and Sixties. Hop Sing was their Chinese cook.'

'I'm not sure Kenny understands,' Jacquie whispered.

'Nonsense. His people invented fireworks and paper money and printing. There's a profound wisdom in the Chinese that goes way beyond *gai pad bai gaprow*. Have you noticed, by the way,' Maxwell leaned towards her and became conspiratorial, 'how the Thailanders are taking over. Siam and China have about as much in common as us and the Bulgarians, but you can't tell their dishes apart these days. It's a sad, sad world, my masters.'

'And talking of sad worlds...'

'Ah, yes.' He reached across to hold her hand. 'You poor darling. Samantha Welland. You all right?'

'Who's having the crab and sweetcorn soup?' Hop Sing was back.

'That'll be me, Hop,' Maxwell said. 'Got a particularly enticing Chardonnay in your extensive cellar? I'm trying to make a lady out of my beer-swilling companion here.'

Kenny winked. 'Got something special, Missy,' he all but bowed.

'Will you stop winding him up?' Jacquie hissed, tackling her crimson-coated ribs.

179

'Mine feel a bit like that,' Maxwell said, pointing at them, 'And I've been on the beach all day.'

'The beach? That's not like you, Max.'

'Michaela Reynolds. Works at the Lilliput Adventure Playground, selling Mr Scrummy ice-cream. More E-numbers than the parson preached about. She knows where Annette Choker is.'

'She does?' Jacquie swallowed quickly and dabbed her mouth to catch some, at least of the falling sauce. She grabbed for her mobile. 'I must get on to Alison McCormick.'

'It'll keep.' He held her hand fast. 'How long have you been on duty now?'

'We never sleep, Max,' she said. 'You know that.'

'OK, Mr Maxwell?' Hop Sing hovered with the Chardonnay.

'Ah, the south side of the vineyard, Hop. Perfect. Thanks.' And he waited until the waiter had gone. 'Shit, this is hot.'

'Anything's going to seem hot with a lip the size of yours, Max,' she said.

Why was it that women, even soft, loving women, could be so bloody non-understanding at times? Had there been a Mrs Michelangelo Buonarroti, no doubt she'd have been standing at the base of a column in the Sistine Chapel, tapping her foot and screaming, 'I've called you three times already. Are you coming in for your dinner or not?' He let it go.

'Henry thinks Sam Welland was murdered.'

Maxwell paused to let his lips recover from the last mouthful. 'Does he now?' he raised an eyebrow. 'And you'd be telling me this, why?' Could this be a turning-point in their relationship?

She threatened to stick a rib up his nose. 'I thought you might be interested,' she said.

'Oh, Woman Policeman mine,' he chuckled. 'How many cases have you and I worked on now – eight? Nine?'

'What's your point?'

'My point is that usually I have to extract information from you with a variety of Inquisition-type instruments of torture. First, I show them to you in the best Torquemada tradition, then I lop off bits of your body, one by one. And here you are, without so much as a turn of the rack, making free with what I'm sure are DCI Hall's most intimate deliberations.'

'He needs your help,' Jacquie said, stone-faced.

'My help?' Maxwell could frown all right. It was smiling that took its toll.

'Several times on the way to Hove,' she remembered. 'Once there and several times again on the way back, he said something like "Ask Maxwell".'

'Figure of speech,' the Head of Sixth Form shrugged, blowing on a particularly luscious piece of crab on his porcelain spoon.

'Uh-huh,' she shook her head, 'I know Henry Hall. There's an historical twist to this case, Max, and he knows it. That's where you come in.'

'You fed him my views on Martin Toogood's computer entries?'

'The *Julius Caesar*? Yes, I did. He's intrigued,'

'We all are,' Maxwell nodded. 'But still, I'm not sure I'm right.'

'It's a lead,' she said. And Leighford nick has precious few of those at the moment.

'What are you doing after this?' he asked, 'when and if I've been brave enough to get my mandibles around Hop Sing's to-die-for banana fritters?'

'Getting some shut-eye,' she said. *'After* I've passed Michaela's info on Annette onto the nick.'

'You are the proud owner of a differencing machine, are you not?' Maxwell was plotting something.

She screwed up her face and rested it in her hand, teasing the last yummy morsel of her ribs into a corner of her mouth. 'I'm sure you can manage the c-word,' she said, 'even if you can't use one. Yes, I have a computer. I won't bore you with the make and model.'

'Brilliant,' he nodded. 'I need to look something up on what you young people call the Internet.' He waved to the waiter. 'Hop Sing,' he called to the odd looks of fellow diners. 'A brace of your lovely hot flannels, please. Just the thing to mop my soup up with.' He leaned forward to Jacquie and said in a whisper, 'Don't think he noticed that I ended that sentence with a preposition, do you?'

'So, Mr ... er ... Maxwell?' Tam Fraser sat in the main tent that Monday morning, surrounded, rather like Dierdre Lessing, with dead men's bones. 'Tell me what you know about Saxon cemeteries.'

'Furnished or unfurnished?' the Head of Sixth Form asked. He had jettisoned the bandages and cream of the previous day, the ones that had jolted Michaela Reynolds and Kenny Hop Sing and had made Jacquie Carpenter love the man even more; and he was bearing his wounds before for all to see.

Fraser was quietly impressed, but he wasn't going to show it. He needed another volunteer at the Leighford dig like a hole in the head, but he was two people down now. First, David Radley. Now, Sam Welland. Henry Hall and a couple of uniforms had been to the site earlier to break the news about Sam Welland to the rest of the team. Fraser had insisted on a two minutes' silence and then it was back to buckets and spades.

'Unfurnished,' he said.

'Usually denotes a Christian burial ground,' Maxwell said. 'Bodies in rows in an east-west orientation, heads to the west, to the setting sun. No grave goods, on the grounds that you can't, in Christian philosophy, take it with you. No cremations either. That little habit didn't come back until the Victorians got rather windy about premature burial. I blame Edgar Allan Poe, myself.'

Fraser chuckled. A bit of light relief was all too missing around here. Perhaps he could do business with this Maxwell after all.

'They are usually concomitant with a church,' the Head of Sixth Form went on, 'but you haven't found one here, have you?'

'Indeed, not,' Fraser nodded. 'Go on.'

'It is unlikely that this site is a continuation of a furnished, that is, pagan, burial site. If it were, you'd go down in the annals yourself, wouldn't you?'

183

'Would I? And why is that, pray?'

Maxwell played the *ingénue*. 'Because there are no recorded examples of that in England.'

'Very good, laddie,' Fraser smiled. 'But you've been to the site before, so you tell me. Pick up all this from Dougie Russell, did you?'

'Emphatically not,' Maxwell bridled. He'd picked it up from some dot.com site on Jacquie's PC, but he wasn't going to tell Fraser that.

'And of course, you know all about poor David.'

'I do,' Maxwell nodded. 'In a way, that's why I'm here.'

'Oh?'

'You're short-staffed.'

'Shorter than you know,' Fraser said grimly. 'What a loss to research that man will be. But this is David's dig. Whatever we find here, my report will carry his name. I'll have it no other way.'

'Unfurnished cemeteries have become quite important in recent years.' Maxwell's memory, even of the Internet screen, was impressive. 'Variants in wood and stone memorials, grave structure, charcoal burial, supine and erect bodies, with arm and leg variations. Of course, at Repton...'

'Repton's Viking, laddie,' Fraser interrupted, testing his man for his ability to think on his feet.

'A winter camp, yes. But it was a Saxon monastery first, founded, if I'm not mistaken, by Haedda, Abbott of Bredon – a double house for monks and nuns. Quite the place to be seen dead, too, if you were a Middle Saxon royal. Aethelbald was buried there; Wigstan, of course;

184

not to mention Merewald, King of the Magon-saetan...'

'Enough, already!' Fraser's hands were in the air, as he laughed out loud. 'You've got the job, Mr Maxwell.' And the great men shook hands. 'But, first things first. How are you at making the tea?'

Jacquie Carpenter spent what seemed like all of that Monday afternoon of Maxwell's half-term on the phone to Hove CID. SOCO had, as promised two days earlier, busted a gut to get what information they could to Henry Hall's people. Their pathologist's initial findings were that Sam Welland had died by strangulation.

'Asphyxia due to a constriction of the neck by force applied by ligature,' were the man's words over the phone to Leighford nick. Text-book stuff. The rope's knot was to the left and behind the dead woman's ear when they found her. The photographs already pinned to an Incident Room in Hove showed Sam Welland as her partner had found her. Her lips and ears were purple, the colour of Peter Maxwell's nose. There was a film of froth around her lips, livid in the camera's flash and her tongue protruded, mauve and grotesque like some ghastly gargoyle leaning out from a Medieval buttress to terrify the world.

There was nothing quick and clean about Sam Welland's death. The macabre science of the judicial executions from James Berry to Albert Pierrepoint allowed for the lightning drop, with Berry's carefully calculated table, worked out to the weight of a condemned man, his height and the length of the rope needed to kill him. Whoever had killed Sam Welland had reverted to the older method, the bunglers like Calcraft, the young Victoria's executioner, who left his victims to writhe at the rope's end, kicking and struggling, fighting for air.

That was how the archaeologist had died; her fingertips were raw from scrabbling at the rough hemp, until, finally, mercifully, her breath had stopped and her eyes bulged and her hands had fallen to her side, her fingers curling in on themselves like claws. She had wet herself in those last minutes, splashes of urine on the kitchen chair and a puddle on the garage floor.

Whoever had killed her had gone into the house freely. There was no sign of forced entry, no broken window, no tell-tale smashing of the lock or door-frame. Ms Welland's upmarket home had a complex burglar alarm system, but no CCTV camera and none of the neighbours had seen anyone come or go at any time over the weekend. That said, The Orchards was set back from the road, with an eight foot brick wall at the front and a ring of cedars around the perimeter. There could have been a quiet pop festival going on in its grounds and the neighbours would have been none the wiser.

So, Jacquie put the question to her Hove oppo over the phone, did Sam Welland know her killer? Had her visitor been the newspaperman, a Mormon, a prospective parliamentary candidate, a four-foot high 'grey' from beyond the known world? Anything was possible. All the accounts of the dead woman that Jacquie had were that she was extrovert, brash even. She wouldn't have been cowering behind a curtain somewhere.

Whoever the murderer was, he had brought his rope with him. Jacquie checked her notes again; Hazel Twigg said that there was none in the house, and apart from the length used to hang the dead woman, she was right. Bruising and a cut on the right jaw suggested that the killer had gone for Sam in the kitchen, where there were slight signs of a scuffle – a ruched mat, a wonky window-blind. In fiction, Miss Marple would have been travelling past in the 4.50 from Paddington at the time and would have seen the lot. As it was, nothing. As Western buff Peter Maxwell would have ruminated, she might as well have been riding the 3.10 to Yuma.

He had lifted her down the stairs from the utility room and laid her down near her car. That meant bodily strength. Sam Welland was muscular and powerful herself. Two tiny blood droplets from her mouth marked the place and one of her earrings had bounced off under the Volvo where her head had hit the concrete. As the pathologist sheared off her thick, blonde hair, he found the bruising, puffy and soft over the parietal bone. The Saturday visitor had strung up the rope from the hook on the wall and passed it, using the chair, across the beams. The height didn't help Jacquie at all. Only a particularly impressive member of the Harlem Globetrotters could have achieved that by standing on the floor. The noose was good and strong. Then he hoisted the unconscious woman's body onto the chair and hauled her upright, securing the loose end of the rope onto its housing, watching her squirm as the pressure on her neck brought her to; and the cold and the terror of imminent death would have made every nerve jangle.

Someone strong, Jacquie doodled on her note pad. Two people? What was it Maxwell had said about Martin Toogood's on-screen doodling? A quote from *Julius Caesar*. That play was all about conspiracy, wasn't it? Not one man, but several, had murdered the dictator. Was that what she was looking at here? Had two or more people conspired to break the neck of David Radley and drop him off at Leighford, among the already long dead? Had one or more of them hoisted Sam Welland to eternity? And how many murderers does it take to fix the brake-lines of a nice guy's car? That wasn't a joke and Jacquie Carpenter wasn't laughing.

Peter Maxwell was a fast learner. By four o'clock, when the sun was still a demon, he'd graduated from making tea to washing pots, well, bones, actually. His *de rigueur* archaeologist's straw hat was tilted back on his hair and he tried not to keep his head down too much for fear it would start the bleeding again. His back ached and he felt such a prat in the pink washing-up gloves Tam Fraser insisted he wore.

'My body is a temple,' he groaned as Derek Latymer brought him another sieve of goodies.

'Long day, Mr Maxwell?'

'Is it always like this, in archaeology, I mean?'

'Ooh, no,' Latymer grinned, wiping the sweat from his forehead and parking his Indiana Jones hat on the corner of a chair. 'Sometimes you get to squat for hours under the blazing sun, getting blisters all over your back and shoulders. That's when you're not knee deep in freezing water, of course, with the rain coming onto your anorak like a fucking waterfall. You're new at this, aren't you?'

'Ssh!' Maxwell winked, putting his finger somewhere where he thought his lips ought to be. 'Don't tell the boss. He thinks I'm a whizzo-wheeze at Saxon cemeteries.'

'I try not to tell him anything,' Latymer said, flopping down into a canvas chair and crossing his booted legs on the table. He whipped out a hip flask from his shorts. 'Hair of the dog?'

Maxwell shook his head. 'I thought you people were all Friends of the Earth,' he said, 'not spraying your armpits and so on, so that the world can be saved.'

Latymer snorted. 'You're mixing me up with the sort of enviro-archaeologist who gives a fuck.' He took a swig.

'Did you know David Radley well?' Maxwell asked.

'I wouldn't say I knew him,' Latymer said, brushing caked mud off his forearms. 'He was a bloody good archaeologist. I was privileged, briefly, to work with him.'

'How did you get the job?'

'Oh, I asked for it,' Latymer said. 'Radley was a legend in archaeology – in the same way old Fraser used to be 200 years ago. I suppose I saw it as a step on the ladder. Still is, in fact. But there's something odd about this site.'

'Odd?'

'Yes. Oh, Saxon cemeteries aren't my field, but, I mean, what's it doing here? You're a local man, aren't you? Historian and all that?'

'Of sorts,' Maxwell nodded. 'Why do you ask?'

'Well,' Latymer leaned forward, resting his trowelling arm on his knee. 'I know the Romans came to Fishbourne, but did the Saxons come to Leighford?'

'Funny you should ask that,' Maxwell said. 'It's not at all documented.' Maxwell had, in his weaker moments, dabbled in the local museum, smiling at the unsavoury chaps and brash, ancestor-seeking Americans who clogged the microfiche in the Leighford Records Office every summer.

'And there's something else.' Latymer was into his stride now, as the Scotch warmed his cockles. 'The ash grove.'

Maxwell peered out through the open tent flap. He could see it in the sharp shadows against the sunlit spoil heaps, the stand of grey-barked trees where they'd found David Radley. 'What about it?'

'We dug a slit trench there on the first day. Geophys were going shit-nuts about it. But David wouldn't let us do any follow up. Said that could wait. Seemed to me that's where we should have started. If this is a church site, that's where the building was likely to be.'

'Have you talked to Fraser about it?'

'The mad professor? He won't have his precious wee David questioned for a moment. Says we'll get to it eventually. But as I understand it, we've only got a week before the bulldozers move in for the golf course and that'll effectively shut

190

us down.'

'Archaeological differences, eh?' Maxwell clicked his tongue.

Latymer got to his feet, pocketing the flask and plonking his hat back on his head. 'Take my advice,' he said. 'You stick to washing bones, mate. At least the buggers can't bite back.'

'Tea?' Peter Maxwell handed a mug that cheered to Helen Reader.

'Oh, you darling man.' She was rubbing her heels, sitting on the tail gate of her estate, trying to get some feeling back into her feet.

'Hometime, eh?' he smiled at her.

'Thank God. I thought David Radley was a hard taskmaster, but Scotland's Gauleiter over there...'

Tam Fraser was ordering people about in all directions, hands on hips, silver-haired chest sprouting out from the crisp white shirt he wore. All he needed was the whip and the boots and he'd have been D.W. Griffith on the *Intolerance* set.

'What are your thoughts, Helen?' Maxwell asked. 'The murders, I mean?'

She sighed. 'I don't know what to think.'

'Aren't you ... afraid?'

'Afraid? Good God, no. Why should I be afraid?'

Why indeed? Maxwell looked at the woman. She had biceps that would put many a man to shame and her thighs looked as though they could crack walnuts. 'Two of the team are dead,' Maxwell reminded her.

191

'Mr Maxwell, I'm what you might call an archaeological groupie. I don't have an official qualification to my name. Ooh, you make a decent drop of tea.'

He bowed low.

'But I've been on more digs than you've written school reports.'

Maxwell doubted that particular piece of hyperbole.

'And when you've been around dead bodies for so long, this sort of thing doesn't faze you. I don't flatter myself that I'm much of a target. Who'd want to kill me?'

'I suspect that David Radley and Samantha Welland would have said something similiar,' he said.

'Sam's lifestyle,' the Groupie said, 'not healthy.' She tucked an errant lock of hair back under her headscarf. 'I don't want to sound too forty years ago,' she said, 'but not everyone is as tolerant of these things as we would like.'

'Are you talking about the fact that Ms Welland was a lesbian?'

Helen Reader bridled at the word, looking rapidly about her. 'I'm sorry,' she said. 'I ought to be comfortable with it and I'm not. Not terribly PC at the moment, I know, to be homophobic, but there it is. We can't help the way we're made.'

'Surely,' Maxwell reasoned, 'that goes for Sam too.'

'It's not for me to say.' She finished her tea with a giant swig for mankind. 'As you said Mr Maxwell. Hometime.'

'Maxwell!' It was Tam Fraser. 'You got a minute?'

The two Great Men sat in the snug of the Kettle that night, Maxwell getting outside a large Southern Comfort, Fraser tackling a double Scotch. The Englishman was paying.

'How well do you know Detective Chief Inspector Hall?' Fraser had shed his director's gear of the day and was back in a tweed jacket again, his lion's mane of silver hair back-combed, his cravat crisp against his white shirt.

'Not as well as I'd like and better than I need to,' came the answer.

Fraser sat upright, frowning. 'Sounds like a bloody Saxon riddle, man,' he laughed. 'Pass it by me again.'

'I've had some dealings with the chief inspector,' he explained. 'The girl I love works for him.

'Does she now? Well, that's handy.'

'It can be,' Maxwell said.

A roar went up from the domino crowd in the corner. 'This the place to be, is it?' Fraser asked. 'In downtown Leighford?'

'You wanted somewhere where we wouldn't be disturbed,' Maxwell shrugged. 'This is the only pub the grocks don't know about."

'Grocks?'

'Grockles,' he explained. 'Tourists. It's a rather charming, onomatopoeic South Coast term for the chattering noise the annoying bastards make. As one of the few people in Leighford who doesn't make my living off them, I can afford a little contempt. Of course, Leighford Cemetery's quieter – mine, that is, not yours. Why do you want to know about Hall?'

'I think the man's grossly incompetent.'

'Ah, now, I fear I'd have to disagree with you there. Henry and I have had our minor run-ins over the years, but he knows his job.'

'So how come he's not taking me seriously?'

'I don't follow.'

Fraser looked around him. The domino gang were engrossed in their game in one corner, two old bags were putting the world to rights in another, probably comparing that nice Mr Chamberlain with that unpleasant, war-mongering bastard, Churchill. The barman looked as if he'd died years ago. 'The Sepulchre Society of Sussex,' he said.

'Come again?' Maxwell winced as a slug of the amber nectar hit his lips. Perhaps alcohol wasn't the wisest choice with a face like his.

'Douglas Russell received a letter four days ago. It came from an organisation called The Sepulchre Society of Sussex and it warned him – all of us really – off the dig.'

'Did it, now?' Maxwell was all ears. 'What did it say?'

'That's just it,' Fraser sighed. 'I'm buggered if I can remember. I gave it to DCI Hall.'

'Who didn't take it seriously?' Maxwell was not *that* surprised. He'd had a similar bum's rush from Woman Policeman McCormick.

'Looked at it like it was my bloody shopping list,' Fraser said. 'I thought it was a pretty important clue, in the scheme of things. David, I mean. Now Samantha.'

'Doesn't explain Martin Toogood, does it?' Maxwell was talking to himself, really.

194

'Sorry?'

'Never mind,' Maxwell shook his head. The waters were muddy enough already. 'What did Douglas make of the letter?'

'Well, I think he was pretty shaken. You'd have to ask him. What's disturbing is the way these people can reach us. How, for instance, did they know Douglas was staying at the Quinton Hotel? How did they know where to find David? Samantha? I'm not easily rattled, Maxwell, but I have to admit, these people have got me peering round corners.'

'What's their beef, then?' the Head of Sixth Form asked, 'the Sepulchre Society?'

Fraser shrugged. 'God knows. Politically correct claptrap. Leave our dead alone, that sort of hogwash. You'd think, wouldn't you, in our spectacularly secular country, that sort of bigotry would be dead and gone.'

'And you haven't come across this group before?'

'Never. As a local man, I thought perhaps you'd know something... You know, petitions, loonies stoning the Town Hall, that sort of thing.'

'Might pay a visit to our local friendly crime correspondent,' Maxwell pondered.

'Could you do that?' Fraser asked. 'As a personal favour, I mean? I'm responsible for my people, Maxwell. And since the local *gendarmerie* are doing fuck all – oh, begging your fiancée's pardon, of course.'

Maxwell gave a smile his best shot. 'I know what this is all about,' he said. 'It's because my bone-washing is such crap, isn't it? You want me

195

off the site.'

'Man, man,' Fraser smiled. 'If I wanted you off the site, believe me, laddie, your feet wouldn't touch the gravel. Is it your shout?'

Chapter Eleven

This was something Alison McCormick wasn't looking forward to. It wasn't so long ago that she'd been a confused kid herself, hating her school, her parents, herself. Somebody had been around to sort her out, hold her hand, put her straight. Had been, in the time-honoured American phrase, there for her. So here she was, this Tuesday morning, sitting in the dark, dismal lounge of the little railway cottage in downtown Leighford, being there for somebody else. Opposite her sat a sulky Michaela Reynolds, pouting under her studded nose. She was still wearing a skimpy top that showed her studded navel. At least, the girl had a sense of symmetry. To her left, equally petulant and with a bandaged left hand, her old man, Shaun, complete with crucifix earring and cropped head. At least he had had the sense of dignity to put on a shirt. Of Mrs Reynolds, there was no sign. She was, to quote both members of her family, 'down the pub', although they both stressed she was working. Pulling pints or pulling customers was not discussed.

'We know you know where Annette is, Michaela,' Alison McCormick was saying. 'You owe it to her to tell us.' The Leighford CID machine had growled into action. Maxwell had told Jacquie; Jacquie had told Alison. All they needed now was for the cow to tell the dairymaid.

'It's no good talking to her,' her dad grunted. 'She's always been the same. Stubborn as all get out. Why don't you tell 'em, you stupid little...'

DC Dave Garstang had met men like Shaun Reynolds before. They beat their wives, their sons, their daughters. They worked if they had to and spent most of their wages on themselves. Saturday night it was down the Sports and Social with the lads, get trolleyed, then home to give the wife one, either a shag or a good kicking, depending on the mood he was in. He was one of those blokes, an old sergeant had once told him, who ought to report to the nick every Thursday for a bit of a smacking. Dave Garstang had never known those days, but he couldn't help basking in a certain glow of their nostalgia.

'Why don't we pop into the kitchen, Mr Reynolds?' he said. 'Let the ladies talk? You can tell me all about your hand.'

'My...? Oh, yeah. Yeah, all right, then.' Shaun Reynolds wasn't a snitch. But that poncey bastard with the stupid bow tie and even stupider hat had got right up his nose. Or was it vice versa? Yeah, he'd tell this copper all about that. He pointed to Alison. 'I'm only next door, all right? You lay a finger on my girl...'

Alison watched him go, Garstang's hand firmly on his shoulder. She waited for the door to close. 'Michaela,' the policewoman leaned forward.

'Did Annette go off with Mr Fry, from school?'

The girl looked at her under sullen lids. This one could go either way. 'Might of,' she said.

'When was this?' Alison saw her way in.

'Dunno. Last week. Week before. Whenever.'

'Where did they go?'

'Dunno.'

'Look,' Alison found this difficult. 'If Annette has gone off with Mr Fry she's in trouble.'

'Why?'

'Have I got to spell it out?' the policewoman asked. 'She could get pregnant. Or worse.'

'How do you mean, worse?'

'What if she annoyed him,' Alison asked. 'Said the wrong thing? Did the wrong thing? He's got a bit of a short fuse. What if he lashed out?' Alison chose her moment. 'You know what that's like, don't you?'

Michaela didn't answer. She just stared dead ahead at the flickering, silent TV screen.

'Michaela, you know Mr Fry's wife is dead, don't you?'

'That's got nothing to do with Annette,' the girl said defiantly, her face twisted, her eyes flashing.

'Maybe not,' Alison leaned back, giving the girl space. 'But he doesn't even know yet. He doesn't know she's dead.'

'You'd better find him, then,' Michaela flounced.

'We're trying,' Alison told her, trying to keep her own cool. 'But you're not helping.'

'All right,' the girl shouted. 'All right. I dunno where he is, all right? She like texted me last Monday. She said she was in London. In a bed and breakfast. I spoke to her on the phone the next day.'

Breakthrough. 'And how did she sound?' Alison wanted to know.

'Okay, I guess,' Michaela shrugged. 'She said it wasn't like she expected.'

'What wasn't?'

'Going away. Getting away from the Barlich-way.'

'That's why she went?'

Michaela nodded. 'You been to her place?'

Alison shook her head. 'No. But I know the estate.'

'Well, her mum's a right cow. You've seen my dad – he's got a temper on him, sure, but he loves us; me and my little bruvver. But Mrs Choker, she's just a scrubber. Annette don't know who her dad is to this day. Different dad every weekend. And more than one of 'em's tried it on with her.'

'Had sex, you mean?'

Michaela nodded. 'She told me about it once,' she said.

'She doesn't have to go back there, Michaela,' Alison told her. 'We've got hostels, places where she'll be safe. She didn't have to run away with Mr Fry.'

'Mr Fry?' Michaela frowned. 'Who said she was with him?'

The people of the *Advertiser* had seen it all, of course. Prize peas the size of a goat's testicles, a kid with a saucepan stuck on his head and, a long time before the local paper was even called the *Advertiser*, a fleeting visit from Karl Marx. Even

199

so, the sight before them that Tuesday lunchtime was odd. A man in a tweed hat pushed on top of a thatch of barbed wire hair, with a face that looked as though it had gone through a mangle, sitting with his head on sideways. Had they been, like Peter Maxwell, film buffs, they might have been reminded of Vanessa Redgrave, the very unnunlike Mother Superior in *The Devils*. As it was, they were simply reminded of a non-technical person.

'Er ... you *can* tilt it, you know.' One of the ladies of the front office hovered by his elbow. 'Just turn this knob.'

'Thank you,' he said, raising his hat. 'Always been a bit of a mystery to me, microfiche.'

Newsprint scudded past him on the screen in the *Advertiser*'s front office, with its smell of coffee and its appalling spider plants.

'What is it you're looking for, exactly?' the busybody woman wondered.

'Damned if I know,' he sighed. 'Ah. Mr James?'

'I'm Reg James.' The man before him was a shambles. He had just crashed his way from the inner office, through a pair of disreputable double doors. He had a piece of newspaper, aptly enough, stuck to a shaving wound on his chin.

'Peter Maxwell.' The Head of Sixth Form stood up to shake his hand. 'Can I have a word?'

'Jesus,' the journalist said, staring at Maxwell's face. 'I'm due in court at two. Come on up. You can watch me eat my sandwich.'

'Thanks,' and the two of them disappeared through the double doors to ascend the spiral twist to the offices on the first floor. More smells of coffee, more spider plants, but this time, the carpet was buried under piles of papers, documents and boxes. Phones rang incessantly and computer screens flickered.

'Want a coffee?' James asked.

'Love one,' Maxwell told him. 'Milk and two, please.'

'Ah. Black, I'm afraid. Janice, have you seen my sweeteners?'

A girl with long blonde hair shook her head without looking up from her computer.

'Thank you, Janice,' James said, rolling his eyes heavenward. He leaned forward to Maxwell. 'Came as a YTS girl eleven years ago. Can't get rid of her.' He was an unmade bed kind of a man, with sparse, straw-coloured hair and incisors that threatened to cross each other – or anybody looking at them funny. Maxwell remembered that William Bonney aka Billy the Kid looked not unlike Reginald James and he killed three of his four men because they laughed at his teeth. Did the infamous outlaw, Maxwell wondered briefly, have a piece of newspaper stuck to his chin, too?

He rummaged in a stash of less-than-savoury mugs and found one for Peter Maxwell. It was probably green. He poured something dark from the percolator on the desk. 'Right,' he passed the coffee to the Head of Sixth Form. 'What can I ... oh, hang on. Sardine paste?' he proffered a limp sandwich, from a polythene bag. The thing sagged even further in the stale air of the newspaper office.

'Thanks, no.' Maxwell did his best to smile.

'You're right,' James hurled the effort into the

nearest bin. 'No imagination, Mrs James. Pleasant woman, up to a point, but no imagination. Of all the unspeakably erotic delights of Mainly Buns in the High Street, she has to pick sardines. So, we'll skip lunch ... again. Mr ... Maxwell, is it? Your phone call said you needed help. Though I should point out,' he peered more closely at the man's face, 'we don't do unsubstantiated assault stories. Whoever put one on you will have to be contacted too. And if it's not really a police matter ... oh, mother of God!' He suddenly grimaced. 'Janice? When did you make this?'

'Ascension Day.' Janice still didn't look up, but she was clearly not the dumb blonde she appeared to be.

'Great. So, the face...'

'No, no,' Maxwell thought it best to forego the coffee and he put the mug down. 'The face is by-the-bye. Have you, in all your long years at the Print-Face, Mr James, come across The Sepulchre Society of Sussex?'

James frowned. 'Sepulchre Society of Sussex? It's an alliterateur's wet dream, certainly, but I can't say... Hang on.' And he wheeled his swivel chair across to a filing cabinet with a series of squeaks and clicks. 'Sepulchre, sepulchre...' he muttered as his fingers dabbled through files without number. 'Look at that,' he tutted. 'The paperless office. Bloody marvellous, isn't it? Seb Coe. Whoops, that should be in the aristocracy file now, of course. Selbourne. Jesus, that boring crap by Gilbert White. Why *did* we print that? Semen. Ah, quite a bit on that, unpleasantly enough. Serial killers. Oh, I remember this. Pretty good, even if I say it myself. No, sorry.' He slammed the drawer shut. 'Nothing on Sepulchre. It's probably some rather downbeat antiquarian group. Having a reunion, are they? Sort of cremation barbecue?'

Only Reg James was laughing.

'I think it's a little more serious than that. What do you know of the dig at Leighford? On Staple Hill?'

'Aha!' James' face lit up. 'Now you're talking my kind of language.' He whipped out a notepad from nowhere. 'Mind if I make a few notes?'

Maxwell quietly took the pencil out of the man's hand. 'I'd much rather you didn't,' he smiled.

'All right.' James leaned back, the pad discarded, and cradled his knee. 'Off the record, is it?'

'Two people connected with the dig are dead.'

'Indeed they are,' James said. 'I attended DCI Hall's Press Conference, of course. Didn't exactly spill the beans, did he?'

'I don't know,' Maxwell said. 'I wasn't there.'

'Wait a minute. Two bodies.' James was leaning forward now. 'Just so we're all singing from the same hymn sheet – you're talking Dr David Radley and DS Martin Toogood.'

And Dr Samantha Welland makes three, Maxwell thought, but no one had gone public on that one yet and he kept it to himself. 'I thought the *Advertiser* might have gone for a scoop on this,' he said. 'Juicy stuff for you boys, isn't it?'

'I hope that's not a criticism,' the journalist chortled.

'Not at all,' Maxwell said. 'I'm sure the police are delighted. They're always telling me how the members of the Fourth Estate are under their feet and up their arses at the same time.'

James narrowed his piggy eyes and clicked his fingers. 'I know who you are now,' he said. 'You're Peter Maxwell!'

'Very good,' the Head of Sixth Form nodded. 'I think I told you that in the outer office and on the phone.'

'No, no,' James was chuckling, 'You're *the* Peter Maxwell. Head of Sixth Form at that venerable centre of excellence Leighford High by day, supersleuth by night. You're the Jane Marple of the South Coast.'

'Dear me,' sighed Maxwell, Joan Hickson to a tee. 'How preternaturally stupid of me.'

'That's bloody great!' James laughed.

'Personally,' Maxwell wobbled his chin as well as he could, only having the one and given the extent of his bruising. 'I preferred Margaret Rutherford.'

'So did I!' agreed James. 'No, you're a legend at my local,' he said. 'Ever since I saw you in the Grimond's School case. The way you demolished that QC wanker in court. I'm surprised he didn't hang up his wig after that. Most fun Winchester's had in a very long time.'

'Flattering, Mr James,' Maxwell nodded, 'but that was then.'

'Ah, yes. Well, this is a turn up,' the journalist sat, grinning broadly at his man. 'DCI Hall know you're on this one?' His demeanour suddenly changed.

'He might have an inkling.' The Head of Sixth Form said. 'What headway have the Fourth Estate made?'

'Well, to put it in a nutshell, fuck all.' He glanced up, hoping to have rattled Janice's cage. She hadn't moved. 'No, at the press call Hall might as well have told us it was a sunny day in June and all the pixies had come out to play. Puts a whole new slant on "No comment" that bloke.'

'Anybody covered the dig from day one?' Maxwell asked. 'Before there was any trouble, I mean?'

'Let's see,' James was off on his travels again, whizzing across the flotex and thumbing his way through a different drawer. 'Hard copy,' he muttered. 'You can't beat it. Okay, let's see.'

And he speed-read the papers in his hand, peering over a pair of specs that had appeared from nowhere on the end of his nose.

'A bloke called Arthur Wimble made the first find, with a metal detector. You'll love him, by the way, invented the word Anorak. He found a couple of coins.'

'At the site?'

'Apparently. This was back in March.'

'That's right,' Maxwell said. 'I vaguely remember it.' Die though he would, rather than admit it, Peter Maxwell was quietly addicted to the *Leighford Advertiser*. He was at a funny age.

'Of course, Mr Wimble met with an accident,' James told him.

'Oh?'

'Fell downstairs one night.'

'Oh, dear.'

'In his bungalow.'

'Ah.'

'One of my colleagues paid him a visit. He wasn't in a talkative mood. Seemed he's sold his metal detector and moved on. New house – one with an upstairs, in fact, which does seem to be courting disaster rather.'

'Police involved?'

'You'd have to ask them,' James said. 'Ah,' the investigative journalist had found something else. 'Another of my colleagues covered the finding of the first body. They called it – and you'll like this, as an historian – that is what you are?'

'It has been rumoured,' Maxwell smiled.

'Called him Frank Pledge. Get it?'

'Got it,' Maxwell admitted, and he was quietly impressed that James had. Frankpledge had replaced tithing in the later Middle Ages and was a sort of promise to be a good boy – electronic tagging of offenders in the days before tags or electronics. 'When was this?'

'Er...' James checked his copy. 'End of April. The body was identified by Dr David Radley of Wessex University as belonging to the mid to late Saxon period. Not a formal burial, in fact, but – and I quote – "a hasty inhumation on a hillside." Radley seemed to think it might have been murder; the skull had been stove in with an axe. Good to see fine old traditions continuing, isn't it?'

'Anything else?' Maxwell wasn't going to be drawn on that one. And, at the moment, no one had actually suffered *that* particular fate. Unless, of course, James knew something that Maxwell didn't...

'Some sort of deal was struck with the owners,' the reporter went on. 'The fields had recently been bought from the local farmer by Cahill and Lieberman Properties who wanted to open a golf course. We covered that, too. Upmarket clients, posh tarts in frocks with G'n'T's in the club-house, you know the sort of thing. Perfect anti-dote to the bloody Barlichway and Tony Blair's Britain, really. 'Course, there were objections.'

'There were?'

James frowned. 'You do read the *Advertiser*, Mr Maxwell?'

'Every word,' the Great Man said. 'Only the old grey cells aren't what they were.' He'd switched effortlessly from Jane Marple to Hercule Poirot. 'This was weeks ago. Fifteen minutes are a long time in teaching.'

James had heard that somewhere, but he couldn't place it. 'Yes. Conservationists. Envious Lefties. Anti-Sports lobby. Saddos all. I enjoy a round myself. Got to be less contentious than fox hunting, hasn't it, when all's said and done.'

'No Sepulchre Society of Sussex?'

''Fraid not,' James smiled. 'I'll get Janice to run you off a list if it helps.'

'Thanks,' Maxwell beamed at the girl but she was miles away, probably up to her modem in Tottingleigh's Flower Festival.

''Course, I don't suppose Messrs Cahill and Lieberman were best pleased.'

'Really?'

'Before I came to Leighford's sunny climes, Mr Maxwell, I worked on a London local – the *Hainault Observer*. Doubtless you've heard of it.'

'Doubtless.' Maxwell tried a wink. It wasn't altogether successful.

'We had a similar thing there.' James was poking about in the briefcase by his feet. 'Do you know, I *know* I've got a yoghurt in here somewhere. Yeah, rescue archaeology. Some kid found a few bits of pot – Roman, if memory serves. They were building a supermarket. Everybody was furious – delays all over the shop, if you'll excuse the pun. They turned Tony Robinson down flat. Told the BBC where to stick it when they tried to steal *Time Team's* thunder. It all got a bit nasty.'

'A bit nasty in the Arthur Wimble sort of way?'

'Could be,' James nodded, holding up the plastic pot in triumph. 'I'm a bit hazy on the details now. Oh, bugger, Janice. Where have all the spoons gone?' Wasn't that an old Edith Piaf number?

Nothing.

'No, I've met Cahill and Lieberman's Mr Anthony Cahill. One of nature's gentlefolk. Like something out of *The Sopranos,* but with an Eton accent. He was probably the school bully.'

'Yes,' Maxwell observed. 'I thought that.'

'Ah, you've had the pleasure?'

'Let's just say his associates and I had a difference of opinion. They wanted to smash my kneecaps and I didn't – call me an old fuddy-duddy if you like.'

'Then, of course,' James was still fishing bits of paper out of his filing cabinet drawer, 'Dr Radley became late.'

'Did you get to the site yourself?' Maxwell wanted to know.

'Can Tim Henman play tennis? There was a

yellow ribbon up around that lot before you could say "Any comment, officer?" That was weird, mind.'

'What was?'

'Well, after we'd taken piccies from beyond the cordon ... oh, nothing we could use; my editor's funny about body-bags on page one, I got back here to the office. There was a message on my answerphone. It said "Beware the wolf, the grey heath-stalker." Spooky, huh?'

'Spooky indeed,' Maxwell nodded. 'Have you still got it? The message, I mean?'

'No,' James said archly. 'Have we, Janice?'

Focus. Fixed stare. No reply.

'No, you can't keep stuff round here. We'd have a bloody warehouse full of tapes and cassettes if we started that game. We get a lot of cranky stuff. The messages we got when it looked like Britney Spears was passing through earlier in the year ... well, even I had to look some of the words up.'

'Do you remember the voice?'

'Now you've asked. Woman, certainly.'

'Accent of any kind?'

James shook his head. 'Not that I can remember.'

'A quotation, presumably?' Maxwell was thinking aloud.

'Do you know it?' the journalist asked, 'Man of letters like yourself.'

Maxwell shook his head. 'It doesn't ring any bells,' he said.

'All right, then,' James said. 'My turn to pick your brains. You're the historian. Tell me about ash groves.'

'The place they found David Radley.'

'Correct.'

'Well,' Maxwell sighed. 'We're talking about a Saxon site.'

'And?'

'And it's not my period.'

James snorted. 'I bet you say that to all your classes.'

Maxwell smiled. 'The early Saxons almost certainly believed woods were haunted. The Celts had regarded trees and stones and water as sacred objects. Even in the late tenth century, the Church was warning people about praying to idols like that.'

'Some sort of ritual thing, then?' James was piecing it together, pentagrams and naked virgins flashing before his eyes.

'It could be.' Maxwell said. 'Of course, if there's a church on the site, under the ash grove, I mean...'

'That's possible, is it?'

'My fellow diggers seem to think so.'

'Your...? Mr Maxwell,' James shook the man by the hand. 'You've been and gone and infiltrated them. Bloody marvellous! Tell me, what's this new bloke like? The one in charge now.'

'Professor Fraser? Old school. Bit of a tartar. Ex-tutor of David Radley.'

'Cut up, is he?' the journalist asked. 'About Radley, I mean?'

'I'd say so,' Maxwell nodded, 'In a cantankerous, Scottish sort of way.'

'So what have you got? Not just dirt under your fingernails, I'll be bound.' He'd unconsciously picked up his pad again.

'Uh-huh,' Maxwell wagged one of those fingers now. 'I came to you, remember, to ask about the Sepulchre Society.'

'Oh, Christ, yes,' James said, plonking the pad down again. 'I'd forgotten about them already. What's the link?'

'Along with the Conservationists, Anti-Sports lobby and Envious Lefties, they don't want the dig to go ahead. The difference is, they might just be doing something about it.'

The afternoon sun was streaming in on Henry Hall's paperwork. He read it again, the letter from the Sepulchre Society of Sussex and he read the lab report on it. No fingerprints. Whoever had typed and posted this, they had used gloves from first to last. Stamp and envelope were both self-adhesive those little improvements in technology that were designed to help everybody and which proved to be such a godsend to the poison-pen letter writer. No saliva, no DNA. No DNA, no point in checking a database of misfits. Then, there was the typing itself. It was Arthur Conan Doyle, bless him, who had first pointed out to a disbelieving world that you could detect differences in type writing machines (in his day, typewriters were the ladies who did the work). But word processors, computers, laptops were as anonymous as the phantom tiddler. The thing could have been written in Henry Hall's outer office.

He checked the clock. Half-past three. It would soon be time for Professor Fraser's daily progress check and he coldly eyed the phone, willing it not to ring. He was out of luck.

'Sorry, guv.' It was Jacquie Carpenter's voice in the ether. 'It's Alison McCormick. I think we may have a problem.'

'That's fantastic!' Peter Maxwell stared in wonder at the object in Douglas Russell's hand.

'Not bad, is it?' the geophysicist said. 'You know, I could get to enjoy trowelling.'

The two men looked at the ornate, chiselled key Russell had brought to the main tent. Maxwell's back was in half. Leaving a gabbling Reginald James flying late to his court session, and starting to bleed anew as he ripped the newspaper from his chin, Maxwell had pedalled like a thing possessed back to the Saxon graves. A knot of sightseers had loafed around the main gate where the ominously black-suited George and Julian were watching them intently from behind their impersonal shades. There was no sign of the police presence that Tam Fraser had hoped Henry Hall could spare him. Henry Hall had no one to spare.

In what might have been psychologically a bad move, the dig director had told his people to be extra vigilant, to take nothing for granted. A man or woman with a trowel, he had observed melodramatically, was by definition in a vulnerable position. Everybody had to watch their backs and, failing that, somebody else's. Whatever those madmen of the Sepulchre Society were all about, Fraser told them, they'd killed already and might do so again.

212

'What are we looking at here?' Maxwell asked.

'Church, I'd say. Certainly, this is a common ecclesiastical design. Late tenth, perhaps early eleventh – Aethelred, Cnut, somewhere around there.'

'Wash and go?' Maxwell asked.

'Why not?' Douglas Russell wasn't a man given to smiling, but he did on that occasion.

'Listen ... er ... Douglas.' Maxwell stopped him, a picture in his pink washing up gloves and yellow goggles. What sort of fare does the Quinton serve? Any cop?'

'Wholesome enough,' the geophysicist shrugged.

'Mind if I join you? The little woman's out on a drug bust or something tonight, beating up Rastas and so on. I could use the company.'

'Sure,' Russell said. 'Can you get there all right?'

'Oh, yes,' Maxwell smiled, waving to the spoil heaps where Surrey lay, bright in the rays of the late afternoon sun. 'I have my trusty steed.'

She turned her head as far as she could in the darkness. She was cold and wet from the dripping wall at her back. She felt the ropes digging into her wrists. Why didn't he come? How long had it been? Night? Day? She couldn't tell. All she knew was that she was alone. Hungry and thirsty and tired. And so very, very afraid.

Chapter Twelve

They did a mean shepherd's pie at the Quinton – in the sense that Peter Maxwell reckoned it probably contained half a spud and a knuckle of lamb. It was tasty enough, though, washed down with an unassuming Carlsberg, from the south side of the hop yard. And anyway, Maxwell was not looking to award any Egon Ronay stars; he had a murder or two to solve.

'I've had another one,' Douglas Russell told him in the snug of the hotel's conservatory as the last of the sun dappled on the old barrack's wall beyond it.

'Oh?'

The geophysicist checked the coast was clear before uncrumpling a piece of paper from his pocket.

'When did this arrive?' Maxwell asked.

'This morning. Or rather when I got back earlier this evening. I think you'd gone to freshen up.'

Maxwell had, but it had been a long and sticky day and, still unable to introduce soap to much of his face, he hadn't altogether felt the benefit. 'Envelope?' he asked.

Russell was impressed. The master was going through his paces. He fished that out too.

'Local postmark,' the Head of Sixth Form peered at it. 'First class stamp – a generous malicious letter writer. Tell me, Douglas, why didn't you mention this earlier? Over dinner, for example, the last enervating hour I've spent in your company.'

Russell shrugged. 'I don't know,' he said. 'I just wish this would all go away. It's the ostrich in me, I suppose. If I left the letter in my pocket, it wasn't there.'

'All very David Blaine,' Maxwell nodded, stony-faced.

'I'm a geophysicist, Max. The electrical resistance of soil – that's pretty well all I know. Polarisation, radiation waves, that's where I'm coming from. I'm out my depth with it all.'

'But you're investigating a murder yourself.'

'What?' Russell looked horrified.

'According to the *Advertiser*, whose extraordinary level of expertise I have come to admire and respect,' he waved crossed fingers in front of the geophysicist, 'the first body at the site was a murder victim.'

'Speculation,' Russell said, digging deep for his pipe. 'You don't mind?'

Maxwell shook his head. 'Nothing like a nice bit of shag,' he said and caught the eye of a confused old spinster knitting in the corner. 'Your speculations don't run that way?'

'Oh, I'll grant you the death was violent,' Russell said. 'It was the first body we found. It was lying on its side in a semi-recumbent form, something like twenty metres from the edge of the cemetery.'

Maxwell winced and it wasn't due to the shepherd's pie biting back. The man was investigating a *Saxon* site, for God's sake; why was he talking in metres?

'The skull had been shattered from above and behind. By an axe, I'd say. And the other bodies show no such signs. They're all fully recumbent, east-west, as you'd expect. So yes, it looks suspect. Could be ritual, though.'

'Ritual?' That word was cropping up a lot recently.

'You're familiar with Lindow Man? The Danish bog bodies?'

'*Comme ci, comme ça,*' shrugged Maxwell, 'as I believe they still say down the Skaggerat way.'

'Most of the corpses found in the peat bogs were ritually murdered – Tollund, Grauballe. In the case of Lindow Man, three methods were used to despatch him – garrotting with a ligature, cutting of the carotid artery with a very sharp knife and stoving-in the head.'

'No chances taken there, then? What we in the business call overkill.'

'Indeed,' but Russell couldn't see the humour in it. 'Of course, that was Celtic. Romano British at best. The Saxons, especially in the later period we're dealing with on Staple Hill, no longer sacrificed. They were Christian.'

'And what about David Radley?' Maxwell asked, bringing his man to more pressing matters. 'Was he a Christian?'

'Right now, I'm more concerned with that,' Russell pointed to the note still in Maxwell's hand.

'I work an awful lot better on a large Southern Comfort,' he smiled, as wide-eyed as his bruises

216

would let him.

Russell took the hint and was gone to the bar. He walked with a wariness that was pitiful. Had a pin dropped now, he'd have died of fright. With a deftness born of long years of confiscating smuggled pornography, Maxwell pocketed the envelope and took in the contents of the note itself. The last incriminating document he'd handled – John Fry's note to Annette Choker – had disappeared into the bowels of Leighford nick via the inexperienced hands of Alison McCormick. He wasn't having this one go the same way.

'"You have been warned",' he read to himself, glad his lips were too swollen to be moving. '"Either you stop the dig or you'll be burying more of your own." Short and sweet,' he handed it back to Russell as the man returned bearing drinks.

'Only Scotch, I'm afraid,' he said. 'Is that all right?'

'I'll stretch a point,' Maxwell said, taking the glass. 'Is that one the same as the first?'

'You haven't seen the first?'

'No.' Maxwell shuddered anew as the alcohol hit his lips. 'Professor Fraser simply told me about it.'

'I wish he hadn't done that.' Russell looked away.

'I think if our lives *are* being threatened, we have a right to know about it, Douglas. He spoke to us all at the site, if you remember, warning us to watch our backs.'

The geophysicist sank back into his Lloyd Loom, blowing pipe smoke to the fan curling lazily and ineffectually above them both. 'I

217

suppose you're right. Sorry, I'm not thinking particularly clearly at the moment. Yes, in answer to your question. The wording isn't exactly the same, but it's got the same letter head.'

'The Sepulchre Society,' Maxwell ran the cheap crystal between his hands. He could get used to Scotch. 'It has a ring to it. Who knows you're staying here, Douglas? At the Quinton, I mean?'

'Um ... everyone at the dig. The University, of course. My mother.'

'You're not married, Douglas?'

'No,' the geophysicist smiled, as if at some long-forgotten joke. 'No, Miss Right never came along.'

'Ah,' Maxwell laughed. 'You're still a young god, for Christ's sake.'

There was a kerfuffle in the lobby beyond the open conservatory doors and a rattled-looking Tam Fraser stood there.

'Thank God you're both all right,' he said. His hair was standing on end and his eyes flashed wildly around the conservatory. The old girl with the knitting needles sat transfixed at the apparition. He looked like he'd just spent three minutes plugged into Old Sparky.

'What's the matter, Professor?' Maxwell asked.

'*This* is the matter,' and he slammed a skull down on the coffee table. 'I've called the police.'

The old girl with the knitting needles screamed. 'For God's sake, madam,' Fraser yelled at her. 'It's how we'll all end up one day. Dinna distress yourself.' Maxwell noticed how much more ethnic the man became when he was scared.

'What's this?' Maxwell was glad it was Russell

218

who asked the obvious. Like you do when part of a person almost lands in your lap.

Fraser leaned to him. 'It's a fucking skull, man,' he hissed. 'Somebody's head. Oh, I forgot! You're a geophysicist!'

Where was it?' Maxwell wanted to know, looking at the thing from various angles.

'On my bed. The police are on the way.'

'Alas, poor Yorick... Douglas, get the professor a drink, will you?' Maxwell asked. 'And perhaps a Babycham for the old girl with the knitting needles. Here...' and he reached into his pocket.

'No, it's fine,' the geophysicist said and hovered briefly at Fraser's elbow, before scuttling back to the bar, glad to be away from the man for a while.

'What happened?' Maxwell asked.

Fraser was still looking transfixed at the macabre object on the table, while one of the hotel staff was comforting the old girl with the knitting needles.

'Perhaps you'd better cover that up,' Maxwell suggested.

The professor whipped off his jacket and draped it over the grey cranium. 'Good idea.' He was calmer now and he sat down. 'Sorry, Maxwell. I don't mind telling you, this business has got me jumping at shadows.'

'From the top, then,' Maxwell said softly.

'From the top,' Jacquie sprawled in Maxwell's bed, wrapped in Maxwell's arms. 'Fraser had been working late at the Museum – we've yet to confirm that, of course – and got back to the Quinton about half-eight. He checked his mail.

Nothing. Went straight up to his room.'

'That's on the second floor.' Maxwell was filling in what the professor had told him.

'And the door was slightly ajar.'

'Forced entry.'

'Jemmy,' Jacquie nodded, nuzzling her hair softly against her man's chest and adding her professional precision. 'Clumsy, too. Amateur job.'

'He went in...'

'He went in and found the skull on the bed, the lower jaw locked open with a twig.'

'As though the skull was laughing at him,' Maxwell noted.

'Or screaming.' Jacquie's imagination was running in a different direction.

'What did he do?'

'Seems to have panicked. Came hurtling through the hotel like a banshee, waving the skull around.'

'How is the old girl with the knitting needles?'

'Still in casualty last I heard. Heavy sedation.'

Maxwell nodded. He'd never had much faith in the curative properties of Babycham. 'I'd never have pegged Fraser for a panicker,' he said, risking pain by kissing the girl's sweet-smelling hair.

'You can never tell,' she smiled up at him in the half light, 'what people will do until they're faced with something like this. The call to the station said somebody had been decapitated. You were lucky I was on my own, or you'd have had the heavy mob, SOCO, Jim Astley, the works. You could have knocked me over with a feather when I saw you sitting there.'

'Ah,' he smiled. 'The bacon sandwich at a

Jewish wedding.'

'Asking for a lift was a bit cheeky,' she tapped his chest. 'Policewoman on duty and all that.'

'Well, I did toy with taking you roughly on the conservatory floor then and there,' he confessed. 'But no, no. Public schoolboy and all that. I waited.'

'Not for long though.' She tweaked his nipple between her forefinger and thumb.

'Ow. Shite. You always told me you enjoyed being groped in hotel lobbies. Tell me about the skull. You've seen more of them than I have.'

'Well, it's a real one,' she started. 'There's so much around these days for Occult weirdoes and snuff movie oddballs.'

'Must be a woman; the mouth's open.' It was pure Harry Secombe as Neddy Seagoon.

She craned her neck to look at him, never ceasing to be amazed at the evidence she was collecting to have him put away.

'The Goons, dear girl,' he explained. 'A Fifties comedy show of monumental social importance.'

'Before my time,' she purred smugly.

'And mine,' he purred back.

'Liar!' she laughed. 'The skull wasn't from the site. Or so Fraser said. It's not Saxon, apparently; although, seen one skull, you've seen 'em all, I should think.'

'You'll be checking that?'

'Oh, yes,' she yawned. 'Come sun-up.'

'Right, then,' Maxwell nudged her. 'Your best case scenario.' He was beginning to sound like Henry Hall.

'Person or persons unknown brings the skull to

the hotel.'

'Chummy,' Maxwell smiled as well as he could. 'Let's call him "Chummy".'

'All right,' she sighed. 'Chummy.' Having reminded Maxwell that he was a child of the Fifties, she now had to suffer that decade's terminology. 'Chummy comes into the hotel.'

'Is he a guest?'

'Could be.'

'Who's on the desk?' Maxwell was closing his eyes, picturing the scene.

'Two spotty youths. Terminal halitosis meets eternal sniff.'

'Castor and Pollux,' Maxwell said. 'Let's call them "Castor" and "Pollux".'

Her eyes rolled heavenward. 'Yes,' she said. 'Those were their names, spookily enough. Not ex-yours, are they?'

'Mercifully, no,' he chuckled. 'It's quite a treat to find an institution in this town that's not run by old Leighford Hyenas.' It was. Seaside havens like Leighford relied on the cheap labour of kids. And Peter Maxwell had been around for so long that generations of waiters, chambermaids, Adventure Playground operators and Dotto train drivers had passed through his hands. 'Say on, Woman Policeman. You have me in thrall.'

'The youths ... Castor and Pollux ... keep a note of new customers, obviously, because they sign in. Other than that, security is, to say the least, lax.'

'No CCTV of course.'

'Of course,' Jacquie confirmed. 'This is the Quinton. They only installed a lift three years ago.'

'I remember,' said Maxwell. 'It instantly became one of Leighford's main attractions. Is Chummy a handyman?'

'Doubtful.' Jacquie shook her head. 'The only handyman who turned up was the bloke to measure for the new lobby carpet. Castor knew him. Been before.'

'You'll check the company, of course.'

'Look,' she finally snapped. 'It's like being in bed with a DCI.'

'So,' he flung her from him by a few inches. 'You've been to bed with the DCI.'

'No,' she scowled. 'And he's *not* a public schoolboy. Anyway, I distinctly said *a* DCI, cloth-ears.'

'Oh,' sobbed Maxwell, '"teach not thy lip such scorn, lady".' It was an immaculate Olivier as Richard III.

'I'll be onto Caring Carpets as soon as I've checked with the Museum,' she said. 'Bloody good Ian McKellen, by the way.'

'Bitch!' he hissed, wrapping her auburn hair round her neck and pretending to pull tightly. 'Right, so we're back to Chummy. Whether he's a carpet bagger or a grock, he's a member of the Sepulchre Society.'

'Seems that way,' Jacquie said.

'But we've got no description?'

'None. A jemmy or whatever he used on Fraser's door isn't difficult to conceal.'

'As in "is that a jemmy in your trouser pocket or are you pleased to see me?"'

'Quite. It's a conventional burglar's tool. Designed to be unobtrusive.'

'All right.' Maxwell was ignoring her disinterested slur and thinking aloud. 'So Chummy sends a second threatening letter to Douglas Russell and the next day leaves a calling card of an altogether more sinister kind for Tam Fraser. The net's widening.'

'Are we actually talking about the same guy?' Jacquie asked. 'I mean, why post a threat one day, and deliver a threat personally the next, to the same address?'

'Don't know,' Maxwell shrugged. 'But it sounds like overkill.' That word again. 'Before you came to Leighford we had a lot of brouhaha about the flyover. A petition against it was handed in to the Town Hall. Contained over 5000 names. Except that all of them were written by a Magnus Potter using both hands, often simultaneously and various colours and types of ink. He was a one-man pressure group.'

'So they built the flyover anyway?'

'Sure,' Maxwell nodded. 'Rumour had it that Magnus Potter is part of the cement footings on the west side. It's how he'd have wanted to go. As it happened, Potter was not a psychopath – just a guy with a mission.'

'This Sepulchre Society, Max...' Jacquie was frowning, 'Are they for real?'

'Three dead bodies, two threatening letters and a skull, dear heart? No, they're a figment of somebody's imagination. Just a nebulous concept.'

Jacquie Carpenter left the love of her life sleeping the next morning. He still didn't look well in the half-light of his bedroom, the sun shaft shining in through the window of 38 Columbine. She gingerly lifted her bra and knickers from the chair before taking the rest of her clothes and tip-toeing down the stairs.

The great Behemoth that was Metternich sat in the archway to the kitchen, crouched on his haunches, tail thrashing slowly. Mother of God, what was this? In place of a crusty old fart waddling about in dressing gown and slippers, a slip of a thing with strange wobbly bits at the front ran past him, making for the lower stairs, climbing into her clothes as she ran.

'I'm late, Count,' she told him. 'Your Master will be up later. He'll sort you out.' She was, no doubt, talking breakfast.

Metternich rose to his full one foot two and turned tail. His Master had sorted him out years ago, with a quick and terrifying trip to that place we mustn't mention, the one with the men in white coats and rows of cages; the hell where youth and testicles go. Thanks, but no thanks. He'd rip seven kinds of shit out of a rodent instead. The brown, crusty stuff in the packet he'd have for lunch.

'No, Jacquie,' Sergeant Wilson was saying. 'Jack Shit, I'm afraid.'

'Thanks, Tom.' She snapped her mobile shut, swinging the Ka left along the sea front as a seaside town came to life. The flags of the new season fluttered in the breeze stirring from the west and the Biffa lorry trundled its way along Wendover Street, pausing to collect the black bags as it went, its operatives, with their sign

225

proclaiming they were working in its rear, roaring the odds to each other with all the panache of people who think they're free and powerful, not slaves of a post-modernist society. Someone was watering the pretty hanging baskets outside the Royal and awnings were coming down against another scorching day, to cloak their shopfronts mercifully with the cool of shade.

She jammed on her anchors outside the Piece of Cod Fish 'n' Chip Bar. 'Jerry!'

The town's most hated man was only ever spoken to by police officers and people about to hit him. But somebody had to be a traffic warden.

'What-ho, Jacquie!' he waved back, more Fifties than Peter Maxwell. He was a little man, who only sported a moustache on his first day in the job because somebody said he looked like Hitler.

'Have you seen Alison McCormick this morning?'

'No, I haven't.' Jerry was a martyr to ill-fitting dentures, his own teeth having disappeared under a barrage of motorists' right crosses and left hooks over the years.

'Yesterday?'

'No.' The warden frowned. 'No, come to think of it, I haven't. Off sick, is she? Rest day? Something?'

'Yes, that'll be it,' she said and drove off.

But Alison McCormick wasn't off sick. And it wasn't a rest day. It was something all right, but what? She should have been prowling this area of the town that Jacquie was driving through now. And yesterday afternoon, she should have been at the nick organizing the search for Annette Choker. But she hadn't been there either. Jacquie hadn't mentioned it to Peter Maxwell because other events had taken a certain priority. But the cold light of dawn brought it all back. Alison McCormick had just vanished.

One more time. Just in case. Jacquie parked the Ka, flicking her police sign in the window. Just let Jerry slip a ticket on that and it was no more Miss Nice Policewoman. You could add her name to the list of people who wouldn't have pissed on him had he been set alight. Alison McCormick lived on the second floor. And Jacquie Carpenter was far too young to remember the Cliff Richard song – Alison doesn't live here any more.

Kids go missing. They fight with Mum or Dad or both. They row with boyfriend/girlfriend. They get in over their heads with drugs or shoplifting. One or two of them, both sexes, go on the game. They vanish. Then, they're found, skulking in a friend's house, trying to rough it in the wild. Now and again, they're found dead. One too many needles; from mainline to flatline. Hitching a ride with the wrong driver whose wife didn't understand him and who just wanted some company.

Adults go missing. They row with the wife, husband, boyfriend, girlfriend. They get in over their heads with drugs or embezzlement. One or two of them are already on the game, both sexes. They vanish, then they're found, in Rio or Warsaw or Nairobi, on the run, out of luck. Now and again, they're found dead, killed for their trainers, their mobile phones. Hitching a ride with the wrong driver...

Police personnel do not go missing. Not unless...

Jacquie was still rationalizing that fact as she used her pass key to get into Alison's flat. Alison, the policewoman who had gone missing. She'd been here yesterday, had the detective sergeant. And now she was back again, just in case she'd missed something, returning to what she hoped this wasn't – the scene of crime. She'd caught sight of herself in Alison's hall mirror. Christ, what a mess. Yesterday's clothes, her hair a tawny tangle piled high on her head. She should have gone home first, for a shower and a change. She could have showered at Maxwell's, but she'd been running late. And anyway, she found herself smiling, she still smelt of him, his warmth, his love, so that was okay. Slight bulge round the middle? Nah. Trick of the light.

She stood in Alison's lounge. What had she missed? A note on the coffee table? "Just popped out." "Help – abducted by fairies." If only it were that simple. There was nothing *Marie Celeste* about this place. No half-eaten meal, no half-drunk cups of coffee, no telly still playing in the corner. Everything was neat. Disgustingly so. Jacquie cringed a little remembering her own place and how it would look this morning. Okay, so she'd meant to do the washing up last night, but then she'd got the station call about the hooha at the Quinton and she'd gone running. And there was Mad Max, looking at her with those sad, purple-rimmed eyes and how could she go home after that? But that was real life – the peck of dirt her granddad had always told her, a little bizarrely and for what reason she could never understand, you had to eat. *This* was scrubbed, sanitized as though the House Doctor had whirled through the place with a mop, a bucket and a tin of mauve emulsion.

She checked the kitchen. Spotless. Dishrack empty. Cupboards full. Cups hanging on hooks. A toaster and no crumbs. Weird. She turned right up the little stairway that led to Alison's bedroom. Sheets turned down like an army exercise. Books neatly stacked on a bedside shelf, Danielle Steele. Robert Ludlum. The usual suspects. The wardrobe contained the woman's police uniform, hanging immaculately on a hanger. How many civilian clothes had gone, Jacquie didn't know. Some, certainly. Shoes, probably. Maybe jeans, a couple of blouses. A shirt or two. Undies were unknowable. Some women had hundreds; others made do on far less. Had Alison McCormick just taken some with her. Or was some pervert adding to his collection?

The detective wandered back into the lounge. A beaming Alison looked at her from a gilt frame, flanked by loving parents, Mrs McCormick the pod from which the pea had sprung. Jacquie hadn't contacted them yet. She'd only been gone ... what was it? Twenty-six hours now. But she couldn't put it off much longer. Perhaps they knew. Or knew a man who did.

'What did she say, Dave?' Jacquie was going over her conversation of the previous day with DC Garstang, in her mind.

'She had to follow up some leads,' he'd told her.

'Didn't specify. I didn't ask.'

Jacquie couldn't blame him. How many cases had they both seen like this? When the last words one person says to another are crucial. Yet they seem so ordinary. Seem so ordinary because you don't know they *are* the last words and by the time you do, it's too late.

She turned back into the hall. And that's when she saw it, sticking out from under the airing cupboard door. The something she'd missed yesterday. She clicked the door open. Snugglers.

A stiffish breeze had come from nowhere, blowing Douglas Russell's papers all over the tent. Peter Maxwell had graduated by that Wednesday to trowelling. He was grateful that the heavy stage of the dig was already over, with the serious tools slicing the clay and carting it away, to form the tell-tale spoil heaps that littered Staple Hill like the work of giant moles. The only down side was that he couldn't do his relief of mattocking joke – perhaps it was just as well.

Robin Edwards, with his 2:1 from Lancaster University, knelt beside the Great Man, his face dark under the broad-brimmed hat. It made a change – most people knelt in front of Peter Maxwell.

'What've we got here then, Robin?' the Head of Sixth Form asked.

Both of them were crouched, looking at the reddish-brown slabs emerging from the centuries of soil that had covered them until now. Edwards' trowel scraped them clean.

'Difficult to say,' the archaeologist said, 'but it

could be the curve of an apse. I want to get those trees cleared and start work over there.' He was pointing his trowel at the tangle of ash trees. 'If I'm right, that's where the nave will be.'

'No chance, I'm afraid,' Maxwell said.

'Oh,' Edwards bridled. 'Expert in late Saxon ecclesiastical architecture, are you?'

'I know my transept from my triforium,' Maxwell was proud to admit, 'but that's not the point. The ash grove is a murder site. You won't be able to dig there until Detective Chief Inspector Hall says you can.'

'Look ... er ... Mr Maxwell,' the archaeologist leaned back on his heels, his climbing boots a dull yellow with the Leighford clay. 'You're not a sort of spy, are you? Undercover cop? Only, I think that's called entrapment.'

'Heaven forfend,' Maxwell leaned back too, but thought better of it as a vicious cramp in his buttocks forced him forward on all fours again. 'But I do have a nose for murder.' He thought of tapping it, but it was too soon. In the pain stakes, he just wasn't ready. 'What do *you* think's going on, Robin?'

The man became conspiratorial, glancing around him as he spoke. 'Russell,' he whispered.

'Sorry?'

'Douglas Russell.' It was his turn to tap his nose. 'Not all he seems.'

'What does he seem?' Maxwell could play the ingenue to perfection.

'Gauche geophysicist with a rather grating Brummy accent. I live for my work type. Great unwashed. I mean,' he pointed to his sodden

231

shirt, 'we all get a bit pongy in this line, but have you stood downwind of him lately? He always wears the same ghastly jumper. Reminds me of my bloody Art teacher at school.'

'All right,' Maxwell nodded, tapping listlessly at a rocky outcrop. 'So that's what he seems. What is he?'

Edwards leaned forward again, so that his head was near Maxwell's. 'This Sepulchre Society nonsense. The stuff Fraser told us about.'

'What about it?'

'How do you know it exists?'

'Er ... is this a philosophical one? Like "how do you know you're really there?" Sound of trees falling in forests. Black polar bears. That sort of thing?'

'No,' Edwards scowled. 'I mean, we only have Russell's word. That the letter is genuine, I mean. I asked him about it yesterday. He was vague; in fact, he was downright evasive. Fraser made his usual over-the-top announcement – never one not to make a drama out of a crisis – but it was Russell who got the letter.'

'And Fraser who got the head.'

'What?' Edwards stopped in mid-trowel.

'A skull – human, of course, to maximise impact. Somebody left it on his bed yesterday.'

'Jesus!'

'I suppose the half horse in *The Godfather* was more dramatic, but it does rather leave your theory...'

'All right,' the archaeologist shrugged. 'So Fraser's a target too. But I'm still betting on Russell.'

'Why?'

'He hated Radley.'

'Did he now?' Maxwell asked. 'Any particular reason?'

'You'll have to ask him,' the lad said. 'Pass me that brush, will you? Got some debris here.'

Maxwell had been reading nuances all his life. The lad's tone had changed, the timbre in his voice. The two of them were not alone. He glanced up to see the elegant brogues of Professor Tam Fraser.

'Any joy, Maxwell?' he asked, his fluster of the previous night having left him.

The Head of Sixth Form-turned-rookie-archaeologist knelt up in the gravel pit. 'Not yet,' he smiled at the wild-haired man silhouetted against the sun. 'But I'm getting there.'

Chapter Thirteen

Henry Hall had been in his office before day or battle broke. He'd discarded his jacket, rolled up his sleeves and slogged through old cases. He'd had these brought up from Records in the bowels of the earth, where spiders crept silently over the paper remains of people's lives. On the desk in front of him sat all the work Martin Toogood had undertaken in his eighteen months with the West Sussex CID.

A Detective Chief Inspector would normally leave minutiae like this to his underlings. But this was different. This was DS Toogood, one of Hall's own. This one was personal. All day, he'd been shifting papers, checking reports, cross-referencing cases. He'd interviewed anybody who had worked with the dead man, looking for a pattern. Something. Anything. Anybody bear Toogood a grudge? No one special, it seemed. Any copper was a target for people he'd put away; it went with the territory. But no one stood out. There'd been no threats, explicit or implicit. No one had dramatically stood up in the dock screaming 'I'll get you, copper!' What about ex-colleagues? Colleagues, even? Hall was on difficult ground here and he knew it. One by one they trooped before him, the men and women who knew him best, the ones who'd watched with him in the waking hours, on surveillance teams, the house-to-house enquiries. People who had stood by his elbow as he uncovered the bodies of dead children and later as he told the parents of those children what had happened to them. Nobody in that company bore him a grudge. Nobody had a bad word to say. Would no one speak ill of the dead?

'What about girlfriends?' Hall was doing the part of the job he hated most. In front of him, by the evening, as the shadows lengthened and one by one, the lights came on along the flyover, sat Bob and Jane Toogood, close together, their fingers clasped, their faces blank, trying to come to terms with why their only son wasn't here any more.

'No one serious,' his father said. 'Not for some time.'

'He *was* engaged,' his mother said. 'She was a lovely girl, Angie. But she broke it off.'

'*She* broke it off?' Hall checked, still looking for a motive.

'That's what he told us,' Bob shrugged. 'It was a few years ago now.'

'He was still at university.' Jane told Hall. 'At Oxford. She was studying Medieval English too. I never quite found out why it didn't work between them. We liked her, didn't we, Bob?'

The father nodded. Then he leaned forward to stare into the reflecting lenses of Hall's glasses. 'You will find some reason, won't you, Chief Inspector?' he asked, squeezing his wife's hand, harder. 'We're not vindictive people. Honest, we aren't. We don't need a person necessarily. Just a reason. There has to be a reason.'

'Still here, guv?' Jacquie Carpenter dumped her handbag onto a spare chair.

Henry Hall had long ago abandoned the stifling confines of his office. He'd interviewed Toogood's parents, given them what tiny crumbs of comfort he could and he had seen them out, watched them drive off along the road their boy had taken days before on his last journey. No, he couldn't show them a killer. No, he couldn't offer them a reason. And no, he couldn't let them have their son's body for burial. Not just yet. All he could give them was his condolences and his No-stone-unturned speech. And it didn't matter a damn to them that, this time, he meant it. For the last two hours, he'd been glued to a video screen, CCTV footage of the nick car park on the last day of Martin Toogood's life. No, that wasn't quite true; for the last hour he'd been staring at a wall.

'Look at this, Jacquie.' He rewound with the remote, as he'd done dozens of times already. 'Camera Three, angled to the north-east corner of this building. Got your bearings?'

'Yes.' She grabbed a bottle of water and found a chair next to her boss.

'There's Martin's car. The Mondeo. Next to the van.'

'Okay.'

'Right. Here he comes now. Look at the time. Eleven forty-nine.'

She watched the fuzzy figure going through its paces on the screen.

'He gets into his car.' He did. 'Drives away.'

'Okay,'

'Now,' he rewound again. 'Look at this.' The screen exploded with a flurry of time-lapse activity, vehicles darting in and out, figures bustling across the concourse. 'There. It's nine thirteen.' He froze the frame. 'What's that?'

Henry Hall was pointing to a shadowy figure moving furtively east to west across the tarmac, following the line of trees that ringed the nick.

'Looks like ... a bloke in ... what? Drizabone – one of those Aussie stockman things? Big hat?'

'Drizabone and big hat,' Hall nodded. 'That's what I see too. What I can't fathom is why no-body's seen him before. The footage *was* checked, presumably?'

'Don't know, guv,' Jacquie said. Of all the times when Hall's team was falling down on the job, it

236

had to be now, when they were all looking for the killer of one of their own.

'He's going to the van,' Hall was forwarding the picture, still by still. 'He's about to get in, into the driver's seat. Then ... there,' he froze the moment in time. 'He disappears. Where's he gone?'

Jacquie squinted. In the shadows of the twilight trees as he was, the night visitor had vanished.

'He's gone,' was all she could say.

'Not exactly,' Hall corrected her. 'He's under Martin's car with a jewel saw in his hand, working on his brake cables.'

Jacquie got nearer. 'Do we see him leave?'

'We do not. At least, not by the front or side entrances.' He switched the remote to freeze frame. 'I've checked this footage and Camera Two's.'

'Side door?'

'Right. Nothing. The world and his wife were calling in that day, but there's nobody, at the relevant time or not, that remotely resembles our man in the duster coat.'

'Which means...'

Hall was nodding. 'Which means he actually went back into the building.'

'Through the bloody nick.' Jacquie was incredulous.

'And out of the back door.'

'Camera One ... oh, shit.'

'Precisely.' Hall was ahead of her. 'The one we wipe daily because we all regard the back door as home territory. No need to monitor that one too closely. Only we use it. Well, that stops, as of now. I want a tape there tomorrow morning, first thing. Tom Wilson still around?'

She checked her watch, 'Went off half an hour ago.'

'I want him here. Eight sharp. Unless I miss my guess, Martin Toogood's murderer walked right past our Sergeant Wilson without so much, no doubt, as a "by your leave". I want to know why.' Hall was rewinding and stopping time to focus on the killer's shadowy form. 'What is he? Height-wise, I mean?'

'He's always stooped over, guv.' Jacquie's eyes were better than Hall's. 'Could be anything from five six to well over six feet.'

'Could be the invisible man,' nodded the DCI. Time to call it a day.

It rained that night, giant drops bouncing like tears off Peter Maxwell's rooflight. He sat hunched over the fallen body of Private Ryan of the Eighth Hussars, his face lit eerily by his modelling lamp, his cheeks still purple and puffy, his nose with its distinctive crimson line.

'You know, I keep thinking about that cryptic message of Martin Toogood's, Count, the one he left on his computer screen. "The affairs of men." Mean anything to you?'

Metternich had been caught in the downpour. You'd think, wouldn't you, with all his cunning and experience, he'd have sensed it, read the twitching in his whiskers aright and got the hell in through the cat flap before the heavens opened? But no, he'd waited, full of bravado, as the clouds rolled and the stair-rods descended. Why did he have to show off to all the females?

After all, whether they were on heat or not was of little consequence to him; he could not deliver. So, here he was, on Maxwell's pouffe, in Maxwell's attic, steaming quietly as he dried. "Affairs of men"? What had he to do with any of those?

'Who had Toogood interviewed by the time he died?' Maxwell was gluing Ryan's little plastic pouch into the small of Ryan's little plastic back. 'He'd talked to all the archaeologists – that's Douglas Russell, Derek Latymer, Robin Edwards, Helen Reader. He'd been to interview Tam Fraser, Samantha Welland, Susan Radley. So what do we know about the marital status of any of them? Good question, Count. Eight out of ten. Level Six.' He looked up at the feline. 'Your CAT score.'

Metternich wasn't laughing.

'Well, the first question is, did Toogood literally mean affairs and did he literally mean men?'

Metternich yawned.

'No, no,' Maxwell wagged his paintbrush at him. 'Stick with the plot. I shall be asking questions later. Let's say "yes" to both questions. Douglas Russell – is he married? No. "Miss Right," and I quote rather cornily, "hasn't come along." Derek Latymer. Don't know. Robin Edwards...Yes, all right.' He threw the paintbrush down. 'I don't know. In fact, the only relationship we know about, thanks to darling Jacquie, is Sam Welland. She was not as other archaeologists, Count. There,' he sat back, tilting the gold-laced pill-box forward over his eyes. 'Now I've shocked you. Or at least, she shocked Helen Reader. Shocked her enough to make her take a rope to

239

her, I wonder? Lived with a woman named, unbelievably, Hazel Twigg… Count!' Maxwell hurled the cap into the air and caught it expertly on the way down, 'Your master is some kind of idiot.'

So, what's new? Metternich was reaming his bum.

'No Maxwell this morning?' Tam Fraser was doing the rounds of the dig as usual, hair flashing silver in the sun.

'Haven't seen him, Professor,' Helen Reader said, the glow already trickling into her eyes. 'God, that rain last night barely touched the sides. It's like soup this morning.' It was. Humidity had reached an all time high at Leighford and while holiday-makers lolled on the beach a mile away, on the scraped and scarred hillside of the dig, the work was unbearable.

'You should try this in Egypt!' Fraser laughed and waved his wide awake hat in an ingratiating gesture.

'He's a patronising old bastard,' Derek Latymer muttered when the old bastard was well out of earshot. 'Somebody's going to put one on him one of these days.'

'Well, I'm not sure it's a breakthrough, Chief Inspector.' Lily Boydell always looked swamped in her white coat and that Thursday morning was no exception. The pair were standing in the police lab in Littlehampton, a new, red-brick monstrosity of the kind that made the Prince of Wales despair of modern architecture. The ghastly Venetian blinds, in regulation pale green, were closed against the fierce heat of the day.

'You're looking at a man clutching at straws, Ms Boydell,' Hall told her. And she was. Whenever a crime was getting the better of him, Henry Hall was banished by his long-suffering wife to the spare room. Here, he could pace and prowl about all night long if he liked, instead of complaining that she kept him awake with her snoring. And that's where he'd been since he'd said his farewells to Jacquie Carpenter in the early hours. He looked like shit, but Lily Boydell was too polite to say so. She was one of those unfortunate people with a cheerful, even bubbly personality buried by a face that looked like a smacked arse. 'About now, I'd settle for anything.'

'All right,' she said. 'Have a look.'

Henry fiddled with the microscope's focus. He wasn't exactly *au fait* with these, and Lily Boydell had eyes so close together they practically overlapped.

'Fibres?' He looked up at her hopefully, but wouldn't have been surprised to be told they were spirochetes.

'Rayon,' she said. 'Mid-tan, dull brown colour. Waxed.'

'Where did you find these?'

'On Dr Radley's left sleeve. And they took some finding, I can tell you.'

'What's your diagnosis?'

The pair stood facing each other now on either side of the lab stools, she in her boffin's coat, he in his grey two-piece; both of them, in their different ways, trying to catch a killer.

'Well,' she screwed her face up more than

241

Mother Nature had, 'I don't like sticking my neck out. But,' she winked at him, 'just for you ... My guess is that our perpetrator killed Radley indoors. There's no sign of soil, clay or any other Staple Hill debris on his shoes. He wrapped him a black plastic bag or bags, some sort of sheeting anyway and bundled him into a vehicle. I'm guessing the last bit. How much did Radley weigh?'

'Er ... Jim Astley says thirteen stone.'

'Right. You don't lug that sort of dead weight around the countryside for laughs, do you? But while he was bagging him up, he brushed Radley's sleeve against his coat.'

'A Drizabone,' Hall nodded.

'Could be,' Lily agreed. 'But I can't guarantee it.'

'What about the change of clothes?'

'Yes, that's odd, isn't it? Jim Astley's quite right on this one, though it sticks in my craw to say so. Unless David Radley was the sloppiest dresser in the world ... or marginally, in a tearing hurry, someone dressed the body.'

'Which could mean he was naked beforehand.' Hall was thinking aloud. 'Is this a sex thing, then?'

Lily Boydell looked at him wide-eyed. She didn't get many offers. 'If it was,' she switched off the microscope, 'why re-clothe him?'

'To put us off the scent,' Hall told her. 'If we'd found Radley's body naked, that would automatically take the investigation in a certain direction, wouldn't it? As it is, well, we're looking for other motives.'

The boffin flicked through the rather dog-eared sheaf of paper on the counter-top. 'There's nothing in Jim's report about sexual activity,' she said. 'There again,' she pulled off her owl-like glasses, 'there's Edgar Allan Poe.'

'Who?'

'The American Gothic horror writer. He was found dead in a Baltimore street in October 1849, if memory serves, wearing somebody else's clothes.'

'Was he now?'

'He was. And there's something else. Did you notice?'

Hall was getting old; what was she talking about now?

'All the clothes were brand new.'

'Have another look in that magic ball of yours,' Hall waved to the microscope. 'You don't see a tall, dark man in a duster coat, do you? And he doesn't happen to have an address?'

Small knots of students wandered the campus that sunny morning. Most of them had gone down, or up, or sideways, whichever direction students went these days. Only a few remained, the overseas people whose visa situation was far from clear and those neurotics taking their Masters and trying to look cheerful through it all.

The man bestriding their narrow world like a colossus looked rather old to be a student. He *could* have been a lecturer, but there was something of a *presence* about him which no lecturer had possessed since they'd allowed women into the universities. Then there was the spread nose with the purple centre and the swollen lips. Not yer everyday Don, with or without a luminous nose.

'Could you tell me where I might find Ms Hazel Twigg, please?' he asked at Admissions.

'I am Hazel Twigg.' A stumpy, unprepossessing woman with glasses and a thatch of silver-grey hair ending in a severe fringe looked up from her desk.

'Ms Twigg,' he raised his unseasonal hat. 'Good morning. I'm Peter Maxwell. Is there somewhere we could talk?'

'You say you're a private investigator?' She stirred her coffee with a certain world-weariness.

'Of sorts,' he nodded. He'd taken her out of her office with its rows of box-files and its computer banks and she'd taken him to the staff canteen, a relatively palatial pad by Leighford High standards, in that it had curtains and glass at the windows and they sat facing each other across an upright, formica-topped table.

'For whom are you working?' she asked. He liked her sense of syntax, suddenly bereaved though she had been.

'Justice,' he said, a little portentously. 'I've already expressed my sincere condolences about Ms Welland. You were close?'

Hazel looked her man in the eye. 'Did you know her?'

'No,' he said. 'Our paths never crossed. I joined the dig at Leighford after she ... died.'

'If this is some sort of insurance scam...'

'As I said, Ms Twigg, I am looking into this sad

business for my own, impartial reasons.'

'And they are?'

'All right,' he sighed. 'A man I rather liked – David Radley – invited me and some of my students to his dig site. Then somebody killed him. There's something red-raggish to a bull about that – well, there is to me, anyway. I don't get maudlin – I get even.'

'You believe that David and Sam died by the same hand?' she asked.

'Don't you?'

'Mr Maxwell,' her eyes dipped to the still-swirling coffee in front of her. 'I'm not sure what I believe any more.'

'You loved Sam?' he asked.

She still didn't look up. Just nodded.

'And she didn't take her own life?'

'No.' The voice was firm, the eyes steady as they came up to meet his. 'No, of that I am sure.'

'Let's draw some threads together, then. Two colleagues, both dead within a week of each other. What's the connection?'

Silence.

'Are you all right, Ms Twigg?' Maxwell asked her. 'To talk about this, I mean.'

'Oh, yes.' She almost willed herself to do it. 'They'd known each other for about three years.'

'As colleagues?'

'Yes, of course,' she frowned. 'What do you mean?'

'Tell me, Ms Twigg, was Dr Radley happily married?'

The silence once again, but frostier this time. 'I believe he was,' she said. 'You must realize, Mr

245

Maxwell, that Dr Radley was Professor of Archaeology I am merely an administrative assistant. We never actually discussed personal relationships.'

'No, of course not. Did Sam ... I mean, was Sam ever...?'

'Was she bi and did she ever have a fling with David Radley?' Say what you like about Hazel Twigg, she knew how to cut to the chase.

'Something like that,' he nodded.

'No,' her reply was louder than she'd meant it to be and a professor of Comparative Religions in the corner woke up from his end of semester doze as a result. 'No, no,' she said more softly. 'Nothing like that.' She found herself smiling. 'She liked to flirt with men, to tease them. For instance, she told me the detective who came to see her was rather dishy.'

'The detective? You mean, DS Toogood?'

'Was that his name? I don't know. He came to see her at the Club. The Campdens.'

'Yes.' Maxwell nodded. 'That was his name. Did Sam tell you anything else about him? Toogood, I mean?'

The woman sighed. 'I really can't remember,' she said. 'He was asking her about David, of course, and Tam Fraser, I believe. I got the impression he was grilling everybody in the Department. I suppose he'll get around to me eventually.'

'No, Ms Twigg,' Maxwell shook his head. 'I doubt he will. What about ... and please forgive me for asking this, but ... other women?' Maxwell was chancing his arm.

Hazel took a deep breath. 'No,' she said. 'Definitely not.'

They looked at each other for a moment.

'Mr Maxwell,' she broke the silence first. 'I loved Sam Welland. And she loved me. Fifty years ago, our relationship would have caused raised eyebrows, revulsion even. It may even have been a motive for murder. But today? Today people can't even be bothered with the old jokes. You're looking in the wrong direction.'

'About now, Ms Twigg,' the amateur detective said, 'I have no idea in which direction I'm looking. What do you know about the Sepulchre Society of Sussex?'

'The what?' she frowned.

'Nothing,' he shrugged. 'Forget I mentioned it.'

She already had.

There had to be a way out. And she'd lost track of the hours in which she'd been thinking of it. Her eyes had long ago become accustomed to the dark. When she was little, her mum had taken her to the old Morwellham copper mine in Devon and she had never known blackness like it. They took you deep underground in a little train and the man turned off the lights. It was impenetrable, mysterious. She had clung to her mum in the infinite silence of that blackness. Now, she had nobody to cling to.

She could feel the chain that chafed her ankles, knew the extent of the links that held her. She'd counted the links and she'd counted the paces she could move from the wall – twenty-three; just enough to reach the hole in the floor she was using as a loo. Was it night? Was it day? She still didn't know. Her watch had gone, so had her shoes.

She'd tried it before, of course. And it hadn't worked. But it was all she had and she had no choice but to try it again. She swung the chains that held her wrist against the near wall, screaming at the same time with all that remained of her strength. Nothing. Nothing but the dying echo of her own voice.

Where was she? Where had she been buried that no one could hear her?

Peter Maxwell was usually a shower man. But that Thursday night, he lay soaking in his bath until his finger-ends wrinkled. He didn't normally do his best thinking while carrying out his ablutions. His shower control was a bitch and he either came out frozen or scalded from the experience and, either way, he had not thought beautiful thoughts. Metternich never ventured into Maxwell's bathroom. The steam and the sickly-sweet aromas of oils and lotions played merry hell with his olfactories. And anyway, he secretly suspected Maxwell of doing things in that white porcelain jobbie which *real* cats did in the garden. It was all rather unsavoury. Especially since he'd never once seen him try to cover it up.

Maxwell was paying the price of trowelling all day and never being able to see fifty-five again. His shoulders ached, his fingers throbbed and he couldn't feel his back at all. They didn't have a bath-foam called Dig Relief, so he had to settle for something green and slimy and lay in it, eyes

248

closed, hands clasped across his chest.

Names whirled in his fevered brain. Scenarios. Places. Men with shotguns and dark glasses prowled the hillside of death. Helen Reader waved to him with her trowel flashing silver in the hot sun. Tam Fraser stood, full-kilted like some latter-day Rob Roy, barking orders to his minions. Douglas Russell waved threatening letters at the dozing Maxwell. Derek Latymer sneered at him, Robin Edwards at his elbow; two men on the make; Castor and Pollux, Brutus and Cassius. He tried to picture the dead Sam Welland twirling at the end of a rope, but he only had Jacquie's second-hand version and love her madly though he did, it was never *quite* the same. David Radley's face would haunt him for ever, like Banquo's at the feast. It was calm and still and dead. As if he'd stood in the centre of that silent, swaying stand of ash trees and given up the ghost. He had lain down like the frozen figures of Pompeii under their grey coats of death and he had stopped breathing. David Radley, whom everyone respected. David Radley, whom everyone liked. David Radley, whom some people loved. One day, Mad Max would stumble onto a murder case that would make him construct a bad sentence.

He opened his right eye and glanced out onto the landing. The great black and white beast lay there, like his master, dozing the evening away.

'No chance of you passing me a towel, I suppose?' Maxwell asked. Metternich turned over and went back to sleep.

The place had 'Geek' written all over it. Maxwell

had parked White Surrey around the corner and checked the address under the street light. Redan Street was a cut above the grim railway cottages where Michaela Reynolds lived with a psychopath in a string vest. The terrace was built to celebrate the growth of Leighford as a Victorian seaside resort. Paris had its Champs Elysee, Amritsar its Golden Temple; Leighford had Redan Street.

He rang the bell of number 41, the number given to him obligingly by the Gentleman of the Press who'd turned out to be a fan. There had to be a catch, of course, and that catch was that Peter Maxwell had to give an exclusive, should he succeed in catching a murderer, to Reginald James, Pulitzer Prize pending. It was nearly nine; past his bedtime, sure, but he had a murderer to catch. Nothing. He tried again. The window to his right was clearly the lounge of number 41 and it was in darkness. There was a glimmer though, as if from a room at the back and he noticed that light dim as he pressed the bell. Somebody was in and somebody had closed the door, or handled the dimmer switch, or both. He'd done it himself, pretending not to be in, most Christmases when carol singers came; not because he was mean, but because he was so embarrassed by a confront-ational, in-your-face rendering of God Rest Ye, Merry Gentlemen. It all seemed so point-blank somehow.

He crouched, as far as his shooting pains would let him, and called through the letterbox, 'Mr Wimble?'

Nothing.

He had another go. 'Mr Wimble. My name is Peter Maxwell. I'd like to talk to you.'

'What do you want?' the voice was muffled, wary.

Maxwell waved his bicycle pump in the air, its end wrapped in sacking. 'I'm having trouble with my metal detector. Somebody said you might be able to help.'

There was a pause.

'Who?' the voice came back. 'Who said?'

'Tony Lyman, at the Museum. He said if anybody could fix it, you could.'

Another pause.

'Mr Lyman said that?'

'Said you were the best south of the Piddle. I took that to be a compliment.'

So, evidently, did Arthur Wimble. This time, there was a visual sighting. Maxwell watched the man hobble through his narrow hall, what appeared to be a baseball bat in his hand.

'Who did you say you were again?' The voice was right behind the door now. In fact, whether he wanted to or not, Peter Maxwell had a pretty good view of Arthur Wimble's groin.

'Peter Maxwell,' he said again. 'From Leighford High School.'

'Are you a member of the Society?' Wimble asked.

'About to be,' Maxwell bluffed. 'Sent off my application a couple of days ago.'

There was a sliding of bolts and the door swung inwards. Arthur Wimble was an unprepossessing shambles of a man, wearing what appeared to be an old jumper of Frank Bough's and a pair of

251

trousers that might once have been worn by Fatty Arbuckle.

'Good Lord!' he whispered when he saw Maxwell's face.

'Yes,' the Head of Sixth Form could *just* about smile by now. 'I have that effect on most people. Mind if I come in?'

'That's not a metal detector!' Wimble half-stumbled backwards, both hands gripping the baseball bat above his head.

Maxwell reached out a defensive arm. 'No, it's a bicycle pump,' he said quickly. 'But I didn't think you'd let me in if I told you the truth.'

'You're a liar!' Wimble screamed, his face crimson, his eyes wild behind his glasses. 'You're a lying bastard!'

'Well, yes and no,' Maxwell hedged.

He ducked quickly as Wimble swung the bat. It hissed over Maxwell's head and crunched into the plaster behind him. So far, so good, but Arthur Wimble's back-hand was a blow too far and not only did he miss, but he stumbled badly and Maxwell wrenched the bat from his grip, thrusting the business end of his bicycle pump up under his chin with the other hand. Wimble cowered, half kneeling in the corner, his glasses dangling off his ears, his hands raised in supplication.

'Please,' he whispered, clearly terrified. 'I haven't been well.'

Chapter Fourteen

'How are you feeling now?' Maxwell sat opposite his man, watching him closely.

'All right,' Wimble said. He was still sniffing. 'I don't suppose you even know Tony Lyman, do you?'

'The Museum man? As a matter of fact, I do,' Maxwell said. 'Tony and I go back more than a few years. Look, I'm sorry about the subterfuge.'

'That's all right.' 'Wimble was still trying to retrieve the bit of his glasses that went behind his ear.

'Tea all right?' They were sitting at the Anorak's rather nasty kitchen table, drinking from his Woolie's cups.

'Fine, ta.'

'I've got to say, Arthur ... you don't mind if I call you Arthur?'

The man shook his head. Peter Maxwell had inveigled his way into the castle he called home, disarmed him in a vicious baseball bat attack, sat him down and made him a cup of tea. Arthur's mum had believed you had to marry people if you had a relationship like that.

'That's all right,' he said.

'Well, I've got to say, going for me with that was a bit OTT, wasn't it?'

The blunt instrument stood propped against the door jamb. If push came to shove, Maxwell reckoned he could reach it first. But there was no response.

'Did you think I was a rent-collector or something? Prospective parliamentary candidate for the UK Independence Party?'

Wimble looked like frightened ferret behind the glasses. 'I thought you were from them,' he said, 'I thought they'd tracked me down. They've got my number, you see.'

Everybody had. Reg James at the *Advertiser* had warned Maxwell about this one. Sudden, hysterical welcomes were his stock in trade. 'Them?' Maxwell asked. He knew the film, of course – black and white Fifties tosh about mutant ants on the rampage in Nevada; James Arness being lantern-jawed, a young Leonard Nimoy getting his first taste of something wicked from outer space. But somehow, Maxwell knew that Arthur Wimble wasn't talking about those 'them'. Wimble had paled noticeably and ripples were forming on the surface of the tea in his cup.

Maxwell pursued it from another direction. 'A moment ago,' he said, 'when we were having a conversation through the door, you mentioned a society. I said I was joining.'

'That wasn't true, was it?' Wimble's lip was trembling.

'Alas, no,' Maxwell confessed. 'But I had to say something to get to talk to you. What society were you talking about?'

'The Metal Detectives' Society,' Wimble told him. 'It was founded in 1995 in Littlehampton.'

'Metal detectives?' Maxwell frowned.

'You're not actually an archaeologist at all, are

254

you?' Wimble's eyes narrowed as he peered at the man.

'Technically, no,' Maxwell said. 'But I have got my knees brown recently.'

Wimble sighed. 'I'm going to get up now,' he said. 'I'm feeling a little stronger.'

Maxwell steadied the man as he put his tea cup down and got shakily to his feet. 'I don't normally invite strangers into my bedroom,' the metal detective said. Maxwell could believe that. 'But, apart from all that unpleasant bruising, Mr Maxwell, you've a kind face. I suppose I ought to be more concerned about the man who gave you that face, shouldn't I? So come on up.'

Maxwell followed the man up the creaking stairs with their single twist and their early Sixties carpet. If Arthur Wimble had 'fallen downstairs' in his previous bungalow, what *would* happen to him here? He led his night visitor into a box-room. It was full of boxes.

'There!' Wimble stood triumphant.

'You collect cardboard?' Maxwell wondered. It was difficult to take all this seriously.

Wimble tried to wither him with a stare, but he didn't really have what it took and relented with a series of blinks. 'In these boxes,' he said, 'are a lifetime of archaeological remains. Bones, pot-sherds, coins – they come from all over southern England.'

'I see,' Maxwell said. 'Shouldn't you have...?'

'Handed them in? Oh, no,' Wimble said quickly. 'You see, the law is a highly complex beast. Most objects found belong to the landowner, except gold or silver. I've never yet met a farmer who

255

wanted bits of bone or pot – in fact, they chuck 'em away with vandalistic regularity. Hence, my little collection. *I* prize them. But these...' He opened a box to his right to show Maxwell a collection of coins, 'are mine. I found them.'

'I thought the law of Treasure Trove meant that the finder *might* be offered the *value* of the goods, not the goods themselves.'

Wimble closed the box quickly. 'That's a very narrow interpretation,' he said. 'Shall we go back down? I don't have much of a head for heights.'

Maxwell descended, careful to keep his hand on the banister. Somehow he didn't really like turning his back on Arthur Wimble.

'Well, basically, Count,' the Great Man was sipping a large Southern Comfort in the quiet of his lounge as Thursday ticked inexorably into Friday. 'Arthur Wimble is as mad as a tree. But he *did* open a can of worms.' He raised an eyebrow at the cat. 'Not mixing too many metaphors for you, am I? I had the lecture of field archaeology versus metal-detecting and how it used to be a free for all and that many irresponsible metal detectives ruined important sites in their headlong, speedy rush for gold. That was the good old days, of course, California '49 – get it? Gold rush? Oh, never mind. It was before satellite television and before Tony Robinson stopped being Baldrick and became an intelligent, if slightly irritating frontman. That's why the Metal Detectives' Society was formed.' He lapsed into his best Mid-West, hand on heart in a presidential salute, 'To do good for the sake of archaeology, to go hand in hand, professional and amateur, in a mutual quest to unearth the past … boldly.'

He took a swig. 'Well, yes, of course it's bollocks, but I suppose I approve. Of course,' he wagged a conspiratorial forefinger at Metternich, 'when Wimble mentioned society, I thought he was talking Sepulchres and Sussex. I tried him out with that. Nothing.' Maxwell looked almost disappointed. 'Either he's up for a BAFTA or he's never heard of it. Bitch, isn't it?'

He reached across and poured himself a top-up. Metternich munched something tasty in his left armpit.

'Anyway, to cut a long story short – yes, this is the shortened version, Count – friend Arthur knows every bit of Leighford and its environs like the back of his metal detector. Sorry, I did fall asleep during the technical stuff about which one he uses and why, I will admit. Anyhoo, one of the sites he was working on back in March was Staple Hill. Oh, you know it, Count, where the dig is. In the good old days, the Leigh used to run that way before Squire Whatsisarse enclosed the place circa 1735. Well, Arthur was up there one night – he couldn't precisely remember when, but it *was* a Tuesday, he assured me. He was feeling pretty pleased with himself because he'd just made a find – when he felt cold steel in his neck. Oh, not the cold steel you, Errol Flynn and I know, buckling our swashes through this wicked world, but the muzzle of a twelve-bore.' He moistened his still-tender lips. 'Precisely,' Maxwell nodded. 'And I'm glad you're still following all this, Count. At the other end of said twelve-bore was a customer

257

whose description sounds suspiciously like one of Anthony Cahill's goons; Julian or Sandy or whatever. The men in black. What of it? I hear you cry.' Maxwell sat up to engage the cat more closely. 'Because of the different way said goons treated me and Arthur Wimble. I was nosing about at the dig too, if you remember, after dark and minding somebody else's business. And whereas I was given a load of verbal and dragged before the beak, Mr Cahill himself, Arthur had his kneecaps removed. Well, not literally, but he did roll up his trouser-leg, mason-like, to show me the scars. Quite nasty, actually. They gave him a smacking. The hospital said he'd never walk without a pronounced limp.' Maxwell looked the black and white beast straight in the smouldering green eye. 'I set 'em up, you knock 'em down,' he said. 'But I don't think this is a matter for levity, Count. Now,' Maxwell lolled back again, staring at the ceiling in the warm lamp-glow, 'why, you may ask, did Arthur get such different treatment from me? Was I just luckier? Julian suffering from a spot of PMT the night he caught Arthur red-handed? No, Count, I think not. You'll remember, of course, that our metal-detecting friend had found something else not far from the knife-blade? Now, Arthur's a keen field walker and he knows torc from butter, but his Latin ... well, Count, I'm afraid Arthur went to a bog standard Comprehensive school. He doesn't speaka-da-lingo. All he could do was spell out the letters of his second find that night. And mighty interesting reading they make too. H-I-C-J-A-C-E-T-A-L-F-R-E-D-U-S-R-E-X. Exactly, Count,' Maxwell winked at the animal. 'And I'm glad you went to a good school, too. *Hic jacet Alfredus Rex*. Here lies King Alfred. Now there, companion of my mile, is a motive for murder.'

Freya's day began with a fierce sun gilding Columbine from a cloudless sky. Great revision weather, Maxwell observed ruefully to himself; Goering's economic policy in the Third Reich or flat out under the great, fiery ball on a glorious sandy, EU-approved beach? What a facer! He shovelled something brown and crunchy into Metternich's bowl. The Great Beast never came down to breakfast. The freeloader that he was had several homes, each of them believing the well-nourished stray was theirs. He would stroll in for elevenses later.

Maxwell dressed for the fray – a tatty pair of gardening trousers, a loose shirt, a broad-brimmed straw hat not unlike Tam Fraser's wideawake and all the other Indiana Jones headgear at the site, but rather more homespun. He grabbed a coffee and a piece of toast. Then he rang Jacquie. No answer. Damn. He must have missed her. He checked his watch and the kitchen clock. Eight thirty. She shouldn't have left yet. Still, a policewoman's lot was not a regular one and she *was* up to her eyes in murder. He'd catch her later.

He pedalled over the rise and turned right, skirting the flyover to the west. The sea was a glittering, shimmering blue and the tiny dots that were sun-worshippers were already taking their positions on the white beach; the Germans were first, of course. Year Thirteen would drift in later, clutching a folder of notes on, appropriately, Bismarck's foreign policy that would remain unopened, as the combination of sea, sand and sun worked a more alluring magic. Cycle-clips flashing, Maxwell straightened his legs and crouched low over the handlebars, driving every sinew as he took the gradient of Gravel Hill, making for the stand of ash trees.

He hadn't intended to, but he found himself wheeling in to that sad, ominous gap in the fence where Martin Toogood's doctored car had left the road. The council had put red ribbon across the gap to warn other motorists and the gorse bushes were ripped and flattened way down the hill. But other motorists had not had their brakes cut and had not fallen foul of a murderer. The twenty-first century's symbols of public grief lay scattered on the verge – roses curling already in the heat. One in particular caught his eye – 'Miss you, mate, love, Jacquie.'

Just another score to settle. He pedalled away.

There was the usual litter of paparazzi at the gate. They'd been banned by Tam Fraser, Anthony Cahill and his heavies and, fearful for their cameras, recorders and teeth, were dutifully staying their side of the wire. The police tape still fluttered there and a solitary copper, already sweating in his shirt sleeves and flat cap, wandered the lines of the perimeter. It was an uneasy truce arranged between the Professor and the DCI – one had a dig to finish; the other a murderer to catch. So the tape and the copper stayed, but the digging continued.

The paparazzi were fewer. Nobody is famous for more than fifteen minutes, not even murder victims. David Radley's obit had already appeared in *The Times*, whose man was one of those long gone from the perimeter fence in search of stories new. As far as the Press knew, Sam Welland was officially a suicide and although the *Mail* had speculated on a plausible link between the two deaths, nothing had yet been established. The *Mail*, after all, had umpteen Spanish villas to give away and there were priorities.

Maxwell waved to them all as he arrived with a flourish of the hat. He hitched Surrey to a post, and because they were journalists, he'd brought his padlock along. 'Mind my bike,' he called to them, but no one was old enough to remember the reference, so he let it go.

'You're at it early, Helen,' Maxwell's feet crunched on the clay, baked hard in the June sun. There was no mistaking that backside, hemispheres of iron.

She turned, wiping the glow from her forehead with a gloved hand. ''Morning, Max. Kettle's just boiled.'

'Elixir!' Maxwell ducked into the Social Tent and brewed up, moving aside somebody's femur to find the tea bags. His head popped out seconds later. 'Can I get you one?'

'No thanks. Tannin.' She pointed to her sizeable frontage. 'Doesn't agree with me.'

Maxwell nodded. He knew the feeling well. There were whole days when nobody at Leighford High agreed with him. He perched on the edge of Helen Reader's trench, sipping the tea as he took in his surroundings. 'Nobody about today?'

'Appalling, isn't it?' she chuckled. 'You and I the only amateurs here and the professionals nowhere in sight.'

'That's odd, surely.' Maxwell blew on his tea as someone once told him the working class did.

'Way of the world, I think you'll find.'

'No, I mean, in my – admittedly limited – experience of digs, they're usually crawling with volunteers, mostly Americans desperate for somebody else's history on account of how they haven't got any.'

She laughed. 'Yes, I suppose it is. But David was adamant. I'd worked with him before, so I had special dispensation. But that was it; there was to be nobody else.'

'Did he say why?'

'You don't ask geniuses like David Radley to justify their decisions, Max. You read his obituary in *The Times*?'

'I did.'

'Mealy-mouthed, I thought. He deserved better.' She leaned back on her haunches, her bare shoulders already flaking from days under the Sussex sun. 'Look at this,' she said, pointing around with her trowel, trying to ignore the policeman, the tape, the paparazzi at the gates of dawn. 'Difficult to imagine how it all must have been in the Saxon period, isn't it? A little church, probably, over there by the trees. Graves where we are now. Leighford ... what, a cluster of wattle and daub huts where the river shallowed. Do you remember your first dig?'

'I do,' Maxwell smiled. 'Warwick. I'd just left school and Bristol University – there wasn't one at Warwick then – were looking for Medieval post holes along the line of the town hall.'

'How exciting!' Helen trilled.

'Not when you're eighteen,' Maxwell corrected her. 'I was filling in before going up to Cambridge and I think we all expected to find something astonishing. You know – Tutankhamun comes to Mercia or something like that.'

'And all you found was post holes?' she asked.

'More or less,' he chuckled. 'Although I was lucky enough to find an unbroken Bellarmine jug. Still don't know how a Bohemian seventeenth century artefact found its way into somebody's cellar in little old Warwick, but there you go. No, what I remember most about the dig was guzzling cider and fish and chips in Priory Park. Feeling muscles for the first time. I even grew a beard that summer – just because I could, you know. The weather was just like this – glorious. We were all chaps on the dig as it happened – behaving like idiots taking wheelbarrows of slag up the planks at silly speeds. Girls we vaguely knew would hover by the wire, whistling at our muscles.'

'Forgive me if this sounds ageist,' she said. 'But did girls do that sort of thing in your day?'

'Ageist?' Maxwell bridled in mid-slurp. 'Madam, I'll have you know that Ladette culture goes a helluva long way back. Back to Boudicca in fact – whose PMT, by the way, was very badly timed for several thousand Romans.'

Helen laughed and got back to her trowelling,

263

scraping away the debris of years.

'Fast forward a little in time,' he said to her. 'What do you know about King Alfred?'

'The Great?'

'I would imagine so. It's not my period.'

'How often have I heard that!' She wagged her trowel at him. 'Well, remember, Max. I'm not a historian...'

He leaned forward to her, patting her gently on her sunburnt shoulders. 'That doesn't make you a bad person,' he said.

'Well, he was a great hero; that I do know,' she said, resting back again. 'Let's see. Fought against the Danes – that was the Great Army, wasn't it? Forced Guthrum, their leader, to be baptized and recaptured London. Winchester was his capital of course, as king of Wessex. He's buried there.'

'Is he?'

'Of course. Asser says so; so does the *Anglo-Saxon Chronicle*.'

'Asser?' Maxwell repeated.

'His first biographer, a monk from St David's in Wales. He wrote the work in 893. Some of it's pinched from the *Chronicle*, but he knew the king personally and must have added lots of touches of his own. But Max, you know all this, surely?'

'Yes,' the Great Historian said. 'I find that I do, but you know how it is. That huge mistake the National Curriculum means that all I teach is the modern period. In fact, my putative boss, the Head of History, though a lovely man, thinks that his subject began in 1900. Heigh-ho.'

'Why your sudden interest in Alfred?' she

asked. 'He's got nothing to do with this site, surely?'

'No, no,' Maxwell smiled, reaching for his trowel for a good day's scraping. 'Nothing at all.'

'Has anybody contacted her?' Henry Hall was waist-deep in statements already and it was only midday. He'd sent somebody out for a baguette – no slur intended, of course, on the nick canteen – which he'd get round to if he had time. He couldn't remember what he'd ordered, but it would taste the same, anyway.

'We've tried her home and her mobile,' DC Steve Holland told him. 'Nothing.'

'What about Maxwell?'

'Guv?'

Hall looked at the lad, assessing the quantity of liquid behind his ears. Holland was the new kid on the block. He didn't know Peter Maxwell or Jacquie Carpenter's relationship with him. 'Boy-friend,' Hall said. 'Fiancé, live-in-lover, Svengali – I really don't know how to classify him in the context of Jacquie. Or any other context, come to think of it.'

'Got an address on this Maxwell?' Holland asked.

'38 Columbine,' Hall said. It was engraved on his heart. 'But he won't be there. I'm reliably in-formed he's joined Professor Fraser's dig on Staple Hill.'

'Want me to try there? PC Scragg's on this morning.'

'No,' Hall said. 'There has to be an explan-ation, a rational one, that is... And if there isn't, I don't want Maxwell involved in any shape or form.'

In the rest of the Incident Room it was business as usual. David Radley's corpse was in a chilled locker in Leighford General's morgue, his body carved with a 'Y' in the macabre graffiti of a pathologist. Dr Jim Astley always took a pride in his suture work and Radley was no exception. Would archaeologists of the future, Astley had wondered briefly, find this man's body and wonder who he was and why and how he died? Astley shook himself free of it. Romantic cobblers. He was getting old. Conversely, Jim Astley was no further ahead on the forensics of murder. The Incident Room knew that the sterno-cleido-mastoid muscles of Radley's neck had been badly pulverized by a blow from the left which had broken the skin, caused huge bruising and dislocated his vertebrae. Whoever had killed him was his height, had stood in front of him when the blow was delivered and was right-handed.

Lily Boydell had found fibres on Radley's clothing and on the soles of Radley's shoes. The latter came from a carpet that wasn't Radley's and the former from the same brown stockman's coat found on the corpse of Sam Welland. The shoes, like all the clothes on Radley's body, were new and they didn't fit too well. They had never trod the Leighford clay. Under the guv'nor's strict instructions, the official line was still that Sam Welland had taken her own life and Hazel Twigg was asked, in the interests of finding her lover's killer, to go along with this, at least for the time being.

A unit in the Incident Room was working on Martin Toogood's car and the CCTV footage of the dark man in the broad-brimmed hat. Jacquie Carpenter was working on Toogood's notes and his computer area. Except that Jacquie Carpenter had broken off briefly and gone looking for Alison McCormick; and Jacquie Carpenter, by that Friday afternoon, could not be found.

'This is unbelievable,' Hall was muttering as he swept through the room, checking on tasks, leads, case status. 'Listen up, everybody.' He clapped his hands for quiet. Peter Maxwell would have approved.

The room's buzz stopped, like closing a window in high summer.

'Jacquie Carpenter. Anyone seen her?'

Puzzled faces. Question marks. A certain, creeping unease.

'She should have come on duty three hours ago and we've had no word.' He told them. 'Tom, duty log.'

The silver-haired sergeant fumbled through his ledger. 'Went to Alison McCormick's place yesterday. Signed out at ... three twelve. Back by four thirty-eight.'

'And?'

'Worked here in the Room, guv,' Dave Garstang said. 'Her usual station.' He waved to the empty desk, the dead VDU screen.

'Get to her area,' Hall ordered. 'Find out what she was working on. What time did she leave yesterday, Tom?'

'Six fifteen.' Wilson was tracking the girl's

267

progress in his ledger.

'Nearly hit me in the car park,' somebody called.

It lightened the moment.

'Was she going home?' Hall asked. 'Anybody know?'

'Said she had a lead to follow up,' Garstang said.

Hall turned to face him. This was something he didn't want to hear just now. 'Did she say what?' he asked.

Garstang knew all eyes were on him. He shook his head. 'Sorry guv. She said it was probably nothing. I didn't give it a second thought.'

Hall nodded, hoping that those words would not come back to haunt either of them. Second thoughts were what good policing were all about. That and second sight. 'Right,' he said, leaning back against a desk and folding his arms. 'Where are we on Alison McCormick?'

DCI Henry Hall's Incident Team were nowhere on Alison McCormick. She'd been sighted last on Tuesday afternoon. That was the day she and Dave Garstang had gone to the Railway Cottages to talk to Michaela Reynolds. Afterwards, the pair had grabbed a quick pasty and pint at The Moorings and got back to the station by two. Like Jacquie Carpenter, the girl had driven out of the nick car park and vanished into space like the girls who had got into Ted Bundy's yellow beetle, the women who had gone for a chat with that nice Mr Christie at Rillington Place, the harlots who had waved a cheery 'Hello' to Jack...

Missing coppers were not the norm, and they posed one hell of a problem. Advertise the fact that they're missing and it sends a shock wave through the community. One half will laugh themselves sick that the police can't even trace their own; the other half will panic for the same reason. Peter Hitchens in the *Daily Mail* would go berserk. On the other hand, *not* to advertise put the missing officer at extraordinary risk. There had been no ransom demand of any kind; no corny letter made up of cut-out newspaper clippings; no weirdo with a heavy-breathing delivery on untraceable phones.

Alison McCormick had a mother somewhere near Basingstoke. Someone from Leighford had been to see her; assuring, calming, softly softly. No cause for alarm at all, but her daughter had gone missing. Janet McCormick didn't scream or get hysterical. She carried on with her washing, glancing out occasionally to the garden, where a pram was parked. Alison was always doing this. She'd always done it, ever since she was a kid. She'd be back, when her cash ran out or she got bored. This wasn't *quite* the same, the somebody from Leighford pointed out. Alison wasn't a kid anymore. She was a policewoman, missing from her post. That seemed to cut no ice with Janet McCormick. The girl would be back. Whatever she was up to, she'd be back.

She sat up suddenly, a horrible smell in her nostrils and over her face. She recognized it at once. Chloroform. And she felt the pain again as she tried to move her jaw. The pain of a rough hand over her mouth, the pressure of a cloth pad over her nose. But she couldn't open her mouth. It was taped shut and she could feel saliva dribbling down her chin.

Her hands were roped together, in front of her, as though in prayer. She couldn't move her legs either, because they were anchored via a chain to something – a wall, was it? She couldn't see in the blackness.

She tried to think, to rationalize what had happened to her. She remembered driving out of the station, turning left along the High Street. She remembered what was playing on the radio – Jeff Wayne's *War of the Worlds*. The red weed had still been on her mind as she got home. She had backed into the garage, had closed and locked the door. Then it had happened. She was just thinking she ought to ring him, touch base with this new information when the hard hand had slapped around her lower face, a powerful arm wrenching hers behind her back. She'd seen the clouds scurry for a moment, then reel and twist. She'd felt her lungs tighten as she fought against the pad, trying not to inhale. But the pain was too much and the grip too strong and darkness had come to her.

And in the darkness she still was, chained to a wall, her clothes damp and clammy. It was June, she told herself. In the middle of a heat-wave. But here, it was like being below ground. She groped forward, as far as the ropes and the chains would allow. She felt wetness on her fingertips, a slime that was cold and dead.

Her whole body shuddered as she realized it. Jacquie Carpenter was lying in a grave.

270

Chapter Fifteen

It was lunchtime before Douglas Russell turned up at the dig, Maxwell's sandwiches wilting in the midday heat. He mused to himself that he really should have brought them up from Surrey's pannier a little sooner, but it had given him the chance to chat to Julian the Heavy.

'Not packing today, Julian?' he had asked cheerily, well within earshot of the patrolling policeman and the remnants of the paparazzi, smoking and sipping Pimms like spectators at a summer event.

'I don't know what you mean.' Julian had shrugged, his eyes black behind the dark glasses, beads of perspiration standing out on his shaven head, a mad dog and an Englishman, all in one, in the midday sun.

Maxwell had gone through the motions for him, a little over-the-top perhaps, of pumping a pump action rifle and blasting the air in front of him. Julian had looked on amazed. He didn't own a pump-action and the shotgun he did own he only carried at night, so what was all the pantomime about? George had thought temporarily about putting one on the cheeky bastard, but it *was* a little open for that.

'Heard of one Arthur Wimble, Douglas?' Maxwell was lying against a spoil heap, his straw hat down over his eyes in best Randolph Scott tradition, out on the studio prairies, with his saddle for a pillow.

'Wimble?' Russell was getting outside a can of lager. 'No, I can't say I have.'

'What about the Metal Detectives' Society?'

'Oh, them,' the geophysicist chuckled. We were back with the mutant ants again. 'Yes, them I do know.'

'In what context?' Maxwell asked.

'Well, in many ways,' Russell told him, 'they're the best of a bad bunch. God knows how much important material has been destroyed over the years by these vandals with metal detectors. As a geophysicist, you can imagine I don't see them as anything but rank outsiders. Well, about ten years ago, a sort of truce was called. Rather than these herberts creeping about at night wiping evidence and us having to lock, bolt and otherwise protect our gear, we invited them on board. They would have the thrill of the chase, plus the cut of the particular Treasure Trove and we would reap the benefits of their searches. The deal is that at the first series of whee-whees on the old electro-magnetic device, they're on the phone to their nearest university or field office. It actually works quite well. Don't tell me they've got to you?'

'Got to me?'

'As soon as we moved in here, they were pestering David, wanting to volunteer their services. He sent them packing.'

'He did?' Maxwell asked. 'Why?'

'Well,' Russell said, 'I don't want to speak ill of the dead, but...'

'Douglas!' Tam Fraser announced his arrival. It

wasn't quite a fanfare or a hundred gun salute, but it didn't need to be when you had a voice like Tam Fraser's. 'After lunch, can we go over those reports of yours? I'm finding anomalies all over the place.'

'Of course, Professor.' Russell finished his drink. 'If there are anomalies...'

'Oh, there's no "if", laddie.' He sat down with his feet in Maxwell's trench and fanned his fiery face with the wideawake.

'Then I'd better go and re-check them.' Russell saw his opening and left.

'Aye, do that, dear boy.' Fraser called after him. 'That man,' he turned to Maxwell with a broad smile, 'hates my guts.'

The Head of Sixth Form lifted the hat from his face. 'I'm sure not.'

'Oh, yes,' Fraser sighed. 'He's new school, y'see. He's all amino acid racenization and uranium series disequilibrium. Me? I call a spade a spade,' and he winked at his man. 'There aren't many of us left, are there, Maxwell?'

'Us?' Maxwell repeated, not sure if Tam Fraser would appreciate the old *kemo sabe* joke.

'Dinosaurs, man; dodos, whatever vanished analogy you'd care to use. The point at issue is that our standards, our ways, were certainties. They were absolutes. Do you not sense that?'

'Perhaps our walks of life are different,' Maxwell tilted back the hat and sat up. 'In my profession there are always a load of initiatives with different acronyms. They all boil down to re-inventing the wheel. I must admit, I am beginning to sound like an old 78 – "We did that in 1982"; "it didn't work then and it won't work now"; "that's all right in the private sector"; "fine, if we had the money". Sound familiar?'

'Indeed it does,' Fraser laughed.

'But in archaeology, surely, it's different. New techniques really *are* new techniques, taking us forward to a new understanding.'

'Ach, that's symposium twaddle, laddie. I'd hoped for better from you. No, take my word for it – it's all just a reinvention of the wheel.'

At the end of a long day, Peter Maxwell threw his warm plastic lunchbox into the pannier of White Surrey and sauntered out of the gate. The paparazzi had gone now. Tam Fraser had given them their quote of the day – which wasn't actually quotable in a family newspaper – and the on duty PCs had done their respective impressions of statues in not responding to them. George had replaced Julian on the late afternoon shift and they'd lap each other again in the wee, small hours. Did those men, Maxwell wondered, ever sleep?

'Arthur sends his regards,' Maxwell told him, buckling down the panniers.

'Who?' George remained rock solid, legs planted firmly apart, incongruous in his black suit and black shades. Maxwell's hot, tired form reflected back at the Great Man in each of the lenses. Maxwell cloned? Now, there was a prospect.

'Arthur Wimble. You know, metal detective here one night back in March. You or Julian or both dented his kneecaps, probably with the shotgun butt you keep tucked down your tights.'

274

He saw George's lip curl. 'I'd be very careful if I were you, Maxwell.'

'Oh, I will,' the Head of Sixth Form said. 'Which is why we're having this little conversation in broad daylight with a boy in blue standing over there. Incidentally, I think I'd fancy his nightstick against your shotgun butt any day. They're really dinky things. Ever seen one in action?'

'No,' George scowled.

'Pray you don't,' Maxwell scowled back. 'Where is it, by the way?'

'Where's what?'

'The object you took from Mr Wimble.'

'What'd that be, then?' George asked.

'Don't play dumb with me, George. There were two things actually. One was a Saxon dagger, four inch blade, bone handle – although I believe most of that had gone. And I know where that is – it's in a packing case in Leighford Museum; I washed it myself a few days ago and labelled it up. So, presumably, you kindly returned that to Dr Radley at some point. No, the other thing is a piece of stone or marble, Mr Wimble couldn't remember which. It had a Latin inscription. How's your Latin, George?'

'I don't know what the fuck you're talking about. Fuck off out of it.'

'You see, *that* was quite an important find.' Maxwell was wiping dust off Surrey's saddle.

'Well, it wasn't his,' George growled. 'It was on private property and he was trespassing.'

'Indeed, but it wasn't yours either, was it? Or Mr Cahill's. It's the job of a coroner to decide

275

ownership of finds like that. So you think seriously about handing it in, all right? And I just might forget you and your oppo jammed a gun barrel into my neck the other night.'

'We're entitled to protect Mr Cahill's property.'

'Oh, sure, and you're just obeying orders, eh, a bit like fifty million Nazis. You disappoint me, George. This is the twenty-first century – I thought you might have something more original to say by now. Oh, by the way,' he swung his leg over Surrey's crossbar. 'No point in trying to put the frighteners on Arthur Wimble again. He's not in the bungalow any more. I had the devil's own job to find him. You have a nice evening now, y'hear?'

Peter Maxwell cycled over the flyover and headed north. This was not the way home, but he wasn't going home. He was going to Jacquie Carpenter's to find out where the hell she was.

'Peter Maxwell!'

'Jesus!' The Head of Sixth Form hadn't turned that fast in a long time. His back jarred and his pulse raced. He'd just left Surrey champing at the bit against Jacquie's wall and had dutifully rung her bell. Nothing. No familiar shape beyond the frosted glass, no call of 'Hang on. Won't be a tick.' 'Henry Hall,' he said, collecting himself. 'Not conducting at Ally Pally tonight then?' The DCI had been here a little while, lurking in the privet, testing the alertness of Neighbourhood Watch and finding it singularly lacking. Then it hit Maxwell. 'Where's Jacquie?'

'It's your key in the lock,' Hall reminded him.

'So it is,' Maxwell said and turned it. The door swung wide. 'Jacquie? Jacquie darling. It's Max.'

He found himself pushed gently back against the door by the DCI. 'Better let me go first,' he said. 'I get paid to do this.'

Maxwell had seen it done countless times on the telly. Good cop and bad cop; rookie and old hand; black man, white man, Clint Eastwood, Tyne Daly. The Magnums came out and one went high while the other went low, arms locked ahead, gun cocked, nerves like tensile steel. Maybe Henry Hall didn't watch shows like that. He just sauntered into the lounge and looked around, then he sauntered into the kitchen, felt the kettle and cooker and doubled back to the stairs, halting Maxwell in mid-step.

'I don't make a habit of this,' he said and was gone up the curve of the staircase, out of sight onto the landing. 'Mr Maxwell, you'd better come up here.'

Peter Maxwell didn't remember, in the years he had left, how he got to the top of those stairs, how he flew into the main bedroom, two at a time. On a wing and a prayer? Who knew? All he knew was that he found himself standing alongside Henry Hall, both of them staring down at an envelope on the double bed.

'She didn't have time to make this,' Hall nudged aside a pillow with his pen. Then he tucked the biro end neatly into the space at the top of the envelope and handled the thing with his fingertips. 'Fan mail,' he said to Maxwell. Both of them could see it was addressed to him.

'Mr Maxwell,' Hall said softly. 'I want you to go

into all the other rooms. I want you to check carefully in drawers, wardrobes and cupboards. I want you to touch as little as possible and I want you to give me the roughest of ideas of anything that's missing. Can you do that?'

'Yes.'

Hall looked at his man. He knew Peter Maxwell of old. He knew him to be a maverick, a madman even, given to strange whims and doubtful tilts at windmills. But he also knew him to be one of the strongest men he'd ever met. But this ... this was different. This was Jacquie Carpenter. And one man's DS is another man's life.

'But what's that?' Maxwell hadn't moved, but was pointing to the envelope in Hall's hand.

'That,' the DCI reminded him softly, 'is addressed to me.'

Maxwell spun on his heel.

The other rooms were as empty as the downstairs. Jacquie's clothes were still in the wardrobe. Winter coat, scarves, gloves, boots. Lacy bras and knickers lay neatly in one drawer; more of them tumbled untidily out of laundry basket in the bathroom. Various lotions graced the shelves; her toothbrush dangled on its rack. Maxwell checked the airing cupboard. The immersion heater was off and Jacquie was a stickler for that. In more petulant moments she'd berate him for never turning his off and what a waste it was. An open pack of sanitary towels lay half-hidden under a pile of sheets.

'She didn't go of her own accord.' He'd returned to Hall.

'I know,' the DCI said. He'd torn open the envelope and, still with fingertip precision, read the letter it contained. "We have your policewoman. Stop the dig or she dies.""

'The Sepulchre Society of Sussex,' said Maxwell. He didn't have to look at the letterhead.

'The same,' nodded Hall grimly.

Time for a council of war.

The lights burned blue at Leighford nick that night. As the wind rose, moaning through the ash trees on Staple Hill and chiselled moon-silver ridges out to sea, a tired group of men and women sat hunched in the Incident Room, blinds drawn, emotions ragged.

'What've we got SOCO-wise on Jacquie's flat?' Hall asked. Everybody knew it was not, technically, a scene of crime. Nothing had been disturbed. But Henry Hall had an officer down and two others missing; one, at least, an apparent kidnap victim. He'd drafted in new people, closed other cases, put yet more on hold. He needed officers out there, knocking on doors, asking questions. He'd square the cost with the Chief Constable later.

'No sign of forced entry,' Dave Garstang spoke for the mysterious Men in White who had spent hours going over the woman's life. 'We're working on prints now, but apart from hers and Peter Maxwell's, there aren't any more to go on; one set's fairly apparent, which we're assuming is mother or cleaning lady – unless, of course, they're the same.'

Levity wasn't working this time. To lose one policewoman might be carelessness, but to lose two ... and this one was Jacquie Carpenter. Could any of them, they'd secretly asked themselves all day, learn to cope with losing *her*?

'Her car was in the garage. Garage was locked. Again, no unaccountable prints. She's taken nothing with her that might indicate a sudden flit. No clothes. No suitcases.'

'What about the letter?' Hall was taking them down every avenue.

'Same as the others,' Steve Holland took up the story. 'The others in the Sepulchre series. The paper and the envelope are both Wiggins, bog standard stationery available in any W.H. Smith's and office suppliers throughout the land. The paper is ninety-gram and the printer is probably a Canon.'

'Shit!' It wasn't like DCI Henry Hall to lose it, but the ridge in his jaw was proof he'd lost it now. 'Know what's so irritating about this case?' he asked the room. This was the DCI asking, the guv'nor; and they all sensed the question was historic; a milestone in the history of Henry Hall and his people. They prepared to be enlightened. 'Everything,' he said, calmer now. 'Everything is so bog-standard, as you put it, Steve, so ordinary. David Radley and Sam Welland – nice people just getting on with their job. We've found nothing in their past, no secrets, no foibles. Even forensics have produced nothing. How can anyone break a man's neck, hang a woman, fix the brakes on a man's car and kidnap one, possibly two people, without leaving any trace at all?'

They all knew the guv'nor was simplifying. Microscopic evidence *had* been found, linking

Radley and Welland. There had to be *some* DNA on the envelopes, the letters, *something* – didn't there? They glanced at each other, afraid of the hopelessness in each other's eyes.

Nobody was going home.

Maxwell hadn't slept. By the time he caught the 8.21 to Newbury, he looked and felt like shit. Southern Trains didn't help. In place of the ancient retainers who would walk the stately aisle offering Brown Windsor soup and fillet of salmon for a paltry sixteen shillings, an incompetent floozy aged four gave him a hot plastic cup in exchange for a second mortgage. His knees were under his chin for most of the time and an exec hunched next to him was clicking implacably on his laptop. Six carriages away, another was talking Big Business on his mobile, declaring to the world how he and Paul Getty were 'like that'. Maxwell didn't doubt it for a moment. But it was a Sunday, for God's sake. Why were these people still talking money on the Sabbath? At least, some of the trains were still running.

But Maxwell wasn't actually listening. He had other things on his mind than the awful coffee and the congested jungle that was commuter travel in the twenty-first century. The woman he loved had gone, into the hands of a bunch of madmen. And, he realized as dawn had crept up over Columbine, he didn't have the first clue how to get her back.

They'd fought not one, but two battles near Newbury, in that pointless war to decide who had the more clout – king or parliament. Since both institutions had survived, cheerfully co-existing, it all seemed rather a waste of time. Maxwell found a cabbie anxious to fill him in on exactly how Gordon Brown would take down Tony Blair and if he did, he would personally be voting British National Party next time out; but, more importantly, he found 93 Wentworth Way.

The house before him had sad windows, blinking in the scurrying clouds of the morning. He heard his feet crunch on the gravel of the drive, heard his heart pounding even louder. He rang the bell and waited. A woman, not much older than he was, stood there.

'Mrs Carpenter?' he tipped his hat. 'I'm Peter Maxwell.'

Jacquie had lived half her life in this house. Her father had died eight years ago and her mother rattled around the place, time on her hands and memories in her heart. She sat Peter Maxwell down on the swinging seat in the back garden. He knew this place; knew it because Jacquie had talked about it. There'd been a rabbit hutch in the far corner where the compost now lay and to its left, the home of Anstruther, the tortoise. Her dad had told her that Anstruther was 400 years old and she'd believed him. She'd believed him too, when her dad had said he'd never leave her; see her married with kids of her own. But that hadn't been true either. Cancer had seen to that.

'I didn't want you to hear it first from some spotty kid of a policeman, Gwen,' Maxwell explained, grateful for the tea and the shade now that the clouds had gone and the sun was a demon again.

'I'm grateful to you,' she said. There was *something* of Jacquie in Gwen Carpenter, though from the photos he'd seen in Jacquie's flat and again in Gwen's living room, she was mostly her father. The grey eyes, the smile – they were his. Only flashes of Gwen came through, when she was angry, brittle, short. 'So, you're Peter Maxwell.'

'Guilty,' he smiled. 'And, believe me, you don't know how sorry I am that we've had to meet under these circumstances.'

'I could have wished it otherwise,' she said. What do *you* think has happened?'

'The Sepulchre Society.'

'No, no, no,' Gwen held up her hand. 'That's nonsense. That's bad melodrama. What's *really* happened to Jacquie?'

He took her hand and held it. 'I don't know,' he said. 'All I know is that she's got great colleagues. They won't stop looking until they find her.'

'And you, Peter Maxwell,' she frowned at him. 'You must know from Jacquie that she and I are not ... close. Never have been, really. Not, anyway, since her father died. But if anything were to happen...' She looked up at him sharply, correcting herself, keeping it all in check. 'You'll look for her too, won't you?'

Peter Maxwell along with fifteen-sixteenths of the county's teaching profession always prayed for five-day weekends and two-day weeks. It was pie in the sky of course, all part of that never-never land where marking was unheard of and children ran merrily into school shouting 'Yippee, the term is here!' But this weekend, Maxwell wanted to last for ever, just to give him a chance to find the little girl lost. That was three of them gone now – in order of disappearance: Annette Choker, Alison McCormick, Jacquie Carpenter. Three little maids who, all unwary, got mixed up with a Saxon cemetery. Well, it didn't scan very well, but there was more than a modicum of truth behind it.

Maxwell prowled Leighford that Sunday afternoon, wheeling Surrey up and down the High Street, down the back doubles, along the Front. This was pointless, he realized for the umpteenth time, as various kids waved to him for the umpteenth time. Was this it, some of them wondered? Had Mad Max at last literally earned his nickname? He even toyed with nipping into the Ladies by the adventure playground, but discretion and probable arrest were the better part of valour.

At night, like most of the south coast, Leighford became another place. Girls from Year Nine slunk past him into the shrubbery with older lads, tottering on Fuck-Me shoes, with jewellery glittering in their navels. Lads whom Maxwell used to teach argued with each other outside the Taj Mahal Curry House. One of them chucked up in the gutter.

'Evening, Mr Maxwell.'

The Head of Sixth Form spun round. He wasn't really in the mood for social chitchat, even if it was with a boy he used to teach. Except it wasn't a boy he used to teach. Mad Max prided himself on his ability to put names to faces and this young man was a stranger.

'Dave Garstang, Leighford CID.'

Maxwell waited for the flash of the warrant card. 'Sorry,' Garstang sensed it. 'I'm off-duty.'

'Do I know you?' Maxwell asked.

'No,' the young man said. 'But I know you.'

'That could be scary,' Maxwell said.

'What are you doing, Mr Maxwell?' Garstang asked. 'Having a night out?'

'You might say that,' the Head of Sixth Form nodded. 'You?'

'Much the same,' Garstang said and they began to wander down the High Street. 'You're looking for her, aren't you?'

Maxwell stopped. 'You might say that too,' he said. 'You?'

'Much the same,' Garstang said and the two men, strangers till now, laughed out loud, exhausted, worried. 'Can I buy you a drink?'

'No, you can't,' Maxwell slapped the man on the shoulder. 'Let me buy you one.'

The Vine was enough off the beaten track of under-age drinkers for neither Maxwell nor Garstang to be constantly on their guard against fourteen-year-olds at the bar. The carpet had a repellent yellow and red swirl and the jukebox had seen decidedly better days. At least, there was no live music tonight – the Yawning Hippos having been lured down to the Isle of Wight Festival for a weekend of birds, booze and extortionate ferry prices. The low, grunting microphoned questions of the Exciting Quiz Nite were not grating enough to be a nuisance.

'Jacquie often talks about you,' Garstang said,

285

wiping the pint's froth from his lip. 'How's the face, by the way?'

'I'm fifty-five,' Maxwell said. 'I've got used to it now, really. Oh, I see what you mean. No, it's fine. I thought what I was doing was pretty useless, tonight.'

'Looking for Jacquie in all the old, familiar places?' Garstang asked. 'Yeah. Well, call me stupid too. Mind if I ask you something?'

'Go ahead.'

The microphone droned, 'In which year was the Crystal Palace burned down?'

'1936,' Maxwell couldn't help answering.

'Do you actually *live* with Jacquie?'

Maxwell guffawed over his Southern Comfort. 'Impudent young puppy!' he roared. Then, himself again, 'No, I don't. Too long in the tooth, I'm afraid. Anyway, she doesn't approve of my habits.'

'Really?'

'What is known as the ship of the desert?'

'A camel,' Maxwell replied softly to the Quiz Master's question. 'I can't help thinking though,' he closed to Garstang, 'that if I did, Jacquie wouldn't be missing now.'

'How so?' The lad took another sip.

'Look, Dave, is it? Dave, how much can you tell me? I mean, I know it's difficult. You're a copper. I'm a civilian...'

'We're both after the same thing,' Garstang cut him short. 'After the bastards who've got Jacquie Carpenter.'

'Right,' Maxwell nodded, smiling. It looked as though he had somebody else on the inside.

'What is the last man-made object to be seen from Outer Space?' the Quiz Master wanted to know.

'The Great Wall of China,' Maxwell told nobody in particular. 'So?'

Garstang took a deep breath. 'We think she was taken from outside her garage.'

'At the back of the block?'

'That's right.'

'When?'

'Well, that we don't know. Our best guess is as she returned home on Thursday night.'

'Two weeks after the death of David Radley.'

'You think there's a link?'

Maxwell looked up at the lad. 'Don't you?'

'I don't know,' Garstang said. 'We've been kicking ideas around for days. You get a bit punchy in the end.' Maxwell knew that feeling well enough; the hours staring at brick walls, sharpening pencils, marking exercise books.

'What level of hardness has a diamond?' the microphone grated.

'Ten,' Maxwell muttered. 'Could she have known her abductor?' Maxwell could multi-task for England.

'Why?' Garstang asked.

'If she was taken by force in the garages at the back, someone, surely, would have noticed. Not only does Jacquie pack a mean left hook, she carries Mace in her bag or pocket and her scream can shatter glass. Try it yourself. Stand in front of that garage block and yell. It'll bounce back at you from eight different directions before twenty windows fly up and you're told in no uncertain terms to eff off.'

'Christ, you're good,' Garstang whistled. 'Wanna job?'

Maxwell smiled grimly. 'With Henry Hall? No thanks. I'd rather gargle barbed wire.'

'Traditionally,' the microphone echoed, 'how many lives has a cat?'

'That,' Peter Maxwell was telling his nearly empty glass, 'no one knows.'

Chapter Sixteen

Monday. Monday. Hate that day.

'Think positive,' Ben Holton winked at Peter Maxwell as he met him in the corridor as the day after D-Day began. 'Only six weeks to go and we're out of this place for the summer hols!'

'Yippee!' muttered Maxwell, flicking his cycle clips into his pocket.

'Good God, Max,' the Head of Science looked his colleague in the face for the first time in the full light of the staff room's neon. 'Bit of a rough half-term, eh? Jacquie keeps you in line, I see.'

Maxwell looked at his man. He and Ben Holton went back more than a few years. Initiatives had come and gone. So had Heads and their Deputies. But he and Ben had grown old disgracefully together, letting all the bollocks and the educational hogwash roll over them like the breaking tide. But one more mention of Jacquie Carpenter and Mad Max would put one on him.

'Max,' Bernard Ryan was brimming with bonhomie as he hurtled into the room, memos clutched in his fist. 'Good God.'

'Yes.' Maxwell decided to stop this now. 'I walked into a door. What price this cheer, Bernard, unless you're taking a greater delight than usual in a colleague's misfortune?'

'Not at all,' Ryan bridled. 'I was about to congratulate you.'

'Really?' Maxwell said. Not another Most Difficult Teacher award from the DES? He was running out of space on his mantelpiece.

'Well, John, of course.' Ryan looked a little nonplussed but he was still smiling. 'John Fry. He's back. James is over the moon. We all are. Well done!' But Bernard Ryan couldn't quite bring himself to slap the man's back; he'd planted too many knives there in the past.

'Oh,' Maxwell said. 'It was nothing. Really.'

And he was gone, marching along the main corridor, barking at children, collecting baseball caps. He was on his way to that centre of mediocrity, the Business Studies Department.

If there was one thing guaranteed to get firmly up the still-swollen purple nose of Peter Maxwell, it was open-plan schools. In the brave days of the Seventies, when comprehensives were new and Jack was as good as his Master, the educational bashaws of Whitehall had believed that all kids were equal, they could all get to Oxbridge and they all could be taught together in one huge room; literally a jungle, in that there were no doors or walls. That was long before, of course,

Political Correctness had kicked in, when social misfits were allowed to sit in the same room as nice people, adding to the chaos. Some of the kids were worse. The business Studies Department at Leighford High was like that. Peter Maxwell had briefly met the architect of the new block when he'd come to discuss his visual conceptualisation a few years back. Funnily enough, after that meeting, he had not returned, but by then it was already too late. The money had been allocated and the bulldozers had moved in, together with trannie-playing, whistling contractors and a great deal of chipboard, specifically designed to enable sound to carry from area to area. Nobody used the word 'room' any more. It was all 'areas' and 'space' and 'circulation vectors'. Plain English died in the 1980s and no one, except Mad Max, noticed.

Nevertheless, that Monday morning, John Fry was in a room and it may as well have been a rubber one. He was sitting slumped, with his head in his hands, out of sight of the chattering classes that made up his department. None of his minions was with him. Only, sitting close and patting his arm, Sylvia Matthews, the School Nurse. She looked up as Maxwell came in, alarm etched on her face.

'John,' Maxwell said quietly. 'How's it hanging?'

'She's left me, Max,' he muttered, eyes wild with disbelief. 'Eleanor. She's gone.'

The Head of Sixth Form sat down opposite them both. 'Yes, I know,' he said. 'I'm so very sorry, John.'

Fry sat up, squaring his shoulders, focusing on Maxwell. 'Well,' he said. 'It's not the end of the world. Ben Holton's wife left him, didn't she, a couple of years back? Came crawling back, I seem to remember he said. I'll go and see Ellie. She'll be at her mother's. I rang there last night. No reply, of course. But I know she was there. Playing her usual little games.'

'Er ... John...' Maxwell looked at Sylvia, who was shaking her head.

'The devil of it is, I can't find my lesson plans for Year Ten this morning. My Schemes of Work. I didn't leave them in your office, did I, Max? The other day?'

'No, John, no,' Maxwell said. 'Look ... um ... Jenny can handle all that, can't she?'

'Jenny?' Fry looked confused.

'Jenny Clark, your Number Two,' Maxwell explained, as though it were the most natural thing in the world that Fry should have forgotten.

'Handle all what? What do you mean?'

'Well, it's just that Sylvia gave me a call a minute ago, didn't you, Sylv?'

The Nurse knew Peter Maxwell of old. Like Paul Moss and all his colleagues and kids who loved him, you didn't question, you didn't doubt; you just went with it. 'Yes,' she smiled, cheerily. 'Yes, I did.'

'There's something going round, John,' Maxwell said. 'A bug of some sort.' He closed to the man, peering into his eyes. 'Looks like you've got a touch of it, old son.'

'What are you talking about?' Fry looked more confused than ever.

'The thing of it is, it's highly contagious. Oh, Nursie and I are all right. We've both had it. But young people are particularly vulnerable; aren't they, Sylv?'

'Absolutely.' She was with him now. 'Teenagers. They're notorious. Pick up every damned infection known to man.'

And a few that aren't, Peter Maxwell mused. 'So, the bottom line, John, is that we've got to get you to a doctor, old son. Oh, not so much for you, of course. It's for the kids.'

'The kids,' Fry repeated as if their existence too, were a closed book.

'Yes,' Maxwell patted his hand. 'How about it, eh? If Sylv takes you to the hospital. Just for a check-up. Hmm?'

Fry looked at them both, from one to the other. 'Oh, all right,' he said and stood up, Sylvia with him. 'But they won't keep me long, will they?' he asked her. 'Because I've got to get in touch with Ellie.'

'No,' Maxwell patted the man's shoulder. 'No, John, they won't keep you long. Sylv – are you all right with this?'

Sylvia Matthews nodded. She'd seen it all before; not often it was true, but she knew the symptoms. She led the man out of his office and through the open-plan throng of kids, clacking away on computers. His staff, one by one, broke off from their teaching, to watch him go.

'In layman's terms, Headmaster,' Maxwell was saying, 'a nervous breakdown.'

'My God,' James Diamond sat back in his

opulent office swivel, ordered from the County Consortium only last month. Cut backs. 'But he seemed fine earlier.'

'What time was this?' his Head of Sixth Form asked.

'Just before school started. Half eight, quarter to nine.'

'You spoke to him?'

'Of course. Look, Max, I don't understand any of this. I thought you'd found him.'

Maxwell snorted, still not an altogether agreeable experience. 'The furthest I got down that road was somebody's skull in my face. It wasn't my finest hour, Headmaster.' James Diamond didn't want to go down that road either.

'So he just came back of his own accord?' Diamond was checking.

Maxwell shrugged. 'Appears that way. What did he say to you? Or you to him, for that matter?'

James Diamond wasn't given to offering his staff much in the way of hospitality, especially pains in the proverbial arse like Peter Maxwell. This morning, though, he felt bound to make an exception and crossed to the coffee percolator. 'You like it black, don't you? No sugar.'

'Close, Headmaster,' Maxwell leaned back on Diamond's settee. 'White and two. But, hey, who's counting? John Fry.'

'John Fry. Right.' Diamond poured for them both, ferreting in his fridge for the milk. 'Well, Bernard tipped me off. Saw John Fry crossing the car park on his way in.'

'Christ!' hissed Maxwell. 'He drove?'

'Possibly. I asked to see him and we had a bit of

293

a man to man, as it were.'

Hardly appropriate in the circumstances, Maxwell thought. But he was a public schoolboy and public schoolboys didn't bitch. Much. Diamond got back behind his desk, where he had a barrier against the wickedness of the world, where he felt safe. 'I asked John outright where he'd been. He said he'd been away for a few days. Half-term break and so on. All very vague.'

'What about Eleanor?'

'Well, quite,' Diamond sighed. 'I didn't know how to handle that at first. He didn't mention her and I felt I had to say something. I offered him my condolences.'

'Which he didn't accept?'

'No. In fact, he got a bit shirty, saying it was none of my damn business. Got a bit of a short fuse, hasn't he, John?'

'Do you remember his exact words, Head-master?' Maxwell asked, sipping his coffee gingerly so as not to disturb the relative composure of his lip. 'This could be important.'

Diamond frowned in concentration. 'Er ... I think I said something like I was so sorry to hear about his wife and he asked me how I knew. Well, that was rather odd, I suppose, with hindsight – and in view of what you've just told me.'

'What did you say?' It was like pulling teeth.

'I said I'd read it in the *Advertiser*. He was not pleased.'

'Of course he wasn't,' Maxwell muttered. 'As far as he's concerned, Eleanor has left him. Gone back to mother. Not even the *Advertiser* carries stories like that. Unless you're a film star, rock legend or frocked priest, of course, in which case it's all fair game.'

'Max...' Diamond was struggling to come to terms with all of this. 'You've been in teaching now how long?'

Maxwell made a big thing about counting on his fingers. 'Three hundred and twenty-eight years,' he said. Diamond, of course, didn't crack so much as a smile. 'Ah,' the Head of Sixth Form wound him up still further, 'but think of the Enhancement.'

'The point I'm making,' the over-promoted pedant went on, 'is that I've never actually witnessed this before. A full-blown nervous breakdown, I mean. Oh, you hear stories, of course. There was that physics teacher found wandering stark naked in his labs a few years back, at that school on the Isle of Wight. People who can't face coming in, getting clammy palms and palpitations at the door, that sort of thing. But this ... it's quite ... well, scary in an odd sort of way.'

'Zen,' agreed Maxwell. 'Unreal. You didn't get round to Annette Choker, I suppose, in your little chat?'

'No,' Diamond shook himself free of it. 'No, John began rabbiting about setting strategies. Ironically, it was the first bit of the conversation I actually understood. So, Bernard's optimism was misplaced.'

'It was,' Maxwell left his coffee. 'Because now, you'll have to find yourself a new Head of Business Studies. It's going to be a bitch, isn't it?'

Sylvia Matthews closed her eyes as she let her

head rest against her chair back. Tommy Wiseborough had hobbled away with his bad knee that she'd redressed. Alex Brannon had taken her tablets under supervision and Jade Granger had come to moan about her mum, her period pains and that fucking horrible Mr Ryan. Just another Monday.

A strained, purple face appeared round the door. 'Nurse! Nurse! I've got this facial problem.'

'You certainly have,' Sylvia the tired woman immediately switched to Nurse Matthews, the competent carer. 'Sit down, Max, for Christ's sake. It was hardly the moment to talk earlier, but what the hell happened to you?'

'That's not important now,' he aped the worst line from the worst movie he'd ever seen. 'Tell me about John Fry.'

She closed the door to her dingy little office, as Maxwell perched on the edge of her trolley-bed. He wasn't certain about this – God knew what examples of humanity had sprawled here before him. He knew, in his heart of hearts, that you couldn't catch things from toilet seats. But trolley-beds in school sick bays? Well, you couldn't be too careful.

'Where do I start?' she asked. 'Jenny Clark gave me a call shortly after nine. She was worried about John; he was behaving irrationally.'

'I'm amazed she could tell.'

'Max!' Sylvia growled. 'Don't come the cynic with me. You're as concerned as the rest of us.'

'More,' he said. 'Jacquie's missing.'

'What?' Sylvia's eyes were wide.

'DCI Hall doesn't know where she is. Nor does

her mother.'

'Max,' she held both his hands, her heart going out to him. 'My God, this is awful. Here I am, burbling on about John Fry, and you ... what are you even *doing* here? Go home, for God's sake. There may be news.'

'I'm not going to sit by the phone like some ineffectual old biddie,' Maxwell snapped. Sylvia knew it was fear talking. 'I'd rather be here, doing something. Besides, I can't shake the idea that John Fry has something to do with Jacquie's disappearance.'

'Did Hall say anything?' Sylvia asked. 'I mean, is there a ransom note or something?'

'Nothing.' Maxwell shook his head. 'Nothing as of yesterday, anyway. Hall agreed to keep me in the loop. He'll let me know if anything breaks. Annette Choker's not back, I suppose?'

'Don't think so,' Sylvia sat next to Maxwell on the low bed. 'I did raise her with John, when I took him to the hospital, I mean.'

'You did?' Maxwell looked up. 'What did he say?'

'Well, I'm not proud of myself, Max,' the Nurse said, 'but it's totally obvious that John has no idea that Eleanor's dead. He was talking non-stop in the car. A lot of it was rambling, repetitious. It's funny. He seemed quite rational at first, when Jenny called me over, but by the time we'd got to Leighford General, he was a basket case. He told me he'd had a few days away. Needed a break. Said it was all getting a bit on top of him.'

Maxwell nodded grimly. 'Business Studies'll do that to you, every time.'

'No, no,' Sylvia was adamant, shaking her head. 'No, whatever John's problem is, it's not school. At least, not directly.'

'Meaning?'

'He said...' Sylvia was trying hard to remember. 'He said he'd come home to find the house empty and Eleanor gone. He knew at once what had happened, that she'd left him.'

'Did he say why he thought she'd left him?' Maxwell asked.

'Oh, yes,' Sylvia said. 'It was because of the girl.'

'Annette Choker,' Maxwell nodded. It all fitted.

'No,' Sylvia corrected him. 'No, I don't think so, Max. I asked him about Annette. Oh, perhaps I shouldn't ... after all, the man has just lost his wife, whether he's aware of it or not.'

'What did he say?'

Sylvia looked at Maxwell. 'He said "She's a good girl. She won't let us down".'

Maxwell looked at Sylvia.

'Us, Max?' Sylvia said. 'What's all that about? I suppose he was just confused, out of it.'

'Yes,' muttered Maxwell. 'Yes, I suppose he was.'

'Hello!'

No answer.

'Hello, the Museum!'

'Sorry,' a voice answered somewhere to the rear of the Victorian chemist's shop front. 'Ah. Hello, Max. Good God!' He was staring at the man's face.

'Yes, yes.' Maxwell shook the man's hand. He'd

298

been hearing similar outcries all day. 'That goes without saying. Tony, how the hell have you been?'

'Better,' the Museum curator said. 'Better than you, by the look of it.'

'Look, I know you're about to lock up...'

'Ah, the lad will do all that.' He bellowed through to the portico, 'Alan. Shut up shop, can you please? Enough is enough. I do believe...' he checked the ledger at the front desk. 'Yes, four people and a junior school today. That's probably a personal best for June. Come on through.'

Leighford Museum stood in the town square. It was one of the oldest buildings the place possessed, a merchant's pad built in the 1820s when that nice William Huskisson at the Board of Trade was reducing duties and opening up foreign commerce with assorted foreigners, which was good news for merchants in the 1820s. Tony Lyman had been Curator here for nearly four years, but he and Peter Maxwell spoke the same language and it felt as if they'd known each other all their lives.

'Southern Comfort, isn't it?' Lyman had led his visitor into his inner sanctum, a dark, stuffy room crammed with papers, charters, maps and a legendary amount of dust. It was a graveyard for anybody with allergies.

'It is,' Maxwell was impressed. 'Well remembered.'

'Oh, I haven't got any,' Lyman told him. 'I just pride myself in remembering these little things about people.'

Lyman was a little round pudding of a man,

ideally suited to working in the cramped, musty corners of a museum. He looked as though, if you could bear to look closely enough, he had mouldy bits somewhere.

'What do you remember about Alfred the Great?' Maxwell settled for tea.

'Alfred?' Lyman clattered the kettle, sliding some title deeds aside. 'Bit before my time.'

'I'm particularly interested in his death.'

'Well,' Lyman was looking for teabags. 'You're in luck. I've got a book on it. Four, to be precise.'

'That'll be the *Anglo-Saxon Chronicle*,' Maxwell lifted the brass Heavy Cavalry helmet from the chair. 'This is rather fine. Can I take it off your hands for a song? Give you a bit more room.'

Lyman took it from him with a deft movement. 'That belonged to Colonel Sir Edward Lacey, Fifth Dragoon Guards. The family used to own...'

'...Staple Hill; yes, I know. That's actually why I'm here.'

'Oh?' Lyman found a temporary home for the helmet, not altogether happy with the envious gleam in Maxwell's eye, purple and puffy though it was.

'One thing at a time,' Maxwell eased himself into the chair. 'Alfred.'

'Right. Alfred. Just dunk that, would you?' Maxwell took command of the teabags while Lyman fished about in a book case. 'Here we are,' he said. 'Which text do you want?'

'Which text have you got?'

'Oh, all of them. Um...' he flicked the pages. 'Here we go. "Here died Alfred, Aethelwulf's

300

offspring, six days before the Feast of All Hallows." As always with the *Chronicle*, of course, there's a brouhaha over the dates.'

'Really?'

'The Winchester Manuscript says 901, whereas it was actually 899. The Peterborough and Worcester texts give October 26, which would be right, and they say "and he held the kingdom healfum laes ?e xxx wintra ... " That's 28 and a half years to commoners like thee and me, Max.'

'Thank you for that,' Maxwell wasn't up to smiling for all sorts of reasons; nor with wrestling with the complexities of Old English. 'Where was he buried?'

'Winchester,' Lyman told him, putting the *Chronicle* back. 'Old Minster.'

'Does it say so there?' Maxwell passed his cup to the man.

'No. Thanks. In fact it's very sparse on the passing of Alfred, bearing in mind how important the man was. National hero, saving our bacon from the Danes ... oh, that's rather good, isn't it?'

Is it? Maxwell wasn't really listening. 'So how do we know?' If he was nothing else, Peter Maxwell was consistent.

'Asser,' Lyman told him. 'The king's biographer.'

'But Asser wrote in 893,' Maxwell said. 'Six years before Alfred's death. Anyway, come in for a bit of flak, hasn't he, old Asser, authenticity-wise?'

'Well, yes,' Lyman had to admit. 'Yes, I suppose he has, but... Look, Max, what's all this about? I didn't think you taught this stuff at Leighford High.'

301

'Oh, we don't,' Maxwell told him. 'So, where was Alfred buried?'

Lyman had planned to sit down and have a well-earned cup of tea. Tottingleigh Juniors had been little short of a nightmare that afternoon. Now, however, Peter Maxwell had got right up his nose, setting him a challenge, questioning his authority. Did he know what it was like running a museum? Did he? Did he? 'I've got a copy of his will somewhere,' he said.

Three or four minutes ferreting through papers produced results. 'Here we are ... um ... "I, Alfred, by the grace of God and on consultation with Archbishop Aethelred and with blah ... declare how I wish to dispose of my inheritance" ... blah, blah ... "And all the booklands which I have in Kent" ... Ah, here we are ... "And there to be distributed for me and for my father and for the friends for whom he used to intercede and I intercede" ... blah, blah ... "fifty to the church in which I shall be buried"... There you are.'

'Yes?' Maxwell waited in mid-sip.

'Yes, what?'

'Which church?'

'Well,' Lyman shrugged. 'The Old Minster, Winchester.'

'Does it say so?'

'Well, no, but... Look, what is this all about, Max?'

'I'll get to that,' Maxwell promised, pinning his man with terrier-like tenacity. 'Why Winchester?'

'Well,' Lyman conceded, 'actually, there's only one reference to Alfred being there. He certainly set the place up as one of the burghs that defended Wessex. And we know it was the head-quarters of Aethelred and Cnut...'

'That's guilt by association,' Maxwell told the Curator. 'What's the reference?'

'A couple of crews from Viking ships washed up on the south coast ... er ... hang on.' He fumbled through the *Chronicle* again. 'Here we are... This is 896...'

'Three years before Alfred's death.'

'Yes. The Winchester manuscript says "They" ... that's the Viking ships ... "were then so damaged that they could not row past the land of Sussex, but there the sea cast two of them up onto land; and the men were led to Winchester to the king and he ordered them to be hanged there."'

'The land of Sussex,' Maxwell mused. 'Leighford.'

'Oh, come on, now,' Lyman laughed. 'That's stretching it a bit, all right. I'd love it to be Leighford, but it could be anywhere.'

'Could it?'

'Look, Max,' the Curator put the book back for what he hoped would be the last time. 'Everybody knows that Alfred was buried in the Old Minster in Winchester. When they opened the new one across the road in 903 his remains were removed there. And when Hyde Abbey was consecrated in 1110, they were disinterred again. There's even a plaque there, for God's sake.'

'Oh, really?' Maxwell said. 'What does it say?'

'Well, it's been a while since I've been,' Lyman was patience itself. 'But if memory serves, it's got a Latin inscription "Alfredus Rex" and the date

303

871, the year of his accession.'

'And the plaque was made...?'

'Eighteenth century.' Lyman knew exactly how Maxwell was going to demolish *this* little piece of tosh.

'Ah, yes.' The Great Man tried to beam. 'That'll be the century in which they said Alfred burnt some cakes, Cnut tried to stop the incoming tide and little "Noll" Cromwell had a punch-up with the Prince of Wales, later Charles I. Oh, and Boudicca was really called Boadicea and built Stonehenge. We're talking Fairyland here, Tony.'

'Yes, all right,' Lyman couldn't leave it there, 'but...'

Maxwell interrupted, in full flow now. 'Let's say you're right,' he said, one hand held in the air. 'Alfred dies in Winchester and is buried in the Old Minster. Count with me – that's burial one.'

'Yes.' Lyman had no idea where this was going.

'He is disinterred, according to you, four years later and buried in the New Minster. Burial two.'

'Agreed.'

'And then, a hundred and seven years later, they dig the poor bastard up again and plant him at Hyde. I make that burial three.'

'What's your point?' Lyman asked.

'Two-fold,' Maxwell said. 'Three burials leaves room for doubt as to exactly which body is being shifted. Especially with over a century intervening between the last two.'

'Well, yes...'

'And secondly,' Maxwell was stabbing the air, 'and much more importantly, how do we know where Alfred actually died? And, for that matter,

304

which church got his fifty quid.'

'Well, I suppose, technically, we don't...' Lyman had to concede.

'Let me,' Maxwell settled back with his steaming mug still in his hand, 'bring you altogether up to date with someone else altogether better known than Alfred the Great. Arthur Wimble.'

'Who?'

'Precisely. Scion of the Metal Detectives' Society and all-round snooper. Says he knows you.'

'Oh, God, yes. Wimble. What about him?'

'Has he brought any finds to the Museum? Recently, I mean?'

Lyman shook his head. 'I don't think so,' he said. 'Why?'

'Nothing Saxon?'

'No. We've had Professor Fraser here a couple of times, that Latymer chap. You were here washing pots last week, I understand – sorry I missed you. Conservancy symposium at the University of Bradford.'

'Bad luck,' Maxwell commiserated. 'But not Wimble?'

'No. Oh, he's often hanging around, I'll grant you, but not recently. Maxwell, will you *please* tell me what all this is about?'

'What if...' Maxwell was thinking aloud really. 'What if someone – an archaeologist; professional, amateur; trained, lucky – I don't know yet. What if someone found an undisturbed grave? A Christian burial of a late ninth century king of Wessex, complete with body and some absolutely foolproof provenance?'

'You're talking Alfred,' Lyman nodded.

'In the grave, yes,' Maxwell said. 'And the amateur, lucky archaeologist who found it, Arthur Wimble. What, in your estimation, would such a grave be worth?'

'Name your price,' Lyman shrugged. 'If the grave contained artefacts like the Alfred jewel, crown, sword, armour, it would be fabulously valuable.'

'It would contain grave goods like that? A Christian burial?'

'Sure. There are other examples. Whoever was buried in the ship at Sutton Hoo – probably Raedwald – had two apostle spoons with him, with the effigies of saints Peter and Paul. Are you seriously trying to tell me that Alfred the Great, King of Wessex, was buried at Leighford?'

'Before I answer that, Tony,' Maxwell said, 'let me ask you one more. What would such a find be worth to the archaeologist, professional this time, who excavated it and presented their findings to the world?'

Lyman laughed. 'He'd be another Schliemann with Troy, Carter with Tutankhamun. There'd sure as hell be a plaque put up to them. It would absolutely make him.'

'The bubble reputation,' Maxwell mused.

'So, in answer to my question?' Lyman persisted.

'Am I trying to tell you that Alfred the Great, King of Wessex, was buried at Leighford?' Maxwell smiled. 'No, Tony, I'm not. But somebody is.'

And he thanked the curator for the tea, eyeing the glittering, plumed helmet for one last time before sweeping along the corridor in his way out, past the dull brown duster coat, with its classic shoulder cape and split up the back, hanging on its hook.

She'd worked out his routine. He'd taken her watch, her shoelaces, her pen. Anything she could have used to harm herself with or to record the passage of time. Her eyes had grown used, at last, to her surroundings. She knew she was in a cellar, maybe ten or twelve feet square. She could reach nearly every corner at the end of the chain that held her. He had come to visit twice in the time she'd been here. She'd heard his footfalls approaching, hollow, metallic. Stairs. Whoever had taken her, outside her own garage, with the chloroform pad over her face, was walking down an iron spiral staircase. The last time he'd come he'd pulled the chain from behind, yanking her backwards against his legs and he'd ripped off the duct tape.

'Ssh!' was all he'd said in the darkness and she was so grateful to be able to breathe properly again that she did as she was told. He left her a plate of food and a tumbler of water. It smelt like cottage pie and tasted like nothing on earth. Her hands were still pinned in front of her, bound together and she had to eat with her fingers. But it *was* food and she had to eat.

The water she gulped down; then, realizing it would have to last her for hours until his next visit, she saved the rest, nudging it carefully against the damp, plastered wall so that she didn't spill it.

She reckoned it was seven hours between his visits. She assumed it was a man, but she couldn't be sure. He was strong, that she knew. Wore trousers and smelt odd. But the whole place smelt odd, dank, dead.

And despite herself, she felt the tears trickle the length of her cheeks and drip and splash onto her neck. Was it night? Was it day? Up there, above the ground, traffic roared, birds sang. People went about their daily business, unaware of her. But two men, at least, would know. And they'd be looking. One was a bland bastard with badly developed smiling muscles and blank glasses, a copper's copper. The other was an infuriating, loveable wreck of a man, an unmade bed with the strength of ten. 'Mixing metaphors again, Woman Policeman?' she heard him say and she sobbed out loud.

'Oh, Max,' she mumbled under the tape. 'Where are you?'

Chapter Seventeen

The lights in the main tent threw lurid shadows out onto the graves on Staple Hill. They were in sharp relief now, with the new security lights installed by Cahill and Lieberman blinding Peter Maxwell as he parked White Surrey and clambered over the gate.

From somewhere in the woods a barn owl swept silent and ghostly over the slope that arced, black and lonely, down to the valley of the Leigh and the sea beyond it. For a moment, Maxwell stood there, looking out at the silvered ridges of the Channel. He saw, with his historian's imagination, the wrecks of two Viking ships washed up on the Shingle, their dragon prows high in the water, their timbers and splintered oars scattered like matchwood at the water's edge. And on the ridge where he stood, arms folded, cloaked and helmeted, the king himself, Alfred of Wessex. 'One day,' he imagined Alfred saying to his thegns at his elbow, 'One day, bury me here. In that little ash grove. Build me a church on this ridge. Away from the cares of state. Away from the clash and the slaughters. Here, within a walk of the sea.'

'Evening, Douglas.'

'Jesus!' the geophysicist was half out of his seat as Maxwell popped his head around the tent flap. 'God, Max. I didn't hear you arrive.'

'So much for the high-tech surveillance gear, then.' Maxwell pulled off his cap and found a seat somewhere among the debris, 'that's what a bike'll do for you every time.'

'Oh, that's the professor's idea of saving our lives. You've just proved him wrong.'

'Indeed,' Maxwell said. 'If I'd been a fully paid-up member of the Sepulchre Society of Sussex...'

'Quite. Any news?'

'I was hoping you'd have some.'

'Well, for the last day, all this gear's been put in with contractors coming out of our ears, but the professor told us today we've been given our notice to quit. Week Saturday.'

309

'Can you finish in that time?'

'If he lets us tackle the ash grove tomorrow, yes, I think so.'

'You think he won't?'

Russell shrugged. 'David didn't.'

'Tell me about David,' Maxwell said, settling himself down.

'I already have,' the geophysicist said.

'Tell me again,' Maxwell said. 'You can't have said it all.'

'I told you,' Russell explained. 'I didn't know him well.'

'But you didn't like him.' It was not a question; it was a statement.

Russell looked at the man, blinking in the lamp light. 'Who told you that?'

'You did,' Maxwell said. 'By your body language.'

'Body language?' Russell scoffed.

'Don't knock it,' Maxwell warned. 'You use it all the time. I never saw you in Radley's company; not while Radley was alive, anyway. So I don't know how you behaved then. But I know how you behave now. Whenever I mention him, whenever *anyone* does, your back straightens, your eyes dip, always to the left...'

'Are you saying I killed him?' Russell was staring at the man.

'Not at all,' Maxwell assured him, hands spread on the table in front of him. 'Are *you* saying you did?'

'Of course not,' Russell shouted.

'But you didn't like him.'

'All right,' Russell snapped. 'No, I didn't like

him. Happy now?'

'I merely wondered why,' Maxwell said, 'when everybody else did.'

Russell looked at his man, 'It's none of your damned business,' he growled.

'Oh, I think it is,' Maxwell closed to him. 'You see, the woman I love has been kidnapped by whoever killed David Radley. That sort of makes it my business, don't you think?'

'I'm sorry,' Russell's tone softened. 'I didn't know.'

'No, I don't suppose you did,' Maxwell said. 'Women aren't really your thing, are they, Douglas?'

'What do you mean?'

'When I asked you who knew you were staying at the Quinton, you said only a few people – the University. Your mother. How old are you, Douglas?'

'I'm forty-two,' Russell told him. 'What of it?'

'Forty-two.' Maxwell nodded softly. 'Telling Mummy where you are and – I quote "Miss Right hasn't come along". Am I making an assumption too far?'

'All right!' Russell snapped. 'I'm gay. All right. That hasn't been a crime for a long time now, Maxwell, whatever cheap capital you want to make out of it.'

'I'm not here to make capital out of anything, you prat!' It was Maxwell's turn to snap. 'You can have sex with your pet hamster for all I care. But if I think any of this gives you a motive for murder, than believe me, you're going down for ever. And if you've got Jacquie, then I'm not

311

inclined to bother with the expense and effort of that judge and jury bollocks! I'll hang you myself.'

Russell's face was frozen in a half smile. 'You can't scare me, Maxwell,' he shouted. 'You're a teacher, for God's sake. Civilized...'

'Oh, don't let this benign old exterior fool you, Douglas. You wouldn't, for example, like me when I'm angry.'

Russell was lost for words. There was something in the man's dark, smouldering, purple-rimmed eyes he didn't like. 'I don't know what I can tell you,' he said.

Maxwell thumped the table and several bones jumped, along with Douglas Russell. 'How about the truth?' he growled, his nose inches from that of the geophysicist.

Silence.

Maxwell leaned back. He'd got Russell in his headlights now and he wanted to keep him there. 'Did you know that David Radley had been stripped?'

'Stripped?' Russell blinked.

'Somebody either killed him bollock naked or removed his clothes post mortem, as the pathologists have it. Now, why do you suppose they did that, Douglas?'

'I really don't know.'

'Yes, you do,' Maxwell wheedled. 'Picture the scene. David Radley is not as other archaeologists. He gets his kicks off Route 66. And I bet his poor, distraught wifey knows nothing about it. So, there's David, dreeing his weird with someone of a similar persuasion – let's call him Douglas Russell – when suddenly, there's a row; tiff; call it

312

what you will. That someone – oh, we're calling him Douglas, aren't we? Douglas loses his cool over something, a lovers' spat. But it turns ugly and Douglas smashes something,' Maxwell picked up a grey femur lying on the dusty table in front of him, 'into the side of David's neck, killing him instantly. But now,' Maxwell's left index finger was in the air, 'Douglas has a problem. And it's the perennial one of murderers the wide world o'er: how to get rid of a body. Now, of course, all this depends on where David and Douglas were mutually engaged, doesn't it? His place or his place. Either way, you can't leave a body there. It raises too many awkward questions. No, the body has to be moved. And you can't just dump him naked, because that raises questions of a different sort. And that might point the finger at Douglas. So, what does Douglas do? He redresses the corpse, scattering a whole shoal of red herrings in his wake...'

'Shut up!' Russell suddenly roared, descending into great sobs that shook his shoulders. 'For God's sake, shut up.'

Maxwell relented. He'd got him now, as if he'd broken him on the rack. 'That wasn't how it was, was it, Douglas?' he said.

Eventually, the geophysicist shook his head and looked up at his inquisitor, sniffing. 'I've never been the predatory type, Max,' he said. 'All right, so the law has changed. Big deal! People's attitudes haven't. Not really. I was always brought up to believe that *that* sort of behaviour, as my mother called it, was worse than revolting. Well, we can't help how we're made.'

'You fancied David Radley?'

Russell nodded. 'It was awful,' he whispered. 'For three months, working with the man day after day, wanting to... I persuaded him to move into the Quinton. That way, I'd be able to see more of him. Oh, I knew he was married, of course. But he didn't wear a ring and he hardly ever talked about his wife. One night...'

'You tried it on,' Maxwell was ahead of him.

Russell half turned away. 'We'd both been drinking, I thought ... well, to cut a long and not very pleasant story short, he turned me down. Oh, he was kind, considerate, but absolutely adamant. Yes, Max.' Russell turned back to look the man in the face. 'David Radley was what everybody said he was – a nice guy. I didn't hate him. In the last weeks of his life, I may even have loved him, just a little. But not in the way you mean.'

Maxwell sat back, reading the man as well as he could in the eerie light of the tent, with bits of dead men for company. 'It's still a motive for murder, Douglas,' he said softly. He stood up, sliding the chair back. 'But not in my book.'

He sat with the forage cap tilted on his head, too many Southern Comforts inside him for what he'd got – a teacher's salary. Private Ryan of the Eighth Hussars was all but finished, sitting his bay with all the calm he could muster on that cold, grey October afternoon, his pipe in his free hand, his eyes watching the Fedioukine Heights for the tell-tale thunder of the guns and the wisps of battery smoke.

'Your master wasn't very pleasant to a nice man tonight, Count,' Maxwell said, not looking at the behemoth in the corner. 'Not something I'd want to repeat. But it had to be sorted.' He slammed down the uniform book he was consulting and Ryan and his horse jumped imperceptibly. 'Where is she, Count?' he whispered, fear suddenly tearing like hot iron through his chest. 'Where is she?'

DCI Henry Hall sat in his office long after midnight, staring at his own reflection in the window. He'd rung home to say he might be camping out here. Margaret Hall was used to it. She sighed and hung up. A DCI's got to do what a DCI's got to do. He'd be home when the time was right and she'd know by his tread on the gravel how it had gone.

Hall's people were in the business of overturning stones. Two policewomen were missing. No ransom notes. No ransom call. Nothing electronic. Missing, presumed dead? It had been days in both cases; Alison McCormick, Jacquie Carpenter. Even so, presumed dead – it was too early for that. You had to remain optimistic. You had to keep focused. And all day, Henry Hall had been telling himself that.

His boys and girls in blue had been out in the flame that was June all day, knocking on doors, asking questions. They'd taken the dogs to Alison's flat and to Jacquie's house, to give their keen, wet noses some scent to follow, some trail. The coppers had bashed their way through woodland, flattening ferns and grinding grass, walking in rows like the infantry Peter Maxwell knew all about. They'd opened lock-ups, crawled through sewer pipes, gone back to Professor Fraser's dig twice, checking his graves, his spoil heaps, the dark tangle of the ash grove.

And, like all coppers with a seaside beat, they'd combed the beaches, sifting the seaweed and the driftwood, coping as best they could with the appalling smell at low tide. And always, they watched the tide, as it ebbed and flowed along the coastline of King Alfred's Wessex.

Peter Maxwell had rung in sick the next day. Tuesdays could get along without him at Leighford High. Temporarily, his beloved Sixth Form had ceased to exist, melted away into that Great Absence that was Study Leave. He had assured Thingee on the school's switchboard that Paul Moss could cope without him for a day or two and Paul Moss had little option but to try to prove him right. The reason? Ah, the Great Man's old trouble; his bad back. Dierdre Lessing fumed; Bernard Ryan was not surprised. Only Sylvia Matthews understood. And, as always when it came to Peter Maxwell, Sylvia Matthews wasn't talking.

'Maxwell!' Tam Fraser was prowling his trenches, clipboard in one hand, dowsing stick in the other. 'We missed you. Back at the chalk face, I assume?'

'Sort of, professor,' Maxwell said. 'And sort of not.'

'There you go again,' the archaeologist said. 'Those damned riddles of yours. You're not

316

dressed for the chase.'

Indeed he wasn't. He was dressed in his work clothes, the tweed hat and jacket slung across Surrey's panniers, but the poncy bow tie firmly in place no matter how sticky the season. 'I'm off to the station,' he said. 'Well, two, actually. Police, then railway. But I wanted a word first.'

'With me?'

'Please.'

Fraser looked at his man. Maxwell seemed to have lost some of his sang-froid since they'd last met. At least his face seemed to be returning to what Tam Fraser presumed to be its former self.

'Come away in, then.' He led the way into the main tent, where Helen Reader sat with artefacts various and a toothbrush. 'Oh, Helen, could you give us a minute?'

'Of course.' The woman was on her feet. 'How are you, Max?'

'I'm well, Helen, thanks,' he nodded, giving her the broadest smile he could manage. The woman I love has been kidnapped, may be dead and I'm treading water in three murders, but hey, that's Africa. No – he couldn't say any of that.

'Tell me, professor,' she paused at the tent flap. 'Are we going into the ash grove tomorrow?'

'Possibly, dear lady,' he said. 'Possibly.'

The men sat down when she'd gone. 'Amateurs, eh?' Fraser scoffed. 'Oh, nothing personal, of course. Will you have a dram, Max? I don't think the sun's gonna be over the yard arm for quite a while yet, but I'm game if you are.'

'Thanks, professor,' Maxwell raised his hand. 'I'm cycling.'

'Well, what can I do for you? Did you make any headway with your journalist contact?'

'Some,' Maxwell said. 'I found Arthur Wimble.'

'Who?' Fraser was pouring himself a stiff one.

'A metal detective.'

The Scot scowled at him. 'Oh, one of those.'

'Yes and no. In terms of his metal detecting, he's a sinner turned saint.'

'Is that right? What's he got to do with us?'

'No one of that name has been to see you, here at the dig or at the Quinton, perhaps asking to join in?'

'They'd get short shrift if they did,' Fraser told him. 'Sinner turned saint or not, I won't have their kind tramping all over my site.'

'David's site.'

'Come again?'

'You said it was David Radley's site. Anything found here would be his.'

'Well, that's right. So it will be. I can't imagine David giving this Wimble character the time of day either.'

'No,' Maxwell confirmed. 'He didn't.'

'Well, there you are.'

'Which is odd, isn't it?'

'Odd?' Fraser frowned. 'In what way?'

'So few volunteers. I haven't done much in this line as you know, but I've never known so few trowels on a site. Any idea why?'

'David's choice,' Fraser shrugged. 'Everybody has their methods. You don't need 'em, to be honest, not once the heavy stuff's done. Volunteers just get in the way.'

'What do you make of this, professor?' Maxwell

318

produced a crumpled piece of paper from his back trouser pocket.

'What is it?'

'A drawing.' It was going to be a long day.

'Aye, laddie, I can see that. Not exactly Rubens. Who did it?'

'A small thing,' Maxwell bowed in his canvas chair, 'but mine own.'

'Well, well,' Fraser chuckled. 'Not even a pretty face. No, sorry, Maxwell, I shouldn't mock. You used, what, charcoal here?'

'Er ... pencil,' Maxwell corrected him.

'Should be HB,' Fraser suggested. 'You've used a shovel. Now, perhaps you'd like to tell me what it's supposed to be.'

'Well, it's a working design only,' Maxwell explained. 'Working in fact from a description given to me by the self same Arthur Wimble I mentioned a moment ago. And he only saw it briefly and in the dark.'

'You're losing me,' Fraser said, shaking his head.

'All right,' Maxwell leaned back. 'Arthur Wimble isn't quite as saintly as I may have suggested. He was on this site, exactly where I don't know, but my guess would be on the edge of the ash grove one night back in March.'

'Was he now?'

'The dig had only just started. He remembers one, perhaps two slit trenches.'

'Uh-huh,' Fraser was leaning back too, still trying to make any sense of Maxwell's drawing.

'He found a knife. Dagger. Something. This was higher up the hill, not far, I suspect, from

319

that first body David Radley found. That's in Tony Lyman's museum now, isn't it, awaiting shipment to your university?'

'I believe it is,' Fraser told him.

'Wimble also found this,' Maxwell tapped the drawing. 'It was about two feet long, made of stone or marble – he couldn't remember which – and it was carved with the letters you see there.'

Fraser fished his glasses out of his shirt pocket and held them up to his nose. 'Here lies King Alfred,' he shouted.

'Precisely.'

There was a silence, then Tam Fraser exploded with laughter. 'Man, man. I don't know who this Arthur Wimble is, but he's on a par with whoever faked the Piltdown skull.' He suddenly leaned forward, deadly serious. 'It wasn't you, was it Maxwell?' and he burst out laughing again.

'You don't buy it, then?' Maxwell asked, when the Scotsman's mirth had subsided.

'What, that Staple Hill in West Sussex is the last resting place of Alfred of Wessex? No, laddie, I do not. And if I were to go public with any hint of this, my fellow archaeologists would laugh me to scorn and rightly so. I don't know whether it's the hours toiling under the hot sun or the blow to the head you received, but whatever it is, man – go and have a nice lie down. You'll feel better in the morning.'

The campus at Petworth shimmered in the afternoon sun, green fields wobbling under the cloudless blue. Maxwell had called in to Leighford nick, to touch base, to look for comfort, however crumby. The ever-on-duty Tom Wilson had just looked up and had shaken his head.

'Nothing, Mr Maxwell,' he said, as though the man had popped in to check on his lost cat.

The Great Man didn't stay to question. The boys in blue had their methods. He had his. And he'd put his trust in Team Maxwell any day. Now, he was making his determined way up the garden path to the Archaeology Department, David Radley's name still prominent on the staff list on the wall in the admissions office. The grim-haired Hazel Twigg looked up at him as he arrived, breath in fist, at Reception. He held something brown and sticky in his left hand.

'Mr Maxwell,' she said. 'What's this?'

'It's a stick,' he answered her. 'More precisely, a twig.'

Her face said it all. She glanced across her office to where her colleagues were all trying desperately hard to mind anybody's business but hers.

'I'm sorry' she said tartly. 'You'll have to be more explicit.'

'Here?' he said. 'Wouldn't you prefer somewhere else?'

She hesitated for a moment. Then she lifted the counter and let him through. He followed her through double doors and along a maze of corridors until they came to what appeared to be a rest room of sorts. There were soft chairs all around the walls. It was deserted. Neither of them sat down.

'I'm not really in the mood for cryptic nonsense,' she turned on him. 'I have lost the woman

I love.'

'So have I,' he snapped back. 'Careless of us both, isn't it? The difference is that, at the moment, I may still be able to get mine back.'

Hazel looked flustered. What are you talking about?' she asked.

'Did Professor Fraser tell you about the skull?' He was asking the questions.

'Skull?' she repeated. 'What skull?'

'The one you sent to the Quinton.' He was at full throttle now. 'The one you placed so carefully on Fraser's bed, its mouth propped open with this – or at least something like it. A twig – your calling card, Ms Twigg. One piece of arrogance too far, I believe.'

She was staring at him, her mouth open. 'You're mad,' she whispered. 'Raving mad.'

'Hazel, I wonder if...' Both of them spun round at the sound of a voice. An attractive young woman stood there, her dress as black as her short-cropped hair. 'Oh, I'm sorry, I didn't realize you were busy.'

'Um ... that's all right.' Hazel Twigg was the first to find her composure. 'Mr Maxwell, I'd like you to meet Mrs Susan Radley.'

They walked together along the line of the river where the horse chestnuts gave the shade. Susan Radley barely reached Maxwell's shoulder as she wandered beside him. It reminded him, for a moment, of a long, long time ago, when he walked with the girl he loved, to Grantchester along the Cam, fancying for a moment, along with Rupert Brooke, that his ghostly lordship still swam the pool below the mill there. The sweet, unforgettable river smell...

'David lost count of the students who've had to be fished out of there.' She saw his eyes trained on the brown eddies of the water, its ripples glittering in the afternoon sun.

'Yes, I'm sure,' he said. He glanced back across the fields to where the tractor belched black, slicing the grass behind it and sending a fine green spray of allergies into the air. 'You know, I've made a fool of myself in universities before. But never quite so glaringly as I did in there.'

'Don't reproach yourself, Mr Maxwell,' she said. 'I know the pressure you're under.'

Maxwell looked at her. He'd talked to widows before, women suddenly alone, having to cope in a world of one where once there had been two. He recognized the courage, the determination and the hopelessness behind those bright eyes.

'It's good of you to take me out,' she said. 'I needed the fresh air.'

'No, no,' he held up both hands. 'It is I who should be thanking you. That's Southern Rail, for you, you see. I had too much time on my way here, for reflection. I'd half-convinced myself that Hazel Twigg was a murderess. Quite how a woman of five foot two was supposed to hoist...'

'A six foot husband?' she finished the sentence for him. 'Yes,' she smiled for the first time. 'It was a bit unlikely.'

'You know,' he said, 'David was a lucky man. You really are an extraordinary woman.'

'No.' She shook her head and carried on walking. 'No, I'm not. I'm carrying on with my life as best I can, but it's not easy. Do you know, today is the fourth time I've tried to go through David's things in his study. Everything has such associations, doesn't it? Books, finds, silly mementoes.'

'No.' he shook his head. 'Not silly. I lost my wife and child.'

'Oh, no.' she stopped suddenly. 'Oh, Mr Maxwell, I'm so sorry.'

'Oh, it was all a long time ago,' he said. 'But I'm afraid the bad news is you never forget.'

'Nor would I want to,' she said, holding her head high. 'The years with David were the best of my life.'

'Tell me, Mrs Radley, did David ... talk to you about the dig?'

'At Leighford? Of course.'

'How did he get involved? Nearest Archaeology Department?'

'Not exactly,' she told him. 'It was more complicated than that. He was approached by someone, another archaeologist, who thought there was something pretty special about Staple Hill.'

'Really? What was special?'

She looked at him. 'You're an historian, I understand, Mr Maxwell?'

'That's right,' he said. 'Of sorts.'

'Saxon expert?'

'Lord no. I'm just assistant to the assistant pot-washer at the dig.'

'David ... David thought there may be some connection with King Alfred – Alfred the Great.'

It was his turn to stop walking. 'What?' he said.

'What connection?'

She shook her head. 'Now, that he wouldn't be drawn on. Said he needed more evidence. He was a careful man, Mr Maxwell, my David. Some people said he was a genius. And Professors of Archaeology geniuses or not, do not stick their necks out without hard evidence.'

Peter Maxwell looked at her. Her husband had stuck his neck out all right. In the wrong place, at the wrong time.

'Mr Maxwell,' she said. 'Do you believe in fate?'

'Fate?' he chuckled. 'With its fickle finger... It's difficult not to believe in it sometimes.'

'I do,' she said, folding her arms and frowning. 'I do absolutely. And I had a bad feeling about Staple Hill. David took me there once, in the early stages three months ago. I didn't like it. I didn't want him to take it on.'

'Can you explain why?' he asked.

She shook her head. 'Oh, you'll call it a silly female thing.'

Now he was shaking his head. 'No, I won't,' he said. 'Really.'

'The day after David ... was found, I had a dream. The doctor had given me something ... sedatives or whatever. Mum and Dad were marvellous as always, on hand to do all they could. But I had this dream. I was standing on Staple Hill, but there was no dig. No trench. No spoil heap. It was as though ... as though I was back in time, to the Hill as it was centuries ago. It was night. I remember the wind in the trees, the distant rush of the sea. It was all so vivid. I saw men, horsemen, in helmets and mail. They were carrying something I couldn't make out at first. Then I saw it was a body, wrapped in a shroud.' She looked deep into his dark, sad eyes with dark, sad eyes of her own. 'It was David's body, Mr Maxwell. They were burying him in the ash grove... It was the sedatives, I suppose.'

He nodded because, astonishingly for Peter Maxwell, he had no words to say.

'Then, as they were laying him in the ground, I saw it. A wolf, a grey wolf, fast, proud, wild. He loped out of the ash grove and made for the high ground. It was the wolf. The wolf, I knew, had killed David.'

'"Beware the wolf,"' Maxwell quoted, '"the grey Heath-stalker."'

'That's right,' her eyes widened. 'Do you know it, Mr Maxwell?'

'I know of it,' he told her. 'It was an anonymous message left on the answerphone of my local paper at Leighford. What's it from?'

She shrugged. 'That's just it. I don't know. David was always quoting it, but I can't remember the source.'

She turned to walk on. 'It was you, wasn't it?' he asked. She stopped, staring into the darkness of the river. '*You* left the message on the *Advertiser*'s answerphone.'

For what seemed a long time she didn't move. Only the river breeze blew her soft hair from her lovely, oval face. 'Yes,' she said softly. 'Immediately after David died, I wasn't thinking rationally. I don't know why, but I didn't trust the police to get their job done. That was silly.'

'DS Toogood spoke to you?'

'Yes,' she said. 'Yes, I believe that was his name.'

'And you told him about the wolf?'

She nodded. 'My dad was a journalist,' she said. 'Fleet Street, nearly thirty years. He was all for getting involved himself, but his heart... He doesn't get out much any more. He suggested I contact the *Advertiser*. What possessed me to leave that silly, cryptic nonsense, I can't imagine.'

'Mrs Radley,' Maxwell said to her. 'Susan. I want to ask you one more question. And I want you to be absolutely sure about the answer you give. All right?'

She nodded.

'The archaeologist, the one who persuaded David to take on the dig at Leighford; who was it?'

'Oh, that's easy,' she said. 'It was Derek. Derek Latymer.'

Chapter Eighteen

Hove CID had checked all the DIY and hardware stores in the area. The rope used to hang Sam Welland was bog standard – it could have come from anywhere.

Leighford CID were working on David Radley's clothes. The last person who admitted seeing him alive was Douglas Russell when the soon to be dead man had taken the phone call at the dig. And he had given his best description to DC Steve Holland, desperately trying to fill the infuriating little gaps in a man's last day. Gone were the Gucci loafers, the Cotton Traders slacks, the Millett's shirt. And gone where? They were not, certainly, at Room 13, the Quinton. Neither were they at Radley's house. Nor in his office at the university. His attic, his cellar, his dustbins, even the remains of a bonfire in his garden had been checked and rechecked; West Sussex's finest going through their paces with meticulous care.

What of the emperor's new clothes, the ones his murderer had so thoughtfully provided for him? Nothing out of the ordinary. The shirt, the trousers, the shoes, the underwear – it was all middle of the road high street stuff. And the boys and girls in blue who trudged from Next to Top Man to Matalan all drew a blank. Yes, they had sold dozens of those, but when and to whom? The till rolls alone could take months.

That afternoon was broken by the rumble of intermittent thunder, as though the gods themselves were angry that no progress had been made. It point-blank refused to rain however. Just great grey banks of cloud forming thunderheads that never developed, except perhaps far out to sea. The grass and the leaves took on an unnatural greenness at the edge of Tam Fraser's dig and Helen Reader felt twitchy from her toes to her trowel-hand. Something was going to happen. And it would happen soon.

John Fry roamed the special room they'd put him in, arms folded, eyes to the ground. He ignored the view out onto the sloping lawns, the trees bright and luminous against the angry grey of the sky. He had to plan lessons for God's sake and get home to see if Ellie had come back yet. There was just so much to do. He didn't register the bars at the windows, the white coated nurses watching him through a grille in the door. And even as they'd wheeled him past it in his dressing gown and slippers, he hadn't noticed the sign that read Psychiatric Department, Leighford Hospital. It was difficult for the watchers to know where John Fry was really; but he sure as hell wasn't here.

Dave Garstang was back in the High Street as they closed the shops. He'd been working the town all day, officially checking the clothing that the body of David Radley had been dressed in. But all the time he was actually looking for Jacquie. Alison McCormick was on his mind too, but it was Jacquie whose face he saw, whose voice he heard, whose perfume wafted past him occasionally on the wind. He'd walked this way already and had bumped into Peter Maxwell, on an equally futile quest. But surely, he reasoned, somewhere, somehow, something had to crack.

He watched them slide back the summer awnings and drop the mesh behind the glass and go home, the stolid, dependable shop-keepers of Leighford. They'd have their tea and watch the telly and maybe nip out to the pub for a pint and a game of pool. It would be hours before dark when an altogether less stolid and dependable coterie would be on the streets – the lawless kids who, God help us all, were to be society's future.

He wouldn't go home just yet. Maybe grab a half at the White Ferret, a few bar snacks; see what came up. There was no Mrs Garstang to wait up for him. Two of his colleagues were missing, a third was dead. Maybe, tonight would be payback time.

Margaret Hall knew all the signs. The last minute change of plan, the phone call in the dead of night, the half-eaten plateful pushed quietly away. The boys had grown up with this. It was just dad and he was a copper and sometimes, it all got a bit much for him. And he'd been there for them when he could, kicking a football around, exploring rock-pools, sitting quietly petrified on death-defying rides in Disneyland, Paris.

That night was no exception. Henry had rung her at something past eight. There were complications and he didn't know when etcetera, etcetera. She told him she loved him and plated up his dinner ready for the microwave and sat in the conservatory with her sewing. Somehow, she didn't feel like eating either.

Mad Max was back in town as television stations all over the country reached the watershed and the nightly effing and blinding began. He was hot and sticky and tired and the electrical storm that had swept across the campus at Petworth had left him feeling oddly on edge. He needed to get to the Quinton and fast, but the taxi rank outside the station was empty. He waited for a while, prowling like a caged panther. He toyed with ringing for a cab, but that would probably take longer than if he hoofed it. So off he went. He took the slope of Tavistock Street at a dead run, until he felt his legs buckle and his lungs feel like lead. He'd often read about 'the wall', the impassable point that long-distance runners reach after miles on the road. And he'd reached it now, just short of the Asda Superstore where the road bends.

He was still sagging here, holding the brick-work with one hand and the stitch in his side with the other, when he saw them, clattering round the corner in their Fuck-Me shoes. His eyes narrowed against the glare of the headlights hurtling towards him, then swinging away as the traffic made the turn. Somehow he hauled him-self upright and continued his trot, less focused now, more splay-footed. His throat was tight and his back in half and he realized that his shoes on the pavement would attract too much attention. So he slowed down, grateful for the reason.

The two girls were ahead of him as he reached the High Street, laughing and chattering as they went. One of them stopped to look in a shop window, pointing out something to her friend, their young faces lit by the tawdry display. Max-well dodged sideways, behind the bus stop near the Town Hall. They were making for Winchelsea Street and that could only mean one of two destinations – the Baptist Church or Dante's Nightclub. Tough call.

Peter Maxwell remembered when Dante's had been the Seamen's Mission, but perhaps there were just too many bad jokes about that and they closed it down. Or perhaps there weren't any seamen any more, with or without a mission. Or perhaps mission statements had all been hijacked by comprehensive schools. The permutations were endless.

The girls had been swallowed up by the blaring music and the flashing lights before he could get there. Shit! Even so, he *had* to talk to them. He was Mad Max, for God's sake and the bouncers on the door had room temperature IQs at best. He ripped off his bow tie, stashed his tweed cap into his pocket and sauntered up the steps with the dwindling panache still at his disposal.

'ID, granddad,' one of the guardians of immorality stopped him with a hand on his chest. The lad was chewing gum with a monotonous vigour and the neon lights were bouncing off his shaven head. Looking at them both, like gargoyles on the neo-Gothic door, it seemed for all the world as if George and Julian had pupped.

Maxwell flashed a tenner which disappeared immediately into the lad's inside pocket. The doors of Dante's opened and Maxwell stumbled into the Abyss.

'Dirty ol' bastard,' the gum chewer muttered to his mate.

'You know who that was, dontchya?' his mate asked.

The gum chewer shook his head.

'Only Mad Max from up at the school!'

'Never!' the gum chewer was nineteen. He must be getting old.

'Dirty ol' bastard,' they chorused.

The dirty old bastard found himself clinging

onto a rail that went downwards. He couldn't see the steps under his feet for the fug and the dry ice and the writhing couples draped over each other and the banisters. The music wasn't music at all – it was a wall of sound, crushing him, driving him back. The bass thumped in his chest and his head and the whole room seemed to swirl in a riot of smoke and colour and strange, indefinable smells.

It was Undead Night, according to the posters stuck badly on the building's frontage. But in fact, had Maxwell been a regular, he wouldn't have noticed much difference. Weird people with dyed black hair slid past him, like latter day Alice Coopers, hinged metal on their fingers and lips, with ears like sieves. One or two of them writhed past him, quietly impressed that such an old geezer should have gone to the lengths of making up. He hadn't *quite* got it right. It was Beaten Up Night last week; perhaps he'd got his dates wrong. But no one who recognized him could believe that. This was Mad Max. He *never* got his dates wrong.

'Wanna dance, Mr Maxwell?' a tall Goth sidled up to him, chains dangling from the most unlikely places. She jutted her nipple-rings at him in some sort of ritualistic, nymphet challenge.

'Thank you, Maxine,' he shouted, somewhere vaguely near where he thought her ear might have been. 'I'm more your Military Two Step man. Did you have those at school, by the way?' he was pointing at her breasts.

'Tits, yes. Rings, no,' she screamed back.

That was quite promising. Maxwell was sorry

she hadn't applied for the sixth form; it now looked like the girl could quip for England. 'I'm looking for two 15-year-olds,' he roared, hoping the music wouldn't suddenly stop in the middle of that sentence.

'Taking a bit of a chance, aren't you?' Maxine shouted. 'You being a teacher an' all.'

'No, no,' he found he could almost smile now. 'It's nothing like that. Tell me, Maxine,' instinctively his arms came up in a reasonable pastiche of the Mashed Potato circa 1965; trouble was he couldn't get either end of the rhythm on this one, 'are you a regular here?' He thought the question a little less crap that 'do you come here often?'

Maxine's chin was bobbing about on his hairline. 'Sorta,' she yelled.

'Do you remember Mr Fry from Leighford High?'

'Wanker in Business Studies? Yeah.'

'Have you,' he ducked backwards as her chains threatened to garrotte him. 'Have you ever seen him here?'

'Nah.' Her head thrashed violently from side to side as she closed and lashed out with a leg that would look good on Jonah Lomu. 'He's married, ain't he?'

'Not any more,' Maxwell told her.

'No, that's right.' Maxine was bending over now, her long black hair a mask over her face. She looked like Cousin It from the Addams Family. 'Wife topped herself, didn't she? He's knocking off that stuck-up copper, ain't he? What a wanker!'

'Is he?' Maxwell had lost all sense of rhythm

334

now and just stood there.

'Gotta get with the beat, Mr M.,' she shrieked.

But Mr M. had seen his targets as well as the light and he bowed before Maxine before taking her hand in his and kissing it tenderly. 'You've made an old man very happy, Maxine,' he said. 'I'll be sure to book you later for the Teacher's Excuse Me,' and he was gone into the swaying, lurching crowd as the lights flashed green and yellow and the dry ice swirled.

'Ladies,' Maxwell sat himself down on the polished oak bench, thrusting out his hip so that the girls skittered sideways, to be wedged against an Inbred with the bulk of a JCB on one side and Mad Max on the other. 'Michaela,' he found himself able to wink at her. 'Always a pleasure. And, of course, and at last, Annette Choker.' His smile froze as he stared the girl down. 'How the hell have you been?' he asked. 'Not to mention where.'

'Fuck off!' Michaela screamed at him above the music. 'I'll tell. I'll say you were hitting on us.'

'What a very silly American phrase that is!' Maxwell shouted back. 'And I'm not sure that down here anyone is going to take a blind bit of notice. Now, I want some answers from you two. The only question is – do I get them here or down at the police station?'

'We ain't done nothing!' Annette told him. She was a pretty girl, taller and more statuesque than Michaela, but her eyes were black with makeup and she smelt of cheap perfume.

'Oh, yes, you have,' Maxwell growled. 'You've lost a man his job and his mind and you're prob-

335

ably at least partially responsible for killing his wife. I'd say it was detention time all round, wouldn't you?'

Mad Max put his career on the line for the umpteenth time. He grabbed Annette Choker's wrist and dragged her upright, pulling her behind him as he made for the stairs. Shrieking hysterically, Michaela followed him, trying ineffectually to pull her friend away. Mad Max had gone mad.

'Go for it, Mr M.,' Maxine waved at him, still gyrating mindlessly in the centre of the floor. The lights flashed red and blue on their shoulders and their hair, and Maxwell pulled them both up the steps and on to the door.

''Ere, 'ere,' the gum-chewer stopped him on the threshold, holding the Great Man by the lapels. 'Was'all this?'

'What this is, Terence – nice to see you again, by the way – is your old History teacher removing two under-age girls from the permissive and unhealthy influence of what your employers laughingly call a night club. Now you and I – and your employers – know that on the grounds of underage drinking, under-age sex and the dealing of dodgy substances, I could close you all down in half an hour. So, is that the road we go down? Or do I just walk away for a quiet little chat with the girlies here?'

The gum-chewer hesitated, blinking first at Maxwell, then his oppo, then the girls. 'Oh, well, put it that way, Mr Maxwell – you have a nice night.' And he let the man's lapels drop.

'You too, Terence,' Maxwell smiled. 'Give my

336

love to your mum.' He glanced across at the oppo. 'Lewis,' he nodded. 'Got the old trouble sorted out now?' Maxwell jerked his head in the direction of the lad's genitals. It never failed.

The Head of Sixth Form had just reached the bottom of Dante's steps when a car pulled up and a head appeared out of a window. 'Can I give you a lift?' it said.

'Well, yes, Count,' Maxwell said. 'There were a lot of tears and there was a lot of screaming. And that was just Dave Garstang. I don't believe he just happened to be passing, do you?' The Great Man had slipped off his shoes and his socks and lay sprawled on his settee as Tuesday night ebbed away and Wednesday morning hovered on the Leighford horizon. 'No,' he sighed, sipping his Southern Comfort, 'I think our DC Garstang was either casing Dante's or he was following me – both perfectly legitimate pastimes, of course, if you're a copper. But you're quite right, he may well have saved my bacon.' His eyes swivelled sideways to look at the cat. The bastard hadn't moved. Maxwell had mentioned the 'b' word and the bastard hadn't moved. Normally he'd have been up on his haunches, doing his meerkat impersonation and purring loudly as the smell of sizzling rashers hit his nostrils. Maxwell thought it safe to continue. 'I can imagine the *Advertiser* headlines, lovingly assembled by my number one fan Reg James. Oh, he'd hate himself for doing it, but he'd do it all the same. "Pervy Teacher in Night Club Nymphet Rap" – "Three in a Bed at Leighford High". Young Garstang saved me from a fate worse than death, not to mention the reputations of two luscious lovelies of Year Ten. Viz and to wit, Miss Annette Choker and Miss Michaela Reynolds. Yes, one of them has been AWOL for a couple of weeks and yes, the father of the other one rearranged my face recently – your point being?'

Metternich rolled sideways, in that sudden and pointless way that cats do, and lay on the carpet as though dead.

'It's actually quite bizarre, Count, and more complicated than I realized. And the hell of it is, I was wrong. There; I've admitted it. Not my finest hour, I concede. The great Mad Max!' He toyed for a moment with hurling the crystal at the wall, but such flamboyant gestures were, in the end, pointless and quite expensive, really. 'Let me take you through it,' he said, resting his glass on his chest and closing his eyes. 'When Sylvia Matthews came to see me – yes, you do remember Sylv. She's the school nurse, for God's sake – stick with the plot. When she showed me John Fry's note, I made a wrong deduction, Count. Yes, me. Max Almighty. I assumed – as did Sylv, I'll grant you but remember, it's never a lady's fault – I assumed that Fry was knocking off young Annette of Ten Eff Ell. Oh, you wouldn't understand, Count, in your physical condition – you, poor bugger, don't get these urges. But some do, you see. The note talked about...' and he switched on his total recall, '...it said "See you tomorrow night, usual place." No, no, quite,' Maxwell nodded, though the cat hadn't moved. 'Fair's fair. So far, so innocuous. But then, you see, the damning line. "There'll be enough room, we can all have some fun. No knickers." Well, exactly. I had the two and two and I made them make four. In fact, of course, they should have made five.'

He glanced again at the cat. If the beast had been purring, he'd certainly stopped now. Maxwell *was* beginning to sound a little like Jonathan Creek. 'What threw me, of course, and confirmed me in my own stupidity, was John Fry denying it like that. When I went to see him, if you remember, he denied the writing on the note was his. That was because his wife, poor old Eleanor, was there. If only he'd run after me or taken me aside the next day and *explained* ... well, we're talking horses and stable doors, I know.'

Maxwell reached down to the bottle of Southern Comfort on the carpet. He freshened his glass. 'Dave Garstang and I settled the girls down between us. I was Nasty Policeman; he was Nice. Gave them both a soothing ciggie, which I thought was going a bit far. I was all for crushing their knuckles in a Corby trouser-press. You see, what we're talking about here, Count, is one very small coincidence and it led me, not to mention half the county's police force, on a wild goose chase of epic proportions. John Fry wasn't having a thing with Annette Choker; he was having a thing with Alison McCormick. That's right – little dumpy copper out of Leighford nick. Annette came into the picture by earning herself a few bob. Turns out that Alison's got a baby – whether it's actually John Fry's or not, I don't know. But Annette was her babysitter. No one at the nick seems to know about this – Garstang was certainly flabbergasted when Annette broke the news tonight. So ... poor Eleanor Fry may have killed herself for all the wrong reasons. If she thought hubbie was playing away with a schoolgirl, she *was* wrong. But he was playing away, and perhaps that, in itself, was too much for her, I don't know.' He sighed, resuming the position on the settee again, 'I didn't know the woman. My guess – and it's really time I stopped doing that, isn't it? – is that the Frys' marriage had been on the rocks for some time. He was going under too – stress of the situation, hard time at work, the complication of Alison – whatever. It sent him over the edge and he wandered away. I wonder if we'll ever know where he went and why.'

Metternich rolled upright, twitched an ear and played dead on the other side.

'Annette on the other hand did an altogether more prosaic flit. She told Garstang and me she met this boy on the Front – Giuseppe. He's from Walthamstow, by the way, before you ask. They eloped together – my word, not hers – and shacked up in a bedsit somewhere in Grotland. No doubt it was love's young dream for a couple of days, away from tarty mum, moody sister, niffy-nappy sibling and yapping dog. But, as I'm sure you're aware, Count, you can take the girl out of the Barlichway Estate, but you can't take the Barlichway ... yes, well; complete the missing words. She dumped Giuseppe – although, of course, he begged her to stay – and she seems to have been sleeping ever rougher until she came home last night. Good of her mother to let us all know, wasn't it? The woman gave her daughter a

340

belt in the gob – I'm quoting here, by the way – and grounded her. Which is why I'll bet she wasn't in school yesterday and why she was in an over-eighteen nightclub earlier tonight.'

Maxwell took a sip of the amber nectar. 'Good bloke, Dave Garstang. He took the girls to the station, handed them over to a Woman Police-man and sent a couple of uniforms around to the Choker and Reynolds establishments. I'd have liked to have been a fly on the wall in either place really. So, there you have it. A mystery, certainly, but not the one I imagined.'

He sat up suddenly. 'The thing of it is, Count,' he said, 'is threefold. I was wrong – and that mistake, I am acutely aware, may have contri-buted to a woman taking her own life. We still have absolutely no idea where Alison McCor-mick is...' He looked the standoffish animal in the smouldering, green eyes, 'And worse,' he heard the break in his own voice, 'I don't know what's happened to my Jacquie.'

By now, he realized, he didn't need her any longer. He'd spent time with her, asking ques-tions, going over and over the same points. She clearly knew nothing. And she was wasting his food, his water, even his air. It was time for her to go. He checked his watch in the half light on the spiral stairs. Half-past one. It might as well be now. He'd go to work on the other one tomorrow, when it was daylight. The other one was cleverer, more experienced. She'd been the real danger all along – why hadn't he seen that? He took the spade from the corner, unhooked the iron door and slid it back. He saw her eyes widen above the tape stretched taut across her mouth, saw the tears glisten wet on the cheeks. Then he swung the spade sideways, thudding dully against her skull. He kicked her legs out of the way and locked the door again. He didn't have time for disposal now. This one was complicated. And there were things he needed. Firewood. Matches. A little petrol.

Year Thirteen were sitting their European History exam that morning as Peter Maxwell pedalled like a thing possessed over the flyover, making for the dig. Last night was like a dream, yet he knew he hadn't slept. He saw Jacquie Carpenter's face wherever he looked – in the clocktower as he cycled past it, bobbing with the dinghies in the marina, swaying with the hanging baskets along the Front. She was crying, silently as in an old black and white. And his heart, as always, went out to her. But his heart would not be enough.

He'd been on his way to the Quinton when he'd caught sight of Michaela and Annette. And by the time he'd extricated them from Dante's and he and Garstang had got the truth out of them, it was too late to go anywhere. But now, he was on the road, burning up the miles and the rubber, putting things to rights. Surrey sprayed gravel as he swung into the elegant curved drive of Messrs Cahill and Lieberman, Property Developers. He threw the bike to the ground and dashed up the front steps, two at a time, and Anthony Cahill's secretary was in the act of asking who he was, when Peter Maxwell kicked open the door marked Managing Director and stood there, a piece of paper in his hand.

Cahill was sitting behind his desk, mouth open, hand poised over the intercom. Maxwell slammed the door behind him as a terrified secretary began dialling frantically for Security.

'Mr Maxwell,' Cahill slimed. 'You seem a little hot and bothered.'

The Head of Sixth Form threw the paper down in front of his man.

'What's this?'

'You tell me,' he said.

Cahill clasped his hands quietly. He'd dealt with madmen before. You just had to stay calm. 'It's a drawing,' he said. 'And not a very good one.'

'Like Herr Hitler,' Maxwell growled, 'I wasn't quite good enough to get into the Vienna Academy of Fine Art. Of what is it a drawing?' Maxwell was standing in front of him now.

'Er ... there you have me.'

Red mist. Peter Maxwell was not a violent man. He was actually a very gentle one. But the woman he loved had been taken, abducted in broad daylight by a psychopath. The gloves were off. He launched himself at Cahill, grabbing both lapels and hauling him upright.

'You know what this is, you money-grabbing creep,' he snarled. 'And I want the original. Now.'

Cahill's eyelids flickered. The colour had drained from his face. To his horror, he realised that Maxwell's kick of the door had locked it and all Security could do was hammer ineffectually

343

on the outside.

'What's the matter, Mr Cahill?' Maxwell growled. 'No goons today? No heavies to beat up harmless metal detectives in anoraks?'

'My heart...' Cahill had gone a very funny colour.

'My arse!' Maxwell snapped and slapped the man around the face. 'Where is it?'

'In ... in the safe.'

Maxwell relented, then pulled the man from behind his desk. 'Open it.' Cahill needed no second bidding. He crouched, fumbling and shaking until the safe door swung back. The knocking on the office woodwork was thunderous. 'Take it out,' Maxwell ordered.

The Managing Director of Cahill and Lieberman, Property Developers slid out a slim, rectangular block of marble, perhaps two feet long. Maxwell looked at it on Cahill's opulent Axminster.

'*Hic jacet Alfredus Rex*,' he read before the marble sheared off and the inscription ran out. He squatted on his haunches, his face inches from Cahill's. 'Now, you tell those rather loud gentlemen in Security to go away,' he said. 'And leave you and me to have a nice little chat.'

'They'll have called the police by now,' Cahill warned.

'Good,' Maxwell sat back on Cahill's opulent leather sofa. 'That's good, Anthony. It will save me having to tell Henry Hall all about it.'

Chapter Nineteen

Derek Latymer was in his trench when they came for him. He was furious that there was still no sign of that old idiot Fraser. Today was the day they were supposed to go, at last, into the ash grove, to look for the church. The professor had cleared it with the police and the yellow, fluttering tape had come down. The chain saws were lying idle near the dumper trucks ready to roar into life.

'Oh no,' Helen Reader's shoulders sagged at the sight. 'Not again.' A large white patrol car prowled along the site fence before rolling to a halt by the gate. Two suits got out. One was a man she'd seen before, talked to, had been interrogated by. That one was DCI Henry Hall. Tall, square, bland, unknowable. The other she didn't know either, but in the literal sense. They both flashed their warrant cards at all and sundry.

'Mr Latymer,' Henry Hall ignored the others. 'This is DC Campbell. Can we have a word?'

Secretly, they all longed to creep nearer to the main tent, to use their softest brushes rather than their loudest trowels and to rest their tired, sweating heads against the rough canvas. But nobody wanted to be first and so they kept away, trowelling, measuring, recording: Douglas Russell, Robin Edwards, Helen Reader, looking for still more bodies in the noon-day heat. Extreme archaeology.

Tony Campbell dropped the marble slab heavily down on the dusty table in front of him, the one he and the DCI had taken from Anthony Cahill's office not an hour ago. The policemen were still standing, the archaeologist sitting down.

'Perhaps you'd like to tell us all about this, Mr Latymer,' Hall said softly.

Latymer looked up at him, the square, silent, sanctimonious bastard. What did he know about archaeology? About anything, really? He was just a thick copper. What do you want to know?' he asked.

Hall pulled back the canvas-backed chair and sat down opposite his man. 'The grave of Alfred the Great,' he said. 'Let's start with that, shall we?'

Latymer smiled. 'A scam, of course.' He raised his knee and cradled it with both hands, rocking back in his chair. 'And it almost worked, didn't it? And on more levels than one – that was something of a bonus.'

'From the beginning?' Hall was patience itself.

'The beginning was David Radley,' Latymer scowled. 'The Alpha and Omega of archaeology. Everything the man touched turned to pure gold. Did you know he was the youngest Professor of Archaeology in the world? Broke record after record. He couldn't fail. Or could he?'

'You were jealous of him?' Hall said.

'Oh, please, Inspector,' Latymer said. 'Don't belittle it with such a petty, demeaning motive. Radley was so smug, so holier-than-thou. I wasn't fit to walk in the shadow of the patronising bastard. So ... I thought – right. Let's see,

346

shall we? Let's test this paragon of brilliance. Let's see what he knows.'

'You planted the evidence?' Hall nodded at the marble.

'It was so ludicrously simple,' Latymer laughed. 'It worked like a bloody dream. Some local had found some bones, so they set up the site. I was supposed to co-ordinate the dig and then I thought ... why not go for it? All my academic life I've had David Fucking Radley rammed down my throat. "When you grow up, you'll realize how good he is", "It's such a privilege to work with a man like this", "He is, of course, a genius." Christ, it makes you want to puke. So I hit upon a cunning plan,' – it wasn't a very good Baldrick, but it had to be said – 'Let's test him, I thought. Let's see how good this genius really is. I got some period marble from my own university and got a local stonemason to inscribe what you see there. It was silly, really. Bit like a typed edition of the Domesday Book or the watch of William the Conqueror. Nobody'd fall for it in a million years. The idea was to discredit Radley, of course. If just one of his minions on the dig – any of those no-hopers outside – found it and got on to the Press, Radley would become a laughing stock. It would be Piltdown all over again.'

'But something went wrong,' Hall said.

Latymer nodded. 'Some Anorak found it.'

'Arthur Wimble,' Campbell chipped in.

'Whatever,' Latymer said. 'And that's where Cahill got involved.'

'Ah, yes,' Hall said. 'Is that what you meant by succeeding on several levels?'

'Exactly,' Latymer told him. Maybe this copper wasn't as thick as he had assumed. 'I was just amazed. Cahill came to the site one day and I overheard him and Radley talking, here, in this very tent. Not only was Radley himself buying the authenticity of that fake, but you could almost see the pound signs in Cahill's eyes. *That* was why the genius wouldn't let us dig in the ash grove. He was psyching himself up to find the grave of Alfred the Great there. It just goes to show – want something hard enough and you start to believe any old rubbish, even someone with a reputation like his.'

'So what happened?' Campbell asked. 'Radley rumbled you and you killed him?'

Latymer looked horrified. 'I didn't kill him, you moron,' he growled. 'It was the man's reputation I wanted, not his head. What do you take me for?'

Henry Hall leaned to his man until his nose was inches from Latymer's.

'I'm trying to find the words,' he said.

He rang the doorbell a little after four that afternoon, watching the cab purr away on the gravel. There was a rattle of bolts behind him and a rather dishevelled Tam Fraser stood there.

'Gardening, Professor?' Maxwell asked.

The Scotsman had a spade in his hand and mud on his green wellies. His lion's mane of silver hair was speckled with what looked like ash. 'Maxwell?' he said. 'Good God, man. What are you doing here?'

'Oh, Professor,' the Head of Sixth Form said. 'Such a cliché. I'd expected more. Don't mind if

I come in?' and he barged his way into the hall.

Fraser's house was, in its own way, as impressive as Sam Welland's. It was what estate agents used to call a Gothic pile, before 'pile' acquired an altogether different connotation. An olive-brown Drizabone hung on a hook in the hall and a broad-brimmed leather hat just above it.

'Van Helsing,' Maxwell flicked its brim.

'I'm sorry?' Fraser was confused.

'Oh, association of ideas,' Maxwell said. 'I was talking to that nice Mr Cahill today; you know, of Cahill and Lieberman, Property Developers.'

'Oh, him,' Fraser was full of disdain. 'Met him once. Didn't like him.'

'No, well, I'm with you there. Oh, I say.' Maxwell had wandered into Fraser's study, heavy with velvet-flocked wallpaper and piled high with leather-backed tomes and sheaves of paper. 'Wiggins,' Maxwell said, holding a single sheet of paper up to the light of Fraser's tapering, leaded windows. He rubbed it between his thumb and forefinger. 'Ninety gram, I'd say.'

'Look ... er ... Maxwell...'

'Sorry,' Maxwell smiled. 'I do ramble, don't I? It's my age, I suppose. That's what this is all about, isn't it? Age? Where was I?' Maxwell threw himself down in a huge armchair. 'Oh, yes. Mr Cahill. Well, you're obviously aware that Mr Cahill has two vegetables working for him as Site Security – Dumb and Dumber, better known as George and Julian.'

'So?' Fraser was still standing, still holding the spade.

'So, in their nightly perambulations recently,

George and Julian saw a rather weird character flitting about, phantom-like, from grave to grave. Now, they're both your down-to-earth, level-headed sort of idiots, not much imagination. But this figure, well, he put the wind up them both, according to Mr Cahill.'

'I don't see...'

'The figure was wearing a duster coat and a hat not unlike the gear worn by Hugh Jackman in the latest piece of Undead tosh, *Van Helsing*. Not unlike your hat and coat in the hall out there, Professor.'

'What are you getting at?' Fraser asked.

Maxwell looked at him. 'Does the name Hugo Prentiss mean anything to you, Professor Fraser?'

'Sir Hugo Prentiss,' the archaeologist nodded. 'Emeritus Professor of History at Cambridge. Yes, indeed. A very great scholar. Dead, isn't he?'

'Well, he wasn't an hour ago,' Maxwell said. 'When I spoke to him on the phone. Detective Chief Inspector Hall actually let me use his carphone. That was kind of him, wasn't it? It's funny, I wasn't very impressed by Prentiss when I was at Cambridge. You know how it is...' Maxwell chuckled. 'Of course you do ... the folly of youth. I was a young Turk. He was an old fart. Even then, I supposed he was a hundred. And Saxon England, well, it wasn't my period. I stood it for a term and then got on to something infinitely more interesting.'

'Maxwell, I'd love to reminisce with you, but I...'

'But, you know,' Maxwell ignored him. 'It's odd, isn't it, how the strangest things stay with

350

you. Take, for instance, the affairs of men.'

'The what?'

'Well, it's a quotation, of course, from a sport called Shakespeare – *Julius Caesar.*'

Fraser laughed. 'I really think...'

'But a very good friend of mine found it somewhere else. She found it on a colleague's computer screen ... talking of which, that's a Canon, isn't it?' Maxwell pointed to the silent, grey monster on the archaeologist's desk. 'I don't know one from the other, but it says "Canon" on the side. Anyway, this friend of mine's colleague was a sweet boy. I say "was" because he's dead now. Somebody cut through his brake cables.'

'That's dreadful.' Fraser shook his head.

'Yes,' Maxwell looked up at the man, grim-faced. 'Yes, it is. Where was I? Ah, this damned age thing, eh? Oh, yes. You see, this boy, this dead colleague, he was a Medieval English buff. And that "affairs of men" ... well, it didn't quite make sense.'

'So?' Fraser was bored already.

'So, I said to myself – who'll know? Whose eminence is so great that I'll be able to source that quotation once and for all? And it came to me; the Michaelmas Term in the Granta days and hopeless old Hugo Prentiss. Like you, I thought he was dead. Oh, he's long retired, of course – now there's a lesson for us all. I don't think he could remember who I was, but I soon got over the hurt of that. We got talking, Sir Hugo and I and he, bless him, put it all in context. Just like he did that Michaelmas Term all those years ago. You see Martin – that's the dead boy's name, by the way, Martin Toogood – he got it just slightly wrong. And that's what threw me off the scent. He didn't mean the *affairs* of men. He meant the *fortunes* of men. And that's a whole new ball game.'

'It is?' Fraser was willing to play along.

'Oh, yes,' Maxwell nodded. 'You once accused me of talking like a bloody Saxon riddle and I bet you could have kicked yourself for that, couldn't you? David Radley knew it vaguely and even quoted from it on occasions. Poor Susan remembered one line – "the wolf, the grey heath-stalker". Van Helsing, the wolf-coat, prowling around the yawning graves.'

'This ... er ... the *Fortunes of Men* thing?' Fraser began.

'An anonymous Saxon poem, probably written by a cleric with a romantic inclination. But then, you knew that, didn't you, Professor? You being the author of *Saxon Identities* and all. It's really quite good, describing the chance destinies of the sons of mothers. Having talked to Sir Hugo again, I realized I knew it. I'd just forgotten it, that's all – an age thing, again, I suppose. Let's see,' Maxwell risked closing his eyes. "One will drop, wingless, from the high tree in the wood... Then sadly he slumps by the trunk, robbed of life; he falls to earth and his soul flies from him."' Maxwell opened his eyes again. 'That's David Radley. His body at the foot of the ash trees on Staple Hill. You couldn't kill him there, Professor, not in the way the poem described, because the ash branches wouldn't bear his weight. Anyway, how would you have hoisted him up there? Instead,

352

you rang him on that lazy, hazy, crazy afternoon and invited him here. I'll just bet the fibres Henry Hall's people found on the dead man's shoes match your rather frightful carpet in the vestibule.'

'Are you insane?' Fraser hissed, horror on his face.

'Pots and kettles, I'm afraid,' Maxwell said. 'But you were clever, I'll give you that. Re-dressing the man was pure genius.'

'How so?'

'Well, it's in the poem, in a way – "Often and again, through God's grace, man and woman usher a child into the world and clothe him in gay colours." You knew about Douglas Russell and his crush on David Radley, didn't you? I'd guess because David told you; trusting, naïve soul that he was. And there was a perfect red herring for you. For a few quid and a deliberately careless re-dressing, you could point the finger at a sexual motive, which would keep the police away from you.'

'You know this is nonsense, don't you?'

'Then, there was Sam Welland. How does the poem have it? "One will swing from the tall gallows, sway in death." You made a gallows for her, all right. I expect if I scout around here for a bit, I'll find some of the rope you did it with. She invited herself along to Staple Hill, didn't she? Expecting to take over the dig, using all Radley's scientific techniques. And that would never do. The problem, of course, was Toogood. And that very problem meant that you very nearly got away with it. He'd sussed you, hadn't he? The old

353

English scholar remembered the *Fortunes of Men* – the fall from a tree, so pat, so poetic. Only he didn't remember it well enough. But you didn't know that, did you? How could you? Couldn't take the chance. Just your luck that the only copper in the county with a degree in Saxon was on your case. Life's a bummer, isn't it? Took a lot of nerve, I'll admit, to fix Toogood's brakes on police property. Oh, it broke the pattern, of course – nothing about cars and their brakes in the *Fortunes of Men*. You dressed up as Van Helsing again. Mr Hall has your picture on his CCTV screens. And poor old Sergeant Wilson at the nick. Popped out for a pee, had he, while you doubled back through the nick? Is that why he didn't see you fleeing the scene of the crime?'

'Man, man,' Fraser was shaking his head. 'This is daft.'

'Now, the Sepulchre Society of Sussex was inspired, but oddly enough, I met a nice lady the other day who didn't fall for it. She said it was melodramatic nonsense. And so it was. Derek Latymer, Mr Chip-on-the-shoulder, thought it was all made up by Douglas Russell. But it wasn't, was it, Professor? It was all made up by you. You sent the threatening letters to Russell, knowing he was weak, flaky. And you borrowed one of your own skulls, I'll bet, from the university, to place on your bed. And, if I had my digging hat on, Professor, I'd take it off to you. A BAFTA performance at the Quinton if ever I've seen one. You really did look terrified. And the twig in the mandible!' Maxwell applauded in the stillness. 'Inspired. Hazel Twigg in the frame too.'

He'd stopped smiling now. 'You don't care where the shit lands, do you?'

'I've been patient, Maxwell,' Fraser said. 'Now I must ask you to leave. You do realize there's no place for you at the dig after this?'

'On the dig?' Maxwell frowned. 'Can't you see, man, it's over? Neither of us will be doing any digging again. Professor,' a sudden thought had occurred to Maxwell. 'What were you doing with that spade?'

'"One will suffer agony on the pyre,"' Fraser quoted, an odd glint in his eye.

'Jacquie!' Maxwell was on his feet, brushing past the Scotsman, running through the house. He dashed into the kitchen; nothing. On into the conservatory; empty. Then he looked into the garden, high-walled and secluded, the cedars masking more distant houses and the road. A blazing fire crackled and spat in the centre of the lawn, the tangled branches crumbling to charcoal in its red hot heart. A woman's body lay near, her hands tied together, duct tape over her mouth. Maxwell hurled himself at the French windows and crashed through the glass, shards slicing through his hands, his forehead, as he streaked across the short grass of summer. He dragged the body from the blaze, feeling the heat scorch his battered, bleeding face. He turned her over. It was Alison McCormick. And she was still breathing. He ripped off the tape and she shuddered, breathing in sharply as her eyelids flickered. She was grey and there was foam round her lips and hard, brown caked blood forming a rigid mark on one side of her face.

'Maxwell!' the Head of Sixth Form turned. Tam Fraser was standing there, another woman held firmly in his grip. Her wrists were roped in front of her and there was the same tape over her mouth that had recently covered Alison's. Her shoes were undone and her tights had been removed. Her auburn hair hung lank and cobwebbed round her neck. Jacquie.

She looked at him with sad, trusting, terrified eyes.

'"One will be spear-slain,"' Fraser said triumphantly, '"hacked down in battle."' He nudged the spade-edge into the girl's bruised neck. 'I'm sorry it's not quite a spear. I wasn't exactly expecting you. A spade'll do it, though, don't you think? After all, I've always called a spade a spade.' He looked at Jacquie. 'She's only a wee lass. Bound to have a thin skull. Like that one there.' He nodded at the fallen woman at Maxwell's feet. 'I'll admit to a wee error here, mind.' Fraser was smiling. 'When Toogood talked about his female colleague and how bright she was, I thought it was that little waste of space at your feet. I went to all the lengths to grab her only to find out it was this one here I should have been talking to all along. Find out what she and Toogood had discovered; just how much she knew.'

The Head of Sixth Form surveyed his options. Alison was weak and barely conscious. She couldn't focus, let alone stand. No help there. There were ... what ... ten yards between him and Fraser and the madman could hack off Jacquie's head in that split-second dash. He looked into the grey, clear eyes of the girl he loved and he

356

used his best weapon.

'Brilliant!' Maxwell said. He stood up slowly, shaking his head and smiling. 'Quite brilliant.' He clapped loudly.

'Are you talking about me, laddie?' Fraser asked. In his head, the crowds roared. Men and women of his chosen profession in gowns and mortar boards, stood before him, standing in their ovation.

'Who else?' Maxwell beamed. 'These young whipper-snappers!' he aimed a deft kick at Alison who groaned a little and rolled. 'When will they realize, eh?'

'Realize what?' Fraser asked.

'That they'll never replace the likes of us. Oh, they call us dinosaurs and dodos – you used the phrase yourself.'

'I did,' Fraser nodded.

'But, man, we are the salt of the earth. Initiatives. Bollocks! Reinventing the wheel.'

'Exactly,' Fraser's spade edge was still pressing on Jacquie's neck. 'Geo-bloody-physics, eh? Give me bosing any day.'

'I can see it now,' Maxwell folded his arms. 'I can see it had to be done. Radley...'

'Aye,' Fraser sighed. 'I felt bad about wee Davey. He was a good lad once. When he was under my tutelage. Don't get me wrong – I'd have given him all the credit. Posthumously, it has to be said. But it would be done by *my* methods and not his. Notice how I'd closed down Russell's stupid electronics? The tragedy was, of course, that wee David broke away from me...'

'Like they do,' Maxwell nodded solemnly.

357

'New-fangled ideas. Scientific hogwash. God, the arguments we had. The rows! He wouldn't listen, Maxwell. Not to a word. Nor Sam Welland, silly little tart. She's no loss to anybody.'

'Not at all,' Maxwell said. 'Right. Well, can I give you a hand, then? You're burning this one, yes?'

'Aye. Good of you to help.'

And Maxwell crouched to roll Alison onto the fire that spat and crackled to welcome her in. Fraser held Jacquie firmly by the hair with his left hand and brought back his right with the spade gleaming in the afternoon sun. There was a dull thud and Maxwell looked up.

Professor Tam Fraser lay on the ground where the nightstick had felled him. A large, blond, fresh-faced copper was standing over him, steadying the wobbling Jacquie as he flicked the night-stick back into his pocket.

'Thank you, Dave,' Maxwell said. 'If I'd have known your timing was as crap as that, I'd never have agreed to your coming along.'

Chapter Twenty

Jacquie didn't let Peter Maxwell go. Ever. She held him as he took the tape off her mouth and the rope from her wrist. As he laid her gently down in Tam Fraser's grass and kissed away the tears. Dave Garstang was punching buttons on his mobile, checking Alison as she lay whimpering.

And Jacquie was still holding him that night in Petworth hospital, he sat by her bed in the private room that Henry Hall had booked for her. He'd square it with the Chief Constable later. Jacquie's face, like Maxwell's, was bruised and puffy. The combination of the duct tape and the chloroform had set up a reaction in her skin and she looked like shit.

'I must look like shit,' she said to him, her voice cracked and her throat parched from days without enough to drink.

'Takes one to know one,' he said. 'The important thing is that you're safe.'

'Max,' she smiled weakly, reaching out to stroke his cheek. 'You saved my life.'

'Me and a night-stick and fifteen stone of pretty hunky copper,' Maxwell said.

'What put you onto Fraser?' she asked.

'The poem,' he told her. 'A Saxon riddle called the *Fortunes of Men* – probably tenth century. Martin was onto it too.'

'The affairs of men!' She could still just about click her fingers. 'On Martin's computer. I was getting there too.'

'From the poem?'

'Oh, no,' she said. 'I leave that to you ancient buffs. No, there's a way on a computer, Max, to blank out text.'

'What, some sort of invisible ink?'

'If you like,' she nodded. 'I don't know why I didn't think to check it before, but the day Fraser grabbed me, I went over Martin's area again. And there it was. He'd changed the text colour to white – sort of guy he was, I suppose: careful,

359

thorough. Didn't want to give too much away. It just said "Fraser alibi". The trouble was he had one. We'd checked it. We all assumed he was actually at the London symposium on the day David Radley died because he didn't ring to cancel. On the attendance list at the conference centre, it looked as if he was present. He wasn't speaking, merely one of the guests. So I made a few phone calls. After the eighth person on the conference list couldn't remember seeing him there, I decided to follow it up. Only he got to me first. Poor Martin!'

He reached out to enfold her as the tears started again. The darkness would be there whenever she closed her eyes. She wanted light. She wanted air. She wanted the safe, strong arms of Mad Max.

'There are a lot of casualties in this one, darling,' he said softly. 'Martin Toogood, David Radley, the parents of one, the widow of the other. Not to mention Eleanor Fry.'

'How is Alison?'

'They say she'll mend,' Maxwell said. 'Fractured skull, dehydration, minor bruising. As for her soul, who knows?'

'Does she know about John Fry?'

'Yes,' he told her. 'At least, they told her. Her mother's with her now, along with the baby. That's what I can't handle, Jacquie. Me and my bloody arrogance. If I hadn't gone to see him that day with that nonsense about Annette... If I hadn't made that mistake...'

She soothed the tangle of barbed wire hair, whispering 'hush' in his ear and kissing the

360

bruised head. 'That's not true, Max,' she said. 'Darling, darling Max. Eleanor Fry had been suffering from depression all her life. We were onto that at the nick. She'd attempted suicide twice before. Oh, a *cri de coeur*, maybe. But this time there was no one around to hear it. I don't think she knew anything about Annette Choker or even Alison McCormick. She was just a deeply unhappy woman. Shit happens and it's nothing to do with you.'

'Isn't it?' he said, and pulled a buff envelope from his pocket. 'I cadged this off the casualty desk while you were being x-rayed.'

'Petty theft, Mr Maxwell?' she frowned. 'Tut, tut.'

'It's my resignation,' he said.

'Your...' Jacquie sat there, open-mouthed and wide-eyed. 'Peter Maxwell,' she sat as upright as she could. 'Leighford High is your life. You're not ready to hang up your chalk just yet.'

'I loused up, Jacquie,' he said, his sad, dark eyes brimming with tears. 'All these years I've been playing Jane bloody Marple, playing fast and loose with people's emotions, people's lives. What on God's earth gave me that right?'

She held his face with both hands and kissed him tenderly on the lips. 'I don't know how many lives you've saved,' she told him, the tears trickling down her cheeks. 'And how many scores you've settled.' She sniffed savagely. 'And anyway, you're Mad Max, for God's sake. There are twelve hundred kids out there who are looking to you for guidance. Who's going to take them down the rocky road to the past if you're not there to do it? You're the bloody piper, Peter Maxwell. You can't just stop playing when you feel like it, you know.'

He half smiled.

'Now,' she sniffed, frowning at him and feeling the tears salty in her mouth. 'Are you going to tear that up. Or am I? Or is Legs Diamond?'

Maxwell chuckled. Nobody called the Headmaster that. Nobody except Mad Max.

'Mr Maxwell?' he half turned at the sound of the nurse's voice.

'Miss Nightingale?' he half rose and bowed.

'I must ask you to leave now, I'm afraid. It's time for Miss Carpenter's rest.'

'Yes, yes of course,' he said and reached forward to kiss her.

'Max,' she whispered, 'They said ... they said the baby's okay.'

He stood upright as though transfixed, eyes wide. The nurse had gone, chuckling softly to herself. 'Baby?' he repeated.

She looked up at him, smiling a little sheepishly. 'I was going to tell you,' she said. 'Honest.'

He looked at her, the love of his life on his pillow. He saw as in a film scene, the dark-haired woman he used to love and the bright-eyed baby on her lap. 'I have two questions, Woman Policeman,' he said. 'Boy or girl?'

'One of those,' she said.

He chuckled. 'And secondly – and think carefully about this one – your place or mine?'

She thought for a second that was barely split of the great black and white beast sprawled on the corpses of his kills; of the 54 millimetre horsemen, saddled and ready to ride into hell in Maxwell's attic. And a smile spread over her face again. 'Yours,' she said.

'You know it's ironic,' Peter Maxwell sat alongside Henry Hall as the DCI drove him back through the darkness of the Leighford night. When I met Martin Toogood he said to me "I don't have time for cryptic clues". And that's exactly what he had time for. He was nearly there.'

Hall nodded. 'His funeral is arranged for Monday, Mr Maxwell,' he said. 'Will you be there?'

It was Maxwell's turn to nod. 'It'll be my privilege,' he said.

He bounded up the steps to the mezzanine floor the next morning as Mrs B., the cleaner, was taking charge of her new floor-polisher.

''Ere, Mr Maxwell,' she hailed him. 'I heard a funny thing the other day. I heard you was going to resign. I told 'em, that's bollocks, that is. Mr Maxwell, he's bloody barmy. Wouldn't catch him resigning. After all, where else would he get all them long holidays?'

'Did you, Mrs B.?' he swept on past her in search of Norman, who owed him a fiver. 'Well, yes, it is. I certainly am. No, you wouldn't, and where indeed?'

Chapter Twenty-One

They closed the dig on Staple Hill that weekend. The JCBs rattled and roared away without slicing into the ash grove. The trenches were filled in and the spoil heaps disappeared. Douglas Russell began the job of compiling his report, with the help of Robin Edwards and Helen Reader. It would carry the name of Dr David Radley, now and for all time.

And George and Julian, the men in black, went home and the developers moved in to create a golf club where a man had died. Or was it more?

Go down. Under the tangle of the ash grove, where the earth is dank and dark. Here, as the wind rustles the ash leaves on Staple Hill, a skeleton still keeps its solitary resting place below the stars. Its hands are crossed over its chest, its tarsals collapsed into the rib cage. And on the skull, grey and dust, a crown of solid gold. In the still clasped hand of the long dead man, a jewel, in glass and amber and gold and the legend Alfredus Me Fecit – Alfred Made Me.

Just another Saxon riddle.

The publishers hope that this book has given you enjoyable reading. Large Print Books are especially designed to be as easy to see and hold as possible. If you wish a complete list of our books please ask at your local library or write directly to:

Magna Large Print Books
Magna House, Long Preston,
Skipton, North Yorkshire.
BD23 4ND

This Large Print Book for the partially sighted, who cannot read normal print, is published under the auspices of

THE ULVERSCROFT FOUNDATION